The Conrad Kidnapping

Tom Saine

The Conrad Kidnapping

A Mark Steele Mystery

Tom Saine

Valparaiso Public Library
103 Jefferson Street
Valparaiso, IN 46383

ISBN-10: 1470166429
ISBN-13: 978-1470166427

Front cover photo: Boris Babikov © 2006
Illustrations, page 8, 100, 111, 265, 373-377:
Thomas L. Saine © 2011
Photo of the author page 379:
Faith Duncan © 2004
1st print, 2012
2nd print, 2015

DEDICATION

I want to dedicate this first book to my late mother Leona June Saine. Mom was an avid reader; she could polish off one, and sometimes two, 400 page Regency romance novels (her favorite) in less than a day. She would be very proud that I was able to finish this book. She would also have been the very first person in line at the bookstore to purchase a copy.

Thank you Mom, for all your enthusiasm, encouragement, and assistance; it has certainly been something that I have missed since you left us in 2003

ACKNOWLEDGMENTS

This is my first novel and there are so many people, other than my mother, who deserve my undying thanks and appreciation for making it possible. Without these people this would still be an idea bouncing around in a vacuum between my ears.

Donna Wells

In 2005 I was researching police officer ranking systems and contacted *The Boston Police Department* for information; I was directed to Donna Wells. At that time she was *Records Manager and Archivist* for the BPD; she has since retired. Unfortunately, I've never met Donna, but we have talked several times on the telephone. She has always been willing to talk to me; always willing to answer any inane question I managed to come up with regarding the BPD; and was gracious enough to do a full edit of the book—and for that I'm truly grateful.

Dona is the author of an illustrated biography of the BPD entitled: *Image of America: Boston Police Department*.

Arcadia Publishing: ISBN- 10 0-7385-12302-4.

Anna Arnett

Anna is the Branch Manager at my local branch of the *LaPorte County Public Library*. My thanks go out to Anna for her ever-present smile and encouragement. And for tracking down the multitude of books I used during this writing process; most were obtained through inter-library loan and took extra effort on her part to obtain.

Also, I can't forget some special ladies at the *Main Branch of the LaPorte County Public Library*. Specifically: **Deborah McCish**: Thanks for searching the basement archives, hunting back issues of Life Magazine needed for research. **Elizabeth Johnason**: For helping me copy the pages (from those same Life magazines) while dealing with a cantankerous copy machine, which kept folding copies like an accordion.

Peggy Westergard

Peggy is a fellow writer and a longtime good friend. Lately of California, but recently transplanted—accompanied by her cat *Seamus*—to Kansas. Thank you so much for your friendship, advice, and constant support.

The Blank Slate Writers Group
The members of my writing group here in Valparaiso, Indiana. I want to thank all the members of the group; all have helped my writing tremendously over the last ten years. So, thank you all. But I especially want to thank a few core members individually. All of whom, I imagine, are sick of reading this story in all its various permutations (in alphabetical order): Barbara Funke, Christina Ortega Phillips, Darlene Cohn, David Mason, John Schaub, Joyce Hicks, Marilyn Kosmataka, Mike Ripley, Olga M. Zulich, Peggy Wesrergard, Robert S. Thomas, Stefan Barkow, Stephanie Holloway, and Timothy Cole

William (Bill) Edwards
Bill was a High School friend and one of my biggest fans; regrettably he passed-away before this was published. However, I continue his memory by including a character in each of my Mark Steel stories with the name of *Bill Edwards*. The characters are wide-ranging, both good guys and bad guys. They do not reflect in any way on Bill's character as a person, or his life in general, in any way or manner; the characters merely use his name. Look for Bill within the text.

Faith Duncan
Faith has been my significant other and partner for the last thirteen years. Faith is the one who gets to put up with my childish crap while I'm writing and particularly during the tumultuous, and seemingly never-ending, editing process. Faith also took the photo of me used in my bio.

And last, but not least:
My Editors. These are the special people who were willing to take a copy of the manuscript, read it through, and then mark it up. They are all deserving of special thanks: (listed in alphabetical order) Barbara Funke, Christina Ortega Phillips, David Mason, Donna Wells, Joyce Hicks, Marilyn Kosmataka, Mike Ripley, Olga M. Zulich, Peggy Wesrergard, Stefan Barkow, and Timothy Cole. Thank you all for your very considerable input during the long, long editing process. I could not have completed this, in a form that could be read, without your assistance.

CHAPTER 1

A shot rang out, shattering the silent night on pier 19, in Boston harbor. Jolting pain ripped through Steele's left arm. The wood piling behind him exploded, sending wood splinters flying. Steele fell back, hitting the piling hard. His knees shook. He grabbed the rope lashing of the piling with his left hand. Pain flashed through his wounded arm. Steele's shoe caught on a loose board or protruding nail head—whatever it was threw him off-balance and he's barely able to keep himself from falling into the icy water of the bay. Recovering, he crouched back into the shadows and drew his gun from its holster, eased the slide back to chamber a round and switched the safety off. His eyes searched the darkened pier. He waited, expecting more shots. Who could it be? Not Boomer? Tony Bombari blows people up; he doesn't shoot at people.

The July night only provided a first quarter moon hanging over the bay. It didn't provide enough light for Steele to see who's out there. The only other light on the pier came from the flashing neon sign above Jack's Crab Shack a hundred yards away. It offered its silent flashing message, Fish and Lobster, in bright orange neon to the darkness.

Orange—what a strange color—can't make up its mind to be red or yellow.

Without warning a blinding white light, followed instantly by an explosion, illuminated the outer end of the pier. Flames and debris burst two-hundred feet into the air. The blast concussion nearly knocked Steele off his feet. Fire engulfed what remained of the 'Bloody Mary', the yacht Steele had under surveillance.

How did Boomer get to the yacht before me?

The sound of a screeching cat, coming from behind him, pulled Steele's attention away from the fire. He heard a voice cry out, "Fucking cats," followed by the crash of trash cans. Steele knew that voice. It's Boomer!

Steele ran toward the voice. He found only overturned trash cans and scattered garbage. No cat, and no Boomer. *Tony Bombari, the bastard, managed to get away clean.*

Steele stood there for a moment, the neon sign blinking relentlessly overhead. His arm oozed red and had begun to hurt like hell. He re-holstered the gun and sat down on the steps of the restaurant, withdrew the handkerchief from his breast pocket and began wrapping his wounded arm. He felt a nudge on his leg and looked down to find a scrawny black cat rubbing its head against his pant leg.

"Hi there, little fella." Steele held out a hand to the cat. "So, you're the one who tripped Ol' Boomer up?" The cat sat, his head cocked to one side, looking up at Steele, his yellow-green eyes sparkling in the moonlight. It sniffed curiously at Steele's outstretched fingers, and then began rubbing its head against the side of his hand. The cat had a jet black coat, except the left half of its face and ear, which were brown.

"You did a good job my little friend." Steele said as he tightened a knot in the handkerchief around his arm. He looked down at the cat and scratched it behind the one brown ear. He chuckled, "Looks like this salty sea air has begun to rust that black coat of yours, my skinny little friend." The cat looked up at him and in the silence of the night Steele could hear a low vibrating sound coming from the cat.

In the far distance, Steele also heard the high-pitched wail of sirens. He looked to where the sound came from, and saw the red flashing lights of fire engines bouncing off the surrounding building as the trucks made their way along the wharf road. The pulsating lights give the scene an eerie surrealistic luminance. The firemen would arrive in a minute. There would be an ambulance, and a medic to treat his arm.

CHAPTER 2

The city of Boston rested quietly this November afternoon, except for a lively breeze from the east, blustering its way up the Charles River. Snow had fallen most of last night and the morning, but had ceased a couple of hours ago. The city lay quiet, now snuggled tightly in its blanket of white fluff. The only snowflakes still falling blown from tree branches, power lines, and rooftops by the wind.

Daryl Mark Steele stood, his shoulder resting against the window frame of his third floor office. Holding his pipe in his left hand as he sipped from a cup of hot black coffee, his attention fixed on a red and white bantam tugboat, struggling against the river currents as it attempted to push two rusty barges westward up the Charles.

The river scene awakened fond memories in Steele, memories of good times long ago, when as a boy, he had floated oak leaves and twigs on the currents of the creek that ran through his family's farm in Nebraska.

The dying sun cast long shadows, trailing black tentacles from every tree, lamppost and telephone pole. Gazing out over the river and the city beyond, Steele puffed his pipe. A cloud of silver-gray smoke hovered over his head. He recalled a similar winter day in New York City: The snow had just stopped; he waited on a street corner for the light to change. His ears nearly froze, despite having turned up his coat collar. He recalled being envious of two window dressers in short-sleeved shirts as they constructed an Alpine village scene inside the Macy's window. The men looked warm and comfortable as they went about placing miniature buildings, trees, and sleighs with horses upon yards and yards of white cotton-batting draped over a wooden frame designed to simulate hills. A gentle smile washed over Steele's face as he thoughtfully drew on his pipe between sips of coffee, thinking about his life as a private detective since leaving the Marine Corps in 1946.

The river scene's merely a temporary distraction. Steele's, deep in thought, puffing his pipe steadily.

After seven years in the business, I really enjoy what I do; but it might be time for me to get into another line of work, before I get myself killed. That little incident in July with Tony Bombari's an example; they call him "Boomer" for good reason. He likes to blow things up. Cars, buildings, or people, don't much matter to Tony. Thank God, the jerk tried to shoot me instead of blowing-up my car.

Steele instinctively moved his hand to rub the wound... still sensitive after these many months.

If Boomer, the little bastard, had used his favorite three sticks of dynamite on my car, it would be on the junk heap now and I'd have ended up on a slab at the morgue instead of having my arm bandaged by that pretty nurse.

He looked at his reflection in the window and wondered aloud, "What's her name?" He puffed his pipe, "Ah yes—I remember now—Francine."

Boy, what a looker, even that starched white uniform couldn't hide her feminine charms. She has a petal soft touch as she bandaged my arm. And, how could I ever forget those flirting blue eyes, rosy pink cheeks, and blood-red lips; too bad she'd been married to a professional boxer. He grinned at his reflection in the window pane.

Still, precious things like pretty little Francine aside. After being shot, most rational people might stop for a minute or two and ponder about just what they are doing and why they are doing it. I guess I'm no different.

Until the little incident with Boomer, 1953 had been a relatively uneventful year in the detective business.

I do consider myself a rational person; a fact that my secretary Lois might dispute. She has this maternal side that she tries to hide; I often feel that she sees me as her son—who died many years ago only a few hours after being born—instead of her employer.

The Conrad Kidnapping

Lost in his ruminations, the muted TAP, TAP, TAP of a knuckle against the glass of his office door snapped his attention back from the scene outside the window.

Steele recognized the sound; his secretary Lois was producing it. He turned his head to find her standing in the doorway; he motioned for her to come in.

Lois wore a snug black skirt and a sleeveless woolen sweater in powder blue with a blue and white silk scarf tied around her neck. The outfit highlighted her trim, athletic figure, making her look younger than her age; the scarf also accentuated her new hairdo.

Lois always had beautiful, shoulder length, dark brown hair until last August, when she had it cut, after attending a sneak preview of a new movie. The movie, *Roman Holiday*, with Audrey Hepburn and Gregory Peck. The very next day she had her regular Wednesday beauty shop appointment. She left the office that morning with long hair and when she came back it had been cut. Cut short just like Hepburn's had been in the movie.

The new look surprise Steele; he almost didn't recognize Lois when she walked into his office.

He exclaimed, "Jesus... what happened, Lois? Your hair!"

Lois had a broad smile on her face and began to dance around the office.

"It makes me feel so young and adventurous!" She announced, as she twirled around the center of the office.

"It'll take a little getting used to," he called out.

"Maybe I should go to Rome myself and look for my own Gregory Peck and have my own *Roman Holiday*!"

Steele grinned broadly at her and put his pipe in his mouth; biting the stem firmly, before he blurted out his thoughts.

I'm not sure if I like it or not; but I must admit, it does make you look ten or fifteen years younger.

In the next few days the way Lois dressed also changed. The drab ankle length dresses, had been replaced by a mid-calf length skirts, and bright-colored blouses and sweaters.

He had indeed gotten used to it. In fact, he'd begun to like it very much. Since she had cut her hair, Lois had become a much happier person.

He turned his gaze away from the river again. "Yes, Lois, what is it? I don't have an appointment?" He turned his head, bringing his eyes back to her, "Do I?"

"No, Mr. Steele. Simply bringing you the morning mail."

"Anything important?"

"There's a postcard from your daughter. Nothing else of importance," she laid the postcard along with a half-dozen white envelopes and a copy of the Police Gazette on his desk.

"What does Janet have to say?"

Lois picked up the card, "Shall I read it?"

"Yes, please."

"No mention of stopping in Boston on their way home?"

"No, Mr. Steele—that's all it says." Lois placed the postcard atop the envelopes on the desk, "Had she planned on stopping in to see you, Mr. Steele?"

"No, she didn't say anything about it. But since their ship lands in New York, and Boston's between New York and Vermont, I just thought she and Thomas might come by."

"Perhaps she's planning to surprise you, Mr. Steele."

"Yes, she loves surprises. That's probably what they're planning." Steele turned his head to look at Lois. He smiled, "That another new outfit?"

"Just the scarf is new. I picked it up in town last weekend. Do you like it?" She pivoted in a full circle in the middle of the office floor.

His forehead wrinkled into a frown as he looked in her direction, "I wouldn't know, Lois. You know me, I know nothing about fashion."

"You either like it or don't. Mr. Steele. It's an opinion. You don't need to know anything about fashion to express an opinion." She grinned at him.

"I'm sorry, Lois. You're absolutely right," he smiled. "Yes, I like the scarf. It's a very pretty color for you. That and the sweater, bring out the bluish parts of your green eyes."

She curtsied, as low as her new tight skirt would allow her too, "Thank you, kind sir," and began to giggle, her cheeks turning red in the process. It took her a moment to recapture her composure, and then she said, "See that wasn't too hard. I knew you could do it, Mr. Steele?"

He smiled at her, but didn't reply, directing his attention again outside the window. Not at the river this time, but to movement on the street below. He noted Fred Archer, the building maintenance man shoveling snow off the sidewalk as a brand new black Lincoln sedan pulled up to the curb. The driver's side door opened, and a Negro man dressed in gray chauffeur's jacket and cap got out. He quickly ran around the car and opened the rear passenger side door. The legs of a woman, long and sheer-stockinged, with red shoes appeared through the open door. The chauffeur extended his hand to help the woman from the car. Besides the red shoes, she wore a full-length mink coat and a pillbox hat with a veil. The hat and veil matched the shoes. She stood by the car a moment and studied the building from side to side, then looked up at Steele's window. She looked directly at Steele, raised the veil with a red-gloved hand and smiled at him. Lowering the veil again, she walked toward the building. Steele directed his attention back to the river; the only movement came from a flock of fifteen or twenty seagulls, flying eastward.

"Do you need anything, Mr. Steele?"

"No, Lois. With this storm, I don't think we'll be getting much business today. I'm thinking of going over to the Rivers for a beer or two. Why don't you take the rest of the day off? Go find Superman and see a movie."

Lois flushed red. "Stop that, Mr. Steele... I'm not Superman's girlfriend. I'm nobody's girlfriend. I'm much too old for anybody's girlfriend. And besides all that, I've still got lots of typing to do."

"The typing can wait till later, Lois," Steele turned back to her, "Go ahead now and get your bottom out of here."

Lois' last name of Lain, isn't spelled the same as Lois Lane in the comic strips; nevertheless Steele loved to kid her about it just the same. Every time he suggested she's Superman's Lois she would turn beet-red and counter with the same speech about being too old for that kind of nonsense.

This time Steele decided to call her bluff, "And just how old are you, Lois?"

"You know precisely how old I am, Mr. Steele."

"Let's see," Steele said, "If I had to guess I'd say a healthy thirty-five, Lois."

"That's very flattering, Mr. Steele, but you know that I'm fifty-three and not thirty-five."

"Just the same, Lois, you know it's not the years. It's how you look that counts and with that new hairdo, you look very much like thirty-five to me."

"Now you're pulling my leg. Aren't you, Mr. Steele?"

"Yes, a bit, Lois." He grinned, "but to be perfectly honest you don't look anything like a woman of fifty-three."

Lois chose not to continue the conversation further; her face still red, she left the room. She didn't slam the door, but she did close it with considerable force.

Steele went back to studying the river and the street below. It must have been below zero outside, but the chauffeur went about polishing the front fender and hood of the Lincoln with a rag.

Five minutes hadn't passed when the office door opened again. Lois walked in.

Steele turned to face her, "I thought I told you to go home, Lois!"

"Yes, you did, Mr. Steele. But, um."

"What—Lois?"

"Mr. Steele, there's a young lady outside who wishes to see you."

"Who? She's not a client?" He said as he put his cup down on the windowsill.

"You'll want to see her, Mr. Steele... she's a looker," Lois said, a broad smile on her face, "and from the look of her clothing, she's high class goods." She winked at him.

"Let me guess. The lady's wearing a full length mink coat, with red shoes, hat and gloves."

"How did you know that?"

"I saw her get out of a new Lincoln a few minutes ago. From the look of the car, I figured she came here to see that new accountant guy on the second floor. What's his name? Ah yeah, Fitchburg, Joe Fitchburg."

"Quite a deduction Mr. Detective..." Lois laughed. "But the wrong one, Sherlock. She's here to see you."

"Okay... what's her name?" With a sigh he put his pipe in his mouth and turned his gaze back to the activities on the river.

"A Miss Penelope Sinclair," Lois replied.

"Do we know her?" His attention again to the street and the chauffeur, who had worked his way around to the left side of the Lincoln.

"No, Mr. Steele. She's a new client. But no referral."

"Okay, I suppose I can spare a few minutes to talk with her... have her come in," he said as he picked up his empty cup and turned holding it out to Lois. "Would you mind re-filling that for me... and ask our guest if she would like a cup too."

"Yes... I'd be happy to," Lois said, as she came back to take the cup from his hand.

Steele stood at the window, his attention drawn back to the river. A Harbor Patrol boat with three blinking red lights atop its cabin and trailing a line of white bubbles twenty yards long in its wake moved steadily toward the outer bay. The window glass and the boat's distance muted, but didn't entirely block, the undulating wail made by the boat's siren.

From behind him, a low velvety voice, almost a whisper, said. "Mr. Steele." The words caressed his ears; as the room became enveloped in fragrance—Chanel No. 5.

Those two words immediately drew his attention away from the chauffeur and the activities on the river. He turned to see who owned the sultry voice. A voice that sounded like it should have come from a woman lying next to him in bed, not from a dame in his office.

It's amazing how much a man's imagination can read into just two words.

Steele's jaw relaxed, but he managed to keep his mouth shut. The most stunningly beautiful woman he had ever seen stood in the doorway. His knees felt like rubber and momentarily wouldn't work. He braced himself with a hand on the window frame.

The Conrad Kidnapping

Steele had been a detective for a long time and a man even longer. As a Military Police officer, during the war, assigned to the U.S. Embassy in Washington he met scores of high-ranking politicians, foreign dignitaries, and other famous people. He had attended international functions that drew women from almost every country in the world. He had met many of the most glamorous movie stars, among them: Rita Hayworth, Lana Turner, and Betty Grable, along with dozens of other, lesser known, starlets. He had even danced once, at her request, with Princess Sophia from Denmark at an embassy reception. These women, all beautiful and alluring, had nothing on the woman standing in the doorway of his office.

He stood there, frozen, looking at her. A tall woman, five foot ten, and perfectly proportioned—with fiery red hair cascading to the middle of her back. Her face had hints of amber-colored freckles sprinkled around the hairline and down the valley of her breasts. *Probably Irish heritage,* he thought. She wore a black silk dress that clung to every curve. He recalled Lois' earlier comment about fashion: *This dress looked like the highest of high fashion.* She wore a pair of red kid-skin gloves and a red hat with a gossamer thin veil. The mink coat hung across her right arm. She's the same woman he had seen getting out of the Lincoln.

A sound came from her lips—almost a whisper—as she smiled and spoke again, "Are you Mark Steele... the detective?"

"Yes... who... wha..." he stammered, as he tried to pretend that he wasn't fourteen years old on his first date with a girl. She smiled as if she understood his dilemma. He finally managed to finish the sentence, "Yes... what, can I do for you?"

She walked towards his desk, set her purse on its edge and tossed the mink coat on one of the overstuffed guest chairs in front of the desk "I need your help... there's been a theft."

Before the last word departed her lips and before he could respond, she had seated herself in the other visitors' chair. She sat back in the chair crossed her legs and pointed the toe of her red shoe at him in a provocative manner, as she gently lifted the veil up over the hat. She made no effort to tug the hem of her skirt down.

She looked directly at him, yet he detected a slight nervousness about her green eyes, which probably related to the reason for her visit to his office. Her lips parted in a half-smile and again in that low provocative voice... just above a whisper, "Can you help me, Mr. Steele?"

Steele sat down in his chair, attempting to hide the bulge growing in his pants. He hadn't been this unsettled around a woman since the sixth grade back in Nebraska when a new girl by the name of Mary had come to his school. He sat for a few seconds, trying to get his thoughts back to reality.

He began to speak, but his mouth went dry; he reconsidered for a moment.

Calm down Steele! This woman won't have much confidence in a tongue-tied detective.

Putting his unlit pipe in his mouth, then removing it again, he finally managed to say, "Sure... sure thing, uh... Miss Sinclair. I believe that's what Lois said."

She nodded as she casually brushed a lock of hair back from her forehead. "Yes, Mr. Steele."

Steele swallowed a couple of times and tried to continue the interview. Lois opened the office door, saving him from possibly embarrassing himself, as she brought in a small tray with two cups of coffee, a china sugar and creamer set.

"Just put the tray on the end of the desk," he pointed to a bare spot. "That will be all. Thank you, Lois."

"Would you like a cup of coffee, Miss Sinclair?" he said.

"Yes, coffee would be nice." She smiled, "But first, I insist that you call me Poppy."

Believing that it wouldn't instill much confidence in a new client for him to become tongue-tied at this moment, he said, using the best professional voice he could muster, "Okay, Poppy it will be," he beamed. "But, if I'm to call you Poppy, I insist that you call me Mark."

She smiled and nodded as she put a spoonful of sugar in one of the coffee cups.

"Poppy, now that's an unusual name." He grinned, "How did an obviously cultured lady as yourself, come to be called Poppy?"

"Mother prefers Penelope, but in school my classmates shortened it to Poppy, which I now prefer," she began to laugh, "Mostly because it vexes Mother so."

"Rebellious. I like that in a woman," he said, lifting the cup to his lips.

She smiled at him, batting her eyes.

Steele pulled a pad of paper and a pencil from his desk drawer, "You mentioned a theft earlier. Tell me exactly what's been stolen, and from whom, Miss Sinclair?"

She looked him squarely at him and smiled, "Mark, I thought we had agreed on Poppy."

"Um, yes we had." He shifted his weight in his chair. "Okay, Poppy. What' been stolen?"

"It's, um, ah. You see, ah..." She spoke haltingly and began to squirm in the chair. "It, ah... the item wasn't stolen from me, Mr. Steele. It's been stolen from my stepfather, Roger Conrad. My real father died during the war, at Dunkirk." She cast her eyes down and then up to look squarely at Steele. "I'm embarrassed to say it, but being rather young at that time, may father and I often clashed. We didn't see the world in the same way. He a staunch traditionalist didn't agree with most modern ideas. Now, I consider Roger to be my father."

Steele, seeking to use his best businesslike voice, said, "And you don't know what's been taken? Correct?"

"Yes, that's correct," she said as she began to nervously twiddle with her hands in her lap.

"I see," he said returning the pad and pencil to the desktop and picking up his pipe. "Do you mind if I smoke?"

"No, of course not. Roger smokes cigars, but I prefer the aroma of pipe tobacco."

He smiled at her as he struck a match and put the flame to the bowl of the pipe. Smoke swirled around his head.

"That tobacco has a wonderful fragrance—what's the brand?"

"It's a special blend I get from a little shop near Piccadilly Square in London."

"I was born in London... do you go there often?"

"No, I haven't been there since the end of the war in '45." He pointed to a tin atop the bookcase next to the desk. "The shopkeeper sends me a pound each month."

"I love the aroma." She said in a low seductive voice.

Steele leaned over and peered directly into her eyes again, "You do realize, Miss Sinclair—um, Poppy—I would love to sit here and talk to you all afternoon about tobacco—or even London—but if I'm going help to you, in any way, you must be a little more specific about what you want me to do."

"That could prove difficult... Father refuses to tell me anything more." She began to unconsciously fiddle with the hem of her dress, adjusting it up and then down, with her right hand. She looked conflicted; trying to decide whether seeing more leg would impress him or put him off.

"Have the police been called?" Steele asked.

She stopped fondling the dress and folded her hand in her lap, "Oh, no... heavens no!" She looked shocked at his question.

"And why not?"

"Father said that he can't do that; that's precisely why I came here to ask for your help."

"Then I will need to talk with your father personally. Can that be arranged?"

"Yes, I don't see why not. I'm sure that my Father will be furious that I talked to anyone about this, however I will address that state of affairs when it occurs."

Steele leaning back in his chair, removed the pipe from his mouth, and placed it in the ashtray. He folded his arms across his chest. "Perhaps after I talk with him, I will be in a better position to smooth things over a bit with your stepfather."

"That's very considerate of you, Mark. Perhaps, you might consider coming to the house for dinner this evening. That would be the best time to talk with Father." Her smile broadened, "Would this evening be convenient for you?"

"Okay, let's see," his face flushed as he began to fumble with the pages of his desk calendar. "Today's the eighth, I believe."

Poppy leaned forward, shifting her weight to the front edge of the chair, "No, I believe it's Tuesday, the tenth."

The pink blush on his face deepened. "Right, okay," he fumbled with the calendar pages. "I'm out of the office a lot, I often lose track. But luckily," he smiled as he reached for the intercom switch, "Lois keeps a more up to date schedule on her calendar... Let's see," he pressed the switch and announced, "Lois, can you check my calendar. Do I have anything scheduled for tonight?"

The intercom crackled, "No, Mr. Steele," Lois' voice responded, "I have nothing scheduled for you."

"Good, put down that I'm having a business meeting at the Conrad residence this evening."

He smiled across the desk at Poppy, "What time should I be there?"

"Dinner's at nine. Why don't you come at eight and have a cocktail. It will give you a chance to meet the family before dinner."

He directed his voice back at the intercom, "Lois, put it down at eight. Leave it open-ended."

The intercom clicked and buzzed for a second and Lois said, "Okay, Mr. Steele."

He looked squarely at Poppy, "Good... that's settled then. I'll be there at eight."

"Thank you, Mark," she smiled as she stood up, retrieving her hat and purse. Her smile turned to a grin as she put the hat on her head, drawing the veil down over her eyes, "I'll look forward to seeing you tonight." She flashed a provocative smile.

He also got to his feet, "It will be my pleasure, Poppy," he said, buttoning his jacket to hide the continuing tightness in his pants. "Poppy, um... Miss Sinclair, I don't wish to be presumptuous, but looking at you it's quite obvious from the expensive dress, the mink coat, the new Lincoln down by the curb that you're accustomed to the nicer things in life."

He picked up her mink coat and assisted her in putting it on, as they moved toward the door.

He continued, "I mean there are dozens of private detectives listed in the Yellow Pages. Several are upper echelon and very exclusive... so, tell me why you're here? What made you choose this office?"

Her voice, again low and sensual, "I don't know. I, um, ah..." she stumbled for the correct word to use, "Yes, I did look in the telephone directory. Your advertisement caught my attention. The phrase, 'Discrete Inquiries', struck a resonant chord with me, and I took down your address. And here I am," she said as turned to face him squarely.

"I see. So other than the telephone book, you've never heard of me before—that right?"

"Yes, that's correct. I did however, inquire about you with Mr. Glenn, he's the head of the legal office at father's company. Mr. Glenn's familiar with your work. He describes you as trustworthy and an extremely competent detective."

"I see. Unfortunately, I don't know Mr. Glenn. Did, he by chance, mention how he knew of me?"

"No, he did not."

"I see."

"Should he have told me more?" She said as she snuggled the collar of the mink tightly up around her cheeks.

"No, not at all. It's quite flattering that your Mr. Glenn knows anything about of me at all," Steele smiled.

"My father has always said that if you do good work, the people who matter will take note and seek you out."

"Your father sounds like a very wise man," Steele said

Poppy smiled at him, "Good afternoon, Mark." She held out her hand to him, "Thank you—you've been very kind."

He took her hand, "It's been entirely my pleasure, Miss Poppy." Bending a little at his waist, he drew her hand up to his lips and kissed the back of it. Her smile broadened as she walked out the door. He watched her walk to Lois' desk, where she stopped and looked back at Steele, flashed a broad toothy smile. She handed Lois a folded piece of paper. And, in a voice almost too low for Steele to hear, she said to Lois, "Mr. Steele will need this."

She glanced once more at Steele; turned away she nuzzled the collar of the mink coat up around her cheeks and ears as she left the office.

Steele leaned his shoulder against the door jamb and began to rub his chin with his right hand.

My God, this woman's staggeringly beautiful. And I believe she may she have more on her mind than her father's stolen property!

Lois got to her feet and came to where he stood. She handed him the folded piece of paper.

"What do you think, Lois?"

"She's definitely upper class material, Mr. Steele. That dress she wore cost as much as I earn in a year, not to mention the Italian shoes, bag, and gloves."

"You're joking."

"No I'm not, Mr. Steele. That dress *is* right out of the pages of Harper's-Bazaar. I'm quite sure it's an original

Dior. You need a rundown for the files?" She asked jokingly.

"By all means, Lois. How would you describe it?"

"Let's see..." she paused a bit putting her finger on her chin, "Strapless silk sheath with a fitted shelf bodice, overlaid with black lace kimono-style topper darted under the bust, with a bateau neckline front with a 'V' in back. Cap sleeves and neckline trimmed in scalloped black lace. The pencil style skirt hugs the body from the midriff area to the hem, which strikes the leg six inches below the knee, with a back kick pleat for ease of movement," she smiled broadly at him. "How's that, Mr. Steele?"

"Interesting, and very thorough, too. Have you taken up writing the fashion column for the Cambridge Chronicle?"

"No, Mr. Steele, but I read ALL the fashion magazines and the ladies at the salon love to compare the latest New York and Parisian fashions."

He unfolded the piece of paper and looked at it. "The dress isn't the only thing you're right about," he held the paper for her to see.

"What?" Lois said looking at him and not at the paper.

"You got the upper-class part right too." He pointed his finger to the amount written on the check.

"My god," Lois' jaw dropped. "It says a thousand dollars!"

"Yes, it does," he waved the check in a fluttering motion in front of her face. "And, we didn't even discuss money. Now, that's called class."

"And, look at that address," Lois snatched the check from his fingers and examined it more closely, "66 Beacon Street; that ain't exactly in the slums," Lois quipped as she began to walk back to her desk, then turned back to Steele, with a puzzled expression, "Beacon Street, that's near the Common, isn't it?"

"Yeah, right across the street, on the north side."

Lois opened the drawer of the cabinet by her desk and took out a black metal cash box. She opened the box with a key from her pocket and deposited the check inside.

"Lois, start a file," he called out over his shoulder as he went back into his office, "Label it CONRAD/SINCLAIR."

Lois nodded, "Yes, Mr. Steele."

Steele closed the door and stood leaning against it for a moment. This woman's presence had shaken him, but why? In an effort to cool down, he went to his private bathroom in the corner of the office, and splashed cold water on his face. Wrapping the damp towel around his neck, he moved back to his desk and picked up his coffee cup. He leaned his shoulder against the window frame. He sipped from the cup, completely oblivious that the liquid had gone stone cold. Nothing on the river caught his attention, no movement, not even a seagull flying by. However, movement on the sidewalk below finally drew his eyes down-ward. He caught sight of Miss Sinclair's red hat as she exited the building. She walked to the black Lincoln sedan still parked at the curb. The Negro chauffeur, leaning against the front fender of the Lincoln. He leaped into action, when he saw her and opened the rear door, as she approached the car. Before she got into the car she turned and looked up to Steele's window. Seeing him, she raised the veil of her hat and smiled at him, and then replacing the veil, she got into the car.

The car made a U-turn and drove off toward downtown Boston. Steele watched the car until it rounded a curve in the street two blocks away and disappeared from view.

Normally at ease with people in general, and women in particular, Steele found himself completely overcome by this new client. Her presence had awakened feelings in him that had lain subdued and dormant since his wife's death twelve years earlier.

Miss Penelope Sinclair could be the best thing that ever happened to me—or the worst. And, I'm damn sure going to find out which

CHAPTER 3

Ten minutes had passed since the Lincoln pulled away from the curb. Steele still stood by the window, coffee cup in hand, gazing at the place down the street where the car had disappeared.

He moved to the desk, picked up the telephone and began dialing the police department number. After the first ring a voice said. "Police."

"May I speak with Lieutenant Williamson please?" Several clicks and pops came over the wire; after a few moments of silence, the ringing tone came through.

"Williamson here," Hank's gruff voice boomed from the receiver.

"Hank! Steele here; are you very busy?"

"Nah, nothing much happening today. What's on your mind today, Steele?"

"How about meeting me at Alice's Diner? I'll buy you a piece of apple pie."

"You tryin' to bribe me Steele? Wha-da-ya want now?"

"New case… and I'd rather not discuss it over the telephone. Meet me at the diner in fifteen minutes."

"I guess I could break away from this desk for a piece of Apple pie. But only if it's à la mode." He chuckled.

"You got it. À la mode, it will be. See you in fifteen minutes."

#

Alice's place—a classic diner—built from an old Pullman car. Its location, only two blocks from Police headquarters, meant that a surprising number of policemen frequented the diner.

The diner had been in its present location since 1940 when Oscar Landis, a retired railroad chef of thirty-five years, convinced the railroad to sell him the car. The tracks it stood on had never been connected to an active line; they'd been laid down and the car put atop them. The Rail Road wanted to remove the trucks, but Oscar wouldn't have it, he wanted the authentic look of the car on wheels. Consequently, they'd been chocked and then permanently welded to the tracks.

Oscar died in 1952, leaving the diner to his wife Alice, for whom it'd been named.

Alice Landis, an energetic woman of sixty-two, and her forty year old son, Oscar Jr., ran the diner with the help of one waitress and a busboy/dishwasher. Junior did the cooking, except for Alice's specialty—baking pies. Each evening, before closing, Alice would bake four pies for the next day. Always three apple with the fourth being a banana-cream, lemon or any of a dozen other types. At Thanksgiving she made two or three pumpkin pies and for Washington's Birthday she always made a cherry pie or two.

Steele parked his car down the block from the diner. People may think it strange that a moderately successful Boston detective would drive an older car that his mechanic sees on a more regular basis than he does. But Steele's car is special to him: A forest green 1937 Cord, model 812 Beverly four-door sedan. The car once belonged to Steele's father. It had gotten a little run down over the years and Steele had undertaken the job of fixing it up. It's his only car and he uses it on a daily basis, when Dexter isn't working on it.

The Cord sports several dark gray primer spots on its fenders and doors. The car had a mechanism of gears and levers which opened and closed headlights. One of the gears to the left one had stripped, leaving that cover open all the time and giving the appearance of a sly wink.

Steele walked briskly through the cool crisp afternoon air. His exhaled breath hung in the air like fog. The scent of freshly baked apple pie flirted with his nose.

The Conrad Kidnapping

The fresh pie aroma reminded Steele of the first time he had gone to Alice's diner. It had been 4 years ago—in 1949—before he'd moved to Boston. Steele had first met Hank at the diner.

At that time—Steele still a private detective in New York City—had come to Boston on a case. He had received a tip that the runaway, a fifteen year-old kid by the name of Eric Sampson, he had followed to Boston, had been seen working at the diner.

Alice couldn't help him, the boy had never worked at the diner, but she did introduce him to Hank, a detective with the Boston police department.

Hank and Steele became good friends working together on that case—between them, they wrapped it up in three days. Steele took the kid back to his parents in New York, and later that year decided to move his detective agency to Boston.

Through the window, Steele could see Hank, already seated at the counter.

Hank should be pleased... freshly baked pie today.

As Steele entered the dinner, he saw Alice set a cup in front of Hank and begin to fill it from a coffee pot.

"I could smell the pie a half a block away, Alice," Steele said, smiling broadly at her as he took a seat next to Hank.

"Freshly baked for tomorrow's customers," Alice grinned.

"Any chance of getting a piece for my pal Hank, here?" Steele laughed, "I promised to buy him a piece if he would meet me here." He winked at Alice.

"I usually don't cut them until the next day," Alice said.

Steele leaned close to Alice and held his hand up to shield his mouth and whispered softly into her ear, "Alice, it's a little bribe, I need a little favor from the Lieutenant."

"Okay, if you put it that way, Mr. Steele, perhaps just this once..."

Steele grinned and said, "Make it à la mode, Alice. Ice cream on the side."

Hank looked at Steele, "What did you whisper in her ear?"

"I told her the truth. The pie's a bribe," Steele laughed.

"Okay, Steele. What do you want? And, am I going to get in trouble, lose my job, or worse, if I give it to you?"

"There won't be any trouble, my friend. It's not even a police matter. I just need a little information."

"What kind of information," Hank said as Alice slipped a saucer with a still warm piece of apple pie on it and a bowl with two scoops of vanilla ice-cream in front of him. He lifted the pie up to his nose and took in the delicious aroma. He smiled as he set the plate on the counter and cut off a piece with a fork and put it into his mouth.

"You, okay, Hank?"

"Yeah, hot apple pie always reminds me of being ten in my mother's kitchen," Hank grinned at Steele.

"As good as your mother's, I hope," Alice said, smiling broadly at Hank.

Hank lifted his fork to his mouth and took a bite of the pie, "Mm, mm, mm… much better, Alice. Much better. You know, my mother's pie filling tasted just like yours—delicious. But she tried and tried, and could never get the crust right. Your crust's perfect." He winked at her.

"Flaky pie crusts need lots of shortening. That's the secret. Lots of shorting." Alice grinned. "I could give you the recipe, if you like."

"That would be great, Alice. I'm going to see my mother next weekend. I'm sure she would be thrilled."

Hank took two more bites of the pie and turned his attention back to Steele, who'd been watching, but saying nothing. "How about you Steele, your mother bake good apple pie?"

"No, she wasn't much of a baker, except for bread. She made really great bread." Steele got a far off look in his eye, "and jelly, blackberry jelly—her specialty. The best I've ever tasted." He blinked a couple times and took a sip of coffee. He took his hat off, a snap brim fedora, and laid it on the stool next to him and looked at Hank. "But I didn't ask you to meet me so we could talk about pie and jelly recipes."

Hank slipped a fork full of ice cream in his mouth and swallowed, "Okay, pie bribery aside, Steele. Why did you ask me to meet you?"

"I have a new case and I'm hoping you can provide a little information."

"Who's your client?"

"You know better, Hank. I'm not going to tell you that, unless they say I can."

"Okay, fair enough. So, what do you need from me, Steele?" He took another bite of pie.

"My client maintains that there's been a theft from the Conrad Company. I don't know anything about the company. Can you fill me in?"

"Don't know much. I only know that they used to manufacture electronic gizmos for the government—the Navy. During the war as a beat cop, I used to patrol the place. Back then we looked for spies and Nazi saboteurs," he covertly held his hand up to his mouth, "pretty hush-hush stuff during the war. I don't believe it's still secret; I believe they switched over to televisions and radios after the war."

"What about Roger Conrad himself? I don't know anything about him."

"Yeah, your guy's a big shot, and whatever he did during the war made him a very, very rich man. I've read that he's on the board of directors of several companies: The Boston Ballet, National Heritage Museum and a member of Constitution Restoration Committee. He owns a big house over on Beacon Street across from the Common."

"That's why I don't know him. I don't pay too much attention to the society pages in the newspaper. World affairs, local politics, and the comics, that's my area. I let Lois handle the society stuff. She loves it," he grinned at Hank. "But you know nothing about Conrad or the company that might involve the police?"

"No, nothing." Hank turned his head and looked Steele straight in the eye, "Hey, you have information I should know about—don't you, Steele?"

"Nothing that I can tell you yet. I've only been told that it's missing; I have no idea what *it is*. I don't even know if *it's* anything the police should be involved with." He sipped from his cup, "I'm having dinner at the Conrad house tonight. If the status changes, you'll be the first person I call."

"You know, if it's illegal, Steele. I better be the first person you call."

Steele looked at him and frowned. Laying his hand on Hank's shoulder, he chuckled, "And just who else, my friend, should I call, McDoodle?"

Hank grinned as he cut another piece of pie and brought it to his mouth.

"Can you quietly snoop around a bit?" Steele sipped from his coffee cup. "See if there have been any police reports made either about the family or the company? Even a parking ticket in the wrong place might be a clue."

"I guess there's no harm in that. I'll have McDoodle take a look."

"I'd feel better if you did it yourself, Hank."

"Look Steele, if a Detective Lieutenant starts checking parking tickets, it won't be quiet for long. Nosy people might start asking the wrong questions. It won't raise any eyebrows if Sergeant McDoodle has a peek—he does that all type of thing the time."

"Okay, when you put it that way, I suppose you're right."

"Don't worry; McDoodle does things like this all the time for me. But I will tell him it's a sensitive matter and he should keep his mouth shut. He knows what to do."

"Thanks, Hank. I appreciate it." Steele waved his hand at Alice to refill his coffee cup. "What about you, you got any hot cases?"

"Nah, things are pretty quiet; nobody's killed anyone for a whole week."

"I read in the morning paper about an explosion on a ship in the harbor. Has our boy Boomer been at work again?"

Steele unconsciously began to rub the bullet wound in his left arm.

"No," Hank took in a piece of pie. "Last I heard Boomer left town... gone down to Jersey. And as for the ship that blew up, my friends at Harbor Patrol tell me that an apprentice boiler mechanic tightened down a bolt to tightly or didn't tighten it tight enough and the boiler blew up. The resulting explosion killed him and two other men in the engine room. Made a pretty big hole in the ship, too," Hank laughed.

"I'll bet it did," Steele smiled, still rubbing his arm.

CHAPTER 4

The Conrad house was a three-story red brick structure with an aquamarine patina on its copper roofing. Located in an upper crust neighborhood adjacent to the Boston Common, the building dated from before the Revolutionary war.

Steele parked on a side street around the corner from the front of the house. A two-foot high field-stone wall, topped with a four-foot black wrought-iron fence surrounded the property. Variegated green ivy formed a good portion of the fence.

The house's red brick structure had been tuck-pointed with black mortar. The window frames, mullions and shutters painted black. It had an impressive front door, a double hung affair, with six ornately carved panels. The high gloss varnish allowed the details of the carvings and the natural white oak wood grain to shine through.

Standing under the porch light Steele checked his wristwatch—it read 7:55. He grasped the big brass knocker and gave it a couple of sharp taps. Two minutes later the door-handle rattled and the big doors swung open. An elderly Negro man, wearing a black cutaway over a red waistcoat and sporting a very solemn expression appeared in the doorway.

"Yes, sir, may I help you?"

The man's clipped English accent brought forth a flash of memories in Steele of the time he spent in London after the war.

"Steele... Mark Steele. I believe I'm expected."

"Yes, Mr. Steele, Miss Penelope informed me to expect your arrival. He bowed his head slightly. "Please come in," he said as he stepped aside. "May I take your hat and coat?"

Steele scrutinized his surroundings as he began to remove his camel-hair overcoat. The enormity of the vestibule struck him. The walls of the round room extended to the top of the second floor, and capped by a dome with elaborate plaster work. Hanging from the center of the dome a chain supported an ornate crystal chandelier four feet above a round oak table in the center of the space. On the table a lace runner stretched across its width, anchored in the middle by a large oriental vase, containing two-dozen long-stemmed yellow roses.

"Sure thing." Steele handed the garment and his hat to the butler. "I trust I'm not too early."

The man extracted a pocket watch from his vest and glanced at it, as a grandfather clock began pealing in the distance. "I do not believe you are late, sir. Miss Penelope and the family are in the library."

The man took Steele's overcoat and hat to a doorway near the entrance; he placed the hat on a shelf and coat on a hanger, which he hung on the rod below the shelf.

As he closed the closet door he gestured with his hand toward the rear of the house. "This way, Mr. Steele. Cocktails will be served presently."

The hallway they entered stretched to the back of the house. Both men's shoes emitted noise on the polished black terrazzo floor. Heavy beams crossed the high ceiling of the hallway every ten or twelve feet. Between the beams the plaster ceiling panels displayed scenes of nude nymphs frolicking with young nude men.

Both walls contained a number of closed doors on each side. Between each doorway hung a large painting that almost seemed to glow, obviously painted by a Renaissance master. They went to the library located at the far end of the hallway, on the right side.

Barnaby opened the double door revealing a large room with shelf after shelf of leather-bound books lining three walls. Steele looked around.

Jesus, he thought, *You could fit my whole apartment and my office inside this room and still have enough room to park my car and a city bus!*

Elaborate French doors and windows covered the fourth wall. A group of couches, overstuffed chairs and tables with lamps encircled a good-sized oval coffee table near the windows. The far end of the room contained a tournament sized billiards table with massive carved wooden legs. A Tiffany light hung above the table and a half-dozen upholstered stools stood scattered around its perimeter. A low island wall containing a wet bar divided the room. Two large wing backed chairs stood between the bar and the billiard table.

Several people gathered around the billiard table drew his attention away from the room and its furnishings. An older gentleman and a much younger man played pool. Two women, one being Poppy, were seated on stools at the far end of the table watching a young man and an older man play pool.

As they entered the room the butler announced, "Lady Julia... Mr. Steele." He bowed slightly from the waist.

An elderly woman's face appeared around the side of the wing-back chair nearest the door. "Very good, Barnaby. That will be all for now."

Lady Julia looked about the same age as the older gentleman playing pool. Her clothing looked as if it had come out of the wardrobe department of a nineteenth-century movie set.

Steele held back the urge to pinch himself to make sure he hadn't been magically transported to the lavish set of a Leslie Howard movie, being filmed in an 1870's English manor house.

The lady wore a dark purple satin dress. The skirt went all the way to the floor. The top, a white blouse with a collar which covered every inch of skin to just below the woman's jaw, also had several rows of ruffles on the front.

She nodded her head and held out her hand, "Mr. Steele. Please, do come in."

Steele grasped her hand lightly and smiled, saying nothing.

She turned to face Poppy and said, "Penelope Anastasia, a drink for your Mr. Steele, please." She looked back to Steele, "What will you have, young man?"

Penelope got off her stool and came to where they stood. But before Steele could answer the lady's question, Poppy took hold of his arm and maneuvered him to the bar.

Poppy had changed clothes since their meeting that afternoon. Her choice in dress, now more conservative, undoubtedly influenced by her mother's wishes rather than her own fashion sense. She wore a black pleated wool skirt that fell several inches below her knee. Over that she wore a camel colored sleeveless cashmere turtleneck sweater. A single gold chain with a heart-shaped pendant fell halfway between her chin and the peaks of her breasts. The gold pendant, about the size of a quarter, had the letter "P" engraved in an elaborate script on its face.

"What's everyone else having?" Steele said, as his eyes scanned the room.

"Martinis, except for Mother; she's having sherry... which would you prefer, Mr. Steele, or perhaps you'd prefer Scotch or Bourbon?" She whispered in that voice that made Steele's knees turn to jelly.

"A martini would be just fine," he couldn't help smiling at her, "on the rocks—if you don't mind."

Using a pair of gold tongs she put two ice cubes in a short gold-rimmed highball glass. She filled the glass two-thirds full of clear liquid from a large crystal pitcher. Steele watched her intently, the muscles in her arms, breast, and abdomen tensioning attractively as she lifted the heavy pitcher.

"Onion or olive, Mr. Steele?" She asked.

"Neither," he said, smiling as he took the glass from her outstretched hand. He turned his head from her saying, "Nice place, yours or your parents'?"

"My parents'... but I do live here—upstairs," she giggled a bit as she rolled her eyes up. "In case you're curious." Her eyes conveyed much more than her lips— virtually an invitation. She took hold of his hand, "Come let me introduce you," she whispered, moving her hand up his arm to encircle his elbow with her arm. She steered him toward the pool table.

"Everyone, I'd like to introduce Mr. Steele," she turned and smiled at him, "Mark Steele."

The older man placed his pool cue across the end of the table and walked towards them extending his hand, as he got closer.

"Glad to meet you, Mr. Steele. I'm Roger, Roger Conrad, Poppy's father. You've met my wife, Julia, and that young fellow over there," he gestured to the young man he'd played pool with, "he's Poppy's younger brother Lawrence." He extended his arm, indicating the young woman sitting on the stool behind the table. "The young lady is Lawrence's fiancée, Miss Beverly Manners; Beverly's visiting us from New York City."

Conrad vigorously shook Steele's hand, then put his arm around his shoulder and began to pat him on the back as if they were old Army buddies who hadn't seen each other since the war.

After Conrad released his grip, Steele noticed a severe frown on the face his wife Julia. Penelope noticed her mother's expression too. She put her mouth near Steele's ear and whispered. "My mother was married to Lord Sinclair until he was killed in the war. She insists on being called *Lady Julia*... and my father will hear about that introduction, in no-uncertain terms, later tonight. He also likes to call me 'Poppy', which my mother deplores."

"From our conversation this morning," Steele looked into her eyes, "you have a preference for Poppy over Penelope, as I recall."

"Yes... I do use Poppy. Not because I have a particular preference to it over Penelope, both are acceptable; but 'Poppy' does annoy mother so, and that pleases me to a small degree."

"I see." He grinned holding up his glass in a mock salute, "Then Penelope it shall be, until I have reason to get on your mother's bad side."

"Hmm, mm—that's okay," she snickered almost under her breath, then said; 'I'm not a 'rebellious child'." she smiled, with emphasis on 'child', and winked at him. "I can be a little vexatious at times, perhaps... but aren't children supposed act that way with their parents?" She leaned close and kissed him very lightly on the cheek. "And I simply *adore* a man who knows when being diplomatic is the wisest course of action."

Lawrence approached them, a cue stick in his hand, "Mr. Steele, would you like to play a game?"

Steele sensed a high amount of stress in the young man's voice. The invitation may have been a plea to get him out of the game with his father, which from the look of the balls on the table; he had no chance of winning.

"No, no... maybe later; you should finish the game with your father."

Steele sat down on one of the high stools between Poppy and Beverly, with his drink in hand. He watched as the elder Roger finished the game. He sank all the remaining striped balls. And with a bit of fanfare he sank the eight ball in middle pocket. All of which didn't allow Lawrence a single shot.

Lawrence racked up the balls and started another game, with the elder Conrad breaking. He failed to pocket a ball on the break and Lawrence could shoot for the first time since Steele began watching them play. He walked around the table studying each ball's position from all sides.

He finally decided on a shot. The three balls lay two inches from one of the corner pockets, but the cue ball lay halfway down the table near the far side rail.

Not an easy shot, but quite makeable—for a semi-skilled player.

Lawrence bent over the table carefully lining up the shot; drawing the stick back and forth between his fingers a half-dozen times before he finally struck the cue ball. The ivory ball raced down the table, narrowly missing the seven ball as it caromed off the ten and hit the three, which careened into the cushion and bounced back into the middle of the table. The cue ball disappeared down the pocket at the far end of the table.

"Ha, ha... you scratched, my boy," Roger laughed as he retrieved the cue ball and placed it on the table, aligning it for a straight-in shot of the six ball, which he proceeded to sink into the corner pocket. He set his sights on the four ball which lay near the side pocket. Good aim and a sharp hit sent the ball straight into the pocket. It only took him a few minutes shooting before the remaining solid colored balls had disappeared from the table. The cue ball ended up hugging the rail by a corner pocket. The eight ball lay at the far end of the table about a foot from the rail cushion.

A long shot, but not that difficult for an experienced player.

Roger lined up his stick and struck the cue ball with a loud smack, sending it spinning down the table where it hit the eight ball, which shot directly into the corner pocket.

"Now that's how it's done, my boy. That's how it's done," Roger laughed.

Lawrence replaced his cue in the rack. "I give up. I give up, Dad... I don't seem able to beat you tonight."

Steele noted a brooding expression on Lawrence's face, which flushed red, as he sat down next to Beverly. He grinned at her, but Steele observed that losing in front of his fiancée had embarrassed the young man.

Lawrence didn't like that loss at all. He seemed like a very defensive man. He never went on the attack. Probably because he's played his stepfather, and lost, but that's doubtful. The shots he chose to make, his rigid posture, tell me that losing a pool game is not what's bothering this guy. He holds his cue like a weapon. A weapon he's failed to—or was afraid to—use effectively.

Lawrence and Beverly dressed quite casually in comparison to the others in the room. They looked as if they had played tennis all afternoon and hadn't bothered to change for dinner. For a man of means, Lawrence's wrinkled white slacks, tattered white sweater vest, and the badly scuffed white buck shoes indicate that he's rebelling—probably against his father.

From the way his mother, Lady Julia, looked at him she clearly disapproved of his manner and his dress.

"Okay, okay... but I'm just getting warmed up." Roger laughed as he began to twirl his cue stick like a majorette's baton, "How about you there, lit'l Beverly, would you like to play a game?" He stopped twirling the cue and pointed it at her chest.

"No, I'm afraid I don't play pool," she said.

Beverly Manners hadn't said a word during the introductions nor during the short time Steele had sat next to her. He noted that her voice sounded rather husky; a low baritone coming from a woman of Beverly's diminutive size caught Steele by surprise. Despite her deep voice, he still found her to be a very attractive young woman. She wore her jet-black hair cut short and combed straight back over her ears in a duck-tail. She looked twenty to twenty-five, about five feet six and very slim, not more than a hundred-ten or hundred-fifteen pounds.

"Come then, I'll teach you." Roger said, extending his arm towards her, cue in hand.

"Okay," she giggled, "If you think I can."

"Nothing to it, my child. It's easy. You take this stick and hit the balls with it. Simple as that," he said with a broad grin across his face.

Beverly blushed and began brushing at the sides and front of her skirt with her open palms.

Roger racked the balls, and said, "I'll go first." He jabbed the cue ball with his stick and racked-up balls went careening in all directions. None of the balls dropped into a pocket.

"Now come here, you little thing, and I'll show you how it's done," Roger said as he wiggled his finger in a *come -hither* motion in Beverly's direction. She got up from her stool and went to the table.

Beverly's tennis dress, obviously custom tailored, was made of white linen with a pleated hem. The dress appeared too large for her, fitting loosely about her petite body. It had a round neck with three buttons, all open, and short cap sleeves. She wore a white belt cinched around her waist, which made the hem of the outfit seem that much shorter. The dress showed lots of her legs, which had almost no contour to them, being straight and slim. She wore white canvas tennis shoes and Mary Jane ankle socks with lace trim.

"Now just watch me," Roger said, as he proceeded to bend over and align the stick on his outstretched hand and point it at the cue ball. Moving the stick back and forth along his fingers he gave the cue ball a heavy punch and it flew across the table hitting the seven ball sending it straight into the side pocket. The cue ball came back to almost the exact place it had been before he hit it. "Now you give it a try," he said holding the cue out to her. Beverly bent over the edge of the table in a childlike fashion and attempted to imitate Roger's movements. She poked awkwardly at the cue ball and struck it softly. The ball rolled across the table and hit the three ball, which hit the rail as the cue ball veered off into the side pocket. "That's good, my dear," Roger cheered. "But you scratched."

She looked at Roger with a blank stare and said, "Is that bad?"

Roger clapped his hands together and went over and put his arm around her shoulder and said, "No, not really bad, just another part of the game."

After she took the one shot, Steele thought *I understand why Roger wanted to play pool with this girl—she hikes that tennis dress up high enough for anyone behind her to get a good peek at those tight pink panties with lace trim.*

Steele looked at Poppy trying to project the best poker face he could muster under the circumstance. She didn't exactly flush, but her face took on a rosy glow. She had obvious seen the same thing that he had seen.

Ignoring the situation, as a good gentleman should, he leaned over and whispered into her ear, "I would like to talk to you and your father alone if that's possible."

The color still showed on her face, although she seemed relieved that no one mentioned Beverly's little lingerie show. She smiled, saying, "Surely... but after dinner."

Almost on cue, Barnaby entered the room. He walked to the large wing-back chair where Lady Julia sat. He leaned down slightly to address her directly, "Madam, it's 9:00pm—dinner is served."

# # #

The discussion during dinner centered almost exclusively on national and world politics. Roger believed President Eisenhower had done a good job so far, but expressed skepticism about Richard Nixon's competence as Vice President. He also voiced his concerns with affairs in Indochina, particularly Cambodia's independence from France, believing Cambodia might be ripe for a Red Chinese invasion, as they had done with Korea in 1950.

The women's talk gravitated toward the latest Paris fashions; in particular the fact that the dress hems had risen nearly two and a half inches this last season. The higher hemlines delighted Roger as much as they annoyed

Lady Julia. Poppy favored the shorter skirts, particularly the new styles by Christian Dior.

Steele, being diplomatic, agreed to most of Rogers's concerns, while reserving his doubts over China's interests in occupying Cambodia. He did refrain from getting involved in the ladies heated discussion over hemlines.

Lawrence and Beverly seemed to have their own agenda. They did a lot of whispering to each other. Beverly briefly engaged in the hemline debate; but neither participated much in the other topics of discussions that made their way around the table.

After dinner but before dessert, Lawrence and Beverly excused themselves so that they could go dancing. Then as Zoë and Barnaby removed the dessert dishes, Lady Julia excused herself with a headache, saying she would retire to her room with a headache powder, leaving only Roger, Poppy and Steele at the table.

After Lady Julia left the room, Poppy leaned over to Steele and whispered to him, "Mother doesn't really have a headache, she has just gotten a new color television and wants to go watch her wrestling matches."

Steele looked at her with a shocked expression. "You're kidding?" Then grinned at her.

Poppy giggled, "No, I'm serious." She drew her mouth even closer to his ear and shielded it with her hand, whispered in a low voice, "I'm certain she has a girlish crush on Gorgeous George."

Steele had to cover his mouth with his napkin to stifle a laugh and prevent the mouthful of coffee he had just sipped from splashing all over the tablecloth.

Roger hadn't been paying much attention to Poppy and Steele's conversation. He had been busy clipping off the end of a cigar and lighting it. "Let's adjourn to the library... shall we?" He announced, "I fancy a little brandy myself to go with this cigar. What about you, Mr. Steele?" He held up the open cigar box, "Have a cigar?"

"Brandy would be welcome, but I'll pass on the cigar." He extracted his pipe from his inside jacket pocket. "I'll stick with my pipe if you don't mind." He paused a moment as he began to get up from the table. "And you can drop the Mr. My father's Mr. Steele, I'm Mark... or better yet, my friends simply call me Steele."

"Okay then Steele it'll be; please call me Roger."

Entering the library, Roger went to the bar and began to pour three large snifters of brandy. He lit a candle sitting on the bar in a silver holder. He warmed each snifter in the flame before handing the first one to Steele, the second to Poppy, keeping the last one himself. He held his glass to his nose and inhaled its aroma. As he did so, he said, "Tell me, Mr. Steele... ah, um. I'm sorry, Steele, my daughter wasn't very specific; what's your line of work?"

"Poppy didn't tell you why I'm here?" He said giving Poppy a questioning look.

Poppy blurted out, "No, I um, no I haven't, um ah..." her hand came up instinctively covering her mouth in a gesture of embarrassment. She removed her hand and continued, in a calmer, more controlled voice, looking directly at Steele, "I haven't had a chance to talk to Daddy alone since he returned home today." She looked back to her father, "I'm sorry."

"Okay..." Steele said, eying her across the rim of his brandy glass as he took another sip. Setting the glass down, he said, "Then why don't you tell your father now why you asked me to dinner tonight."

"Yes... ah, Poppy, why don't you tell me what's going on here," Roger said with the cigar sticking from his mouth as he tried to light it and talk at the same time.

Poppy walked over to one of the sofas and sat down, crossing her legs.

"Poppy, are you going to tell me what this is all about?" Roger insisted.

Poppy gave Roger a pouting look, "Okay, okay, I will. But first, come here and sit down with me, please."

Roger did as asked and sat on the chair nearest the couch where she sat. Poppy began to swirl the brandy in her glass. She ran the rim past her nose twice before taking a small sip of the amber liquid. She looked at Roger and said, "Mr. Steele... uh... Mark's a private investigator. And, today I went to his office and hired him to look into the theft."

Roger immediately stood up shaking his finger at her nearly touching her nose with it. "How could you, Poppy? I told you I would handle this."

Poppy stood her ground, ignoring Roger's mock threat and said, "I thought it best to have a professional who's familiar with people who steal things, work on the case."

"But... but... they specifically said NO POLICE." Roger blustered, emphasizing "police" and getting redder and redder in the face as he became more animated.

"Has anyone been in touch with you, about this?"

"Yes, they have. I received a telephone call at the office; a man's voice, a gruff and husky voice, he said that they had something of mine, and they'd let me know, in due time, what it would cost to get it back."

"Have they called you back?"

"No, nobody has called... not yet."

"Has anyone called here at the house?" Steele looked at Poppy, "Has anyone called you?"

She frowned at Steele, "No. And no."

"Still," Roger said, "I don't like getting the police involved, peculiarly since they specifically told us not to call them."

"Daddy," Poppy sat down next to her father, "That's exactly why I engaged Mr. Steele. He's not from the police, he's a private investigator."

Roger looked at Poppy and then at Steele, and back to Poppy. He got to his feet and walked to the bar. His anger had subsided a bit and he said, "Okay, and now?" setting his still half full brandy glass on the bar. He picked up a decanter of scotch and filled a highball glass half full. He came back and sat down in the armchair and took a big quaff from his glass. He looked directly at Steele, squinted his eyes and leaned forward, and as he sat the drink on the table said, "Now-then, Mr. Steele. Tell me what you think about this?"

"Roger, at this point, I don't think much of anything. Penelope told me about the theft. But, she didn't tell me what had been stolen or from where. She gave me no other details when we talked in my office. She thought it best, given your hesitance to speak about it, that I should talk with you personally. I agreed with her assessment of the situation and accepted her invitation to dinner this evening."

But, mostly because I wanted to see her again.

"I see," Roger said while a look of relief washed over his face. "My daughter can be trying at times, Mr. Steele." A scowl returned to Roger's face as he glanced in Poppy's direction. He pulled another cigar from his inside jacket pocket, ignoring the half-smoked one smoldering in the ashtray, and went about lighting it. He didn't say anything. "Father, you shouldn't be that way; I'm certain Mr. Steele can be of help."

"I'm not sure if I should confide in anyone; they sounded quite serious when they called." Roger frowned, as he picked up the glass and drained its remaining contents in one gulp.

"Mr. Conrad, I don't want to interfere and I certainly don't want to force my services on you if you don't want them. But, in a situation like this, I believe I can help you."

"I wish you would listen to what Mr. Steele's saying, Father," Poppy said as she got to her feet and walked to where Roger stood by the bar.

"Okay, perhaps you're right..." Roger said, as he turned, addressing Steele. "You know, Mr. Steele, I've been in business all my life, but I'm at a loss as to what to do in this situation."

"You've probably never had this sort of situation come up before... am I right?"

"Yes, that's correct, *I have not*. I suppose I have every right to be a little confused by what's happening." He took a sip of his drink and smiled at Steele.

"Mr. Conrad, if you can fill me in on whatever *it* might be—then maybe I can help lift your confusion. After that we can formulate a plan to deal with the problem."

"Okay... um... last week I brought a few files from the office to work on here at home. The thing I..." he paused and took a sip from his glass. "I hardly ever do that; bring my work home with me. I prefer keeping my work life and my home life separate. It had been a spur of the moment decision on my part."

"What type of files are you referring to? Assuming of course, it won't give away any national secrets."

Roger walked back to the sofa and sat down, "That's just it, Steele... it may!" He sat his drink on the coffee table and looked straight into Steele's eyes. "The paper dealt with different projects my company has under development for the government. And that's about all I can say about them. I hope you understand."

"Okay then," Steel got to his feet and walked to the bar and poured a drink. He took a healthy slug from the glass. "If that's the case, you shouldn't tell me anymore."

Steele gulped the rest of the drink, "However, regardless of what the thief might have told you about contacting the police, you have to call the FBI immediately. You also need to have me checked out through the FBI and your own company security people. The FBI can call my office; I'll instruct my secretary to make any information available that they might need." Steele reached into his breast pocket, pulled out a business card case and handed it to Roger. "Then after you've done all that, if I can help, you can call me."

"It's not you personally, Mr. Steele, I hope you can understand that," Roger said. "It's just the situation."

"I understand completely, Mr. Conrad. I really do. During the war, I was a Military Police officer in the Marines; I understand fully how these things work. I can assure you, I take absolutely no offense."

Poppy looked at Steele and said, "I'm sorry, Mr. Steele... I had no idea it's such a serious situation. I just thought that Daddy's in such a state... I thought..." Her face and neck began to get a pinkish color, and her eyes welled up. She nearly started crying, but didn't.

"No harm's been done, Miss Sinclair," Steele said as he set his empty glass down on the bar, and pulled back the sleeve of his jacket and glance at his wristwatch. "It's half past eleven, perhaps this would be a good time for me to go."

Poppy got to her feet, a forlorn look on her face. "I wish you wouldn't leave so early," she said in a pleading voice.

He looked at her, "Considering the circumstances..." He turned and started walking toward the door.

She ran to him. "Mr. Steele," she smiled. "My goodness, what kind of hostess would I be if I didn't walk my guest to the door?"

"That's really not necessary, I'm sure I can find my way."

"Don't be silly, I insist." She slipped her arm around his elbow.

They left the library, neither saying a word during their walk down the hallway.

Poppy retrieved Steele's overcoat and hat from the closet near the entry. She stepped behind him and helped him get the heavy coat over his shoulders.

He turned around and gave her a big smile, "Thanks," he said as he put the fedora on his head. "Make sure your father understands that it's important for him to call the FBI immediately." As he put his hand on the doorknob he added, "They do have a night shift at the FBI building, so tonight wouldn't be too soon."

"I'll see that he does it right away," she smiled.

"The FBI can handle everything for your father; but you can call me if I can be of help to either of you."

She took his hand in hers and shook it lightly for a second and then began to squeeze it gently as she leaned into him and kissed him on the cheek, "Thank you, I'll make sure Father calls, if not tonight, then first thing in the morning."

"I will have Lois return the check you gave her this morning."

"No, don't do that. I mean, I wish you wouldn't do that—not yet anyway. Father may still need your help, whether he realizes it or not."

"Okay," he smiled at her, "I'll hold it for a few days, and we'll see what happens."

"Thank you," she smiled back at him. "I'll call you, and keep you apprised of the situation."

The night air seemed much colder now, as Steele stood on the stoop pulling on his leather gloves. His breath hung in a cloud around his face as he walked slowly down the steps and along the sidewalk to his car. He sat in the car for a moment staring out the windshield. He removed the glove from his right hand and felt his cheek: the memory of her warm kiss still lingered.

Jesus, what an enjoyable ending to an evening.

CHAPTER 5

After leaving the Conrad mansion, Steele pointed the Cord towards Cambridge and his apartment. He turned the radio on and scanned the dial to catch the news. There had been a bar robbery and shooting reported earlier in South Boston, but he found no new news reports about it.

A nice hot shower and a cold beer sounds real good right now.

After crossing the river he changed his mind, deciding that a cold draft and conversation might be more relaxing. He headed to the Rivers Tavern instead. The tavern's only two blocks from his office, an easy walk if the one cold beer happened to turn into two, three—or more.

Steele spent a lot of his off time at The Rivers, chewing the fat with Jasper Culpepper, the owner. Almost everyone called him Culp. Culp didn't delegate work easily, and consequently you could find him working behind the bar almost every day, from the time the tavern opened, till it closed. He often quipped, 'I worry about the place when I'm not here to keep an eye on things'. Accordingly, Leo Clark, his other bartender, only comes in to help with the weekend crowds.

The Rivers could not be called a trendy nightspot, like many of the upscale establishments in the downtown area. You're not likely to find a banker, a stockbroker, or a lawyer sipping a gimlet at the bar. It did overlook the river, but not at a scenic spot like the posher places along the south bank. The view from the Rivers Tavern encompassed only tugboats, fishing boats, barges, and docks.

The tavern's a unique institution. A place with a split personality—during the week it draws men who work the river: deckhands, roustabouts, and longshoremen. Rough men who are prone to throw a punch at you for no reason other than you've glanced in their direction. In contrast, when the weekend comes, the rough men are gone and the clientele consists mostly of M.I.T. students. Wealthy kids who have money and whose definition of an altercation would be a heartfelt apology and to buy you a beer after bumping your elbow on the way to the bathroom.

Steele liked Culp because he's not only a good listener; he'd also been a Boston cop until he smashed his knee tackling a young kid who had supposedly robbed a downtown jewelry store. As it turned out, the kid hadn't been the one who robbed the store. He ran from Culp because he had six outstanding speeding tickets and thought Culp wanted to arrest him for that.

Culp's knee had been mangled badly, bad enough that the city forced him to retire early when his leg kept him from completing the required training course. He'd refused to take a desk job.

Culp made a good sounding board when Steele had a tough case. Culp still had connections on the police force and enough people owed him favors that he could often get little things done for Steele that would otherwise be impossible to get done himself.

"How's things going, Steele?" Culp yelled as he entered the door.

Steele noticed that the bar only had two customers other than himself. A man and woman seated in one of the booths that lined the wall nearest the street. The couple didn't take notice of Steele; they seemed to be engaged too deeply in conversation.

"Slow night, huh?" Steele asked as he took a stool near where Culp stood polishing glasses with a bar towel.

"So, so," Culp nodded, putting down one glass and picking up another, "all the regulars, in earlier, have gone on to greener pastures."

A woman with blond hair stuck her head through the door and yelled. "Hey Culp, you gonna need me tonight?"

Steele turned to see Eleanor Dillard, one of Culp's part time bartenders, standing in the open doorway.

Culp yelled back, "Why, you got a hot date, Eli?"

"Yeah as a matter of fact, I do. Not that it's any of your business," she shouted, sticking her tongue out at him.

"He-rump," he muttered, waving a hand at her, "Go have your fun, but be here by seven tomorrow. You know how this place gets on a Friday night."

"Hey, Culp, be a nice guy, won't ya? I usually start at nine," she pleaded as she came through the door and sat down on the stool next to Steele.

"I am being nice," he grinned at her, "would you rather start at six?"

"No, I wouldn't." She got off the stool and headed for the door again. Halfway there she turned, "How about making it eight instead?"

"Okay, but not a minute later. You know one person can't handle this place with a big crowd."

Eleanor brought her hand up to her mouth and blew him a kiss. "Thanks boss. Love you. I won't be late," she called out, then left.

"Expecting a big crowd tomorrow night, Culp?" Steele asked.

"No, most likely it'll be a slow night; but she doesn't need to know that. Most of the river people get paid once a month; usually the first of the month. So it's been three weeks since payday and most of them are flat broke by now, and hoping they have enough to eat on till next payday."

"Must be nice to have everything figured out." Steele mused.

"You just have to pay attention to people, Steele. And besides, I've been here long enough to know when to expect a weekday crowd. Now, the weekends are not as easy to figure out. Those rich kids come and go. This week they may want to hit my place or maybe they'll decide to go downtown. Hard to figure these kids out."

Tom Saine

"I'm sure that if anyone can figure it out, you can, my friend."

"So what can I get you tonight, Steele?"

"A cold draft will do me just fine." Sreele gave him a little smile, "I could use a little conversation though."

"Oh, yeah? So, what's botherin' you tonight, Mr. Detective?" He slid the glass of beer across the bar. "Woman trouble, detective trouble, or both?"

"Maybe both, but mostly a case, or more correctly, a non-case." Steele put the frothy top of the glass to his lips and took a small sip.

"A non-case... what kind of case qualifies as a non-case?" Culp said as he went back to polishing another glass.

"Tell me. Did you ever have a case where the victim of a theft wouldn't tell you what had been stolen?"

"Can't say as I ever did. But under the right circumstance, sounds like it might be interesting."

"Like how?"

"Yes, knowing you the way I do, there's most likely a beautiful woman involved. That alone should make it interesting." He glanced away and then back to Steele. "Back in a sec." He nodded to Steele and went to the booth where the couple sat.

Steele hadn't paid much attention to the couple, but obviously Culp had had his eye on them. Steele leaned over to get a better look. He could see that the woman's blouse had been unbuttoned and man had slipped his inside.

A few words from Culp and the man threw a couple bills on the table and he and the woman left. Culp came back, picked up his towel and again went about polishing his glasses without saying a word.

"Tell them to get a hotel room?"

"Yeah."

"I could see he had his hand inside her blouse. I don't think he's feeling around inside there for a lost napkin," Steele chuckled.

"Yep. I wouldn't have minded watching them go to town. If they'd been in my living-room I'd have let them go all the way and enjoyed the show. But, I have to draw the line when it gets to be to obvious; after all, it's a public place." He grinned broadly at Steele. "Now, what did you wanted to talk about? You mentioned a non-case. What's a non-case? Never heard of such a thing, as a non-case."

Steele gave Culp the story of what had happened, the gorgeous woman showing up at his office, the dinner at the Conrad house, and the father's missing files.

"I knew there would be a beautiful woman involved," Culp said as he held up a glass to the light and began to scratch at a spot with his thumbnail. "But... doesn't sound like there's much you can do about it at this point, my friend. Unless..." he trailed off, but kept polishing his glasses.

"Unless what?" Steele asked, taking another pull from his beer.

"You interested in the case or just the beautiful lady?"

"I guess I'm a little curious..." He paused to sip his beer. "About both."

"Then the lady's the key. Take her to dinner. Talk to her, maybe she knows more than she's saying," Culp said as he turned around and threw a switch on the back wall behind the bar. The jukebox lit up and began to play. The twangy voice of Hank Williams filled the room:

🎵 🎵 *I'm so lonesome I could cry.* 🎵 🎵

Only the first few words had gotten out of the big Wurlitzer's speakers before the front door sprang open. Detective Lieutenant Hank Williamson walked through the open door. He had the usual grin on his face because of the music. As soon as he sat down Culp had a cold beer sitting in front of him.

"Culpepper, are you ever going to stop doing that every time I come in?" Hank asked in a loud enough voice to be heard over the music, "Okay... you've made your point, please turn it off."

"Hank, you know I only do it because I like ya," Culp said as he reached for the switch and threw it. The jukebox went off, "and I always pay for the fun with the first beer on the house, don't I?"

"Yeah, you do that, but I can't help it if my name's Hank, can I? And besides, Williamson's a long way from Williams, don't you think?"

"Maybe not for you. But, it's close enough for me—in spades," Culp laughed.

"Ah, Hank, stop bellyaching, you know you love it," Steele laughed as he patted the big man on the shoulder, "don't you?"

"I like the free beer, so I guess that's reason enough to put up with his little amusement." Hank smiled and took a sip of his beer. "Eventually I'll figure out how you know I'm coming in, and just come in through the back door."

"And you call yourself a detective," Culp laughed. "I always see your car go by out the window. I wait three minutes and then throw the switch. You're very punctual you know."

Hank didn't say anything. He rolled his eyes and put his head down, resting his forehead on the bar. Under his breath he whispered, "I should have known," and sat up smiling. "That's what I get for being predictable. Next time I'll park further down the street and walk slower."

"If you do that, I'll need to figure out another way. Maybe I'll hire me a lookout," Culp said as he continued polishing a tumbler. Hank didn't respond and he and Steele sat in silence.

Culp set the tumbler he had been working on aside and picked up another and began polishing it. "Steele, why don't you tell Hank about your little dilemma?"

"First of all, it's not a dilemma," Steele said.

Setting his beer down with a thump, Hank said, "So what's going on, Steele? You sound a bit defensive tonight.

This got anything to do with the Conrad Company you asked me about?"

"Yeah, it does."

Steele told Hank about the girl, about the stolen files and about the father's reluctance to bring in anyone to help, including the police.

As Steele finished his case outline to Hank, Culp chimed in, "I told him to pump the girl."

"Culp, she's a client, not a bimbo, or gangsters moll," Steele said an indigent voice.

"No, I didn't mean you should screw her, although that might work too," he chuckled. "I meant that you should take her out dancing, buy her a few drinks—I mean lot's of drinks—then see if she knows anything more that she's not telling you."

"That might work," Hank said. "Or I could have McDoodle pick her up and sweat answers out of her down at the station house."

"That's just it. I have a hunch she doesn't know much more than she's telling me now," Steele said.

Hank said, "If the girl doesn't know anything, maybe you need to talk to other members of the family. The brother, for instance; he may know what's going on."

Steele didn't respond, he just sat and finished his beer quietly, then had Culp draw another. Steele hadn't paid much attention until he realized Culp kept leaving to attend to other customers. Three men had taken the place of the young couple in one of the booths. A half-dozen other people had entered since Hank had sat down. The place had started to fill up.

"What's going on, Culp? Kind of late for a crowd like this isn't it?" Steele asked.

"The game just let out. If the Sox won they'll have one drink and all be gone in half an hour; if they lost they'll have two or more drinks—and may close the place up."

"Think I'll call it a night myself," Steele said.

"What about your case?" Hank said.

"Think I'll just sleep on it." He handed Culp a dollar bill, and looked at Hank, "Don't worry, I'm not sending her retainer back just yet; I have a feeling the lady or the father will call me tomorrow with news."

CHAPTER 6

As Steele inserted the key into the lock of his apartment door he heard the crashing of glass inside. He pulled his thirty-two from its holster, released the safety with his thumb and twisted the key silently in the lock. Crouching down by the wall, gun at the ready, he gently pushed the door open. The cat greeted him with a mournful *me-o-o-ow* and a strange look from the cat that sat just inside the doorway, his head cocked to the left.

Steele stood up gun still poised, and stepped over the threshold cautiously; his eyes darting from side to side as he surveyed the interior. He detected no evidence of an intruder. He closed the door quietly and went to the bedroom, then the bathroom, and finally the kitchen. He found nothing out-of-place, apart from the wastebasket in the kitchen. The contents of the overturned basket lay scattered across the floor; including the pieces of two broken beer bottles. Steele turned and looked at the cat who had jumped atop one of the stools in the kitchen.

"This is a pretty mess." He pointed the gun at the broken glass. "Your handiwork, I suppose? Or, did you invite a friend in to help you?" he said as he slipped the gun back into its holster and picked the wastebasket up. "You still like digging around in a trashcan, don't you?"

Rusty—the cat he'd befriended on the pier the night he'd been shot. Steele had given the cat the name because his face and ear looked like a rusted spot might on a black surface. Steele had felt sorry for the creature, scrounging through the restaurant garbage-cans for food, and had brought him home as one might do for a down-and-out buddy. Steele figured that anyone who tripped up Boomer, for any reason whatsoever, earned his friendship. They had become quite close, keeping each other company, during Steele's recuperation from the wound to his arm.

Rusty looked up at Steele, cocked his head to the right, then to the left—as if ignoring Steele's flare-up entirely—the cat began licking his paw and washing his face with it.

Steele looked at the empty food dish on the floor. "I reckon you're hungry—that it? That why you're back to your old habits of digging in trash cans?." He reached down and scratched the cat behind his one brown ear."

Steele found a leftover pork chop in the refrigerator. The cat watched intently as Steele diced the meat and put it into his bowl. The cat jumped down and sniffed at the bowl for a moment, then looked up at Steele.

"What do you want, Rusty? So it's not fish heads from Jack's Crab Shack. It's the best I got."

The cat looked up at him and let out another mournful *me-o-o-ow*.

"You really shouldn't be so finicky, you've gotten pretty fat while you've lived here with me."

Rusty cocked his head to the left.

"You know I should take you back to that pier. I wonder just what possessed me to go back for you anyway. How would you like to go back? Fend for yourself again?"

Rusty rubbed his body against Steele's leg, then left the room, headed toward the living room.

Steele followed the cat into the living room where he found it curled up in his favorite easy chair. Still curious about the bar robbery in South Boston, he turned on the radio and searched the dial for a news broadcast. Finding nothing but dance music he gave up, leaving the dial on a station where the Glenn Miller band played *In the Mood.* He went to the bedroom and got undressed.

The hot shower he'd anticipated since earlier in the evening felt good; he stood under the hot water, his hands braced against the wall, until the water began to get cold, which took nearly thirty minutes. The clock read 2:00am when he finally turned the radio off and settled into bed.

His thoughts about the case kept him awake. After ten minutes of staring at the dark ceiling he sat up on the edge of the bed, turned on the light, and began writing the essential facts in a notebook he kept on the bedside table. This affair wasn't adding up; so-far two and two has come up three. He needed more information. But he didn't even know what questions he should ask. And, why should he be this concerned about a case that wasn't really his case at all?

It must be the girl, Penelope Sinclair? She's certainly beautiful and I'm unquestionably attracted to her. She flirted with me from the time she entered my office, all through cocktails in the library, and throughout dinner. And that kiss. I've had clients kiss me before, but not like that kiss."

He rubbed his temple with his finger, shook his head, trying to clear his thoughts.

Or, am I trying to make a base-hit into a home-run?

He finally fell asleep forty-five minutes later, the light still on, pencil still grasped in his fingers, and the notebook lying across his chest.

# # #

The sound of the telephone ringing woke Steele from a sound sleep at five-thirty in the morning. It rang a half-dozen times before he finally picked it up. His voice erupted angrily into the mouthpiece, "I don't care who you are! Why the hell are you calling in the middle of the night?"

"Mr. Steele." The voice on the other end of the line came from a very excited Penelope Sinclair. Her voice had always been low and calm; now, its intensity and urgency had increased. "Can you meet me?"

"Ah... Miss Sinclair. Um, Poppy! I'm sorry, I didn't mean—"

"That doesn't matter. Can you come quickly?"

"Yeah, sure right-away. Where are you?"

"I'm downtown, at an all-night drug store."

"I'll be right-there. Which drugstore?"

"No, please don't come here. Can you meet me?"

"What's the matter? Are you hurt?"

"No, no... I'm okay. But my Father he's... I need your help, right away."

"Okay. Can you come to my office?"

"Yes, that would be perfect. I'll can be there in ten minutes."

"Okay, ten minutes," Steele said and hung up the phone.

Steele dressed quickly; he didn't even bother putting on underwear. He ran from the building still stuffing his shirt-tail into his pants. He started the car and buttoned the shirt as he drove. It only took him three or four minutes to cover the mile to the office. He parked at the curb in front of the building. His watch told him that it had been precisely eleven minutes since Poppy had called. She hadn't arrived yet. Rather than go upstairs and wait in the office, he decided to wait in the car.

Another five minutes passed before a cab pulled up to the curb in front of the building and Poppy got out.

She smiled at him as he approached her. She said, "Can you pay the cabbie for me?"

"Sure," he said as he removed his wallet and handed the cabbie a five-dollar bill. The cabbie fumbled with a bunch of bills, but Steele said, "Keep it, buddy," and waved him off.

As the cab pulled away Steele finally got a good look at Penelope. She had previously presented herself in a most proper way—sexy but not trashy. Now, however, she wore only a light cotton laboratory smock, its hem falling halfway down her thigh. She wore no makeup, her hair a tangled mess, hadn't been combed.

"Why are you dressed like that?" Steele asked as he turned from the cab.

Penelope stood in ankle-deep snow; her feet bare and dirty, like she's sloshed through a newly plowed field after a rainstorm. She clutched the smock about herself and began to shiver uncontrollably.

"Jesus! You're freezing," he said as he took off his overcoat and began wrapping it around her shoulders. "And what's this?" He touched her forehead with his finger, inspecting a swollen reddish spot. "Who hit you?" She didn't answer his questions. Still shivering, she drew the overcoat tightly around herself and said, "Can we go inside?" Her eyes pleading as her body trembled uncontrollably.

Steele took hold of her arm and led her toward the building. Her bare feet made it hard for her to walk in the ankle-deep snow and ice on the sidewalk. Steele picked her up, placing one arm behind her knees and the other in the small of her back. She hugged his neck as he carried her to the door of the building.

When they reached the door he said, "There's no snow here. I'm going to have to set you down so I can unlock the door."

She didn't say anything, but nodded and he let her feet fall to the concrete. He hurriedly found the correct key. They entered the building, and he locked the door. The building had no lights and the lobby looked as dark as a coal mine. "Wait here," Steele said, "while I find the light switch."

Steele's eyes hadn't had time to adjust to the darkness. And the street light, nearly half a block away, didn't illuminate the interior enough to help Steele find the receptionist desk. He remembered the location of the light switch's—on the wall behind the desk. He found the desk in the darkness, mostly from memory. But not before stumbling and almost falling to the floor causing the object to go skittering across the floor making a loud racket.

"Shit," Steele called out.

"Are you o, o, okay, Mr. Steele?" Poppy's voice quivering from the cold came from the doorway.

"Yeah, just tripped over a wastebasket."

He found the wall behind the desk, but there wasn't enough light to see the switch panel itself so he took out a match and struck it against the wall. The flickering flame allowed enough light to see the switch panel. Not knowing which switch controlled the lobby lights, he turned them all on. The lobby lights came on, and he shook the match to extinguish its flame.

Steele looked at the elevator. It remained dark.

"Only the janitor has the key for the elevator," he said looking at her. "Do you think you can you make it up three flights of stairs?"

"I'm not sure..." Her body still shivered badly. "But I can try." She managed a weak smile.

She managed to make it up six steps, before her legs began to wobble and she fell backwards. Steele caught her before she went down completely. He picked her up in his arms again, carried her up to the third floor and down the hallway to his office. He set her feet down on the tile floor and leaned her against the wall while he retrieved his keys and unlocked the office door. He turned on the lights and brought her into the office.

"Do you have a drink?" she said as she took a seat on the couch next to Lois' desk.

"Yes, but first I'll get you a blanket."

Steele went to his office, pulled open the sofa bed, yanked the blanket off and rushed back to Poppy with the bundle.

She had drawn her feet up under herself and pulled the overcoat snugly about herself. She shivered severely. Steele quickly wrapped her up in the blankets.

Her voice quivered, "I could really use a drink."

"Yeah, sure thing. I keep a bottle of scotch in my office for special occasions, and emergencies..." He went to his office door and turned back, "But, I'm afraid I only have paper cups."

"That's okay. I just need a drink." Her voice quivered severely. "Straight from the bottle would be okay too."

Returning from the office, he looked at her intently as he walked toward her with the bottle of scotch. He started to ask her if she needed another blanket, when he realized that she probably shook from fear as much as she did from the cold. He opened the bottle and poured a quarter of an inch into a paper cup.

Her hand shook so badly that she could not grasp the cup. Steele took hold of her hand to calm it and put the cup into her fingers. Her hand continued to shake and before she got the cup to her mouth she had spilled nearly all of it.

Steele took the cup and refilled it, this time nearly half full. He put his hand on the back of her head, like giving medicine to a child, and put the cup to her lips. She sipped the contents—draining the cup.

He refilled the cup again, this time she took the cup from him and downed its contents in one gulp. She then took the bottle from his hand, removed the stopper, and greedily gulped a hearty slug.

He grabbed the bottle and took it away from her. "Take it easy with that. A little goes a long way."

"I'm sorry, it's just..." her face turned red, "I'm so scared," she cried. "They, they... they took Daddy!"

"Okay, just tell me what happened, as calmly as you can."

Steele poured the cup half full again and handed it to her. She again drank it quickly. She held the cup up to him. He poured another quarter-inch and she drank that down too. She held the cup up again.

"That's enough for now," he said, "If you keep going, you won't be able to tell me anything about what happened."

"You're right," she said as she handed him the paper cup. "Maybe a cup of coffee... if you have any."

"Lois usually handles that, but I'm certain I can find where she keeps the pot."

Poppy's forlorn smile magnified the lost look in her eyes.

"Will you be okay while I find the coffee pot?" he asked as he got up and set the bottle of scotch on the corner of Lois' desk.

"I'll come with you." Her eyes began to brighten a bit. "Maybe I can help. I'd rather keep busy and not think too much right now."

She got to her feet, pulling the overcoat tightly around her still shaking body.

Earlier he had imagined that she had, at least, worn a nightgown under the laboratory smock; he now saw enough of her body to realize that she had nothing on under the smock. He fought to get such thoughts out of his mind.

Down Steele, as much as you'd like to, this is not the time to think about a beautiful naked woman in your office.

He picked up the blanket and wrapped it around her. Then, went to the thermostat on the wall by the door and turned it up to eighty degrees.

"Sorry I didn't think of that earlier. The temperature should come up in a few minutes."

"I'll be okay," she said, knotting the belt of the overcoat around her waist, and pulling the blanket tightly around her shoulders. Her shivering hadn't gone, but it had begun to lessen a bit.

"Lois keeps the coffee pot in the store-room." He pointed to the closed-door on the wall across from Lois' desk. "This way," he said as he opened the door.

He grinned at her. "I don't remember the last time I came into this storeroom; it's more Lois' domain than mine."

The small room appeared even smaller with all the file cabinets and high shelving, covered with office supplies and boxes. Lois had set up a little kitchenette with a hot plate and a small refrigerator on a table by one wall. Steele found the can of coffee in a cabinet over the counter and

Poppy filled the pot with water from the sink in the bathroom. Within a few minutes the coffee pot began to perk on the hot plate.

Making the coffee had a calming effect on Poppy. By the time it'd finished perking, Poppy's anxiety had waned a bit. With their cups in hand, Steele took her to his office. She sat on the couch with her legs pulled up under herself. She no longer looked cold and the fear he had seen in her eyes earlier had mostly faded away.

"Okay now young lady, can you tell me why I have an almost naked woman in my office this early in the morning?" Steele asked with a deliberate glint of lust in his eye. Then he turned more serious and asked her, "and how did you get that bruise on your forehead?"

She flushed a little and tried to smile. "I couldn't sleep last night and I came downstairs to make a cup of hot cocoa. While in the kitchen, the doorbell rang and I went to answered it. When I turned the knob the door flew open and hit me, knocking me down."

She rubbed the bruise on her forehead. "The door must have hit me on the forehead. The next thing I knew a heavy individual had jumped on top of me and held my head down mashing my face into the floor. I heard another person running up the stairs. The man holding me down stayed behind me as he wrenched my bathrobe from my body and wrapped it over my head so I couldn't see anything."

"Did they say anything?"

"No, neither of the men talked. But when the man who ran upstairs came back down, I could hear my father's voice. One of them, I don't know which, tied my wrists behind my back with a piece of rope, and then tore the bathrobe off my head. I tried to see their faces, but they had turned the vestibule light off, and immediately put a pillowcase over my head."

"So you can't describe either of these men?"

"No, not really. I only saw them for an instant, as they burst through the door. Even then, they only appeared as big, vague, dark blurs, coming at me."

She looked pensive. "At first I thought I'd imagined it." Her brow wrinkled. "But I'm positive they wore cardboard Halloween masks. The type printed on the back of cereal boxes for children. It's probably not much help but one looked like Bugs Bunny and the other Porky Pig," she snickered.

Steele chuckled too, "You never know what will crack a case."

Her smiling expression turned again to one of fear. "It all happened so fast I didn't have a chance to see much. I know they were big men. The one who carried me picked me up easily and threw me across his shoulder like a sack of potatoes. I'm not sure, but I believe they carried Daddy too." Her eyes welled up but stopped before she began to cry. "They threw us into the back seat of the car and then drove off."

"Do you have any idea what kind of car they put you in?"

"I'm not sure, I couldn't see anything, but I could feel things. The feel of the seats, door handle, and armrest reminded me of a car my father owned before the war. I'm quite sure it was a Cadillac."

"Did you recognize where they drove—where they took you?"

"They drove around, turning right and left many, many times. I don't believe they went anywhere in particular; they only drove around, trying to confuse us. Then after about ten minutes they stopped. That's when they put me out of the car. They left me there with the pillowcase still over my head and my wrists tied together."

"Where did they leave you?"

"At first I didn't know. I found myself lying in a pile of snow. I heard the door close and the car drive away. A man removed the pillowcase from my head and untied my hands. I had been left in front of the all-night drugstore. The man, the pharmacist at the drug store, gave me this smock and let me use his telephone—that's when I called you."

She began to cry. "They still have my father. He may be hurt, even dead by now!"

Steele sat down beside her and took hold of her hand and let her lean her head on his shoulder. "I don't think they will harm him. They will probably demand a ransom. Till that happens, I'm sure your father's still safe."

"I hope you're right, Mr. Steele," she sobbed. "I'm terribly afraid for him."

"Do you think the man at the drugstore, the pharmacist; do you think he may have seen anything?"

"I don't know, he said nothing to me."

"That's okay; I'll go by and talk with him later. Did the men in the car say anything about what they wanted or your father's location? Did you recognize any of their voices?"

"None of them said even one word—not one word." she began to cry even harder. "What's going to happen to my father?"

Steele got up from the couch and went to his desk and started dialing the phone.

"Who are you calling," she asked with a quiver in her voice.

"It's time we called the police," he said listening to the line ring in his ear.

"You can't do that—what about my father?" she pleaded.

"Your father's exactly why I have to do this—this has definitely become a job for the police."

The phone rang six or seven times before a woman's voice came on the line, "Boston Police, Sergeant Bradford speaking—what can I do for you?"

"Mark Steele here. Can I speak with Detective Lieutenant Williamson, please?"

The voice didn't answer. The line clicked and buzzed before a man's voice came through the receiver, "Squad room—Detective Gilbert."

"Mark Steele here, can you put Williamson on the line?"

"Sure I could, but he's not in yet."

"Okay," he said, "That's fine then, I'll call him at home."

Steele hung up and dialed Hank's home number. The phone rang three times before being picked up. He heard a loud thud as if the receiver had been dropped on the floor; followed by a long pause. Steele could hear voices in the background, indistinguishable but quite animated voices nevertheless.

Then Hank's voice came on the line, "Williamson— what the hell do you want at this hour?"

"Sorry to wake you, Hank," Steele said.

In the background Steele could hear a muffled voice. He could also hear Hank's voice, now also muffled as if Hank had put his hand over the receiver. Then it became a little more distinct. He heard Hank say, "It's Steele, go back to sleep." Then Hank's voice came back full strength. "What's up, Steele? This better be really important to call this early."

"Can you meet me the Conrad mansion on Beacon Street in twenty minutes?"

"Sure. But what's the emergency?"

"Roger Conrad's been kidnapped!"

"You shittin' me, Steele?"

"No, it's true. I'll fill you in when you get there."

"Are you sure?"

"Positive. Meet me at the Conrad house as soon as possible."

Steele, thankful for once that Hank hadn't quizzed him about every detail over the phone. He just said, "Okay, I'm on my way," and hung up.

Poppy looked at Steele. He saw the fear returning to her eyes. "Are you sure calling the police's the best thing to do?" she said.

"Definitely—Yes. Now we need to get over to your house as quickly as we can."

Fred, the maintenance man, must have come on duty at seven, because the hallway lights had been turned on and the elevator worked. They took it down to the lobby. Steele, entirely through rumor and innuendo, had gotten a bad enough reputation with the people in the building. Most had convinced themselves that Steele seduced every woman who came into the building. He wasn't that type of person, but that didn't seem to stop the rumors or even slow them down. The rumors would only be worse if anyone saw him escorting a half-naked, barefoot woman from his office. Luckily none of the other tenants had arrived yet, and he carried Poppy to the car without being seen.

#

They drove to Beacon Street in total silence. Poppy drew her legs and feet up on the seat cushion and rested her chin on her knees. She wrapped the overcoat tightly around her legs and feet. She looked like a small ball with her head against the glass and her body leaning against the door panel.

The morning traffic, heading downtown, slowed their progress, and they didn't arrive at the Conrad mansion until quarter past eight

CHAPTER 7

Beacon Street's a one-way street flanking the west side of the Boston Common. A police car had been parked across the street from the front entrance to the house; headed in the wrong direction it appeared to be unoccupied. Steele parked the Cord directly in front of the house. He got out and looked around—no-one in sight—he didn't see Hank anywhere along the empty street. Steele walked to the passenger door to help Poppy out of the car. As he did so, a second police car, its red light flashing, pulled up and parked behind the Cord.

Steele had barely gotten the door opened when Hank appeared behind him.

"Steele," he said loudly.

Startled by Hanks materialization, seemingly from nowhere, Steele instinctively reached inside his jacket for his gun. Seeing Hank he said, "Where the hell have you been."

"Just looking around. I checked the outside of the house and the grounds."

Poppy swung around in the seat and got her feet outside the car sill, the overcoat opened, showing her bare leg up to her mid-thigh. Hank smiled at her and winked.

"So, you two were out dancing? Ha, ha," Hank laughed.

Poppy glared at Hank, and if looks could actually kill, the look she shot Hank would have killed him dead as the proverbial door nail right there in the middle of the sidewalk. And after he'd died, she probably would have kicked his lifeless body into the gutter just for good measure. Hank's opening remark had aggrieved her and combined with the leering look he gave her legs, made her madder than hell.

"No," she yelled, pulling the overcoat tightly around her naked legs and body.

Steele helped her to her feet but because snow and ice covered the ground, he immediately picked her up and headed toward the house. "I'll explain later, Hank. Right now we need to get her inside."

Hank didn't say anything. He ran ahead and rang the doorbell. By the time Steele had gotten Poppy to the porch Barnaby had opened the door. He saw Poppy in Steele's arms and a look of astonishment came across his face that even his British upbringing couldn't conceal.

"Are you all right, miss?" he asked as he held the door open widely for them to enter.

"I'm fine, Barnaby." She looked at Steele and he set her down on her feet, "I'm going up to my room to take a hot shower and change into cloths more suitable for mixed company," she said it to Steele, but glared, over his shoulder, at Hank. "Barnaby, show the gentlemen to father's office." She looked back to Steele, "I'll only be a few minutes." She started towards the stairs then stopped, "Barnaby, would you also have Susan prepare coffee, juice, and toast for us all. Perhaps scrambled eggs and sausage too, or whatever she has in the kitchen." She turned again and ran up the stairs taking the steps two and three at a time.

Hank and Steele both watched her until she disappeared at the top of the landing.

Hank grinned at Steele. "That one's certainly got a little spunk—doesn't she?"

"Take it easy on her, Hank. She's been kidnapped too. Then they dumped her on street corner downtown, naked, hands tied with a pillow case over her head."

Hank looked up to the landing where Poppy had disappeared a few minutes earlier. His eyes got as big as pie plates. "You're shittin' me, ain't ya, Steele?" He winked at Steele. "Naked, huh!"

"Honest Injun, Hank—like the day she was born. Now if you can put your eyeballs back into their sockets, why don't we go to Conrad's office and have a drink? I'll fill you in on what I know up to this point."

The first door to the right down the hall on the ground floor led to Roger Conrad's office. The office wasn't as large as the library, perhaps half its size. But just like the library, shelving containing expensive leather-bound books covered the walls. A large red oak desk occupied the space in front of the window at the back of the room. A fireplace occupied the center of the right side wall; its oak mantel held many models of ships and aircraft—presentation models—all rendered in silver with black marble bases. Between the desk and the window stood a low credenza with a four-foot long fully rigged model of the *USS Constitution*—the oldest ship in the U.S. Navy, currently berthed at the Navy yard in Boston.

A small sitting area had been arranged at the near end of the room, made up of: A brown leather love seat, two red leather chairs, all positioned around an oval, glass-topped coffee table.

As Steele surveyed the room Hank sat down on the arm of the sofa and watched him for a few minutes, "Steele, are you ever going to tell me what the hell's going on here."

"In due time, old buddy. In due time." Steele started leafing through the papers on Conrad's desk.

Hank frowned, "It's not wise to do that without a warrant or his permission."

"I know, but it's all in plain sight, isn't it?" He glanced at Hank over his shoulder, "besides, he's my client, and if it helps me to find him, I don't think he'll make too much of a fuss about it."

Hank and Steele had been in Conrad's office for only a few minutes when Poppy came through the door. She wore black slacks, black high-heeled shoes and a blue-gray sleeveless sweater. She had obviously dressed hurriedly. The sweater hadn't been fully pulled down and she still worked at knotting the red scarf around her neck when she entered the room. Her hair had been quickly pulled back into a ponytail and tied with a red ribbon that matched the scarf.

Poppy opened her mouth to speak at the exact moment Barnaby appeared in the doorway. "Coffee, Miss," he announced. Barnaby pushed a wheeled serving cart covered with a linen cloth and carrying an ornately decorated silver coffee urn on a pedestal into the room. Cups and saucers flanked the urn along with an expensive looking silver cream boat, sugar bowl and a covered chafing dish over Sterno flame.

"Shall I serve, miss?"

"No, Barnaby, we can serve ourselves. That will be all for now."

As soon as Barnaby left the room and closed the door Hank got to his feet and cried out, "Now, can anyone tell me what the hell's going on here."

Steele waved his hand, trying to calm Hank down. "Rather than me tell you the story, I believe Miss Sinclair should give you a firsthand account of what happened to her this morning."

"Miss Sinclair," Hank said, "I thought you said that your father, Roger Conrad had been kidnapped. Isn't that true?"

"Yes, Roger's also been kidnapped. However, just to be clear, Roger Conrad's my stepfather. My real father died in WWII," Poppy said, as she started to pour a cup of coffee. "Please help yourself, there's warm buttered toast, eggs and sausage under the covered dish."

"Yeah," Steele said. "Hank, I should have introduced you. Detective Lieutenant Hank Williamson," he gestured with his hand in Hank's general direction, "This lovely lady's Penelope Sinclair," also gesturing in her direction as he lifted the silver cover of the dish and retrieved a piece of toast. Looking at Poppy he said, "Penelope, why don't you start from the beginning and tell Hank exactly what happened last night. There are still details that I don't know about myself."

She took her coffee and another saucer with toast on it and walked to the sofa and sat down. She sat the coffee cup and saucer down. Raising a piece of toast to her lips, she took a small bite and put it back on the saucer. Steele could see Hank getting impatient at the delay in her explanation.

Hank sat down in one of the chairs. Steele sat next to Poppy on the sofa. She took a napkin and patted her lips and looked straight into Hank's eyes as she began to speak.

"I couldn't sleep, so at two-thirty in the morning I came downstairs to get myself a snack. At about two-forty-five, while in the kitchen, I heard the doorbell ring.

"I had dismissed Barnaby and the rest of the staff at about midnight, and knew they went to their apartment on the third floor. The doorbell also rings in the servants' quarters, so I went to the intercom and buzzed Barnaby. He answered the intercom and I told him: 'I'm in the kitchen getting a snack. Don't bother to come down, I'll answer the door myself.' He thanked me and I proceeded to the vestibule to answer the door.

"I looked out through the peephole, but didn't see anything because the outside light had burned out. Thinking it might be one of the neighborhood youngster playing a prank, I opened the door a crack to see who, if anyone, it might be.

"As soon as I cracked the door, it flew open, hitting me in the head. I fell to the floor, momentarily stunned." She reached up and touched the black and blue spot on her forehead.

"Do you know who it may have been?" Hank asked.

"No. I only saw them for a second. Two large men—dressed in black and wearing cardboard Halloween masks—the kind they print on cereal boxes for children at Halloween."

Steele cut in, "She told me earlier that one looked like Bugs Bunny and the other one, Porky Pig."

"You're pulling' my leg," Hank laughed.

"No, Mr. Steele's quite correct, Lieutenant. They did resemble Bugs Bunny and Porky Pig."

"Okay, this all sounds a little silly, but I'll take your word for it." Hank wrote briefly in his notebook. "Tell me, what happened next?"

"One of them fell on me and rolled me over, so I couldn't see any more; he held me tightly from behind, putting his hand over my mouth. He wore gloves. I heard the other man run up the stairs. In less than five minutes the man who had gone upstairs came back down with my father. He'd been stripped naked and had a pillowcase over his head with his hands tied with a rope."

"Does your father always go around the house naked?" Hank said.

"No, not always, but I have seen him naked before. He often swims naked in our pool—as do I. And, I do not believe he always wears pajamas to bed."

"I didn't see a pool in the back of the house when I looked out the library windows," Steele said.

"No, Mr. Steele, the pool's not in the yard, it's located in the basement."

"So, you've seen your step-father naked in the basement swimming pool?" Hank said.

"Yes, many times."

"Not your usual family situation, I would think."

"We're all very casual about it, Lieutenant," Poppy smiled. "It's not at all unusual for members of the family to swim together nude. I've also swam with my brother, and occasionally with my mother although that's quite rare lately—mother rarely swims at all these days, with or without a swimsuit. That a problem for you, Lieutenant?"

"Ah, um, I suppose not. If it doesn't bother y'all, I guess I'm okay with it."

"You're not a very good liar, Lieutenant," she chuckled.

Hank blushed, "Okay, ah, um getting back to what happened last night."

"Yes, Lieutenant," she said as she took a sip of her coffee. "The man who went upstairs had brought a second pillowcase down with him and covered my head and tied my hands behind my back. They carried the two of us outside and forced us into the back seat of a car at the curb. I couldn't see, but I only heard the one car door close, so there must have been a third man already in the front seat of the car."

"Can you be sure of that?" Hank and Steele both asked in unison.

"Yes, I'm reasonably confident about it, Lieutenant. The engine started as soon as we got inside, and like I said, I didn't hear another door open or close. I'm almost certain the car's a big car—a Cadillac limousine."

"How do you know that, if you'd been blindfolded?"

"They put my father and me on the seat and the two men sat across from us, facing us. My father had a car like that, until shortly after the war. It has two small seats, across from the back seat—you can fold the seats up and down. I believe they're called 'jump seats'."

"Do you remember anything else about the car?"

"The sound of the engine—it rumbled just like Father's old car. I also felt an ashtray and cigarette lighter on the armrest of the door, similar to Daddy's old car. He doesn't have the car anymore, but I'm sure about it being a Cadillac limousine like the one he owned. Our chauffeur, Alton Johnson, maintains all of our automobiles. He can tell you the exact make, model, and year of the car. He may even have a photograph."

"Yes, we'll talk with him later. Did anything else happen in the car?"

"They drove around for at least half an hour and then the car stopped. One of the men in the back seat got out and dragged me outside with him. He got back into the car and it sped away, leaving me there with my hands tied and the pillowcase over my head. I'd been there long enough to work myself up into a seated position—perhaps three or four minutes—when the pillowcase was pulled off my head and a man untied my hands. The man, also the pharmacist from the drugstore, had seen me struggling in the snow-bank and came out to help me."

"Did he see the car, or the people inside?" Hank said.

"I don't believe so. I didn't see anyone else. Not even another car on the street."

"Anyone else in the drugstore? Maybe a customer?"

"No, I don't think so. Finding a naked woman outside his establishment distressed the pharmacist tremendously. He didn't say anything about seeing anyone, or a car. He brought me inside and gave me one of his laboratory smocks to wear."

"Okay, I'll have to talk to him later," Hank said.

"I finally convinced him I wasn't a crazy person or pervert running naked around the streets of Boston. And, he let me use his telephone—I called Mr. Steele. I also called a cab and had the driver take me to Mr. Steele's office. And that's pretty much what happened."

Hank sat with his mouth open for a few seconds. He finally took a long sip of his coffee and started to talk. "So you don't know very much about these guys or where they may have taken your father?"

"No, I don't know them."

"Which drugstore did you say they left you off at?" Hank asked.

"Boston Family Drug on Charter Street not far from the Old North Church. You can ask the cabbie. He picked me up there and let me off in front of Mr. Steele's office building."

"Which cab company?" Hank asked.

"Bunker Hill Cab Company."

"You said you had come downstairs for a snack because you couldn't sleep—correct?" Hank said as he thumbed through the pages of his notepad.

She nodded at him.

"What were you wearing?"

"My white silk bathrobe."

"What else?"

"Nothing," she said taking another bite of the toast.

"You mean nothing, no nightgown, not even a bra and panties?"

"Yes, that's correct. I always sleep in the nude, Lieutenant. I put my robe on, only by chance last night. Usually I don't bother when I come down late at night for a snack—but the air had a slight chill last night." She smiled at him.

Hank began to flush again.

"That seems to bother you. Nudity seems to bother you Lieutenant?" She flashed him a big smile.

"It's just that most people wear pajamas to bed."

"Not everyone," Steele said, "I often don't bother after a hot shower late at night. I often just go straight to bed."

"I'm not a bit surprised at that, Steele," Hank laughed. "You can be strange yourself at times."

Hank turned his attention back to Poppy "What happened to the silk robe, Miss Sinclair?"

"I have no idea, lieutenant. They stripped it off me before tying my hands behind my back, and then they put the pillowcase over my head. After that I don't know what happened to the robe. You should ask Barnaby, it's possible he found it. Unless they took it with them, it should be on the floor in the vestibule, on the stairs, or on the walkway outside."

"I'll be sure and ask him, miss," Hank said as he scribbled in his notebook. "However, it brings up a point that's been bothering me."

"And what would that be, lieutenant?" Poppy asked. "How did you pay for the cab?" He said as he leaned towards her.

She took another sip of coffee, and said, "I didn't give it a single thought when I called the cab. But, when I got to Mr. Steele's office I asked him to take care of it. Which he did."

Hanks forehead wrinkled into a frown. "Right Steele?"

"Yeah, that's how it happened."

Then Poppy said, "Oh yes... I just now remembered. I did wear a scarf on my head. Do you think it's important, Lieutenant?"

"No, not particularly," Hank grunted. The vagueness in her answers starting to get to him. However he made a note of the scarf in his notebook. "Do you still have the scarf?"

"No. Lieutenant—it's missing."

"Hank, I know there's not much to go on here," Steele said, "Penelope came to my office yesterday afternoon and asked me to look into a theft. It's my opinion that this kidnapping is in all likelihood connected to that theft. I met with Conrad last night, but he wouldn't tell me anything about the theft, not even what had been taken. However, when he told me the files pertained to a secret project for the government I advised him to call the FBI as soon possible. He said he would do it this morning; but, I don't believe he had time to make the call. Maybe that's a lead you can look into officially now that he's missing."

"Okay, I can do that. But I just had another thought. Does anyone else live here? And who are the servants and where are they? Dose his wife know anything about what went on last night?"

"Poppy can fill us in on the *who*. As for the *where*, I guess we'll just have to ask them."

"Okay Miss Sinclair, who all lives and works here in the house?"

"The butler's name's Barnaby, Barnaby James Wallace. He and his wife Susan have a small apartment on the third floor. I dismissed them both early last evening. Not long after Mr. Steele had departed. Perhaps eleven or eleven fifteen. Father and I talked for a while, but we had both gone upstairs by twelve-thirty."

"Anybody else in the house?"

"The chauffeur, Alton Johnson—he wasn't actually in the house—he has rooms above the garage. And Zoë had the night off. I believe she went out; I am not at all sure if she has returned—you can ask Barnaby, he will know.

"Who's Zoë?" Hank asked.

"Zoë Zimmerman. She's the maid. She helps Susan with almost everything around the house—cooking, cleaning, and laundry. She also has a room on the third floor.

"Anyone else?"

"Only my brother, Lawrence. His room's on the second floor, across the hallway from my room. But he went out with his fiancée Beverly Manners last night. They left shortly after dinner and I don't believe he's returned thus far.

"That's all?"

"And of course there's my mother, Julia. Her room's on the second floor. She went to bed early last night." She glanced at Steele, "About nine-forty-five, I believe... wouldn't you say so, Mr. Steele?"

"Yes, I didn't check my watch, but that sounds about right." Steele said, instinctively glancing at his watch."

"Anyone else?"

"No, that's everyone. All accounted for." Poppy flashed a big smile.

Hank wrote frantically in his notebook. He finally stopped and said, "So, maybe I should talk to your mother. I'm pretty curious—just how her husband could be snatched out of their bed and her not know anything about it."

"Oh," exclaimed Poppy, "that's quite easy to explain. They have separate rooms."

Hank's eyebrows went up. "Are they having marital problems?"

"I don't believe so. They don't act as if they are. And they haven't indicated to me in any way that they are."

Hank frowned. "Most married couples I know share the same room, the same bed. So why separate rooms?"

"My mother's health has declined in recent years. She goes through spells when she won't leave her room for days, or even weeks. The doctors call it a phobia. I believe he said... *agoraphobia*. He made it clear that it isn't dangerous to her and she's of no danger to anyone else. We, Susan and I, see that she takes her pills and then mostly indulge her wishes." She smiled as she nibbled on a cold piece of toast.

"Just the same, I should have a talk with her."

"Lieutenant, I would appreciate it if you didn't bother her. I don't plan or telling her about father until we know where he is and if he's okay."

"I don't know if I can do that." Hank said. "She lives in the house."

"I know, Lieutenant. But bad news like this upsets my mother terribly. When my real father died in France, she went into a depression that lasted for months and months—nearly a year."

"Maybe I can delay talking to her for a while. But before long, I'll need to talk with her."

"I understand Lieutenant, and I appreciate your understanding."

"What's going on?" Lawrence's familiar voice said from the doorway where he stood with Beverly. They looked tousled and weary, like they'd been out all night.

Lawrence picked up a piece of toast from the tray and took a bite. "I saw the police car outside, and Barnaby told me about the Lieutenant here."

Poppy got up from the couch and went to Lawrence and hugged him. "It's Daddy. He's been kidnapped."

Lawrence looked shocked, his face turned white, "Are you sure? When did this happen?"

"Yes, I'm sure... it happened last night. They took me too—but they let me go." Poppy began to cry as she stood there, her arms around her brother's waist.

"That's terrible," Beverly, said. "Any idea who may have done such a terrible thing?" she asked the room, rather than anyone in particular.

"What do they want? They want a ransom?" Lawrence asked.

"We don't know yet. They haven't called, and they didn't leave a ransom note," Steele said as he patted Lawrence on the shoulder. "This is Detective Lieutenant Williamson from the Boston police. He's just starting his investigation."

Hank walked over to where they stood, "You the victim's son?" he asked.

"Victim... I don't like the sound of that," he shot a look at Hank.

"Okay, sorry. Force of habit, I'm afraid. How about the *missing person*? Do you like that phrasing better?"

"Yeah... sure... um, ah. Okay. And yes, I'm Lawrence. Roger Conrad's stepson."

"Okay, then I need to ask you a few questions. First, where did you go last night?"

"Am I a suspect?" Lawrence looked perplexed and a little shocked.

"Oh my God!" Beverly squealed.

"I don't think so," Hank said with a shrug of his shoulder. "Should you be?" He gave Lawrence a stare.

"No. Hell, no! I don't know anything about this."

"Okay son, just calm down," Hank said. "It's a question I have to ask everyone."

"Okay, okay..." He removed a handkerchief from his breast pocket and began wiping his brow. He looked at Beverly. "Bev and I went dancing last night. We went to a club—several of them—till after three. Then we went back to Bev's apartment and spent the rest of the night there."

"Can anyone vouch for that?" Hank said.

"I don't know if anyone would remember us or not. I didn't see anyone I know, if that's what you mean."

"You didn't talk to anyone all night?"

"Of course we did. Maybe one of the bartenders would remember us, or one of the cab drivers."

"Can you give me a list of the places you went?"

"Okay, ah, maybe. You see I drank pretty heavily—I don't know." He looked at Beverly. She shook her head. "Let me think," He went to the bar and began to pour himself a tall glass of scotch. "I'll try to remember." He gulped half the drink. "Just give me a minute or two."

"Okay, Lawrence, I'll need a list as soon as you can get it. But I do have one more question."

Lawrence carried his half full glass of scotch back to the couch and sat down. "Yes, Lieutenant, what's your question?"

"Did anyone see you at the young lady's apartment last night?" He gestured toward Beverly.

"I can't say for sure," he growled as he threw back the rest of the drink, "I don't remember seeing anyone I know, they may have seen us, but I don't know." He got up and went back to the bar and began refilling his glass.

Hank turned his attention to Beverly. "How about you, miss? Do you remember seeing anyone in your apartment building?"

"Not last night, but I talked to the manager this morning before we came over here. He saw us both."

Hank looked at her with a scowl. "Okay, write your address here in my book."

Lawrence watched Hank disapprovingly as he talked to Beverly, his expression sullen and his brow wrinkled. He had finished his second scotch and began working on his third.

Hank turned his attention to Poppy. "I'm afraid I'll need to talk to the staff. Can you arrange that, Miss Sinclair?"

"Surely. They will all be in the kitchen preparing breakfast at this time of day. Shall I send them here to Father's office, or would you prefer seeing them in the kitchen?"

"The kitchen will be just fine. I could use a cup of fresh coffee," he laughed as he held up his cup. "Just show me where it's located."

"It's this way, Lieutenant." Poppy started toward the door and Hank followed her out of the room. Only a few seconds later he popped his head back through the door opening and said, "Do you want to come along, Steele?"

"No, I'll stay here. I don't think the servants can give us anything we don't already know," Steele said as he went to Roger Conrad's desk and opened one of the drawers. "I'll poke around here and see if I can find anything that will give us a lead."

"Okay, it's your call," Hank said closing the office door as he left.

Twenty minutes later Hank and Poppy returned to Roger's office. Hank didn't look like a man who had solved the case.

"You're right, Steele; questioning the servants didn't add much."

"Our best bet now is to question the employees at the Conrad Company. I suspect this kidnapping's related to the theft. Evidently, whoever stole the files didn't get what they wanted so they snatched Roger to get answers."

Hank chewed on a piece of toast. "You may be right about that, Steele. There's not much else we can do around here till the kidnappers make contact."

"Yes," Steele said looking first at Hank and then to Poppy, "We should put a tap on the telephone here, if they call." He shifted his gaze to Lawrence, "Would that be okay?"

Poppy looked at Lawrence, who nodded. Poppy came over and sat down next to Steele. "Yes... whatever we can do to help."

"Can you arrange that, Hank?"

"Okay, I'll call the office and get a wire-tap man over here to monitor and record any calls." Hank put his coffee cup down and snatched another piece of toast from the chafing dish. "Steele, are you gonna be here a while?"

"Sure."

He bit into the toast and headed for the door. "I'll go call it in on the car radio so I don't tie up the line if they call in the next few minutes."

The events of the last six or seven hours had begun to solidify in Poppy's head. She suddenly moved very close to Steele and buried her head in his chest. She began to cry. He held her and let it take its course. In about five minutes she sat up and dabbing at her tears with one of the linen napkins from the tray on the coffee table.

"Are you okay? Do you need to lie down for a while?"

"I'm fine... it's just that, I feel so helpless."

He could see the tears welling up in her eyes again.

"As I said to Hank, I'm convinced that this kidnapping's directly related to your father's missing files. I allowed him to be evasive about it when we talked last night, and that's my fault. I should have pressed him a bit more. But, he could have told me more without disclosing any secret to me," he leaned back to look at her, "Did he tell you anything that you haven't told me?"

"I don't think so."

"Think back, it might be a little thing he mentioned. Maybe he received a telephone call. Found a message... maybe it's so small that you don't think is significant.

Maybe a little clue that we need to find to make more sense of what's happened."

"I can't remember a thing that might help."

Steele looked at Lawrence. "How about you, Lawrence. Did you notice anything the least bit suspicious?"

"No, nothing," he said as he sat down in one of the chairs, placing his empty glass on the coffee table. "And if he or the company were involved in a secret project, I'd be the last person my father would confide in about it."

"You do work for him, don't you?"

"Yeah, I do. However, Roger doesn't let me handle anything of any importance related to the business. My primary role at the company *is* to occupy an office in the building. So no, to answer your question, he didn't say anything to me."

Steele noticed Poppy's eyelids flutter and her head slump forward; she'd begun falling asleep. "Poppy, you look tired," he said to her.

Her head snapped upright and her eyes opened wide. "I am, just a bit." She yawned, covering her mouth with her hand.

"A lot has happened this morning. It might be best if you get a little sleep. Maybe later you'll remember a little puzzle piece we need."

Steele got to his feet and helped Poppy get up too. They were about to leave Conrad's office when Hank came back through the door.

"I'll need to talk with the butler again. Is he still in the kitchen?"

"I'll ring for him," Poppy said and went to her father's desk and pressed a button on a small intercom box.

Only a moment had passed before Barnaby came into the room. "You rang, Miss?"

"Yes, Barnaby. The Lieutenant has thought of a few more things he needs to ask you about last night."

"Yes, Miss, anything I can do to help." He turned to Hank. "Lieutenant, what do you need to know?"

"Miss Sinclair has told me that the kidnappers undressed her before they took her from the house."

Barnaby stood ramrod stiff and said, "I'm sure I wouldn't know anything about that, Lieutenant."

"I didn't suppose you would, Barnaby. But my question's this." He grabbed another piece of toast from the tray and took a bite. "Did you happen to find a silk robe belonging to Miss Sinclair, in a peculiar place?"

"Why, yes I did. I found Miss Penelope's robe on the front steps when I went to retrieve the morning paper. I imagined that the laundryman may have unwittingly dropped it. I intended to speak to him about being more careful."

"Why would the laundryman be using the front door? Shouldn't he be using the servant's entrance in back?" Poppy said.

Barnaby turned to Poppy. "Yes Miss, you are correct, he would normally use the back entrance. However, he has a new truck—it's much larger than his old truck. The trees lining the alleyway in back pose a problem for the larger truck. So, understanding that, I granted him permission to use the front entrance until the trees in the alleyway can be trimmed to accommodate the larger truck."

"I see. Thank you, Barnaby," Poppy said.

Hank cleared his throat rather loudly. "Yes, getting back to my other question—concerning Mr. Conrad's pajamas—did you notice anything unusual about them this morning?"

"Why yes Lieutenant, now that you mention it—I indeed did find it a bit curious that Mr. Conrad's sleepwear lay in a heap in the middle of his bedroom floor. Very untidy, and not at all like Mr. Conrad is in the habit of doing."

"Anything else, Barnaby?" Steele asked. "Pajamas discarded in the middle of the room. Isn't that unusual?"

"Yes, it's unusual. Mr. Conrad's normally quite neat about his clothing. And, I also found it strange that one of the sleeve had been torn from the garment along with all the buttons, and the snaps on the waistband, of the trousers, had also been torn. I really didn't know what to make of it all."

"You didn't suspect foul play?"

"Why would I have reason to imagine that, Mr. Steele? After all, they are Mr. Conrad's pajamas, and I suppose he's allowed to do with them as he wishes."

"So you didn't think to question what you had found?" Hank said.

"Lieutenant, I would never presume to question Mr. Conrad about his pajamas. I had, however, intended asking if he wished to have them repaired or discarded."

"Perhaps I should have a look at these pajamas," Hank said in a gruff voice.

"As you wish, sir," Barnaby said as he looked at Penelope.

"Yes, Barnaby, go and get the pajamas for the lieutenant."

Barnaby turned to go to the door. His hand had barely touched the doorknob when Poppy said, "And, Barnaby, if the Lieutenant or Mr. Steele needs anything else will you please see to it."

"Very good, Miss.. I shall endeavor to be of as much assistance as I can be." He bowed ever so slightly at the waist, in Hanks direction, the turned and addressed Poppy, "Will that be all, Miss?"

"Yes, Barnaby, that will be all for now. However, I don't think I will be having lunch today. Will you have Zoë draw me a hot bath?"

"Yes, Miss, right away." He bowed again and left the room.

Barnaby turned to Hank, "Lieutenant, I will have the pajamas ready for your inspection any time before you leave."

Hank waved his hand in acknowledgment, but did not speak.

Poppy turned to Steele and Hank and said, "If you two gentlemen don't have any more questions. It's been a long and weary night. I believe I'll have a long soak in a hot bath and then take a nap."

Lawrence went to the bar and poured another drink. "That sounds like a good idea, think Beverly and I will go up to my room and have a nap too."

CHAPTER 8

Steele's watch read one-thirty when he stepped out of the elevator on the third floor of his building. The chatter of Lois' typewriter keys greeted his ear halfway down the hall as he approached the office door. He knew she'd been there since eight.

"Little late today aren't we?" Lois greeted him cheerfully as he came through the door. "You have a hot date last night, Mr. Steele?"

"Don't start with me, Lois," he grumbled as he hung his overcoat on the tree. "I'm in no mood today."

He shot right by her desk and went straight to the sink in his office bathroom and splashed water on his face and the back of his neck.

Lois followed him into his office. "What's the matter, Mr. Steele? It's not like you, being ill-tempered like that—what has happened?"

He emerged from the bathroom, drying his wet hair with a towel.

"Mr. Conrad and Miss Sinclair were kidnapped last night," he said as he wrapped the towel around his neck.

"That's dreadful! Has Miss Sinclair been taken too?"

"Yes, but she's been released; she's okay." He brought the end of the towel up and dabbed at a streak of water running down the side of his face. "She called me after her release and I've been with her since five-thirty; she's distraught, but unhurt."

"I'm so glad to hear that. She seemed like such a nice person. But, you say, her father's still missing?"

"Yes," Steele sat down in at his desk, still wiping his left ear with the tail of the towel. "Hank has put out an

APB on him. Other than that we don't have much to go on."

He took the towel from around his neck and placed it in a heap on the corner of the desk. "Get your pad, Lois, we need to update the Conrad file, while the facts are still fresh in my memory. A little coffee would be nice, too, if we have any," he added with the most cheerful voice that he could muster.

Two minutes later Lois returned with her steno-pad in one hand and a cup of steaming hot coffee in the other. She sat the cup on his desk and sat down in the chair in front of his desk with her pad on her knee and her pencil at the ready.

"What did you wanted to dictate, Mr. Steele?" She said cheerfully.

Ten minutes later he had finished relaying the story to her, beginning with dinner at the Conrad house the previous evening, Poppy's call in the middle of the night, her arrival nearly naked at the office in a cab, and their meeting with Hank at the Conrad house an hour ago.

"Type that up, Lois, and if you haven't done it already, prepare a folder for Conrad slash Sinclair and file that in the folder. And please start an expense sheet for the same names, starting yesterday."

Lois didn't bother to remind him that they had already started the file and the expense account yesterday. She just said, "Right away, Mr. Steele," and left the office, shutting the door behind her. A few moments later the familiar chatter of her typewriter began its cadence.

Steele laid his head against the back of the chair and closed his eyes allowing the rhythm of the typewriter to still his vague dire emotion concerning Roger Conrad and where he might be, and what had happened to him. The sound of the typewriter stopping snapped Steele back to reality; he remembered a promise he'd made and pressed the intercom key.

"Lois, would you please come in," he announced.

Lois sat down in the other guest chair, crossed her legs, positioned the steno-pad on her knee and, with pencil poised, looked up at Steele.

Steele waved his hand at her and said, "Put that away for a minute. I need to talk to you about…"

Lois placed the pencil and pad on the edge of the desk and sat forward in the chair. "Yes, Mr. Steele. Bad news about Mr. Conrad?"

"No, nothing like that. I haven't received any new news about that yet." Steele said as he began to fidget with his tobacco pouch and pipe.

"Then, what's bothering you, Mr. Steele?"

He stammered, "I don't really like to get involved in things like this but a friend has asked me—as a favor—to assist with a problem he's having. I told this person I wasn't comfortable doing what he wanted me to do but he insisted and made me promise to look into it."

"Is it a new case? Maybe I should take notes," she said as she reached for the pad and pencil.

Steele put up his hand in a "stop" motion. "No, Lois, it's not a case. It's a good deal more personal."

She sat back in the chair. "More personal. What do you mean by more personal?"

"I'm really not comfortable discussing this—but since I made a promise—I guess maybe I should just dive right in."

She didn't say anything, but he could see the questioning look on her face.

"Lois, when's the last time you went out on a date?"

She frowned, a bewildered look came across her face, "I, um, I, ah. Why do you want to know, Mr. Steele?"

"You've been my secretary now for nearly five years and not once during that time have you gone out on a date."

"What brought this up, Mr. Steele? Who in the world would want to know about me dating?"

"We'll get to that in a minute, for now, just answer the question."

She sat up straight. "Not that it's anyone's business, but I have too been on dates. Many dates in the last five years," she said with an indignant tone in her voice.

Steele turned his head so he could look her squarely in the eye. "When, where, and with whom, Lois? You've told me about everything in your life and you've never once mentioned going on a date."

Lois blinked, and slumped back into the chair as if being threatened. She blushed saying; "Bingo... I play Bingo with Barbara and Judy at the VFW every Wednesday night."

"That's not a date, Lois. That's an outing with your girl-friends."

"Fine, let me think." She closed her eyes a moment, then cried out, "Oh, oh! Oh, yes. Just last week, I went to the Rivers Tavern."

"Do you mean when you delivered that report to me?"

"Yes," she said in a sullen voice.

"Lois, Lois, Lois! Delivering a report to me at the Rivers doesn't count. That's not a date. Having a beer with Culp, Hank, and me at the Rivers isn't a date. Just because Culp, Hank, or I buy you a beer, doesn't make it a date."

"Um, ah..." her face began to turn pink then quickly went to red. "I suppose I just don't understand what you mean by a date then."

"A date, Lois, would require that you and another person, presumably of the opposite sex, spend time together doing an activity you both enjoy: A dinner, a dance, a movie, or a walk on the beach in the moonlight."

"Hum," she said making a face.

"How are you and our mailman getting along, Lois?"

"Oh... if you mean Mr. Hudson—we get along just fine." She folded her arms across her chest and frowned at Steele. "Not that it's anybody's business." She uncrossed her legs, re-crossed them and sank back into the chair cushion—the picture of defiance.

"See," he opened his desk drawer and pulled out his pipe and leather tobacco pouch, "I knew talking to you about this would be a bad idea a very bad idea." He opened the pouch and began filling the pipe.

Her facial expression relaxed. "So, it's Jeffrey. He's the friend you refereed to?" she said.

"Umm, ah, yes," Steele struck a match with his thumbnail and put the flame to the bowel. Two puffs sent a cloud of white smoke over his head. He waved the match about, extinguishing its flame and put the burnt end in the ashtray, "I know that he's asked you out many, many times. Now he's asked me for my advice. He wanted to know if I would talk to you on his behalf."

"About what, Mr. Steele?"

"A date, Lois. A date. The man's enamored with you. Can't you see that, Lois? He wants to take you out on a date!"

"He's very nice... but, I..."

"But what, Lois?"

"Every time Mr. Hudson...um, Jeffery asks me out all I can think about is Warren. What would Warren think?"

"Warren?" he paused a moment, puffed the pipe as he thought, "Ah, yes. I remember now—wasn't that your husband's name? Wasn't he a pilot?"

"Yes, he flew P-51's in the war. He..." she didn't finish. A blank look washed over her face. The color drained from her cheeks as if she'd seen a ghost.

"Yes, I see." His pipe had gone out and he struck another match and put it to the bowl. "He died in the war?"

"Yes... May the first, 1945. Just a week before the war ended."

"It's been... I, umm," he looked away from her for a moment, puffing on the pipe as he calculated the numbers in his head, "Eight years ago now."

"Yes, eight years." She withdrew a handkerchief from the pocket in her skirt and began to dab at the corner of her eye.

"I don't mean to sound callous or disrespectful, Lois, but do you feel that Warren would want you to mourn him for this long?"

"I don't know, Mr. Steele. I just know I still miss him so very much."

"Put yourself in his place... if you had died eight years ago and Warren sat here talking to me. Would you want that from him?"

"Of course not, Mr. Steele. That would be very selfish of me."

"Exactly my point, Lois. Isn't it reasonable to think that Warren would want your happiness? Even if it involved being happy with another man?"

"I don't know, Mr. Steele. You lost your wife too. Don't you think about her when you meet a new woman?"

"Of course I do, Lois. It's been eleven years, and I still miss her every single day." He picked up the picture frame on his desk. A double frame in gold which contained two pictures; one of his wife Nancy Lynn, the other their daughter Janet. He looked at them with misty eyes for a moment. "But I also know, deep down, the one thing that would make Nancy happy... would be for her to know that I'm happy; like I would if our circumstances had been reversed." He took the handkerchief from his breast pocket and wiped the glass a few times, then set the frame back down. He turned his attention back to Lois. "So, even though she can't be with me now, I know that whoever I date or whoever I may eventually fall in love with, Nancy would be happy for me. She would approve."

"That's very nice, Mr. Steele," she refolded her handkerchief and dabbed at a tear that had made its way half way down her cheek. "I had never thought about it in just that way."

"I'm equally sure your Warren would want you to be happy too—even though he can't be here with you now."

"I'm sure that you're right, Mr. Steele. He would... Warren's one of the kindest, most generous men I have ever known."

"I'm not saying that you should run off and marry Jeffrey. But you might want to consider at least one date with the man. Who knows, you may find that you like him. You may also find that you really have a lot in common. I know that he lost his wife a few years ago. I know he'll know just what you're feeling; he, maybe better than anyone else, can understand how you feel about your loss of Warren."

"I don't know, Mr. Steele. I do like Jeffrey, he's attractive, and he's amusing—it's just... it's..."

Steele held his palm up to her, cutting her off, "Look, Lois." He placed the pipe in the ashtray and both palms on the desk and leaned toward her. He looked straight into her eyes. "I know Jeffrey really likes you Lois—he's loony about you. Every time I meet him when you're not around in the hallway, the lobby downstairs, or on the street outside, he asks me about you... he doesn't talk to me about baseball or hockey scores, the horse races, or the weather; he only talks to me about you, nothing else—just you, Lois."

"I... I," she sighed, turning her head away from him. Her eyes wide open and fixed, staring transfixed out the window. She said nothing for a few moments. When she turned back to face him, he could see a fresh look about her. Her eyes looked bright and clearly focused. The corners of her mouth had begun to form the beginnings of a smile. "I still don't know, Mr. Steele, I'm not sure what I should do."

"I know you go to the movies, Lois. You give me a report almost every Monday morning. What would be the harm in meeting him at the movie theater? Watch a movie together. Let the man buy you a bag of popcorn for Christ's sake."

"I still don't know, Mr. Steele." She squirmed about in the chair and looked out the window again, seemingly lost in thought for several minutes.

He could almost see her thought reflected in her face as she considered what he'd said. He picked up his pipe and re-lit it, waiting for her speak. An old interrogation tactic he had learned from a detective he worked with in New York; 'Give the suspect the facts and let them stew about them in their own time.'

Lois wasn't a suspect, or anything like that, but the analogy still held up.

A minute later she turned back to Steele, then got up from the chair and came around his desk. "Thank you, Mr. Steele," she said as she bent down and kissed him gently on the cheek. She looked deeply into his eyes, and then smiling at him, said in a low voice, "You've given me another way to look at things; and I will think about what you've said."

"That's a step in the right direction. I will tell Jeffery that we talked; but any decision on the subject is entirely in your hands."

She went back and sat down in the chair. "Jeffrey's a nice man. And, I will give him... um, it proper thought." She grinned, as she picked up the steno-pad and pencil. "Now, you said you wanted to dictate notes, Mr. Steele?"

"No, no notes, we've finished with that for now." He said as he placed the pipe in the ashtray and got to his feet.

"Miss Sinclair called me at five in the morning and I'm a bit bushed. I'm going to lie down on the couch and close my eyes for a while. If Hank or Miss Sinclair calls, or anything important happens, just wake me up.

"Would you like for me to I close the blinds?"

"No, that's not necessary. I'm just going to close my eyes and rest for a bit." He said as he sat down on the couch

CHAPTER 9

Lois shook Steele's shoulder
"Mr. Steele... Mr. Steele, wake up, Mr. Steele."
Steele could barely make out the words in his sleepy fog. *Am I dreaming?* His mind wouldn't focus. *It sounds like Lois's yelling at me. But, Lois never yells. This has to be a dream.* His shoulder began to shake again, and he heard the voice again, "Wake up, Mr. Steele. An important package just arrived for you."

Steele sat up on the couch rubbing his face with his hands. "Okay Lois, I thought I'd been dreaming. How long have I been sleeping?"

"It's been nearly an hour, Mr. Steele."

Steele looked at his wristwatch as he said, "What's this about a package?"

"Jeffery...um, Mr. Hudson, the mailman, just brought it. It's a special delivery letter from Brazil." She held it in front of his face, "I didn't know you knew anyone in Brazil? Do we have a client in Brazil? Perhaps a friend from the Marines."

"I don't believe so Lois—but I'm still half asleep—just put it on my desk and get me a cup of coffee, please. I need to splash water on my face again."

"Yes, Mr. Steele."

Steele struggled to his feet and went to the washroom and splashed his face with cold water. Grabbing a towel from the rack he walked to his desk.

The package really wasn't a package at all; but a five-by-seven manila envelope. The return address, which had originally been printed on the envelope, had been over-typed with X's. Nevertheless, Steele could make out what it said; *The Conrad Corp., 303 Harrison Avenue, Boston, Massachusetts.* A new return address had been typed below the original. It read: *Sandoval, General delivery, Rio de Janeiro, Brazil.*

The envelope hadn't been sealed, only clasp-closed. It also bore *Special Delivery Mail—Signature required* stamped in red ink on the front and back. Steele inspected it more carefully and noted that the envelope contained a *Washington, DC* postmark; mailed at 9:07AM the previous day; it apparently had not been mailed in Brazil.

Lois came in with a fresh mug of coffee, which she set on the desk.

"Lois... Jeffrey still here?"

"No, Mr. Steele. He left right after I signed for the package... um, letter."

"Hopefully he's still upstairs. Will you please take the elevator down to the lobby and wait for him there? When he comes down, bring him back here to my office."

Lois left the office at a dead run. Steele went to his overcoat, took out his leather gloves, and slipped them on. He opened the envelope and withdrew the contents. His suspicions had been correct: the envelope contained a ransom note. The note had been typed on a very badly maintained typewriter.

```
AIR MAIL ALL DOCUMENTS FOR THE ENDEAVOR
PROJECT TO:
     SANDAVAL
     GENERAL DELIVERY
     RIO DE JANEIRO, BRAZIL
DEPOSIT 1 MILLION DOLLARS IN THE FOLLOWING
SWISS BANK:
     ACCOUNT: BANK OF BERN
     ACCOUNT #: 23937 6457 9928
THE PACKAGE AND THE MONEY TRANSFER MUST
BE RECEIVED BY MIDNIGHT MONDAY NIGHT
1953/11/11 OR THE OLD MAN WILL NEVER BE
FOUND ALIVE.
```

Steele laid the paper on the desk and copied its content, word-for-word, to another sheet of paper which he folded and put in his pocket.

Lois came into his office with Jeffrey the mailman close on her heels.

"Mr. Steele, I caught him before he left the building." Jeffrey, out of breath, huffed, "Lois said that you needed my help. What's up, Mr. Steele?"

Steele held up envelope Jeffery had delivered earlier. "This envelope you just delivered. Any way to trace this?"

"No, not really. According to the postmark it came from the Conrad Corp. in Washington, DC. The Brazilian address's probably a subterfuge—a phony. That's about all I could tell you about it."

"Can I see the card that Lois signed? What's the return address?"

"Sure thing, Mr. Steele. It's right here in my bag." He patted the side of his leather satchel.

Steele frowned, "Can I have a look at it?"

Jeffrey fumbled through the bag, pulling a fistful of letters out and laying them on the corner of Steele's desk. "Here," he said triumphantly as he held up the green card. "The return address's Rio De Janeiro, Brazil, Mr. Steele," he beamed.

"Sandoval, general delivery I suppose," Steele said. "Yeah, that's right... Sandoval, general delivery, Rio De Janeiro." He handed the card to Steele.

"Can you stay a few minutes, Jeffrey? I may need your help. But first I need to make a couple of phone calls."

"Sure, Mr. Steele. If it's important Post Office business, I can stay as long as you need me."

"That's great, Jeffrey. It's possibly, very important." Steele slid the small envelope back into the large envelope. "Why don't you have a seat." He gestured to the chair in front of his desk. "Can I have Lois get you a cup of coffee or a cold drink?"

"A Coke would be great." He turned and smiled at Lois.

Steele looked at Lois, "Do we have Cokes?"

"Yes, we do, Mr. Steele," she said. She returned Jeffrey's big smile, "I'll... I'll get you one right away, Jeffrey," her voice faltering a bit.

Steele noted a new sparkle in Lois's eyes and a lilt to her voice as she spoke to Jeffery.

Perhaps my talk with Lois did make a favorable impression after-all.

Steele snapped from his momentary distraction with Lois and Jeffery's romance and dialed the police department number. He waited while they found Detective Williamson. While waiting, his hand over the receiver, he said, "So Jeffrey how's that crusade of yours for a date with Lois coming along?"

"Just fine, Mr. Steele, just fine." Jeffrey grinned. "You mean she's accepted a date?" Steele intentionally looked surprised, because he knew that Lois hadn't. "No,   not exactly, but I'm *slowly but surely* wearing her down. As of today she's only turned me down one thousand four hundred forty-two times. I'm optimistic that she'll come around soon."

"Jeffrey, I believe you're the most optimistic person that I have ever met," Steele quipped, "but, it's likely you may be right this time."

Hank's voice came on the line. Jeffrey opened his mouth, about to speak, when Steele held up his hand indicating he wanted him to wait.

"Hank, there's been a development in the Conrad case. I received a ransom note this afternoon in the mail... Hell, I don't know why they sent it to me... No, I didn't get any fingerprints on it. Okay, I'll bring it over right away." He hung up the phone.

"Okay, Jeffrey, I will need your help."

Jeffrey jumped to his feet and said, "Sure thing, Mr. Steele. What can I do? I always wanted to be a detective."

"But, you're not a detective, Jeffrey."

Jeffrey's shoulders slumped and his smile turned to a brooding grimace.

Steele noticed his expression. "We'll just say a detective's helper, okay?"

"Sure, I didn't mean... whatever I can do to help."

Steele pressed the intercom buzzer. The office door opened and Lois came in carrying an open bottle of Coke.

Steele put the ransom letter back into its original envelope and turned to Lois. "Do we have an envelope large enough for this?"

"Yes, I believe we do, in the store room."

"Would you please find me one?"

Lois left the room and a moment later returned with a large manila envelope. Steele stuffed the small envelope into the larger one.

"Lois, I want you to work with Jeffrey."

Her face showed surprise which immediately changed to a demure smile.

"Lois, call Jeffrey's supervisor and have him come over here. Make sure he understands it's urgent. Show him this return receipt and find out if the Post Office can do any kind of trace on it, see if they can find out anything about the person who sent it. Make sure that he understands this could help in a kidnapping case."

Lois took the green card and turned to leave. Before she got completely out the door, Steele said, "Also, can you take a set of Jeffrey's prints so we can eliminate his prints from the envelope." She frowned again, then turned and left.

Jeffrey had a lost look on his face. Steele gestured with his hand for him to follow Lois. Jeffrey picked up his mailbag and followed her.

Steele dialed the Conrad's number. Barnaby's British accent greeted him.

"Barnaby, Mark Steele—may I speak to Miss Sinclair?"

"One moment, Mr. Steele, I'll see if she's available."

Three minutes later Poppy answered. "Mr. Steele, do you have news of my father?"

"Yes, I have new information. Can you and your brother meet me at the downtown police station, as soon as possible?"

"What's happened, Mr. Steele?"

"I received a ransom note in the afternoon mail."

During the slight pause, he could tell that she'd held her hand over the receiver and spoken to one of the servants. But, he couldn't make out to who, nor what had been said. Poppy came back on the line. "Barnaby tells me that my brother isn't here. He and Beverly left and didn't say where they were going, or when they would return,"

"That's okay—we can find him later. Just meet me at the police station as soon as you can."

"Okay, I'll be right there."

Steele grabbed the large manila envelope and headed out the door. Lois talked on the phone with Jeffrey huddled near her ear listening to the conversation.

"Lois, if you find out anything, call me at Hank's office," Steele said.

Lois had the telephone in one hand and handed him a folded piece of paper with the other. He unfolded the paper and looked it over. It contained Jeffrey's fingerprints and his name, address, and telephone number.

"You're so efficient, Lois, one of these day's I'm going to give you a raise."

Lois looked like she wanted to speak, but then she just smiled. Steele shrugged his shoulders, turned and left the office. He noted that Jeffrey stood closer to Lois than necessary as he wiped the ink from his fingers, and she didn't object.

The thought flashed through Steele's head. *Maybe this'll be just what ol' Jeffrey needs to get that date with Lois.* He smiled. "Ain't love grand," he said out loud just as the elevator door opened. The woman who got off the elevator gave him an *Are you crazy* look as Steele entered the elevator.

"Lovely day isn't it, Miss," Steele said as the door closed behind him. The perplexed expression on the woman's face caused his smile to broaden.

#

Steele jumped into the old Cord and headed to the police station. Light traffic made for a fast trip, until he got three blocks from the station where traffic came to a complete stop. He could see two cars in the middle of the next intersection. A small fender-bender, but it stopped traffic in all directions. No traffic in the opposite lane so he pulled out and drove a hundred yards on the wrong side of the street before turning into an intersecting alleyway. He drove two blocks down the alley till he found a cross street that wasn't blocked up. The detour had cost him only a few minutes.

Steele walked into the station house to find Poppy already waiting in the reception area. It had been almost an hour since he had called her. The on-duty Sergeant knew Steele as a friend of Lieutenant Williamson and buzzed them through the door. The elevator pointer indicated it had stopped on the top floor; they didn't wait for it to come down and took the stairs to the second floor.

Hank's office, if one could call it an office, consisted of a small cheerless room barely large enough to accommodate it's furnishings: A metal desk, a single file cabinet, and two straight-backed wooden chairs, one painted blue, the other green. The office, and even the entire building, hadn't been painted in recent years; the beige paint on the walls had begun to peel in many spots.

A stack of newspapers and magazines stood perilously atop the single file cabinet. Above the desk, a calendar hung on a nail; it displayed the correct month—but dated 1941. A framed, and autographed, photograph of Franklin Roosevelt hung next to the calendar.

As soon as Steele and Poppy entered the office, Steele handed the envelope to Hank. Hank took the envelope and yelled, "McDoodle, come in here."

A second later a heavy-set, bald man stuck his head in the door and said, "You need me, boss?"

"Yeah. Get this down to the fingerprint guys and see if they can find anything on it. And bring me a Photostat of the letter as soon as they can make one without destroying any fingerprints." He put his hands down on the desktop and leaned towards the Sergeant. "And, McDoodle, it's top priority! I want you to wait for it. Bring it back to me here yourself—understand?"

McDoodle grabbed the manila envelope without saying a word, and darted out the door.

Hank looked at Steele, "I don't expect we'll find anything, unless the kidnapper's a complete amateur." He sat down in his chair and immediately jumped back to his feet. "Oh shit! I should have looked at the note before I sent it out... do you remember what it said, Steele?"Steele pulled the folded piece of paper from his pocket and handed it to Hank. "Word for word. I copied it before I put the original back in the envelope. Don't worry. I wore my gloves so my prints won't show up anywhere but on the outside of the envelope. It's been typed on an old and badly maintained typewriter with misaligned type-bars. It looked like it had never been cleaned; most of the closed letters had filled in."

Hank sat down at his desk as he read the ransom note. "Ya know, Steele, I wish I had a few detectives in my unit as quick on their feet as you are." He laughed. "It would save me lots of headaches, not to mention shoe leather."

Hank wasn't the kind of fellow who went around patting his fellow workers, or anyone else, on the back for basically doing the right thing. Steele took his little admission as a real compliment. But knowing Hank as he did, he kept his thoughts about it to himself. Steele knew that if he acknowledged what Hank had said he would get embarrassed and would start denying that he had said it at all. Steele just smiled at Hank and nodded.

Poppy hadn't said a word except "hello" to Steele in the lobby. Now she spoke up. "What's in the note? Any clue as to where my father's being held?" she asked looking directly at Hank and then back to Steele.

"Nothing unusual. They want money. A million dollars, and Conrad Company design files... a project called *Endeavor*. Do you know what that might be, Miss Sinclair?" Hank asked as he passed Steele's handwritten note to her.

She took the paper and studied it for a while, then folded it and handed it back. "I have no idea what they're talking about. My brother may know about it, but I doubt it. He's supposed to work for the company, although I've heard my father chastise him many times about rarely setting foot in his office except at the end of the month to pick up his pay envelope."

Steele turned to Poppy. "You told me that Barnaby said Lawrence wasn't at the house. Maybe he's at his fiancée's place. Why don't you call there and see if we can get him down here to talk with us?"

"That's a good idea," Hank said as he slid the phone across his desk towards Poppy. "Use this."

"Okay," she said and began dialing the telephone.

"Hello... that you, Beverly? She's not home... do you know where she's gone? It's important I talk to her."

Poppy listened for a half-minute, shaking her head several times. "Okay," she said, and then hung up.

Poppy had a far-away, blank look on her face as she stood, not moving, not even blinking an eye. Steele touched her shoulder and she seemed to come out of whatever trance she had retreated to for those few seconds.

"Is everything okay? Your brother okay?"

"I talked with Beverly's roommate, Joyce. She said that my brother and Beverly have gone shopping in New York City," Poppy said as she sat down. "Father's been kidnapped and most likely dead. And my brother's off on a shopping spree to New York with his girlfriend." She began to cry. "What in the world's wrong with him!" she shouted.

Steele could see the tears begin to roll down her cheek. Hank handed her the box of tissues he kept on his desk for times like these.

"Lieutenant... Hank," Steele said, "Do you think the New York Police would be able to pick him up and hold him for a while?"

"On what charge, Steele? While it's certainly strange and unusual behavior for a son to go on a shopping spree after learning of his father's kidnapping—but it's not against the law."

"Yeah, I guess you're right, it's unusual behavior; but as you say he's not breaking the law." Steele got up and began to pace back and forth, but didn't say anything for a moment. He withdrew his pipe from his jacket pocket and began to light it. He stopped in mid-stride and looked intently at Hank who had watched his movements with great interest. "Okay, we can get to Lawrence later. But in the meantime, I believe it's about time the police paid a visit to Roger Conrad's office and got a few disturbing questions answered."

"You're right, Steele... I believe you're right."

Hank looked at Poppy, "Miss Sinclair, would you mind coming with me to your father's company headquarters?"

"I'm awfully tired, Lieutenant, I didn't get any sleep last night. Do you really need me to come along?"

"I would like to interview the employees, and if you come with me I won't have to waste time getting a search-warrant, you can authorize me to search your father's office as well as the office of the other employees."

"Okay, if that's the case, I would be happy to come along—but only if Mr. Steele can come too."

"Sure, that won't be a problem.

"But," Steele said, smiling at Hank, "there will be a problem."

"And what would that be, Steele—you got a hot date tonight?"

"No, Hank, I don't have a hot date. But it's after five, and if you want to interview employees, they've probably all gone home for the day."

"You've got a point, Steele."

"Lieutenant, Mr. Steele's correct," Poppy, said, "hardly anyone will be there at this time of day. I know this is important, for Father's sake, but can we go to his office the first thing in the morning?"

Poppy put her hand to her mouth to cover a yawn.

"Yeah, she needs to rest," Steele said, "And, I need to check with Lois and see if Jeffrey and the Postal Service have any news about that envelope."

"Okay," Hank said as he got to his feet. "I guess we can wait till tomorrow morning. God knows I have plenty of things to do." He put on his hat on as he headed toward the door. "I'll have McDoodle run down anything that's come up on that APB I sent out."

"Thanks, Hank," Steele said as he too headed for the door. "I'll pick Poppy up in the morning and we'll meet you at the Conrad building at nine."

CHAPTER 10

The Conrad Company occupied a whole city block, with its entrance on the corner of Hudson Avenue and Knox Street in downtown Boston. It occupied a ten-story red brick building built in the '20's. In appearance the building looked brand new; however, extensive renovations over the years had added stainless steel and glass to the exterior, making the place look more modern.

For a company involved in secret government projects, the security at Conrad's building didn't exist. No security guard greeted them when they entered the vacant lobby. Two clipboards with sign in sheets lay atop the unoccupied receptionist counter. The sheets carried the day's correct date, but nobody had signed-in today. A large white sign with red lettering hung on the wall behind the counter. The sign read:

CONRAD COMPANY SECURITY

- *All visitors must sign in before entering the building.*
- *A visitor's badge must be worn, in plain sight, at all times.*
- *Visitors must be accompanied by Conrad Company personnel at all times.*
- *All bags and briefcases will be searched upon exit.*

However, despite the stern warning sign, no guard or security personnel manned the reception counter, or could be seen anywhere in the lobby.

A directory by the elevator listed the executive offices as being on the tenth floor. No one challenged the little group when they entered the elevator, not even the operator who seemed completely uninterested in who got into his car. The book he read—a paperback edition of Parade's End, by Ford Madox Ford—had 100% of his attention. He never took his eyes off the page as he manipulated the elevator controls, stopping precisely at the tenth floor.

Poppy took them directly to her father's office, in the northeast corner of the building. Conrad's secretary, Mrs. Frances Stevens, occupied a desk just outside her father's office door. Poppy introduced her to Hank and Steele.

Mrs. Stevens, a woman in her late fifties, was dressed conservatively in a dark blue pinstriped business suit. Under the jacket she wore a white blouse with a starched collar and a thin black tie—a man's tie. Her dress could have come right out of the pages of Mr. Madox's book. The soldiers returning home from France after WWI would have considered the dress high fashion.

Hank held up his badge and identification. "Detective Lieutenant Williamson, Boston Police, Miss Stevens."

"It's 'Mrs.' not 'Miss,' Lieutenant." She pointed to a name placard on her desk.

"Sorry, Mrs. Stevens," Hank said, as he looked down, shifting his weight on his feet like a kid having been scolded by a teacher. "But, this's official police business."

"And just what type of official police business might be of any concern to either the Conrad Company, or myself?"

Hank's posture recovered; he stood tall with his chest puffed out. "Last night, two or more men kidnapped Mr. Conrad from his home."

Shock enveloped Frances's face as she looked at Poppy. "Is this true, Miss Sinclair?"

"I'm afraid it's true, Frances. The lieutenant wants to look for any clues in Daddy's office."

Frances looked sternly at Hank. "I can't imagine what you could find there, Lieutenant. But if Miss Sinclair says it's okay, I guess there's no harm in letting you look around." She opened the door and showed them inside.

"Thank you, Mrs. Stevens," Hank said as he entered the office. "I'm sure that Miss Sinclair can keep an eye on us for now. You may go back to your other duties."

Poppy smiled at Frances. "It will be okay, Frances. I trust the lieutenant. I'll call you if we need anything."

Mrs. Stevens did not reply, just nodded her head and left the room.

The massive office, looked more like a movie set than a corporate office.

"Jesus Christ," Hank said as he looked around the room, "you could fit my whole squad room in here and still have room for a basketball court."

A large cherry wood desk and credenza, polished to a high luster, stood in front of white draperies covering the two windows centered on the wall behind it. The clean desk top held only a telephone, a hand carved onyx desk set, and a blotter. On top of the credenza stood an extensively detailed model of an aircraft carrier. Steele judged that the letters "LEX" painted its deck made it a model of the USS Lexington, which went down in the Pacific during the battle of the Coral Sea during WWII.

Three overstuffed, wing-back guest chairs, upholstered in black leather, stood arranged in an arc, facing the desk. Two black leather sofas separated by a glass-topped coffee table occupied the center of the room.

A bar with a sink and black marble top was built into the wall and displayed an extensive assortment of liquor decanters. A small refrigerator rested below the bar, flanked by a nearly-full wine rack.

Bookshelves covered most of the walls not taken up by windows. Leather-bound books occupied the shelving; interspersed amongst the books sat model airplanes of various types, ranging from WWI biplanes to ultra-modern swept-winged fighter jets from the Korean War.

A long cherry wood topped conference table surrounded by twelve high-backed, black leather chairs occupied the area between the bar and a seating area. On the end of the table nearest the windows sat a telephone, an onyx desk set and blotter—the twin of the one on the desk.

Steele pulled Hank aside as they entered the room and suggested, "Perhaps we… ah, perhaps you, should ask the secretary... Mrs. Stevens, to have the senior staff assemble for a meeting here."

"I was just going to suggest that myself," Hank said,

as he went to the door and gestured with his hand to Mrs. Stevens. She got to her feet and came to the doorway.

"Yes, Lieutenant, did you want to talk to me?"

"Yes, Mrs. Stevens. I need you to assemble the senior staff here for a meeting as soon as possible. Can you do that for me?"

"Yes, I suppose, but... a few of them are out-of-town."

"Okay, do the best you can. If we need to talk to the ones who are out-of-town, we'll make other arrangements later."

Fifteen minutes later Mrs. Stevens returned. She knocked on the door and then came into the office, "Lieutenant Williamson," she announced, "all the executive staff that are in the building today are waiting in the reception area."

"How many are there, Mrs. Stevens?" He asked as he took a seat in the chair at the end of the conference table.

"Eight, I believe. All the others are unavailable."

"Is that unavailable out-of-town or unavailable—like they're on the toilet, or another cockamamie reason?"

"Both, Sir... four are out-of-town, one's on sick leave, and Miss Gelding, the company accountant, she's in a meeting, with bankers. Mr. Becker, the vice president of production, said he was too busy to come to a meeting now. But, I don't know if any of them are on the toilet," she said smugly.

"So, Miss Gelding and Mr. Becker are too busy to meet with the police." He scowled at Mrs. Stevens. "We'll see about that," and he yanked the pen from the writing set. "What are their numbers?"

"Miss Gelding's on extension 302 and Mr. Becker's on 217. Shall I call them again, Lieutenant?"

"No, Mrs. Stevens. I'll take care of this myself."

She turned and walked away as Hank began to dial the telephone.

"Is this Miss Gelding?"

"No, Sir, I'm Susan, her secretary. May I help you?"

"I'm Detective Lieutenant Williamson from the Boston Police department and I need to speak with Miss Gelding."

"I'm sorry, Sir, she's in an important meeting and can't be disturbed."

"Look, you tell her that this is official police business and I need her in Roger Conrad's office right now. Tell her that she can postpone her meeting till later."

"I can't do that, Lieutenant. She won't do that! This meeting's a very important meeting."

"So's this one. Tell her that if she's not in Roger Conrad's office in five minutes, I'll send a uniformed officer to her office and bring her up here in handcuffs. Do I make myself clear enough, Susan?"

"Yes, Lieutenant, it's perfectly clear. I'll give her the message immediately."

Hank looked at Steele. "Jesus Christ, Steele, what a bunch of prima donnas we got here."

Steele looked amused, "If you like, I can go extend a personal invitation to Mr. Becker. It doesn't appear that a simple telephone call will convince him to attend your meeting."

"You're probably right. Think you can get him here without shooting him?"

"I know I can persuade him easily enough—without broken bones," Steele chuckled. "I'll only shoot him as a last resort."

"Okay, go!" Hank glared at him. "But Steele," His glare turned to a smile, "you can slug him, if it becomes necessary."

Steele headed to the door and waved his hand in response to Hank's joking remark.

"And let the others in on your way out," Hank called out just as Steele opened the door.

Steele nodded and left the room, leaving the door open.

The staff had assembled outside the door, huddled into a group talking low enough so no one nearby could hear their conversation.

Steele announced to the group, "Lieutenant Williamson wants to talk to all of you inside." He gestured to the still open door to Conrad's office.

The group as a whole shot Steele suspicious looks, but none questioned his directions as they filed through the doorway.

Steele took the elevator down to the eighth floor to Becker's office. He didn't bother stopping at the secretary's desk; he walked right past her and opened the office door, bursting in. The secretary was hot on his heels.

Becker was sitting at a small round table with two other men. He sprang to his feet as soon as he saw Steele.

"Who the hell are you? This is a private meeting."

"My name's Mark Steele, I'm here representing the Boston Police Department. Your presence *is* required in Mr. Conrad's office. Right now!"

"I told my secretary I couldn't come until I'd finished this meeting."

"This meeting's finished... right now." Steele looked at the other men. "Gentlemen, you may wait here for Mr.

Becker—it won't be more than an hour or two. Or, you can come back later—perhaps tomorrow."

"You can't just barge in here and do that."

"I just did. Lieutenant Williamson wants you in Conrad's office now. He's already threatened other employees with being handcuffed and dragged to the meeting. So I suggest you come with me before he arrests you just on general principles."

Becker looked at Steele, then at the two men. "John, Howard, I guess I have no choice. Can you both check with Miss Billings and see when we can re-schedule?"

Both men nodded but didn't say anything. They got to their feet and left the room.

"What's this about anyway?" Becker said as Steele led him from the office.

"Lieutenant Williamson will explain everything in good time."

As they passed the secretary's desk, Becker stopped in his tracks and looked at her.

"Miss Billings," he barked, in a stern voice, as he bent over and picked up a wastebasket by her desk, "how many times have I told you that you are not allowed to chew gum in this office?" He held the can up to her, "Put that disgusting stuff in here."

She took the gum from her mouth and dropped it into the basket without saying anything. The lump made a distinctive thud when it hit the bottom of the metal container. Becker replaced the wastebasket and continued out of the office.

As soon as the two men left, and door closed, Miss Billings opened her desk drawer, took out a package of spearmint gum, extracted a piece, unwrapped the foil and put its contents into her mouth.

# # #

While Steele was away tending to Becker, Hank took note of the seven men and one woman as they entered Conrad's office. They all appeared to be in their middle to late fifties or early sixties. The men dressed similarly: black or blue business suits, a white shirt and either a blue, yellow or red tie, no stripes or flowers. They all carried a black leather portfolio embossed with *The Conrad Company* in gold lettering on its cover. Hank directed them to be seated at the conference table. The last to come through the door was the lone woman. Her clothing was surprisingly different; she wore a stylish light-gray business suit over a blue blouse, unbuttoned far enough to show a considerable amount of cleavage. She walked to the conference table swinging her hips to garner attention. She succeeded.

When all had seated themselves, Hank stood up. He had just opened his mouth, to address the group, when the door to the office burst open and in came a woman yelling at the top of her lungs.

"Who the hell's this Williamson person? And what the hell does he want with me?"

The woman was young, not more than mid-thirties. She dressed unlike anyone else in the company. She wore a sleeveless red silk dress with a low-scooped neckline and empire waistline. She looked like she had just come from a cocktail party and not an important corporate meeting.

"And who the hell are you?" Hank shot back.

"I'm Veronica Gelding, and I have very important financial people in my office!"

Hank's temper rose, and he struck the conference table with his fist causing the telephone to jump in the air and ring as it landed. In a booming voice shouted, "And, I'm 'the hell' Williamson. Detective Lieutenant Hank Williamson of the Boston Police Department, to you! And I don't care if you have Presidents Eisenhower, de Gaulle, and Winston Churchill himself in your office. I'm investigating a kidnapping and I want you 'the hell' here...

Now shut-up, sit down, and listen!" His temper having lessened, after the short outburst, he gestured calmly to one of the seats at the conference table.

"I'm sorry, Lieutenant. I didn't realize it was a serious matter. I thought it was some kind of lame joke." Her face, shoulders, and chest began to turn as red as her dress.

"I assure you, Miss Gelding, this is no joke," Hank said in a low calm voice.

"I understand now, Lieutenant. May I call my secretary and tell her to reschedule my meeting?"

"Yes, by all means. But make it snappy," Hank said, again in the same calm voice, "Use this phone." He pointed to the telephone on the conference table.

She dialed the phone.

"Melissa, please tell Mr. Simon and Mr. Hall that I've been called away on important business. Reschedule our meeting for whenever it's convenient for them." There was a slight pause while she listened. "I realize that, Melissa, but it can't be helped. Offer to buy dinner for them and their wives. Make whatever reservations that you need to make." Another pause, "Yes, put it on the company account." She gave Hank a sheepish smile and hung up the telephone.

"I'm sorry to inconvenience you, Miss Gelding. I wouldn't have been so insistent if it weren't important. Please have a seat," Hank said as he gestured to an empty chair at the far end of the table.

Hank stood at the end of the table and began to speak to the group. "As you may have surmised from my little exchange with Miss Gelding, I'm Detective Lieutenant Hank Williamson of the Boston Police Department."

The office door opened again, interrupting Hank's speech.

This time it was Steele with Becker in tow. Hank gave Steele an icy stare and waved his hand for them to enter. Neither said a word. Steele stood near Hank while Becker took a seat across the table from Miss Gelding.

"Now, I hope we can get started again, before another person busts in here cussing a blue streak," Hank said firmly, a little aggravation showing in his voice. "For those who have just joined us," he glanced momentarily at Mr. Becker and then to Miss Gelding, "I'm Detective Lieutenant Hank Williamson of the Boston Police Department... I'm here to investigate a kidnapping that took place in the early hours of this morning."

A buzzing of whispers and low voices shot around the table as he spoke.

Hank raised his voice to overcome the sound. "I don't have any details that I can give you at this point other than to say that Mr. Roger Conrad was abducted from his home last night, and we received a ransom note earlier today."

The whispers now turned into shouts as everyone at the table shot questions at Hank, all at once:

"Who did it?"

"What do they want?"

"Is Mr. Conrad all right?"

"Do you have any leads?"

"Do you have any suspects?"

Hank waved his hands in the air to stop the commotion around the table, "Quiet, quiet!" he shouted thumping his hand on the table. "Those are all good questions, people. And, in time, they will all be addressed. But right now, I can't answer any of them for you."

The man directly to Hank's left said, "What can we do, Lieutenant?"

"And who might you be?" Hank inquired.

"My name's John Watson and I am Vice President and Director of Marketing here at the Conrad Company," he replied, as if Hank should have recognized who he was before asking the question.

"Okay... as to what you can do: we'll get to that in due course. But right now, I want to know who each of you are, and what you do here at the Conrad Company. So starting here with the gentleman to Mr. Watson's left we'll go around the table. Introduce yourselves and tell me what you do here. That's all I want from you right now. No comments and no questions."

They started around the table and as each spoke, both Steele and Hank began writing the names down in their notebook.

"Arnold Becker, VP, Production."

"Harvey Alexander, VP, Engineering."

"George Hall, Personnel."

"Gerald Glenn, Conrad Company Attorney and I have a few questions," Glenn said ignoring Hank's previous instructions.

Hank smiled at Mr. Glenn and said, "I'll bet you do, counselor. I've never known an attorney that didn't. But right now I need to know who I'm dealing with here, so if you don't mind, we'll continue with the introductions. When we've finished with that, then I'll answer all your questions the best I can. Now, please continue." Hank pointed to the man sitting next to Glenn.

Glenn snorted. He was obviously a man used to getting his own way, but he didn't push the point any further.

"Clarence James, VP, Research and Development."

When it was Veronica's turn, she smiled at Hank and said, "I'm Veronica Gelding, but you already know that. I am the Accountant for the Conrad Company."

"Dan Harding, VP, Planning."

Now that everyone had introduced him or herself, Hank addressed Glenn directly. "You had a question, Mr. Glenn, did you not?"

"Yes, I did." He stood up. "I would like to know what this is all about."

"Okay, if you'll take your seat again I'm about to tell you what it's all about." Hank began to walk around the table as he spoke, "Last night at about two or three in the morning Mr. Roger Conrad was kidnapped from his home by three masked men. He was taken from his house and driven away in a black, four-door prewar Cadillac. His daughter Penelope was also abducted at the same time, but was later released unharmed. Earlier today, Mr. Steele received a ransom note by mail," Hank pointed to Steele. "Mr. Steele's a private investigator looking into an unrelated matter for the Conrad family."

John Watson interrupted Hank. "What do they want... you said there was a ransom note. What was in the note?"

Steele knew from past cases that Hank didn't like making these kinds of speeches, especially in front of potential suspects. Give him one or two to interrogate and he was great, but put him in front of this many people and he began to unravel pretty quickly. Steele was proud of him this time though. He conducted himself admirably and said calmly, "I'm getting to that. Patients, Mr. Watson."

Hank mopped his brow with the handkerchief from his breast pocket and continued. "The ransom note contained a demand for a great deal of money and all documents related to one of the Conrad Company's projects."

"Which project?" Harvey Alexander demanded.

"We feel at this time that, that information needs to be kept confidential," Hank said, again wiping his brow with his handkerchief, "However... if we feel that disclosing that information to any one of you can help us in our investigation, then we will discuss it with you on an individual basis."

"How much cash?" Victoria Gilding spoke up. "Or *is* that a secret, too?"

"No, we don't feel that's a secret. They're asking for one million dollars."

"What time frame. These things always have a time limit. Don't they?" asked George Hall.

"Yes, as a matter of fact, they usually do. This one's no exception. They want the money in a wire transfer to a bank in Switzerland by the end of the business day on Wednesday, the 11th of November."

"And the project papers?" asked Glenn.

"Same time frame but delivered to a post office in Brazil."

"Has the FBI been informed of the kidnapping, and are they working on it?" asked Glenn in a powerful voice that wasn't loud, but demanding—more appropriate in a courtroom than in a conference room.

"Yes, the FBI's been informed and are working closely on the case with the Boston police. They are working the international aspects; mainly they are investigating what part Switzerland and Brazil are playing in this case." Hank paused and looked around the table. "The FBI may contact you individually—I suggest you give them your full cooperation."

Glenn was about to ask another question when Hank cut him off. "That will be all for now. I want to thank you for your cooperation. Now, either myself or one of my men will be interviewing you individually, so don't leave the building without checking with me or one of my men first."

Surprisingly, they all got up, gathered up their portfolios and left the room without speaking. Once outside the office they split up into groups of two or three and began chattering away. Their reaction seemed like a conditioned response to Steele as he watched them milling about. He thought.

Perhaps Conrad has intimidated these people in past meetings. Now they're reluctant to raise too many questions with any authority figure.

It didn't seem important so he pushed the thought aside.

He walked up to Hank and shook his hand. "A very good job, my friend. I know how you hate being the center of attraction at a meeting like this. Well-done." He patted Hank on the shoulder.

Hank smiled, more from embarrassment than from pride, but Steele could tell he was proud of himself, "Ah, Steele, I've been taking a course in public speaking at night school... do you really think it's helped?"

"My friend... that's a question you'll have to answer for yourself. What do you think?"

"I wasn't as nervous as I have been in the past. I'm sure it has helped." He smiled.

"I believe it has. You showed a lot more confidence today," Steele again patted his shoulder.

They sat down on one of the couches. Steele opened his mouth to speak, but before he could, Poppy came over and sat between them.

"So, Lieutenant, what happens now?"

"I'll talk to each of them individually—see if any conflicts surface."

"What about my brother? Have you located him yet?"

"No, but I've called a friend of mine in the New York Police Department and he's looking into it for us. He's already issued an APB for both Lawrence and Beverly in New York City. That should turn them up pretty quickly."

"I'm just not sure about his involvement," Poppy said, her eyes began to mist over. "It concerns me that he ran off to New York after hearing about Father."

"It's probably nothing," Steele said, "People react to upsetting news in many ways. And then again it could be everything. There's really no way of knowing for sure at this time."

"That's not very reassuring, Mr. Steele." Poppy dabbed at the corner of her eye with her handkerchief.

"Yes," Hank said, "Him leaving town's very suspicious in my book. But I still need a more clear-cut reason to go after him."

Poppy put her handkerchief back in her purse. "I realize it's suspicious," she said, "but my brother never reacts to an upsetting situation the way most people do. This may be his way of handling a situation he doesn't want to contemplate."

"If I were certain of his involvement, then it wouldn't be a problem going down to New York and questioning him. But until I have evidence—even weak evidence—against him the police department would never authorize the trip."

"I was thinking the same thing, Hank," Steele said, "suppose I went down there and nosed around a little. After all I'm still licensed in New York—so that won't be a problem. Of course, it would be unofficial, and we may get a few of our questions answered." He turned to look at Poppy. "I haven't discussed the idea with my client yet, but I'm certain she will authorize a trip to New York. What do you say?"

Poppy smiled and said, "It's a marvelous idea."

Hank wasn't quite as enthusiastic as Poppy at the prospect. "I don't know... it could be tricky. I can't authorize a citizen to do that sort of thing, you know that, Steele."

"I know that. Like I said, it'll be unofficial. After all, I am working for the Conrad family." He looked squarely at Poppy. "Or am I?"

"Yes, you certainly are, Mr. Steele," Poppy said emphatically, looking Hank squarely in the eye, "I will go with him and we can talk to Lawrence as if we're family. Wouldn't that work? And, he already knows that Mr. Steele's working for my father." Poppy smiled.

"I suppose that would be okay... if he's involved that may put him off guard a little."

"And if he's not involved, it won't matter one way or another," Poppy said.

"You're right about that!" Hank said.

"Good. It's all settled then. I'll have Frances make all the reservations. I'm sure there's an express train that leaves Boston every afternoon going to New York, Baltimore, and Washington."

"Do you know the exact time it leaves? You know it's nearly 2:00pm now," Steele said.

"I'm not sure, but Frances will find out," She went to the telephone and pressed the intercom button.

Hank looked at Steele and said, "This could be dangerous, you know."

"I know, Hank. I know. I'll be careful and keep an eye on her, too."

"Good," Hank said, as he pulled a business card from his pocket and began to write on the back of it, "but in case you do need help, here's the number of my friend in New York." He handed the card to Steele. "His name's Jack Moran and I'll call him and let him know you're coming and fill him in on the situation."

Poppy came back into the office. "Frances called the station. A train leaves Boston for New York every two hours. When do you want to leave?"

Steele glanced at his wristwatch. "It's 2:05 now. How about four?"

"That's what I thought, too." Poppy smiled. "So, I had Frances make reservations for the train, and a hotel in New York. The train leaves at 4:30 pm." She gave Steele an even bigger grin.

"Do you really think we'll need to spend the night?" Steele's forehead wrinkled as he looked at her. "I thought we would just pop down, talk to Lawrence, and come right back on the next train."

"I don't think it will be that easy," she said, her smile turning to a scowl. "According to Frances, Lawrence has reserved one of the company's rooms. But if he's involved, he may not want us to find him. He may have made that reservation to mislead whoever may follow him. He could be staying in one of the other hundreds of hotels in the city."

"That's a good point. You're becoming a good detective, Miss Sinclair." He flashed her a toothy grin.

She wrinkled her nose, making a face at him, "Why, thank you, Hank." She curtseyed. "I'm trying to think like a criminal; the way I would if I'd planned this."

"That's generally the way it's done. Right Steele?" Hank said, grinning at him again. "That's quite a lady you have here—don't you think?"

"She's a pistol; surprises me all the time."

Poppy jumped in. "We'll need to stay over at least tonight and maybe even tomorrow night."

"Okay, you're the boss." He looked directly at her with a somber face. "You're paying the bills."

"That doesn't really matter," Poppy, said, "The Company has a contract with the hotels. They keep several rooms open for the Conrad Company; for when a customer or a buyer may need a room."

"A very convenient arrangement, I'm sure."

"Yes isn't it? I use them often myself, when I go to New York on a shopping trip, a new Broadway show, or just a night on the town."

"Okay," Steele said, throwing his hands up, "I give up. I give up. I keep a bag, with clean shirts and underwear in the trunk of my car for just this type of emergency."

Poppy grimaced at Steele, "Okay smarty-pants, I'm not as organized as you are. I need to pack a few things; can go by the house?"

CHAPTER 11

Barnaby was standing near the top of a stepladder on the front stoop as Steele parked the car in front of the Conrad house. Barnaby was in his shirtsleeves with a red apron tied around his waist. He had the overhead light fixture opened and was polishing the inside of the glass with a rag.

"You'll catch your death, Barnaby," Poppy said as they approached the butler.

"Miss, it's hardly freezing." He looked down at her with a stoic face. "It must be nearly forty-five degrees today." He pointed to the dust-covered fixture, hanging from its hinge. "And the glass requires a good cleaning."

"How was the bulb itself, Barnaby?" Steele asked.

"Just fine, Mr. Steele," he said as he continued cleaning the glass with his dist rag. "It had become dislodged from its socket, but it still functions as it should."

"Thank you, Barnaby," Steele said as he turned to Poppy, and in a lowered voice said to her. "It's too bad Barnaby's so efficient. We may have been able to get fingerprints from the fixture or the bulb."

"I'm sure he didn't think of anything like that. The light was out, and he repaired it. That's part of his job."

"I know, I'm not accusing Barnaby of anything. But still," Steele shook his head.

Poppy smiled at Steele and looked up at Barnaby, "Thank you, Barnaby."

"My pleasure, Miss." he said as he placed the dust rag in the pocket of his apron and climbed down from the ladder and began to fold it up.

"Mr. Steele and I are leaving to meet Lawrence in New York. Will you have Alton bring the car around and have him park Mr. Steele's car in our garage while we are gone?"

She turned away, and then turned back, "Would you ask Alton to bring Mr. Steele's bag along, it's in the trunk of his car."

Barnaby stood the folded ladder against the building. "Yes Miss, right away," he said as he opened the door.

Poppy started up the stairs. "Get Mr. Steele a drink and send Zoë up to my room to help me pack a bag."

Steele and Barnaby watched her as she took the stairs two at a time.

"What would you like to drink, Mr. Steele?"

"Coffee... yes, I'd like a cup of coffee, Barnaby."

"Very good, Mr. Steele. Would you like to wait in the library?"

Steele looked Barnaby straight in the eye. "You needn't bring out the silver serving set for me, Barnaby. How about I have a mug in the kitchen?"

The slightest hint of a smile was evident in the corners of Barnaby's mouth, "As you wish, Mr. Steele."

Steele was chatting with Susan at the kitchen table when Poppy came into the room. She had changed her clothes, and now wore a slim black skirt with a sleeveless cashmere sweater in a mint green color.

Alton came in from the garage. "I've moved the Cord to the garage and the Lincoln's out front when you're ready, Mr. Steele."

Alton, I have a favor to ask of you," Steele said.

"Yes, Mr. Steele. What can I do for you?"

"Would it be possible for you to take the Cord to my mechanic in Somerville while I'm in New York?"

"Certainly, Mr. Steele. But, the car seemed to run just fine when I put it in the garage."

"It's not the engine, as you say, its running just fine. But, one of the headlight mechanism's broken and he's going to replace it."

"I see," Alton said. "Sure, I can take the car over as soon as I return from the train station."

Steele held out a five dollar bill, "Here, take this for cab fare."

"That won't be necessary, Mr. Steele, I'll just have Barnaby follow me in the Lincoln."

Steele looked at Poppy, "Will that be okay?"

"Yes, that seems like a good plan."

"Okay, it's settled then," Steele said turning back to Alton, "Dester's garage isn't difficult to find, it's on the corner of Auburn Avenue and Cross Street."

"I'm sure I won't have any trouble finding the place, Mr. Steele."

"Tell Dexter that I'll call him when I get back from New York and make arrangements to get the car."

"Sure thing, Mr. Steele," Alton said as he tipped his cap.

"Thank you, Alton," Poppy said. "Now we have a train to catch. But first, there's a bag in my room. Will you put it in the car, please, and then we'll be ready to leave."

# # #

Alton was very skillful in traffic and pulled up at the train station twenty minutes early. Steele checked in at the counter and picked up their tickets. They went to the coffee shop and ordered Coca-Cola. Steele telephoned Hank from the booth in the back of the coffee shop.

Hank was not in his office. It took McDoodle five or six minutes to track him down. Hank was in the laboratory going over evidence in another case.

"What ya need, Steele?"

"Just checking in before we get on the train. Any new information on the whereabouts of Lawrence and Beverly from your guy in New York?"

"Yeah, as a matter of fact, I just talked to him twenty minutes ago. He hasn't actually located Sinclair yet. However, he knows they're registered at the midtown

Hilton at 53rd and 6th. However, none of the staff his people talked to have seen them today."

"That's great, Hank. At least we have a starting point. I'll call you from New York as soon as we get anything."

While Steele made the call, Poppy had taken a seat at a table in the coffee shop. She was looking in the other direction when he returned. Feeling a little mischievous, he crept up, out of sight, and was able to come up behind her without her seeing him. He leaned as close to her ear as he could get. "Hey, lady..." she jumped at the sound of his voice, almost dropping her glass of Coke. She turned around to face him. He grinned at her, "Can I take that bag for you, it looks heavy."

She went along with his little impromptu charade.

"Sure mister, where ya headed to? I'll bet it's a romantic spot. Atlantic City?"

"No romance and no place romantic. Just a business trip to New York with my boss," he replied.

"You like traveling with your boss?" she asked as he bent over and picked up her bag. They started off walking toward the gate and the platform.

"Yeah, I guess so," he said with a laugh. "Although, he's actually a she; and as far as bosses go, I guess she's okay."

"Sure, sounds to me like there may be a romance going on there," she laughed.

"I couldn't say, you'll have to ask her... I'll never tell."

"I may just do that," she looked away as if aloof—but saw that he was grinning.

They walked towards the gate in silence, both lost in their own thoughts for the moment. Steele was aware of the people around him, but only vaguely; he heard voices, but not words. He heard the steady meter of Poppy's heels as they click, click, clicked on the polished terrazzo floor, the cadence reminded Steele of the melody to a long-lost song he could not recall.

He became keenly aware of the vendors they passed. He had walked through this station, even this exact corridor, many times on his trips in and out of Boston. This was the first time he ever remembered smelling the coffee, the mustard, the hot dogs and popcorn of the vendors as he passed them.

Once they reached the platform itself Poppy was all business. She guided them to the second car from the rear of the train and then to a stateroom near the middle of the car. She seemed apologetic when they entered the compartment.

"I'm sorry; Frances couldn't get a better compartment at the late time we booked."

"No need to apologize. It's fine. Much better than I usually get when I have to travel for a client. I've never booked a compartment; I usually just take a seat in the club car."

The compartment was large with two seats, one facing forward and the other aft. It even had its own bathroom.

They sat across from each other. Neither spoke. The train began to move, Steele glanced at his watch, and it was exactly 4:30. Ten minutes after the train left the station Poppy reached over and put her hand on his knee. She smiled at him and cocked her head to the side as if judging his reaction. She then got to her feet and walked to the washroom door and opened it.

"This trip takes six and a half hours. I'm going to slip into a more comfortable outfit." She flashed him a toothy smile and carried her bag into the tiny washroom and closed the door.

In a few seconds she poked her head out and said, "Have the porter bring us drinks. A martini would be nice." She smiled broadly again. "With two olives, please."

He did as she asked and rang for the porter. When he arrived, Steele asked him to bring a pitcher of martinis, a dish of olives and two glasses.

Ten minutes later Poppy emerged from the washroom wearing a pair of very thin powder-blue silk pajamas, with a matching silk robe. The outfit brought an immediate reaction from Steele; he looked out the window and began counting the passing telephone poles as a distraction.

She's my client. I can't let anything happen, if anything happens it will have to wait until this case's closed.

She sat down beside him. He looked at her and blushed, then said, "Ni, ni... nice outfit."

"Do you like it? I had an idea that you would."

"Um... yes, very blue." He looked away and began counting passing telephone poles again. He muttered, "I, um... I thought you didn't approve of pajamas?"

"Nonsense," she smiled at him, "whatever gave you that idea."

"Listening to the comments you made to Hank the other morning. I guess, I just assumed..."

"Your assumptions are incorrect, Mr. Steele. Yes, most nights, I do sleep in the nude. However, I have all types of sleep-wear. It all depends on the situation and what mood strikes me. Traveling on a train requires a modicum of modesty—don't you agree?"

His blush deepened. "Oh..." Was all he could say, because, at that same moment there was a knock on the compartment door. Steele got to his feet and opened the door; the porter with their drinks greeted him. Steele stepped aside as the porter stepped inside and set up a folding stand to hold the tray he also carried. The tray contained a pitcher of liquid, two long-stemmed martini glasses, and two small bowls, one containing olives, and the other little white onions. Steele thanked the porter, giving him a half-dollar.

"Do you want to do the honors or shall I?"

"You go ahead." Poppy smiled.

He filled two glasses, making sure that one had two olives, which he handed to Poppy. He sat down across from her and holding his glass high, he said, "Guten Freunden."

She smiled and held her glass up too, "Yes, to good friends."

Steele was trying very hard to get his mind off his own bodily reactions to just being with Poppy, alone in the cramped compartment. He diverted his eyes from the bumps her nipples made in the thin fabric and focused intently on her face. Her eyes...

"You continue to surprise me, Mr. Steele, I had no idea you spoke German."

"Just bits-n-pieces I picked up in the beer halls and Hofbräuhaus of Nuremberg after the war."

"You served in the Army?"

His brow knitted. "No, the Marines." He closed his eyes a moment. "Military Police."

"Ah, Nuremberg. Did you have anything to do with those dreadful trials?" She took another sip of her drink.

His eyes narrowed and he frowned, "Yes," was all he said as he looked away from her fixing his gaze out the window.

"You don't wish to speak of it—I understand—it wasn't a pleasant time for any of us to remember."

He looked back in her direction and nodded.

"What, then, shall we talk about?"

"You and your brother don't get along, do you?"

It was her turn to frown. "Um... that's not an easy question to answer. After all, he's my brother and I suppose we battle like most brothers and sisters do. However, most of the time we *do* get along, however we do have our little tussles."

"I believe it goes a little deeper than *little tussles*," Steele said.

"Why would you think that?"

"Nothing specific..." He took out his pipe and began to fill the bowl with tobacco, "mainly it's the way you reacted when you found out he had gone on a shopping trip to New York with his girlfriend."

"He can be quite insensitive at times, and selfish. I do get angry at him for that. His trip to New York at this time is a perfect example... leaving town when Father's been kidnapped. It so callous and uncaring. Don't you think?"

"You're certainly right, I couldn't agree more. It does seem strange. But maybe he has a good reason for it."

"I can't wait to hear what it might be." She drained the last of her martini. She reached over to the tray and poured another, which she drank down almost in one gulp. She laid her head against the back of the seat cushion and closed her eyes. Her eyes still closed, she said, "I didn't get enough sleep last night, I'm going to take a nap. Can you call the porter to make up the berths?"

It only took the porter a few minutes to finish making up the berths and to leave the compartment.

Poppy took off her robe. The sheer silk pajamas barely concealed anything; her breast, nipples and pubic hair clearly discernible through the thin fabric. She got into the lower berth and slid as far back as she could go. With her back to the wall she patted the mattress in front of her with her hand. She whispered, "Are you going to join me?

Steele fought against his natural reaction to such a request and said, "No." He got to his feet and went to the door, "I believe I'll go to the club car. Smoke my pipe and make a few notes about this case."

"You don't know what you're missing," her eyes twinkled, although obviously tired.

"Oh... I'm very certain that I do." Steele looked back at her. "But anything like that will have to wait." He walked over and covered her with the blanket, "You need to rest. As you said, you didn't get much sleep last night."

He went into the bathroom and turned on the light, leaving the door open an inch, and then turned the compartment lights off. Standing at the compartment door he looked back at her in the soft light. Her eyes closed, she appeared to have already fallen asleep.

He smiled and whispered to himself, "See, I knew you were tired."

# # #

The club car made up the last car of the train. Steele expected the car would be crowded at this time of the evening, but found only three people and the bartender; a woman sitting alone reading a book—*Murder on the Orient Express*—and a couple who cozied together like newlyweds.

Steele ordered a Dewar's-White on the rocks and took the drink to the back of the car and through the door. Air streamed around the end of the car, intensifying the cold temperature on the observation platform. Steele pulled his collar up around his neck and leaned against the closed-door sipping his drink. The rhythmic clicking of the wheels on the track had a calming, almost hypnotizing effect as he watched the tracks fall away to a single point far off in the distance.

Jesus, you're a jerk, Steele. Why didn't you crawl into the berth with her? She wanted you to, you know she did!

That's just it; I don't know if she did or not. This whole chasing after me—may be a reaction to what has happened to her in the last few days. And besides that... she's my client. I may be a lot of things, but I do have my scruples, I'll just have to wait and see. Maybe things can change, once the case's over.

He finished the drink and returned to the bar for a second. He sat down in one of the empty chairs away from the other people. He re-filled his pipe and lit it, then took out his notebook and began to read his notes as he sipped his drink. As tired as he was, the notebook didn't hold his attention for long and he dozed off still holding it in his hand.

He awakened abruptly to a man's voice. A loud voice. He didn't understand the words; he scanned the car to find its origin. Except for the conductor, who was leaving the car, and the bartender, the car was empty. Steele got up and went to the bartender and said, "I must have dozed off. What did the conductor just announce?"

"He just made the call for Pennsylvania Station in thirty minutes," the man said, "May I get you another drink?" he went on. "Perhaps a cup of coffee?"

Steele shook his head and left the car, heading forward through the train. Poppy was up, the berths had been stowed away, and she was having breakfast from a tray when he entered the compartment.

"You didn't return last night." She bit her lower lip "Where have you been?"

He sat down beside her. "I went to the club-car to think things through and review my notes. I dozed off—just woke up."

"You would have been more comfortable in my bed," she laughed.

"I'm sure I would have been. It's just that... Look, it wasn't that I didn't want to accept your invitation. But, there are a couple of things to consider. First, you've been put through major trauma in the last couple of days and you may just be reacting to that trauma. And secondly, I have this rule about my clients. I make it a practice to not get involved with them romantically during a case. Now, if you still feel the same way when this case's done and finished—I would be more than happy to accommodate you."

"It all sounds so clinical and calculated when you say it out loud." She paused and took a sip from her coffee cup. "I can also see you've given it a little thought. I'm not sure I agree with your rationale, but I can understand how you feel."

"So what's next?" he said.

"We'll just see what happens, if that's okay with you."

"That's fine with me, as long as you understand the rules and what's going on."

"Yes... I understand how you feel."

Steele returned to the club car and ordered himself a drink. He wanted to forget about Poppy, and his feelings for her, as well as the case for a time—unwind a bit. He filled his pipe, lit it, and sat back in his seat puffing it and sipping his drink till the train neared Penn Station.

The bartender told Steele that the train was rerouted around a small wreck on the tracks south of Providence. Another train, ahead of them, had struck a car at a crossing. The detour had caused them to arrive twenty-five minutes later than scheduled.

CHAPTER 12

It was nearly eleven-thirty when Poppy and Steele set foot on the platform at Penn Station.

"Frances has arranged for a car to meet us at the main entrance on 34th Street," Poppy said as they set out across the enormous lobby.

A man in a chauffeur's uniform called out, "Miss Sinclair," as he approached them.

Poppy turned to the man. "Were you called by the Conrad Company?"

"Yes, Miss. Miss Stevens called the car service."

Poppy looked intently at the man. "Do I know you?"

"Yes, Miss Sinclair. My name's William Edwards, but most folks call me Bill." He reached for Poppy's bag. "Let me get those bags." He placed Poppy's bag under his arm and held her small travel case in his hand. He took Steele's bag in his other hand and gestured with it toward the door. "The car's this way, Miss." They had taken a few steps when he turned his head to Poppy and said, "I was your driver when you visited New York in September."

"Yes I remember now. I did a great deal of shopping that day."

"Yes, Miss."

"Things are a little hectic with the train and all, I'm sorry we're late."

"The train people explained about the detour and the wreck. You don't got no cause to be apologizin' to me, Miss."

She looked at him again, cocking her head to the right and then to the left, "I do recall now. I didn't recognize you at first." Her smile brightened. "Yes, of course. You suggested that wonderful restaurant on 6th Avenue."

"Yes, miss."

When they had almost reached the car Poppy said, "Bill, did Frances tell you where we are going?"

Bill opened the door to the limousine and said, "Yes Miss, she did. We'll be there in about ten minutes. Unless you need to make a stop along the way."

"No, just take us to the hotel."

Once in the car Steele asked, "Which hotel are we going to?"

"The Meridian on 57th Street. Father maintains rooms there, for when he and Mother come to New York. So I asked Frances to make the arrangements for us to use it. That okay?"

"Sure, that's fine, you're the boss. How far is it from the Times Square Hilton?" Steele asked.

"Let me see..." She looked out the car window a moment and back to Steele, "I believe it's only a few blocks, why do you ask?"

"When I talked to Hank on the telephone, at the station, he said his friend in New York told him that your brother registered at the Times Square Hilton earlier today—but they haven't found him yet. The hotel manager said Lawrence and Beverly had been there last night, but they haven't been seen today."

"The Hilton's another of the hotels where Father's company has rooms reserved for the use of customers and clients who need a place to stay in New York. I often use those rooms myself when I come to New York. I didn't tell Frances that we wanted to look for Lawrence in New York, so she didn't say anything to me about arranging rooms for him."

"Maybe he didn't tell her. He could have made his own arrangements."

"Yes, that's true. But still, I should have thought to ask Frances about it." A serious look came across her face,

"Do you really think my brother has anything to do with all this? I just can't imagine it."

"I'm not sure at this point. His actions do seem a bit unusual, people react to crisis in different ways, so how they act in itself doesn't make them guilty of anything," Steele said in as reassuring a voice as he could manage. "I'm sure we'll know more when we've talked to him."

At the hotel, Bill retrieved the bags from the trunk and handed them off to a waiting bell-boy. "Will you need the car any longer this evening, Miss Sinclair?" he said.

"No, Bill, not for tonight." She took two steps toward the entrance, and then turned back. "However, we will need the car in the morning."

"What time shall I pick you up then?"

"I'm not at all sure. I'll call when our plans are more finalized."

"Very good, Miss," he bowed, touched his finger to his cap, then turned and got into the car and drove off.

Steele looked all around as they walked into the hotel. He couldn't place the architectural style, but the building was definitely in the deluxe category. White marble with arches and columns everywhere the eye fell. The lobby looked big enough to accommodate a baseball field, with a ceiling that loomed three stories above their heads.

The man on the registration desk greeted them as they approached the counter.

"Ah, Miss Sinclair, so glad to have you with us tonight. Mrs. Stevens called earlier. Your rooms are ready—as instructed by Mrs. Stevens."

He plucked a key from a cubby-hole behind the desk and handed it to Poppy with a broad smile, "If I may be of any further assistance—please call on me."

"Yes... I'm famished." She glanced at Steele. "Would you have room service send up a platter of cold cuts... ham, summer sausage, crackers, cream cheese, that sort of thing?" She flashed him a broad smile. She turned to leave and then turned back. "And a bottle of wine." She paused, putting her finger to her chin as if musing "Chateau Margaux. 1936 would be nice." She glanced over at Steele again. "Or would you prefer another vintage, Mr. Steele?"

"Coffee... I'd prefer coffee." He put on a gracious smile as he continued his inspection of the lobby and its furnishings.

"Okay." Poppy smiled at the clerk. "A pot of coffee for Mr. Steele. And cheesecake, with that wonderful cherry sauce your chef prepares, for dessert," she added in a giddy voice, acting like a ten-year old kid on her first trip with Mom and Dad.

She turned away from the desk, grabbing hold of Steele's arm and pointing him toward the bank of elevators not far from the desk. Inside the elevator she gave the operator a Cheshire-cat grin and said, "Thirty-eighth floor, please."

"I see you know your way around this place," Steele offered.

Her arm still entwined in his, she said in a voice that sounded more like singing than talking, "Yes, I do, I've stayed here many times in the past." She squeezed his arm tightly.

"Alone?" Steele asked.

"I'd prefer not to say Mr. Steele." She chuckled. "A lady never discusses such matters."

"Of course," he blushed slightly.

The elevator operator glanced at her. She winked at him. Steele saw the gesture, and grinned. The man too grinned broadly as he again faced forward.

She turned her head and looked directly into Steele's eyes. They stood nose-to-nose. "Does that bother you, Mr. Steele?"

He blinked and his cheeks reddened even more. "No, you're perfectly right. You shouldn't discuss such matters. I apologize for being so crude as to ask *the question* in the first place."

The elevator operator took a quick peek at him, and then to her. Steele flashed a broad smile at him as the elevator door opened on the 38th floor.

You know, young lady, two can play at this little game of cat and mouse you seem to want to engage in.

Poppy saw the two men grinning at each other and jerked Steele's arm aggressively, pulling him firmly from the elevator.

The room was large by anyone's standards, reminding Steele of a villa he once visited in the south of France after the war. Very elegantly furnished in cherry and maple. A king-size bed on a raised platform eclipsed everything else in the room. A separate seating area contained a sofa and coffee table; a plushy upholstered seat occupied the space below the bay window recess—flanked on either side by French doors.

He walked to the French doors and opened one. The balcony contained a potted plant, two chairs and a small table and overlooked Central Park located on the far side of the street. The glow of the street lamps provided a grand visual sense of the park.

Steele turned to Poppy who had seated herself on the foot of the large bed. She was busy removing her gloves.

"Very nice," he said as he began to remove his overcoat.

"I like it," Poppy said in the childlike voice she had used on the desk earlier. "I'm glad my brother used the Hilton suite instead of this one," she said as she removed her hat.

"This room has any special memory for you?"

"You might say that." She got to her feet and came to where he stood. She again entwined his arm, giving it a hard squeeze.

"You want to tell me about it... or shouldn't a gentleman or an employee ask such a question?"

"See, it's like this." She began rubbing the back of her hand along his jaw line. "The other suite has two bedrooms and four twin beds. And, as you can see," she gestured with her hand in a sweeping motion; ending by pointing at the bed. "It's a single room with only the one bed."

She broke her grip on his arm and went towards the bathroom.

"Why's that important?"

He watched her disappear into the bathroom. She didn't shut the door. He could hear the water in the shower begin to run.

She called out, "I'm sure that you can figure it out—you're the *detective*." She stuck her head out of the doorway, "And while you ponder it, I'm going to take a shower." She ducked back inside. And, following that short respite, a pair of red silk panties with white lace trim came flying out of the still open bathroom door, landing near where Steele stood.

Steele's first thought was: *The little vixen's trying to seduce me again.* However, he discarded that idea as being ridiculous. He had talked to her about that. She had said that she understood the employer client relationship he needed to keep with her.

She knows I'm interested in her. She's a gorgeous woman, funny and interesting. Never the less, I need to hold my ground—if I allow myself to get involved, it could be a disaster for both of us.

As he sat down on the couch to ponder the question further, there was a knock on the door. A man's voice called out, "Room service," from outside.

Two men, in hotel uniforms, greeted him when he opened the door. The first man pushed a cart full of food; the second man carried a silver bucket with a bottle of wine wrapped in a white cloth in one arm and held a tall crystal vase containing a half-dozen red roses in the other hand. They set it all up in front of the window seat and left.

Steele went to the still-open bathroom door. He could hear the water still running in the shower and called out, "Poppy, the food's here."

"Okay, I'll only be a minute," she replied.

He sat back down on the sofa. A moment later she appeared at the bathroom door. She hadn't dressed; she had only wrapped a pink towel around herself. The towel barely covered her. She used a smaller towel to dry her hair. She walked to the cart and picked up a sausage from the tray and began to nibble on it.

"Figured it out yet?"

"What?"

"The room riddle." She smiled as she continued to nibble on the sausage provocatively as she poured a glass of wine.

Keeping a sober face, he lied, "Ah that... I didn't give it much thought."

"You didn't, huh?"

"No, not too much at all."

She came to within a few inches of him and stood there looking down at him. She brought the last of the sausage to her lips and pushed the remaining piece into her mouth with her middle finger.

"I had one thought," he said, "but I wanted to wait and see what happened." He grinned at her. "See if it was correct."

She didn't say anything. She picked up a glass of wine and backed away a foot or two, pirouetted on her toes, turning around completely two times. When her back was to him, on the last turn, she allowed the towel to drop to the floor. Now fully naked, she looked back over her shoulder in the same pose Betty Grable had struck in her famous wartime photo. She said in a very hushed voice, "Here's a hint... Mr. Detective." She then walked slowly back to the bathroom swinging her hips erotically from side to side.

She hadn't quite gotten to the bathroom door when he caught up to her.

"I just might have. You'll have to judge for yourself," he said as he came up from behind her. His hands found her waist and pulled her body to his. His left hand gently cupped her breast while his right hand caressed the belly. His lips found her ear and kissed it gently, then trailed a string of kisses down the side of her neck and across her shoulder.

She threw her head back and twisted so that her mouth was near his. They kissed lightly as his hand moved from her belly downward. His fingers entwining themselves in the soft damp mound of hair they found there.

She turned in his arms to face him, wrapped her arms around his neck and crushed her naked body against him. Both his hands cupped her butt and pulled her even closer. A moment later she pulled back, breaking the kiss. She whispered, "So, Mr. Detective—were you correct?"

"Yes, I believe so!" he whispered and then pulled away from her. He held her at arm's length, his hands still on her waist. "As nice as this may be, and it's very nice, it's also a big, big mistake. This isn't why we came to New York."

She smiled and drew him into another passionate kiss, whispering, "Are you sure about that?" While her hand was busy massaging his shoulders, back, and his hair. She then pulled her head back a little and whispered, "You got your reasons for being here, Mr. Detective." Looking him straight in the eye, she moved her right hand down and began to move it vigorously up and down the front of his pants. "And I have my own."

Steele's head was spinning. All of his being wanted to romp with her in that bed for the rest of the night, and every night thereafter. But deep down he knew that if he didn't stop this soon that she would be the one to suffer. If she realized later that she had made love to him while her father might be enduring torture at the hands of his kidnappers, she would never forgive herself—or him.

Her finger began to undo his belt, but he caught hold of her wrists and pulled her hands away. He backed up a foot releasing his grip on her wrists. She raised her arms, attempting to encircle his neck. He caught hold of her wrists again and forced her hands down to her side.

The phone rang.

It rang again.

And again.

The though flashed through his head, *Thank God—saved by the bell.* "Are you going to answer that or not?" he said.

She grunted and cried out, "Bumsen!" as she stomping her foot hard on the floor. She stalked, heavy footed, to the nightstand and plopped down hard on the edge of the bed. She sat there a moment, calming herself, while the phone rang three more times. She picked up the receiver. "Hello," she said, and then a pause holding the receiver up to him. "It's for you... it's Hank."

She got up and handed the receiver to him and then walked to the bathroom as he sat down and put the receiver to his ear.

"Hi, Hank, anything new on your end?"

"Anything wrong there? The lady sounded a bit peeved."

"Yeah, she's a little upset—*spoiled*—not used to not getting her way," he said as he watched Poppy through the open bathroom door. "We're having a late night snack. Poppy's changing her clothes." He continued watching her through the open door. She brushed her hair, still naked, in front of the mirror. Her movements with the brush caused her firm breasts to jiggle provocatively.

He looked away. "When she's ready we're going over to the Hilton to talk to Lawrence."

Hank said, "That's good. The FBI has come up with a little tidbit concerning his girlfriend. However, I don't really think it's of any importance to this investigation, but interesting nonetheless."

"So, what might it be?" Steele asked.

"Like I said, it's just a curious finding, I'll tell you later, when you get back to Boston. It's unimportant and I don't think it has anything to do with our case. As for all the employees, they check out. All had satisfactory alibis for the time of the abduction."

Steele glanced at Poppy again. She had put on a black lace bra and had one foot into a pair of black lace panties. He watched as she pulled the flimsy material up over her hips.

Steele forced his attention back to the telephone call. "Could be that they hired it. These people are delegators, not one of them looks like a hands-on type to me."

"You're right about that," Hank said, "We'll keep checking them out just the same. Meanwhile, the FBI's also checking them out."

"Hank, I got to go. Poppy just came out of the bathroom. She looks like she's ready to go. I'll talk to you later when I know more, Okay?"

"Sure, okay," Hank said, and then the line went dead.

Steele hung up the phone. He'd fudged the truth a bit to Hank though; Poppy had indeed come out of the bathroom, but she wasn't nearly ready. She had put on her bra and panties, but nothing else. She sat down on the window seat, the hairbrush still in her hand. She picked up a cracker and dipped it into the caviar and began to nibble on it. Steele got up and walked over and sat down next to her. He also picked up a cracker and began to eat it.

He looked at her and said, "Sorry."

"It's okay." She smiled at him. "Deep down, I know you're right. I should think more about my father's situation and a little less about having sex with you." She picked up another cracker. "Did Hank have any good news?"

"He said the FBI had information about Beverly, but he didn't think it was important to the case. He said it had nothing to do with the kidnapping."

"So he didn't say what?"

"No, he wouldn't say. Said he'd tell me later."

"Must not be too important then," she said, taking a bite of cracker. "But knowing Beverly, it more than likely pertains to one of her past lovers. I believe she's dated a few shady characters, and at least one of them was a jail-bird."

He accepted her explanation with a nod. "You better finish getting dressed. We need to see if we can find your brother before he decides they need to go to London, Paris, or Rome to do more shopping."

"Okay," she said as she got up. She kissed him very lightly on the cheek. "I'm sorry too," she whispered. She turned and went to the bathroom, still brushing her hair as she walked.

She bent over without bending her legs and picked up the red panties that she had thrown out the bathroom door earlier. He had a perfect view of her womanly charms. He felt the stirring in his pants.

My God, my God, my God... this woman has an exquisite looking ass, and she wants to make love to me. What the hell was I thinking!

He watched as she stood in front of the mirror and ran the brush through her hair several more times.

He got up and went to sit on the foot of the bed, out of view of the bathroom. He pulled his notebook out and began to thumb through it, attempting to get his mind off Poppy and her luscious body. He made a few new notes and was just finishing, ten minutes later, when Poppy emerged from the bathroom.

"You all ready to go?"

He looked up to see her standing in the doorway of the bathroom. She was wearing a blue skirt with a matching silk blouse. He smiled at her and then patted the bed next to where he sat with the palm of his hand, beckoning her to come sit down next to him. She smiled and came over and sat down beside him.

He looked deeply into her eyes and said, "You know, Poppy, about what happened earlier."

"What about it?" She smiled. "Have you changed your mind?" She reached for the buttons on her blouse, "Should I get undressed?"

He shook his head, "No, it's nothing like that. It's just this: everyone handles a crisis in a different way. Perhaps, having sex may be a way for you to feel that everything's okay. The world's not really out of sorts or broken. That things can still matter and be okay."

She bent over and kissed him lightly on the cheek.

"What's that for?"

"Just because... that's all." She wrapped her arm around him and said, "Shall we go?"

They walked to the elevator in silence. Steele's finger just touched the down button, when the doors opened. Once inside the car he pulled her to him, wrapped his arms around her and kissed her passionately on the lips.

Her eyes registered big surprise by opening wide, and she said, "What's that for?"

"Just because. That's all," he said and squeezed her tightly as they walked across the lobby.

"Damnez le!" she called out.

"What's wrong? If my German wasn't so rusty, I'd swear that you just hollered *damn it.*"

She stopped and turned to him. "Your right, I did."

"Why? Did that upset you?"

"No, no, nothing like that. I told Bill we wouldn't need the car tonight. I didn't call to have him pick us up."

"It's okay, we can take a cab. It's not that far," Steele said.

She smiled at him and nodded in concurrence.

Nearing the outside door, the doorman saw them coming, opened the door for them and asked, "Taxi, sir?"

Steele nodded to him and the man went off towards the street blowing his whistle at passing cabs.

While standing outside the hotel waiting for a taxi, Steele took hold of Poppy's hand and said to her, "Poppy, I was thinking. After we've finished this case, I hope you'll let me make up for tonight."

She squeezed his hand tightly and said, "You got a deal, Mr. Detective."

A cab stopped at the curb and the doorman opened the door for them. Steele slipped a quarter into the man's hand as he got into the cab.

CHAPTER 13

The Hilton hotel was six blocks from the Meridian, and the traffic was heavy. However, the taxi driver managed to negotiate through traffic, avoiding all the red lights. He made the trip in less than five minutes.

Poppy recognized the person behind the registration desk immediately, as did he, her.

"Mr. Gladstone!" she exclaimed.

"Miss Sinclair. This is certainly a pleasant surprise; I was not informed you would be arriving this evening. What can we do for you? Do you require a room for the night?"

"No, Mr. Gladstone, not tonight. However, I've been told that my brother Lawrence's staying with you... have I been misinformed?"

"Yes, you've been informed correctly. Mr. Lawrence and his companion checked in this morning."

"Is he in?"

"No, I'm afraid you just missed them. He and his lady friend went out about half an hour ago."

"So, they've already checked out?"

"Heavens no, Miss Sinclair. Mr. Lawrence made dinner reservations at the Bowery Taproom in the west village."

"Okay... umm..." Poppy seemed deep in thought for a moment. "Mr. Gladstone," she said, looking at her wristwatch, "It's only half past eleven, would it be possible for you to call the Bowery Taproom and change my brother's reservations to accommodate four?"

"Surely, Miss Sinclair. I would be happy to do that for you," he said as he picked up the phone and began dialing. Poppy took hold of Steele's arm and stepped a few feet away from the counter lowering her voice. "If we hurry, we can get there before Lawrence."

Steele looked perplexed. "How do you figure we can do that? They've been gone for a half an hour."

"Knowing Lawrence as I do, he'll hit a couple of bars between here and the Bowery Taproom."

Mr. Gladstone hung up the telephone and motioned to Poppy. "Everything has been taken care of, Miss Sinclair. Anything else I can do for you tonight?"

"There's one more small thing." she smiled broadly at him. "If you could, Mr. Gladstone."

"Yes, Miss Sinclair. What do you require?"

"I know it's an imposition, and we are not staying here, but would it be possible for the hotel car to take us to the Bowery Taproom?"

"That would be no problem at all, Miss Sinclair." He picked up the telephone and dialed three numbers. "Yes, Mr. Jackson, bring the car around. We have a guest who requires transportation." He replaced the receiver and looked at Poppy. "The car will be out front in just a moment. Do you require anything else this evening, Miss Sinclair?"

"No, you've done enough. Thank you very much, Mr. Gladstone." She held out her hand to shake his. Steele noted that Mr. Gladstone's hand held a five-dollar bill when she withdrew hers.

"Thank you, Miss Sinclair, and please give my best regards to your father." He bowed his head slightly and thrust the bill into his vest pocket.

#

The Bowery Taproom must have been the latest hip place to eat in New York. It was a small place with only room to accommodate twelve or fifteen tables. The bar was in the middle of the room with tables scattered around it.

A jazz trio, consisting of a clarinet, a base and a guitarist performed an upbeat rendition of *Blue Moon* on a low stage, centered against the back wall.

The song brought back memories in Steele; it had been one of his wife's favorites. He also recalled an incident in London—the night he had met Billie Holiday. The promoter of a music hall show he had attended, arranged for a few American servicemen to attend a party after the performance. Steele had met Lady Day, as she was known, at that party. Steele remembered the hauntingly beautiful rendition of *Blue Moon* she had done on stage that evening. He had talked with her for a few minutes at the party—mentioning to her his wife's fondness for the song. She graciously offered to sing the song again at the party—which she did—and dedicated it to Steele and his wife Nancy.

Twenty or more people stood in a line outside the door. The man at the door let them in because they had made reservations. The five bucks that Poppy had slipped Mr. Gladstone, at the Hilton, had paid for itself in spades. Even then, they had to sit at the bar until their table was ready.

Lawrence and Beverly arrived fashionably late for their midnight dinner reservation. He spotted Poppy and Steele immediately at the bar as he and Beverly walked through the door. Steele noted that Lawrence was now dressed very differently from the last time they met at the Conrad house. No expensive suit now. He wore a pair of beat-up old Levis and a cranberry-colored sweatshirt with the yellow-gold Harvard logo emblazoned across the front. Beverly wore a floor length sleeveless red satin dress with a scoop neckline. The dress was remarkable only in the fact that it didn't seem to touch her body anywhere except her shoulders, and hung straight down to the floor. The dress was also slit up one side to mid-thigh and showed her pencil thin legs when she walked.

Lawrence and Beverly stood at the bar next to Poppy and Steele as Lawrence ordered a Manhattan and an apricot-brandy cocktail. His drinks arrived as the maître d' came to announce that their table was now ready. After they were seated and the waiter had taken their order, Lawrence turned to Poppy and said, "So, big sister, why are you two in New York?"

"We came to talk to you about Father."

Lawrence had his drink to his lips, about to take sip, when Poppy spoke. He came close to spitting it out across the table and right down the front of Beverly's dress. His face changed instantly from happy to morose and drained of color. His lips twisted with disdain.

He swabbed his face, chin and the front of his shirt with a napkin. "But," he protested, "I don't know anything."

"Nevertheless, the police need to talk to you." Poppy raised her voice. "You need to come back to Boston and answer any questions they do have."

"But... but..." he sputtered, wiping his chin again with the napkin. "Bev and I are off to Paris tomorrow. One of Bev's friend's, Chloe is showing her new spring clothing line."

Steele looked at him and then at Beverly and said, "I don't think that will be possible." He paused and took a sip of his drink. "The FBI has gotten involved and as soon as you show your passport anywhere you'll be detained and brought back to Boston for questioning."

A serious expression came across Lawrence's face. "So, Snookums," He said as he looked at Beverly, "I guess we'll be going back to Boston for a day or two... What do you think?" He held his glass up in her direction.

"You're right, lover. Chloe 'ill be deathly disappointed if we don't make it to her show, but I suppose that can't be avoided."

"We can send a wire... explain the circumstance." Beverly said, "Surely she'll understand... the FBI and all."

"Okay, then it's settled. The first thing in the morning we'll go back to Boston and talk to the FBI. See what all the fuss's about." He looked at Poppy and beamed, showing his teeth prominently, "How's that, Sis?"

"How much have you had to drink tonight?" Poppy said.

"Not nearly enough, it would seem." Lawrence began to slur his words more markedly, grinning broadly at his sister.

"You sound like you're drunk to me. You most likely won't remember any of this in the morning?"

"I'm not drunk... not yet anyway... but I'll be smashed before I'm in bed tonight." He was waving his drink around and nearly spilled its contents over the lady at the next table. Luckily it only slopped onto the floor. "Besides, even if I don't remember anything, my trusted side kick, Beverly here, who never gets drunk, will remind me— won't you, sweetie pie?"

"Sure, sweetie pie... I'll remind you," the tone of her voice made it clear that Beverly was growing tired of his drinking pretty quickly. "Maybe we should get back to the hotel early so we can get an early start tomorrow morning. What do you say, sweetie pie?"

"That sounds like an excellent idea, my dear Bevy, Bevy, Bevy... Snookums."

Poppy looked at him, and then to her. "Should we come with you and help you get him in bed?"

"No, that's okay. I've done this before. I can handle him. But I could use help getting him outside and into a cab."

It didn't take the three of them long to get Lawrence into a taxi and see them on their way. Poppy and Steele stood in front of the restaurant and watched as the cab disappeared into traffic. Steele turned to Poppy. "Maybe we should follow them? Beverly may need our help again."

Poppy looked at the restaurant and then back to him. "She said that she could handle him. And, it doesn't

appear that this is the first time she's had to do it either."
She flashed him a smile. "Why don't we go back inside and
finish that nice dinner. After all, it's only one and we
already have the table."

Steele waved his hand toward the restaurant door.
"Sounds like the perfect plan," he bowed slightly at the
waist. "After you, Milady." He flashed a toothy smile,
"You're the boss."

Without Lawrence's drunken antics, dinner was
uneventful. The music was soothing and romantic.

"What's bothering you? You have that *I've got a
questioning* look on your face."

Steele put the fork full of salad he had raised to his
mouth back onto his plate. "Just a little." He poked and
prodded the lettuce and bits of cabbage, carrot, and
cucumber on his plate with the fork. "I don't know if it's
anything."

"Can you tell me what?"

"Just thinking about Lawrence."

"What about him?"

"How often have you been around him when he's
been drinking?"

"A few times, but not that much." She took a sip from
her wine glass. "So, what's bothering you?"

"It seemed strange to me that he went from nearly
sober to cock-eyed drunk in a flash, after we mentioned
returning to Boston."

"I hadn't noticed," she said as she dabbed at the
corner of her mouth with her napkin. "But now that you
mention it... it did come on rather abruptly. Didn't it?"

"That's what I thought," he said as he lifted the fork
full of salad again. "Anyone, besides Beverly, who might
know Lawrence's drinking habits?"

"No one that I can think of, perhaps one of his old
college buddies, maybe one of his office workers. But, I
really don't know."

"What about Barnaby?"

"He might, but he's fiercely loyal. He might tell me, and then again, if he feels that it's privileged information, he would not."

"It may be nothing, but it might be significant. We need to check it out when we get back to Boston."

"Do you think his drinking habits are important?"

"I'm not sure... I just don't know." He placed the fork on his plate. "But, to me, his actions seemed unusual, that's all." He took a sip of coffee. "It may be nothing at all, just the nervous impulses of a very cynical, suspicious-of-everything detective."

"Nevertheless, it won't hurt to ask a few questions." She sipped from her wine glass. "Will it?"

"Not a bit." He held his glass up to hers and they touched rims.

They lingered over their after-dinner drinks and then over coffee, listening to the music until two, when the quartet finished for the night.

As they left the restaurant, Steele checked his watch. "You know this city's a crazy place. Look." He motioned with his open palm, "It's two fifteen in the morning and I swear there are as many people out now as at noon."

Poppy grabbed his arm. "Yes, don't you just love it?" she said as they walked to the curb.

A taxi pulled up and a young man and woman got out. Poppy and Steele got into the cab.

"The Meridian," Steele announced to the driver.

Poppy looked at Steele. "It's such a nice night—why don't we take a ride through the park?" she asked as she snuggled up to him.

"Driver, the lady wants to see the park."

"Yes, sir," he said as he saluted Steele in the rear-view mirror.

CHAPTER 14

The hotel was busy when they arrived. A group of nearly twenty people milled about the lobby. "What do you suppose it could be?" Steele said as he looked over the crowd.

"One of the nearby theaters must have just let out," Poppy said as they walked toward the elevator.

"Ah..." He looked around the lobby again, "but, it's kinda' late for the theater don't you think?"

"A little," she smiled at him, "but often, if a show is popular, they will add a midnight performance, on the weekend, to accommodate public demand."

"That makes sense. Good old American supply and demand," he chuckled.

She ignored his attempt to make a joke. "Too bad we have to leave tomorrow; we could go to the theater." She wrapped her arm around his elbow.

"How about a rain check on that? When this whole thing's finished—of course."

"It would be my pleasure, Mr. Detective."

"What kind of theater do you prefer? The dramatic, the serious, or the frivolous?" he said.

"The frivolous—with singing and dancing. Perhaps a comedy, if it's good."

"Yeah," he frowned, "since I know nothing about the theater, I'll have Lois make the arrangements. Unless you'd like to do it."

"Frances's an absolute whiz with theater tickets," she laughed. "It'll be fun."

"Okay, it's settled, I'll speak with Frances about it."

The elevator was empty except for the operator, a young man. Poppy said to him, "Thirty-eight, please."

The boy didn't say anything, he just watched as she pulled Steele to herself and gave him a big kiss. The elevator operator began to turn cherry red.

"You needn't watch, my boy," she said to the elevator man, "just turn your head away and operate the machine, please."

"Yes, Ma'am," he said as he suppressed a giggle.

She looked at Steele. "Nosy neighbors." She kissed him again.

He broke away from her lips, "Poppy, I hope you haven't forgotten our little talk earlier."

"No, I do remember it, in my head, but... my body still wants more." She then grabbed Steele and pulled him into another kiss.

"Ever done it in an elevator?" she whispered, as her hands began to undo his belt.

This caught Steele so completely by surprise that all that came out of his mouth was a long, "G-e-e-z," as he grabbed hold of her wrists. "Naughty, naughty girl." He held her hard to his chest and whispered into her ear, "You'll just have to wait till the proper time, my love. Remember our agreement?"

"You're no fun," she pouted. She drew back and whispered, "I've never done it in an elevator."

"Neither have I," he said. "You'll have that to look forward to, next time, won't you?" He tweaked her chin with his thumb and forefinger.

The elevator boy appeared as surprised as Steele at what went on. He jammed the lever to the side and the car came to an abrupt stop. It was the thirtieth floor. The doors opened, the elevator was half a foot higher than it should have been. The elevator boy's face and neck turned red. He looked out of the open door. There stood a man and a woman in evening clothes.

The man was looking at the floor mismatch.

The elevator boy looked at the floor and then up to the man's face. He said, "Oops," and adjusted the level of the elevator.

After they departed the elevator and the door closed, Steele turned to Poppy and said, "That poor kid. He must think we're quite insane."

"Sure... but, it would have been a lot more fun if I'd gotten that belt off," she giggled. "Besides, it's New York, he just thinks we had a few too many. He probably sees that sort of stuff every day."

As Steele opened the door to the room he said, "You may have had too much to drink yourself. You don't remember anything I said earlier. Do you?"

"Yes, I do. I remember every word, and I'm not dinky dunk," she said, her words becoming slurred. She threw her coat on the floor and began to unbutton her blouse. Next came her skirt, which she let drop to the floor. He blouse came off and went flying across the room. She stood looking at him, her feet spread apart and her hands on her hips. She was still wearing her bra and panties, along with a garter belt, stockings and her shoes. She squinted, grimaced and said, "I also remember what I said. I said I understood, which I do. But what I didn't say was—I don't like it. I hate it!"

She ran to the bed and threw herself across its width, and began to cry.

Steele removed his overcoat and picked up her clothes. He draped his coat and her clothes over the back of a chair, then went and sat beside her on the bed. He was about to speak to her when he realized that she was no longer crying. Her breathing was slow and steady. She had fallen asleep.

He bent down and removed her shoes, undid her garter-belt and removed it with her stockings. He took hold of the edge of the bedspread and gently covered her with it. Picking up one of the pillows and retrieving his overcoat, he made himself a bed on the couch.

CHAPTER 15

The sun coming through the window awakened Steele. It was uncommonly bright for this time of year. He looked at his wristwatch. It was half past eight. Glancing over to the bed he saw Poppy still sound asleep. He called room service and ordered coffee, juice, toast, and bagels with cream cheese and then took a very long, hot shower. While drying himself off, there was a knock at the door.

"Room service," came muffled through the door.

He wrapped a towel around himself and answered the door. The bellhop wanted to bring the cart inside and set it up. Steele glanced over his shoulder to Poppy's naked body stretched across the bed and convinced the bellhop that he could handle it himself. The man yielded quickly when Steele gave him a silver dollar tip.

Steele poured himself a cup of coffee and sat on the window seat sipping it while he watched Poppy sleep. She was lying face down and had thrown the covers off during the night. He marveled at the contours of her legs, how they so smoothly transitioned to her thigh and then rose steeply up to the rounded contour of her butt, and then, dropping down into the valley of her back to slowly rise up to the roundness of her shoulders. She rolled on to her side and he could now see the full roundness of her breast, the ruddy tint of her nipple, and the flatness of her belly as it dove down in a smooth curve—terminating in a tuft of reddish-brown curly hair between her legs.

Steele sat thinking.

God, she's a beautiful woman. I could sit here and watch her sleep for days on end. But we need to go as soon as possible. But, it would be a shame to wake her.

He filled a cup and walked over to the bed. Holding the cup close to her he waved his hand across the cup wafting the rich aroma of the coffee to her nose.

She stirred, opening her eyes and yawning a bit. Putting her hands above her head, she stretched like his cat Rusty did after one of his afternoon naps. Every muscle in her body strained from her fingertips to her toes, all extended to their maximum elastic limit.

"Hi," Steele said. "Want a cup of coffee?"

She moved her legs to the edge of the bed and sat up, raising her arms over her head, stretching again; her mouth formed a wide 'O' in a yawn as she brought her arms down. Resting her hands on her knees she said, "Hi, yourself. What time's it, anyway?"

Steele handed her the cup. She took a small sip.

He looked at his wristwatch. "Quarter past eight," he said as he walked back to the window seat and picked up his own cup. "There's toast, bagels and cream cheese, too, if you want." He pointed to the cart.

She sat on the edge of the bed sipping her coffee. "I've got a terrific headache. Got any aspirin?" she said as she pulled her legs up and folded them under herself Indian style.

"Sure, let me get a couple." He walked over to his bag and retrieved a tin of aspirin which he handed to her. "I'm not at all surprised—you overdid it a bit last night."

"Did I make a complete fool of myself?"

"No, not really. At least nothing of any importance."

"What did I do?"

"Just a little flirting with the elevator man."

"How much flirting?"

He took a bite of toast, "I'm sure he has a great story to tell all his friends."

"I didn't. Did I?" Her eyes widened and her jaw dropped. "Did we... umm?"

"No, my lovely lady. I'm afraid your virtue's still intact."

"You keep waving that thing in my face and it won't be for long because I'm going to attack you!" She smiled as she held up a glass of juice, pointing it directly at the bulge growing underneath his towel.

"I'm sorry," he said as he ran into the bathroom. "Just took a shower," he said peeking sheepishly around the edge of the door.

She began to laugh. "You're so damn cute—do you know that?"

He came out of the bathroom wearing his slacks and buttoning his shirt. "Why would respecting a woman I like be considered cute?" he said as he sat on the window seat and began pulling a sock on his foot.

She held her hand up beckoning him with her finger, "Why don't you come over here and we'll discuss it." She smiled.

"Poppy, seriously, one of us has to show a little self-control. We need to get back to Boston, remember?"

She began to cry and threw herself back on the bed. "I know, I guess I'm just being selfish," she sobbed.

"No, you're not... everything that has happened in the last few days has gotten your world all turned upside down and inside out. You're just confused and scared and can only see this minute. You can't even comprehend the next minute right now. It's okay... you'll get through this."

He went over and picked her up and held her. She continued to cry there in his arms for a few more moments. He held her and let her get it out—she hadn't been able to, until now. Soon she calmed down a little and pulled back, but still held him tightly. She looked up at him. "Thanks Mark. I'm sure I'll be okay for a while." She pressed her head tightly against his chest. Looking up, she touched his cheek lightly.

"Don't worry. I'll still be around when it's all over."

She looked up at him and smiled. "You promise?"

"Promise." He held up his hand with three fingers extended. "Scout's honor."

She pulled away slowly, and scampered to the bathroom. He soon heard the water in the shower running and the sound of her singing an unfamiliar tune with French lyrics. The shower stopped in a few minutes and she called out, "Mark, what do we do now?"

"That depends. Are we flying back to Boston with your brother and Beverly, or are we taking the train?"

"I thought we would go with Lawrence on the company plane." She appeared at the door of the bathroom, still naked, rubbing her wet hair with a towel.

"Okay, then we need to find out when he's leaving."

"Why don't I call him at the Hilton and see what his plans are?"

She wrapped the towel around her head like a turban and walked over to the telephone.

"I just remembered," Steele said, as he rubbed his chin, "I didn't shave. I'll do that while you're on the telephone."

In about five minutes Steele was halfway through his beard when Poppy came into the bathroom. "What?" he said.

"Lawrence and Beverly checked out of the Hilton at three in the morning. The night manager said he overheard Beverly mention sunbathing and boating in the Bahamas."

"You're kidding!" Steele cried out. "Where's the company plane?"

"The company has a hanger at Teterboro Airport, on the other side of the river in New Jersey."

"Okay, good. Call the hanger and see if the plane's still there."

She went back to the phone, and tapped the cradle switch three times. "Operator, can you please connect me with Teterboro Airport?"

Steele came out of the bathroom wiping the last of the shaving cream from his face. "What did they say?"

The telephone was back on its cradle and Poppy had a look of defeat on her face. "The plane's gone!"

"Did they say where it went?"

"The mechanic said that he topped off the fuel. But, I didn't think to ask about their destination." She looked even more disappointed.

"Okay, that's not a problem," he wrapped the towel around his neck, "They would have no reason to tell him anyway." He took a brush and comb from his bag and began to brush his hair, "We can call the airport tower and see what they put on their flight plan.

Steele dialed the hotel operator, "Can you please connect me with the Teterboro Airport again?"

Steele was sitting on the edge of the bed looking up at Poppy who was still naked with her hair wrapped in a towel.

He smiled at her. "I love seeing you that way." He waved his hand at her. "But don't you think it might be a good idea to put your clothes on?"

She didn't say a word. However, her chest, neck, and cheeks flushed pink. She stiffened her back and standing very straight, she thrust her breasts out, turned and headed toward the bathroom swishing her hips provocatively as she moved.

The hotel operator was able to get the airport control tower on the line in record time.

"You in flight operations?"

A short pause, a raspy man's voice said, "Yes, you're talking to flight operations—Teterboro Airport. Can I help you?"

"Can you tell me if the Conrad Company plane has filed a flight plan?" Another short pause, "Just a minute," Steele put his hand over the receiver mouthpiece. "Poppy what type airplane does your father own?"

Poppy came to the bathroom door; she was wearing a white bra and panties, and was holding a white silk blouse, "It's, a twin-engine Lockheed L-18."

Steele spoke into the phone, "Lockheed L-18." He listened for a moment, and again with his hand over the mouthpiece, turned to Poppy again. "Do you know its number?"

Her face brightened and she ran to her purse and took out a small notebook. She opened it, located the correct page, and handed the book to him then returned to the bathroom.

Steele read the number, "NC-481C." After a short pause, his forehead wrinkled with a frown. "Ah, yes... they did... Okay, thank you." He hung up the telephone.

Poppy emerged from the bathroom. She was now wearing the white blouse and a pair of black wool trousers. "What's wrong?" she asked.

"The flight plan has them going to the Bahamas and then on to San Juan."

She looked like her favorite pet had just been killed. Then she said, "Damn—that's not good."

"Steele shook his head and began to dial the telephone. "I'm calling Hank to fill him in. After that we need to get back to Boston."

#

Hank picked up on the first ring.

"Hank—Steele here. We talked to Lawrence last night and he said that he would come back to Boston and talk with you but during the night he and Beverly took off in the Conrad Company's Lockheed L-18 aircraft. Their flight plan has them headed first to Nassau, Bahamas and then going on to San Juan."

"I got it, Steele. I'll get a cable off to Nassau right away."

"Okay, you do that. Poppy and I will get back to Boston as soon as we can."

Poppy sat on the window seat and sipped a cup of coffee.

"Hank's going to contact the police in Nassau and see if they will hold the plane till the FBI can get there to question them. He also said that he would call whoever's in charge at the Conrad Company and see if they will classify the plane as being stolen," Steele said as he sat down beside her, picked up a bagel and took a bite of it.

"You know, the Bahamas destination's probably a ruse. They may have gone directly to San Juan," Poppy said rather dejectedly.

"I know, but Hank has both destinations. He's a real bulldog when it comes to tracking people. He'll find them wherever they land. Meanwhile, we need to get back to Boston as soon as we can."

"I'll call Frances and have her make arrangements to get us home." She got up and went to the phone. Steele went to the mirror in the bathroom and began tying his tie. A few minutes later Poppy came over and wrapped her arms around his waist and laid her head against his back. "Frances said that there was a big storm last night and Boston airport's temporarily closed to all arriving flights. They don't expect the runway will be cleared till tomorrow morning. Our other choices are a car or the train. So, I told her to book us on the train again."

"Sounds good to me. What time does the train leave New York?"

"There's one leaving Penn station every hour. If we hurry we can make the one leaving at eleven."

"Okay."

"I also called Barnaby and told him we're leaving on the eleven o'clock train and to have Alton pick us up at South Station."

Steele called Hank back. "Make sure that if they didn't catch Lawrence in the Bahamas, that they notify the San Juan police."

"Steele, what do you take me for, a rookie?" Hanks voice became indignant. "All of that's been done."

"Sorry, Hank... just ticking things off in my head and momentarily forgot who I was talking to."

"Okay, Steele, I often get my thought sidetracked."

"A simple case of two great minds thinking alike," Steele chuckled.

Steele had not unpacked; he had changed his shirt and underwear and returned the used items to his bag. He helped Poppy pack and in a few minutes they rode the elevator down to the lobby. The man at the concierge desk—his name tag identified him as Bengerman Howell—graciously made arrangements for the Meridian limo to take them to Penn Station. Steele also noted that another five-dollar bill discretely slipped from Poppy's hand to Mr. Howell's and then directly into Mr. Howell's breast pocket.

The limo driver knew his stuff. He was a master at judging the lights going south along Seventh Avenue. He didn't have to stop once from the time they left the hotel garage till the car pulled up at the curb outside Penn station.

The five-dollar bill Poppy slipped the driver as they got out of the car seemed more than justified. They had settled into their compartment fifteen minutes before the scheduled departure time.

CHAPTER 16

A half hour after leaving the station, Steele went to the club car and brought back ham sandwiches, potato chips, and cold bottles of beer for them both.

"I've been mulling things over," he said to her as he opened the compartment door and set the tray of food down on the table.

"What have you been *mulling* about? Me, I hope," she grinned at him. She pointed to the tray. "You know the porter would have brought that here for you."

"I know the porter could have done it. I just like to do things for myself and it gave me a chance to think. It's about time to review what has happened, especially things that happened the night of your father's abduction."

"If you think it will help. But, I don't know what else I can tell you."

He sat down and took a bite from one of the sandwiches. "Did your father ever mention this Endeavor project to you?"

"Not that I remember... he rarely discussed company business with me... perhaps with Lawrence, but never with me." Her demeanor was matter-of-fact, showing little emotion. She picked up the other sandwich and began to eat it, getting mustard on her nose.

Steele leaned over the table with a napkin in his hand, "You've got mustard..." He dabbed at her nose with the corner of the cloth, "on your nose."

She giggled.

"Okay, now seriously," he put the bottle of beer to his lips and took a sip. "Your father never talked about anything to do with the company. Not even things that happened in the past? You know, a little friendly boasting over cocktails about the deals he's especially proud of. A project that made the company a lot of money; it may have happened a long time ago and turned out badly for him or for the company. He never talked about any of it?"

"Now that you put it that way—I do remember one story. It happened when the business had just started. In the story I heard it happened twenty years ago. One of the men that started the company with Roger became furious about an idea he had come up with—an invention—or a patent. He thought the company wasn't giving him full credit for what he'd done."

"That could be significant. But, I don't know how it might fit in at this point."

"But it all happened over twenty years ago. As I remember it, there was a hearing and a trial, and the judge awarded the man a great deal of money. Nothing more happened after that."

"I have a feeling it's important—but how?" He ran his fingers through his hair. "Can you remember anything else about the incident? What was the man's name? Anything at all might help."

"I believe the man moved to England or France, or maybe it was Italy. I've never heard the complete story, just snippets now and then from different people." Her brow furrowed momentarily and then her face brightened, "Mother probably knows nothing about it." Her brow furrowed again. "And, she's in such a state that she doesn't know what's happening most of the time."

"What about his secretary, Frances. Would she know this man's name?"

"No, that's unlikely. She hasn't been with Father that long." She took a sip from her bottle of beer. "However, she would know exactly where to look in the files to get the answers."

"Good. As soon as we get back give her a call and have her start looking for that name." He finished his last bit of sandwich. "Does anything else come to mind?"

"No... I can't think of anything else."

"Okay, but keep thinking about it. Go over every detail in your mind. Even a small thing, a detail that may not seem very important to you, that could be just the thing we need—the piece of the puzzle that completes the picture."

"I'll try." She looked as if he had asked her to have a tooth pulled without anesthetic. She reached over and picked up his bottle of beer and put it to her lips.

He took hold of her other hand. "Try to relax. In fact, don't think directly about it. Just let your mind work on the details by itself for a while.

"Try thinking of an activity you and your father did together that you enjoyed. For instance, did you ever go on a trip together? Did he ever take you to a place that was especially fun for you? The circus? The zoo? You know, that sort of thing."

"Yes, I see what you mean—let me think." She closed her eyes in deep thought for several minutes. Then she said, "I do remember one time he did take me to the office. It was summer time and I was home from school. It was a day when all the employees brought their children to work to see what their parents did all day. I don't remember much about it. I was about sixteen at the time and not much interested in anything to do with business. I do remember meeting several of the other kids and their parents. They gave all the younger kids paper and Crayola's; they drew pictures in the large conference room."

"That's good, just keep that day in your mind for a while and think over what the other kids did, what you did. What did they draw? Did you draw anything? Just silly stuff like that."

"Do you really think this will help?"

"I don't really know. It may not prove anything, or it may help a lot. In any event it gives your mind a rest, time to focus on unrelated things. I often do it when I'm up to my eyeballs in a case and can't see any sort of solution. I often remember times back in Nebraska when I was a carefree kid. Walking barefoot through a field of tall grass, swimming in the creek with my friends—it helps to clear my head."

"Does it work?"

"Yes, most of the time it's effective. But even when it doesn't work, I feel rested and more able to manage whatever comes along."

Poppy had put her elbows on the table and propped her head on her hand, closing her eyes. After a few moments, she opened her eyes. Steele realized that she looked tired and drained. Her eyes sad and puffy. Her cheeks flushed, like she could start crying again any second. Not so surprising, since she hadn't gotten a good night's sleep since this all began.

"You look tired."

"Just a little," she replied.

"Why don't I have the porter make up the bed so you can get a little sleep before we get back to Boston?"

She didn't say anything. She closed her eyes again.

# # #

Steele had the porter make up the upper berth. It took him less than five minutes. Poppy crawled up the ladder and lay down. She was sound asleep almost immediately. She hadn't even bothered to get undressed. Steele sat down on the seat below the berth and used the opportunity to go over the case. He withdrew the notebook from his inside jacket pocket and began to leaf through the pages.

The most obvious fact that emerged was that he still had no really solid clue about who had kidnapped Roger Conrad. Lawrence was certainly acting suspiciously, but so far, there was no evidence implicating him or his girlfriend. Because he liked Poppy, Steele didn't really want her brother implicated in this awful thing. But Steele had to follow the facts wherever they might lead him.

Steele decided that his biggest problem with Lawrence was that he couldn't figure him out.

The man's an enigma. Is he just a jerk, as he appears? Or, is he very clever and playing the jerk to throw off suspicion? Why the trip to New York? Running off like that just focused more suspicion on him.

Steele needed to ask Poppy more about her brother. How was he as a kid growing up? The way he's acting now may be just the way he *is*. He needed to know more details. Perhaps the servants at the Conrad house could shed more light on Lawrence.

There was an element that eluded him. He couldn't put his finger on what it could be. He also knew from experience that—whatever it was—it would surface sooner or later.

The only other people who had raised any suspicions in his mind had been the chief accountant at Conrad Company and Arnold Becker, the production manager. There was no real evidence against either of them; just the feeling in his gut that had started when they made such a fuss before the meeting in Conrad's office. Then again he thought, maybe it can all be chalked up to their abrasive personalities— they're both annoying schmucks—nothing more than that.

Right now he just didn't know. He took out his pen and made a note in his book:

1) Have Hank look closely at Veronica Gelding and Arnold Becker's past. <u>See if they have any skeletons lurking in their closets.</u>

But he thought *Hank probably doesn't have enough evidence against her to get a warrant to look at her bank account. But, a deposit here or a withdrawal at a suspicious time can often break a case. I'll have to talk with Hank about it. Now—this new man Poppy mentioned also interests me.*

He continued writing in his notebook:

2) Who's this man who Poppy has remembered?
3) Was he Conrad's partner in the past?
4) <u>If so, find out when?</u>
5) Is it realistic to believe he could he be involved after twenty years?
6) Did he really move to Europe? 7) Or is he still in Boston? In the US?
8) <u>Find out his name and check his background.</u>

Steele, like many detectives, relied heavily on his gut feelings—correct most of the time—and also capable of leading him down the primrose path to a dead-end.

He put the notebook back in his pocket and, after gazing out the window a few moments, he decided to go to the club car and have another beer.

Twenty minutes later he returned to the compartment. Poppy opened her eyes as he closed the door.

"Just went for a drink." He held up a bottle of beer. "You want one?"

She stretched her arms over her head and yawned, again reminding him of Rusty when he wakes up from one of his frequent afternoon naps.

"No, no beer. But, a cup of coffee would be nice."

"Okay... I'll get it," he said. "Be right back."

She reached out and put her hand on his shoulder, and in a still sleepy voice said, "Wait, I'll go with you."

Steele ordered coffee for Poppy and they took a seat at a small table in the rear of the club car. They sat and watched the scenery until Steele finished his beer. He went to the bartender to order another.

"Sorry, sir—bar's closed. Railroad regulations, I have to close the bar twenty minutes before reaching the station."

"So, how soon will we be in Boston?"

The man pulled a pocket watch from his vest. "We'll arrive at South Station in eleven minutes, sir."

CHAPTER 17

Alton was at the station right on time. Poppy spotted him first. He was standing in the foyer between the inner and outer door of the front lobby. As soon as he saw them coming, he opened the door and came toward them. He tipped his hat to Poppy, smiled without saying a word and took both their bags. After exiting the building he pointed to the car, which was waiting at the curb. The weather had improved since the reports they had heard in New York. It was no longer snowing but there was a foot and a half of new snow on everything in sight. The snow on the sidewalk had a hard frozen crust. It made loud crunching sounds under their feet as they walked to the car.

Alton opened the door for them and then put the bags in the trunk. After he had taken his place behind the wheel, Poppy told him, "Alton, we need to stop at the downtown police station before going home."

"Yes, Miss Sinclair."

The car moved out into traffic.

Fifteen minutes later the car stopped in front of the police station. Steele got out while Poppy spoke to Alton.

"Alton, we'll be here for a while. Why don't you take a coffee break at Alice's Diner; Mr. Steele tells me the apple pie's delicious. I'll call you there when we're ready to leave."

He nodded his head and said, "Yes, miss."

Alton waited at the curb till they'd entered the station before he drove off.

Steele didn't recognize the new officer at the reception desk. He called Hank and a few minutes later McDoodle was escorting Poppy and Steele to Hank's office.

Hank was going over reports with a dozen open folders scattered around his desk when Steele walked into his office.

Tom Saine

"Guess your little trip to New York was a bust," Hank said as he put his feet up on the corner of his desk.

"No, I wouldn't say that, Hank; we did get a little from Lawrence, just not what we had expected."

"You think this trip to Nassau and San Juan's an admission of guilt?"

"Not necessarily," Steele said as he pushed the fedora back on his head. "I just can't figure out how this things going to work. Hank, you and I both know that a victim in a kidnapping has about a 90% chance of being killed, and 99% of the time the kidnapper doesn't end up with the loot."

Poppy burst into tears, "Oh no! You mean Daddy's already dead? You said, you said..." she stammered between sniffles, "they... they wouldn't hurt him if the ransom's paid. Would they?"

Steele took her in his arms. "I'm still hopeful." he held her at arm's length, "Poppy, I—we haven't given up yet."

"But, but you just said..." she sniffled.

"Those are just statistics. Every case's different. And until we find your father we won't know anything for sure." He gave her his handkerchief and began helping her out of her overcoat. He hung both coats and his hat on the coat tree in the corner and sat down in the chair next to her.

"Steele, you also know that most crooks are as dumb as a fence post—don't you?"

"Yeah, I know, most crooks aren't the smartest apples in the crate. But there are parts of this case that just don't feel right. It's off kilter, and I can't put my finger on why."

Poppy looked at Steele, then to Hank, and back to Steele "What do you mean, it doesn't feel right?"

"The whole thing looks as if it's been planned by a complete idiot. The ransom note doesn't make any sense—too much money—and the file they want—it's for a nothing project. I'm beginning to suspect it's a personal thing, having nothing to do with the project files at all."

"You're probably right, but that still doesn't get us anywhere—does it?"

Steele ran his fingers through his hair. "Still no line on that production manager—what's his name—Becker? The more he evades us the further I push him up my list. How about phone records? Anybody checking who called who?"

"I've got people on that. So far they have calls between Becker and Lawrence on several different occasions, but that could be related to their business. No way of knowing what they discussed."

Steele got up and began to pace back and forth in front of Hank's desk. "Has the FBI come up with anything?"

"Only the bare minimum. The Argentine police have put a surveillance team into the post office in Rio De Janeiro. But there are problems in Switzerland."

"What kind of problems?"

"You know how the Swiss are," Hank threw his feet up onto his desk. "They get pretty testy when it comes to their bank transactions and their numbered customer accounts." He took out a cigarette and lit it, took a long pull on it, and blew out a perfectly round smoke-ring that shot off toward the ceiling. "Anyway, Steele, all the stuff about the Swiss isn't entirely made up from the movies. Privacy for account holder's a real thing with them. They won't monitor the account or allow surveillance inside the bank. The FBI has set up a surveillance unit outside the bank. But they can only let us know if there's any suspicious activity around the bank by the people we suspect. They plan on following all of our suspects after they leave the bank."

"That's all fine and good, but what if a transfer comes by letter or telegram? The money could end up in Beirut, Shanghai, Moscow, or Outer Mongolia—anyplace in the world."

"I know. But right now we can only hope that the FBI knows how to handle this sort of thing and then keep our fingers crossed. Besides, that's not our biggest problem..."

"What else has happened? Another kidnapping?" Poppy called out, concern showing in her voice.

"No, nothing like that," he gave Poppy a reassuring smile. "It's just that the people at Conrad—Miss Gelding in particular—say that the company doesn't have that kind of money. It might take more than a month to raise that kind of money."

Steele looked at Poppy and then back to Hank. "And, that makes finding Conrad even more important." He reached over and took hold of Poppy's hand. "I had hoped that we would at least learn a little from Lawrence. But we didn't. We don't know a hell of a lot more now than we did before we went to New York."

"How about the car?" Hank asked, looking at her, "Didn't you say it was a limousine, Miss Sinclair?"

"I originally thought it might be a limousine, like my father once owned, but it could have been a four-door sedan—I can't be sure."

"Didn't you say it was black or blue—can you remember now which color it was?"

"No, I didn't say, lieutenant. I had a pillowcase over my head and couldn't see anything." Her brow furrowed. "It may have been pink for all I know." She paused a moment then her face brightened, "The druggist who untied me. He may have seen the car. Have you talked to him yet?"

Hank didn't answer the question but began fumbling through a sheaf of papers on his desk. Finally, he pulled one free from the pile and began to scan it.

"Yeah, he said he wasn't completely sure of the color; under the streetlights it looked dark blue, but it could have been black. He goes on to say that the license was from New Hampshire and not Massachusetts."

"Did he get the license plate number?" Steele said.

"It says here that he wasn't sure. He thought it might have started with nine and two, but the car was a long way off and he couldn't be positive." Hank's face brightened and he sat up in his chair. "I hadn't noticed that before... that's a good lead." He had a broad grin across his face as he began dialing the telephone, "Yeah... Williamson. I have a partial plate number and a car description. Can you check it for me?"

He held his hand over the receiver and took a drag on his cigarette. This time he blew two smoke rings, one after the other in the air over his head. "Yeah, we're looking for a New Hampshire plate beginning with nine and two. The car's a black or dark blue four-door Cadillac." There was another pause as Hank listened to whoever was talking on the other end of the line. "I don't know the year, but we believe it was prewar." A pause.

"Okay—get back to me as soon as you can. The car's part of a kidnapping investigation and every minute counts." He hung up the phone. He looked at Poppy and then at Steele, "They tell me it'll take till tomorrow afternoon to process the information through Concord motor vehicles."

Steele pulled out his pipe and began to fill the bowl. "Okay, while they are doing that, I have another angle we can investigate." He looked at Poppy and squeezed her hand. "On the train trip back from New York, my able-bodied assistant here remembered an incident in the past that's worth checking out."

"And what would that be?"

"It seems that many years ago Conrad had a partner and the partnership ended badly," he looked at Poppy again, "but maybe it would be better if she tells you about it herself."

Poppy uncrossed her legs and moved forward in her chair, looking at Hank. "There's really not that much to tell. Only what I've heard from other people. It all happened many years before Mother met Roger. I don't even know the man's name."

"I see," Hank said scratching his chin. "Then, tell me what you do know."

She leaned closer to him like she wished to share a deep dark secret. "It was told to me like this: About twenty years ago when Roger started the business, he had a partner. They had a big argument over the ownership of the inventions and patents and when it was over, his partner left the business."

"Did you say you didn't know this man's name?"

"I only heard Roger mention his name once, but I don't remember what it was. Since I mentioned it to Mark in New York I've been trying, but I still can't remember the man's name. I do remember it was a foreign-sounding name."

"What else happened?" Hank asked, "Did he make threats against Conrad?"

"I don't know about any threats. This all happened years before I even met Roger and years before he married Mother." She sat back in the chair and crossed her legs. "However, I do know that there was a law suit and that the judge made Roger pay this man a great deal of money."

"How much money?"

"I believe the sum was $50,000."

"Whew…that's a lot of money," Hank said as he exhaled a billow of smoke.

"A hell of a lot more when you consider it was twenty years ago," Steele said.

"Yes, it was, Poppy said, "I believe Roger had a difficult time keeping the company going, until the war started. Since then the company has been quite successful."

Hank looked at Steele. "You really think it's important, Steele? I mean it was twenty years ago and the man got a healthy court settlement. You think this guy could still be carrying a grudge?"

"I don't know." Steele struck a match with his thumbnail and put the flame to his pipe. "Things like that are often more about principles than money. Oftentimes this kind of thing doesn't get resolved by winning a court case and being awarded a lot of money in a settlement— no matter how much it might be."

"You may have a point there. Still, twenty years? That's a long time to hold a grudge. Don't ya think, Steele?"

"I don't know about that, Hank. Look at the Hatfields and McCoys; I understand that feuds been going strong for nearly a hundred years."

Hank laughed. "You're joking, Steele. Those are just stories and folk tales."

"I don't think so," Steele, grinned, "the graveyards down there in the West Virginia and Kentucky hills are chock-full of folks who wouldn't agree they're just stories."

"Just the same, you really think it's worth looking into?"

"All I'm saying it seems like a reasonable lead. It may be a good lead; maybe not. But we won't know which until we do a little checking."

"Okay, I'll have McDoodle pull the court records and see what we can dig up on this guy. See if we can track him down and ask him a few questions. Does that satisfy you, Steele?"

"Sounds reasonable to me. But, that still leaves us with the question: Where do we go from here?"

Hank sat back in his chair and ran his fingers through his hair. "Unless McDoodle makes a fantastic discovery, my prime suspect still has to be Lawrence, at least until I find a better one."

Hank looked at Poppy and gave her a quick smile and a nod. "Not because I have any real evidence against him, mind you, but mostly because he's avoiding talking with me, or anyone else for that matter, about the case. That makes me very suspicious of him."

Poppy smiled at Hank. "I can't believe my brother could do such a thing. However, you are correct. He's acting strangely, and I'm becoming more suspicious of him myself."

"Still," Hank, said, "other than him, our best bet's to go back and re-interview everyone involved. I'm positive one, or more, of the company employees knows more than they're letting on."

Steele got up and went to the coat tree and retrieved Poppy's overcoat and held it up for her. He got his own hat and coat and put them on, saying, "Okay, Hank, why don't you start on the people at the company and Poppy and I will see if the servants know any more than they told us the other night."

"Sounds like a good plan. I'll have my boys round-up the bigwigs and bring them in here for a little talk; getting them out of their element may shake them up enough to loosen a tongue or two." he said. Fumbling around on his cluttered desktop, he finally pulled two sheets out from the middle of the pile and yelled, "Sergeant McDoodle! Come in here."

The Sergeant stuck his head through the open door. "Yes, boss. What ya need?"

Hank handed him the two sheets of paper and said, "Have the people on this list brought in for questioning. And get me a copy of the court records of a lawsuit brought against the Conrad Company about twenty years ago."

McDoodle took the papers and said to Hank, "Ya, okay. But Lieutenant—it's Saturday... how can I get any records—everything's closed up for the weekend."

"McDoodle, use your imagination," Hank growled. "Send an officer to get whoever you need to open up the records office if you have to."

"And what about the people on this list; where do I find them?"

"They'll be at the Conrad Company, or at their home—just find them," Hank barked. "McDoodle, I told them not to leave town. So, if any of them are gone, put out an APB and have them brought in—in cuffs—from wherever they're found. Understand McDoodle?"

"Yes, Lieutenant. I understand perfectly." He turned and raced out the door like his tail was on fire. A minute later he ran back into the room.

"What now, McDoodle?"

"This court case... do we know which year it was filed?"

"No, I don't," Hank hollered, "Check between 1925 and 1940. Just, find the damn thing for me."

McDoodle didn't say anything more and ran out again just as fast as he had before.

"Little hard on the guy, aren't you, Hank?" Steele said.

Hank sat back down, "Nah... he's a good kid... just a little slow on the uptake... he just needs a little nudge now and then, that's all."

He took out another cigarette and lit it with the stub of the one he had smoked, blowing another smoke ring in the air.

The telephone on Hank's desk rang. He picked it up and said, "Lieutenant Williamson here. What can I do for you?" The expression on his face began to change from sullen to a grin and then back to serious. He listened for a moment, and then wrote a few lines on a notepad on the desk. "Right, I'll be over in a few minutes."

Steele's questioning expression got a response from Hank.

"FBI. They want us over there right away. Seems they've got information on Lawrence."

Hank retrieved his gun from his desk drawer and slid it into his shoulder holster.

"Let's go see what they have to say," Steele said and headed for the door.

"May I come along?" Poppy said, "After all," she smiled, "he's still my brother."

"I don't see any reason why you shouldn't come along, Miss Sinclair," Hank said as he put his hat on, "They said that they had information. They didn't say that they had him in custody. And even if they do they probably won't let you see him."

"That's okay, I'll take my chances. I still want to come with you, just on the off-chance he's there and they will let me see him."

# # #

The Federal building was only two blocks away—if it had been spring they would have walked—but since the temperature had peaked at twenty-nine—they decided it might be smart to take a car. Hank checked out a marked squad car so that they wouldn't have any problems finding a place to park.

The Federal building was a new building with clean, stark lines. Unlike past government structures, this post-WWII modern had no fluted columns or fancy cornice works adorning its exterior. The building had a few tall, narrow windows. The windows reminded Steele of arrow slits in castles he'd visited in Europe. If the building had been constructed from granite blocks instead of concrete it might have been mistaken for a medieval castle; it only lacked turrets at its corners and parapets along the roof line, and a moat with a drawbridge at the entrance.

Hank showed his badge at the desk and in a few minutes a security guard came to escort them to a third floor conference room. The security guard informed Hank that Special Agent Alex Jarvis, the agent in charge of the investigation, would be with them in a few moments.

They sat down and immediately two men in black suits came in and sat down in front of them. The larger of the two men put a stack of manila folders on the table and introduced himself as Special Agent Alex Jarvis and the other man as Special Agent Jack Kelly.

Hank showed his badge and again introduced himself. "Miss Penelope Sinclair," he said indicating Poppy. "Miss Sinclair's the older sister of Mr. Lawrence Sinclair."

Poppy extended her hand to Kelly. He shook her hand and turned his attention to Steele. "And you might be?" he asked.

Hank spoke up before Steele. "That's Mark Steele, a local private detective. He's been employed by Miss Sinclair—and he's working closely with me on the case."

Jarvis opened one of the folders and started talking. "Sinclair and Manners are being held at the US Embassy in San Juan. We have arranged for them to fly to Boston on a military transport aircraft. They should arrive in Boston late this evening or early tomorrow, depending on Air Force schedules."

Hank spoke up, "When will we be able to talk with them?"

Agent Kelly seemed to ignore Hank and continued, "Both Sinclair and Manners have made preliminary statements. They say that they had nothing to do with the kidnapping and theft of items from the Conrad Company."

"I would expect that," Hank said, "In my experience, suspects hardly ever confess at the first interview."

"We'll keep after them," Kelly said, "if they're guilty, we'll get it out of them."

"Miss Sinclair," Hank nodded in her direction, "wasn't sure if she could identify any of them by their voices... she said they only whispered when near her. They never talked out loud."

"That true, Miss Sinclair?"

"Yes. But, I'm positive the man who kidnapped me was not my brother. I'm certain I would have recognized his voice, even in a whisper."

"He still may have been the driver," Steele said as he looked at Poppy. "You did say the driver didn't talk."

"Yes, that's correct," she flushed, "the driver didn't speak."

"We can put him in a line up just the same. We'll simply blindfold you and have the suspect whisper a few words or phrases you might recognize. You can never tell what might happen," he said.

"Okay, I'm willing to try it," Poppy said, "I'm not sure I'll be able to recognize anyone... but, I'll try my best."

"I'll call you in as soon as we have a suspect. Can you make yourself available?"

"I'm sure I can," she looked at Steele, "you have my telephone number, and Mr. Steele's."

"Okay, Miss Sinclair, as soon as we have a suspect we feel fits the bill, I'll call you in."

#

"What do you think, Hank?" Steele asked as he opened the door to the police station and then followed Poppy and Hank inside.

"About the FBI?"

"Yeah, they didn't really tell us anything that we didn't already know."

"Hard to say. If anyone can get those two to talk, the FBI can. They take kidnapping and extortion pretty seriously over there at the Federal building."

"But that whole meeting could've been handled with a telephone call."

"You know the Feds; they typically play their cards very close to the vest. They like to make local cops jump through hoops for them, makes them feel superior. I've always considered myself lucky if they tell me anything at all."

Hank was about to sit down in his chair when McDoodle came running into the office waving a sheet of paper. "Just got a Telex from the Border Patrol in response to our APB on Arnold Becker. They have a record of Arnold Becker using his passport to enter

Canada at Champlain, Vermont, into Montreal last night at 1:00 AM." He handed the paper to Hank.

Hank read it, "Are they sure that it's our Arnold Becker, and not another Arnold Becker?"

"They're pretty darn sure it was him, sir," McDoodle said.

"Why didn't they stop him at the border?"

"Says on the paper there that his passport was valid and correct, lieutenant. They had no reason to stop him."

"What about our APB? Don't these people read these things?"

"I guess that's our fault, Lieutenant. We listed him as a possible witness and not as a suspect or a fugitive. They only found him by going over the lists that they keep of people entering their country. Just sheer luck that anyone caught it at all."

"Okay, McDoodle... anything else?"

"No, sir."

"Damn bureaucrats," Hank muttered as he sat down. He took a cigarette from the pack on his desk and lit it.

"Can hardly blame the Canadians, Hank. Until now we didn't really consider him a suspect, we just wanted to talk to him. We didn't have enough to label him as a fugitive— which would have raised a red flag and the Canadians would have held him."

"I know that, Steele. It just makes me feel better to blame someone—anyone."

"I understand that." Steele said looking at Poppy, "Maybe we should leave before we get the blame too."

"Hank wouldn't do anything like that, would you, Hank?" Poppy said as she got to her feet.

"No, I usually don't pick on my friends, mostly just politicians, bureaucrats, and criminals."

"I guess we're safe then, since we don't fall into any of those categories." She laughed.

"Okay... I'll call you later," Steele said as he took hold of Poppy's hand and walked to the door.

"Yeah, sure." He waved his hand at them. "Get the hell out of here so I can get back to work."

When they had gotten two steps outside the door, Hank yelled, "Close the door."

Steele went back and closed the door. The sergeant was busy on the telephone at his desk just outside Hank's office. When he hung up Poppy asked, "May I use the telephone? I need to call my chauffeur to pick us up."

"Sure thing, Miss Sinclair." He smiled cordially and pointed to an empty desk about eight feet away.

"I should call Dexter about my car too," Steele said.

"Sure thing, Mr. Steele," the sergeant said, as he pointed to a telephone on the other desk. "Use that one over there."

"Thanks, Sergeant," Steele said as he picked up the receiver and began to dial.

"Dex, Steele."

"Y'all back from New York okay Mr. Steele?"

"Yeah, we got back this morning... have you finished with the Cord?"

"Sure thing, Mr. Steele. The fender arrived from Elkhart two days ago. We replaced the headlight parts yesterday afternoon and she's all fixed-up and already to go."

"You mean I have two headlights now that actually shine on the roadway?"

"Yes, sir. They open and close and are properly adjusted and as bright as ever. Just like they come off the assembly line," Dexter chuckled.

"That's great... Say, I'm just leaving police headquarters now. Can you bring the car to the Rivers later? I'll buy you a couple of cold ones."

"Sure you can afford a beer and to pay for this car in the same week, Mr. Steele?"

"My client was exceedingly generous with her retainer." He looked at Poppy. "I've got enough to pay the bills and buy a few beers."

"Okay, what time should I be there?"

"How about ten o'clock—late enough for a beer and too early for the college crowd to show up."

"Sounds good to me. We'll be there fur-sure—the car an' me."

CHAPTER 18

Steele and Poppy waited in the reception area for about ten minutes before Alton pulled the big Lincoln up to the curb in front of the station. He got out and opened the rear door for them. A minute later his voice came over the intercom, "Where do you wish to go now, Miss?"

Poppy pressed a button to lower the separation window, "Alton, we'll be going to Mr. Steele's office first... you remember where it's located?"

"Yes, Miss—Memorial Drive, not far from the University," Alton said as the car moved away from the curb.

They had gone over the Longfellow Bridge and had turned onto Memorial drive when Alton said, "Miss, I believe we're being followed."

"Alton, are you sure?" Steele said as he sat up in the seat and looked out the rear window.

"I believe so, Mr. Steele. A tan Chevrolet, parked across the street from the police station, made a U-turn when we pulled out. He's been behind us ever since—he's two cars back now."

"Alton," Steele said, "make a right turn at the next intersection and see if the car stays with us."

"Yes, sir," he answered and immediately changed lanes and turned right at the next street. The side street had been plowed earlier, but was still slippery with packed snow and ice. Rounding the corner a little too fast the big Lincoln fishtailed, seemingly out of control, but Alton was able to get it straightened out.

"Don't speed up yet, Alton. Just see if they follow us."

"Yes, sir," he answered and the car slowed.

Steele was now looking out the back window and said, "You're absolutely right, Alton. I can see a tan car and it just made the same turn we made. He wasn't so lucky. He hit a patch of ice and rammed a car parked at the curb. But it didn't slow him down much. He's still coming on strong. Make another right at the next intersection."

Alton didn't answer this time but the car made a right turn at the next street. It swerved and fishtailed again down the side street, barely missing two cars. The Lincoln had gotten about half way down the block when the tan Chevrolet came around the same corner, fishtailing violently. The driver wasn't as good as Alton. He sideswiped one of the cars that Alton had missed. The Chevrolet accelerated quickly.

"Okay, Alton. You can punch it now. They're definitely after us. They've hit two cars and are still coming," Steele said as the big Lincoln began to accelerate.

"Alton, do whatever you can to lose them," Poppy shouted.

The Lincoln immediately jumped forward, thrusting Steele and Poppy back into their seats. Two blocks later, Alton made a left and then a quick right. Again on Memorial Drive, a much wider primary street, which allowed Alton more room to maneuver. Because of its heavier traffic it had no ice and snow and gave the tires better traction.

The Chevrolet came around the last corner, its tires screeching loudly as they met the dry pavement. The scream of its tires could be heard even inside the Lincoln. Looking back, Steele could see billows of smoke coming from the rear tires of the Chevrolet as it accelerated. Within a block the tan Chevrolet had caught up to them. A man wearing a black Halloween mask leaned out the passenger door with a revolver in his hand. He began shooting at them. Two bullets shattered the rear window of the Lincoln. Luckily Alton had his window down which created enough pressure inside the car to blow the rear window out sending fragments of glass flying back over the Chevrolet.

Steele shouted, "Get down!" and at the same time pushed Poppy down to the floorboards.

Steele yanked his gun from its holster and stuck his head up over the rear seat far enough to see where the Chevrolet was. Its front bumper was nearly touching the Lincoln's rear bumper. Steele got off two shots through the gaping hole where the rear window had once been, before ducking down again.

The man in the Chevrolet had traded his revolver for a Thompson machine gun. The rat-tat-tat chatter of the machine gun started. Bullets ripped through the Lincoln's trunk and rear fenders. The Chevrolet pulled out and into the oncoming lane and along-side the Lincoln. Slugs peppered the side of the car, raking it first from the front to back and then from back to front. Glass from the side windows flew in all directions and the Lincoln began to slow down. It swerved sharply to the right. The car bounced over the curb, flying three feet in the air. It came to an abrupt, bone-shattering stop. Steele got bounced around violently by the impact. He landed on top of Poppy, who was still face down on the floorboard.

The big Lincoln had jumped the curb and collided with a telephone pole.

Steele raised his head in time to see the tan Chevrolet as it zoomed off down the street. He got off two more shots at the car, but wasn't able to read the plate number. He did see that it was the distinctive green and white color of a New Hampshire license plate.

Steele bent down to check Poppy. She was moaning but appeared unhurt. He looked forward over the front seat to Alton. He could not see him. He tried to open the door but it was stuck. He lay back on the seat and kicked the door as hard as he could with both feet. The door sprang open on his second attempt.

The car was a mess. Two rows of bullet-holes ran down its entire length. The rear, and all the side windows had shattered and a dozen holes pierced the windshield safety-glass.

A geyser of steam spewed from under the hood with a loud hissing sound. The hood, buckled in the middle like a kid's pup tent, sitting up on the fenders of the car. The force of the collision had pushed the front of the hood back nearly two-feet.

The front bumper now hugged the telephone pole like a long-lost lover. The force of the impact had bent the pole over at a thirty-degree angle. If the car hadn't held it in its grip it would have fallen over. Several wires hung down from the transformer. None of the wires came in contact with the car. Two wires bounced across snowdrifts thirty feet down the street spewing a shower of sparks in all directions as they jumped about—like a living entity. Steele could see no wires near the car.

He looked into the driver's window at Alton. He found him slumped over on his right side, laying across the center of the seat. It didn't look as if he was bleeding, but Steele couldn't see him clearly enough to tell for sure. He went to the back door and looked in at Poppy who was still down on the floorboard but sitting up. She looked dazed.

"Are you hurt?" he yelled at her.

"No, I don't think so," she replied with a quivering voice.

"You have blood on your forehead and your arm, which looks like it may be broken."

She felt her forehead and then looked at her arm. She held her arm with her hand. "No, it's just a scratch."

Steele went back to check Alton again. The driver's door was also jammed. Bracing his foot against the door pillar, he pulled on the door with all his strength. The door popped open on his second attempt. He raised Alton from the seat and placed him upright against the seat back. He was unconscious and bleeding badly from a wound on the forehead. Steele pulled the handkerchief from his breast pocket and applied pressure to the head wound. He looked for other wounds but didn't find signs of blood anywhere else. He looked at Poppy. She was sitting upright on the seat now, still looking confused and dazed.

He called out to her, "There's a phone booth over there." He pointed at a booth on the corner, ten yards behind the car.

She looked in Steele's direction, and then turned to look behind the car.

He yelled again, "Poppy, you need to call the police— we need an ambulance."

This time she appeared to understand what he was saying and got out of the car, but just stood there, not moving.

He yelled again, "Poppy, snap out of it. Alton's been hurt. And, it's serious."

CHAPTER 19

Forty-five minutes later Hank found Steele and Poppy in the emergency room of the hospital. Poppy was sitting on an examination table; she had a large white bandage on her forehead. The doctor had just left after applying half a dozen stitches to a cut on Poppy's right leg, just above her knee. Her skirt had bunched up on her lap while a nurse applied a bandage to the wound. Steele was sitting on a stool nearby as another nurse applied bandages to a series of cuts on his head and neck. He had a black eye and his shirt contained large splotches of blood.

"What the hell happened, Steele?"

"It would appear that our snooping around has earned us a little attention," he said with a somber look on his face.

"Are you okay?" He looked at Poppy as she got down from the table and adjusted her skirt. Besides the large wound she had several smaller bandages on her knee, legs and arms. The one on her forehead now sported a red spot where blood had seeped through the gauze. "And Miss Sinclair—is she okay?"

"We're both fine, just minor cuts and bruises, nothing serious. But the chauffeur, Alton, has an extremely bad head wound. He was still unconscious when the ambulance got him here."

"Was he shot?"

"I couldn't tell—maybe—but, he did have a rather bad head wound. I couldn't tell if a bullet did it or his head hit part of the car. I didn't see any other wounds—but who knows?"

"I saw the car—it's a real mess." He removed his hat and wiped his forehead with a handkerchief. "I had it towed to the police garage. Maybe it'll give us a clue or two, but I wouldn't hold your breath." He looked Steele right in the eye, "Jesus, Steele, I counted forty-six holes in the side of the car. And that's not counting the ones that went through the windows. They must have used a Tommy gun?"

"Yeah, they did. I'm surprised there weren't more than a hundred... I thought for a while there that we'd gotten mixed up in a Jimmy Cagney movie with a bunch of Chicago gangsters after us." Steele couldn't hold back a chuckle.

"This ain't funny, Steele—it's serious."

"I know... I know it's serious. It's the absurdness of the situation that's gotten my funny bone, he said," still with the smile across his face. "A Thompson machine gun in broad daylight. It's insane. Ludicrous."

Poppy had gone to the restroom and came back to join the two men. "Lieutenant, anyone in the street injured?" she said.

"No. But many of the store windows down the street got shattered by stray slugs. And besides the Lincoln, six other cars are now sporting bullet holes. I don't know of any other injuries; just you, Steele, and your chauffeur."

"That's good," she said as she turned and sat down on a stool next to Steele.

"D'yeah think this had anything to do with the Conrad affair or is it related to one of your other cases?"

"I have no idea." Steele said as he ran his fingers through his hair and rubbed the back of his neck.

"You pissed anyone off particularly badly lately?"

"I don't think so, but in this business, it's hard to tell." He looked directly at Hank. "You know as I do—the bad guys don't always think rationally. Most of them have a screw or two loose from the beginning."

"I know. But still... when did you first notice the car following you?"

Steele's tone turned more serious. "They waited for us to leave the police station. Alton saw the car parked across the street. It made a U-turn and came after us."

"You're kidding. Who knew you'd be at the station?" Hank asked.

"That's just it... no one could have known. We came straight from the train station. Unless..."

"Unless what, Steele?"

"The only one who knew we would be at the train station was Frances Stevens, Conrad's secretary. She made the train reservations. The only other person who knew was Alton; Poppy called Barnaby from Boston to have Alton pick us up at the station."

"We can probably rule out the chauffeur since he was in the car with you," Hank said as he began to pace back and forth.

"If you want to know the truth, it could have been anyone. Our travel itinerary wasn't exactly a top-secret operation. Alton, Barnaby, Susan, Zoë, or anyone. Like I said, the trip was not a secret. Even Dexter, who was fixing my car, knew about the trip to New York—although, I don't think he knew when we'd be back. And, who knows who Frances may have told at the Conrad Company. Almost anyone could have found out just by overhearing Frances make the reservations over the phone, or looked at a note on her desk."

"Do you remember anything about the car?"

"It was a brand new tan-colored '54 Chevrolet sedan. I didn't get the license number, but it was definitely green with white numbers, like they use in New Hampshire."

"New Hampshire again. The same as the druggist said was on the kidnappers' car?"

"Yes, it was. But it's probably a red herring."

"What do you mean?"

"I bet if you check with the New Hampshire State Police, you'll find both cars had been stolen in the last few days. Meant to throw us off the track—send us on the proverbial *wild-goose-chase*. Most crooks, as we just agreed, are idiots. But even the stupidest of them know enough to steal a getaway car and switch plates. And, out of state plates are even better."

"You're probably right. Just the same, I'll put a man on it and check it out."

"Did anyone talk to the people on the street? Anyone get a good look at the men in the car?"

"The two patrolmen on the scene talked with about two dozen people and have about two dozen different stories. Most heard screeching tires and the machine gun, after that the stories pretty much go to shit in all directions. Everyone was ducking for cover, and scared. They don't remember much—and, what they do remember seems all screwed up and contradictory."

"You can't blame them, Hank. I'm trained for these types of situations, and I didn't get a good look at the guys, either. As soon as the shooting started, I threw Poppy to the floorboard and covered her. I did get off a few shots, but still, I don't think I could identify either the driver or the guy with the gun."

"Damn lucky you did cover her, from the looks of the holes I saw in the car, she would be in surgery, too."

"Have you been able to talk with any of the Conrad Company people you pulled in?"

"No. We could only locate five of them. None of them had arrived at the station house when the call came in about the shooting. I still have people looking for the other three or four."

"You think any of them skipped town?"

"No, not yet. According to relatives and servants we've talked to, most are either out shopping or gone to dinner. Dan Harding, for instance, was at a hockey game downtown with his two sons."

Hank was just about to leave when a man in a white lab coat walked over to where Steele and Hank stood.

"Are you Miss Sinclair?" he asked, directing his comment to Poppy.

"Yes, are you Alton's doctor?

"Yes, Dr Newly."

"I'm Mark Steele," Steele shook the doctor's hand. "Detective Lieutenant Williamson—Boston Police." Hank said.

"Is Alton okay?" Poppy said.

"He's stable now but still in serious condition. He has a bullet wound to his head—a grazing wound—not that serious. It did probably knock him unconscious. But he also has two other bullet wounds. One in the back, where we believe the bullet entered," Dr. Newly placed his fingers against Steele's back, "about here, just under the scapula and exited the chest. Just here," he pointed his fingers to a spot on his own chest, "which missed his heart, but it did collapse the left lung—he has already gone to surgery to repair the lung and other tissue damage."

"No, no," Poppy sat down and began to cry.

"What are his chances, doctor?" Steele asked.

"I would say they are excellent," he said with confidence, "but he'll be in the hospital for at least two-weeks."

"When can I talk with him?" Hank asked.

"Because of the anesthetic, I don't think he'll be conscious and coherent till late tomorrow morning."

"Okay, doc," Hank said, then added, "Make sure you call my office as soon as he's able to talk." Hank pulled a business card from his inside jacket pocket and handed it to the doctor. "Here's my card."

The doctor looked at the card and slipped it into his breast pocket. "Sure thing, Lieutenant Williamson."

"Doc—I'm putting a uniformed officer outside his room till we find out exactly what's going on."

"I don't see how that could hurt anything," the doctor said. "Now if you will excuse me, I need to get back."

Without waiting for a reply he turned and headed off down the hallway.

Hank said, "One last thing, Doc."

"Yes, Lieutenant?"

"The bullet... if I understand you correctly. There was no bullet recovered. That right?"

That's correct, lieutenant. It went in and then out again. He was lucky the bullet missed the rib in the back, on entry, and only nicked the one in front as it exited." He smiled at Hank.

"Okay, doc, that's all," Hank said.

The doctor disappeared through the same door he had come out of earlier.

"Hank, do you really think Alton's the target?" Steele asked.

"I don't know, I'm not taking any chances until I know more about what happened."

From far down the hall footsteps could be heard running in their direction. It was a uniformed patrolman who obviously knew Hank. He came directly up to him and said, "Lieutenant, we've just received a report. We've just received a report that the tan Chevrolet on the APB has been found. It's stuck in a snow bank, half a mile from where your shooting took place."

"Think it might be our car?" Hank asked the man as he leaned towards him to read his name tag, "Conley."

"Pretty sure, Lieutenant. It has New Hampshire plates and about a hundred forty-five caliber shell casings in the back seat, and two bullet holes in the trunk. There was also a lot of blood covering the back seat."

Hank looked at Steele. "Looks like you might have hit one of them, Steele."

"I hope so. Might make them easier to find."

As the little group stood there discussing things, Lois arrived. She came up from behind Steele. Poppy had seen Lois walk up and waved her hand, but Steele had not seen her.

Lois had taken a place behind Steele and Hank, not saying anything but listening to the exchange between Hank, the police officer and Steele.

When she heard them talking about the shooting, she began to shout, "Bullet holes! Blood! Oh, my god! Mr. Steele, are you and Miss Sinclair all right?"

"How did you get here, Lois?" Steele said.

"I took a cab. Lieutenant Williamson called from his office. He said there had been an accident! But bullet holes! Blood!" she cried out again. "He didn't say there was shooting. Are you and Miss Sinclair all right?"

"We're just fine," he said in a reassuring voice, "but Miss Sinclair's chauffeur, Alton's been injured."

"Is he hurt badly?" Lois said.

"We don't really know. He's still in surgery," Poppy said as she began to cry.

Steele held Poppy, walking her toward a bench near the wall. He sat her down and, along with Lois, sat down beside her.

"Look after her, Lois," Steele said as he got to his feet, "I need to talk more with Hank."

Lois nodded her head but didn't reply.

"Okay, Conley. Make sure that the car arrives at the police garage," Hank was saying as Steele approached the two men, "and have the lab guys go over it with a fine toothed comb. Don't forget to have them test all the empty shells for fingerprints. Our shooter may have gotten careless."

"Yes sir. I'll check with the towing company, and put the police garage on alert. Remind them to collect all the shell casings and check them for fingerprints. Anything else, Lieutenant?"

"That'll be all, Officer Conley. But, when you get back to the station house tell McDoodle to get a man over here on the double to keep an eye on a witness for me. Have the officer contact Dr. Newly." Conley pulled a small notepad from his breast pocket and wrote in it, and left. Hank looked at Steele. "I need to get back to my office. You and Miss Sinclair come by as soon as you can and we'll fill out an official report."

"Okay, Hank," Steele said then added, "How 'bout we meet later at the Rivers instead?" He pointed to Poppy on the stool. "She's pretty shook up now; later would be better. I'll buy you a sandwich and a beer."

"That'd be okay—but it'll be late. Will half past ten be okay? I'll bring the forms." He waved a hand, as he took off down the hallway in the same direction officer Conley had gone.

Steele sat back down next to Poppy. She had her head down, bent over and resting on her hands with her elbows on her knees. Lois was patting her lightly on the back. She had stopped crying. When she finally raised her head to look at Steele the whites of her eyes showed red veins, her face flushed red, was puffy and swollen and streaks of black mascara ran down her cheeks. A dark purple spot had begun to appear over her right eye. She had hit her head pretty hard during the accident. Steele looked at her for a moment then took his handkerchief and wiped the dark streak of mascara from her cheeks.

She looked at him and took his hand and said, "Thanks," and started to cry again. He wrapped his arms around her and held her tightly until she stopped. She asked, "What's wrong with me... I can't stop crying."

He pushed her a small distance away, so he could see her face and said, "Let's see... you've been involved in a high-speed car chase through slippery snow-covered streets. You've been shot at with a machine gun. You've been involved in a bad car crash. You have a severe wound on your head and numerous cuts and bruises on your body. And on top of all that, a friend of yours was shot and in the operating room right now. Nah, none of that qualifies you to be bawling." He winked at her and smiled.

Lois got to her feet. "I'll get her a glass of water," she said as she hurried off down the hall.

Poppy giggled. "Okay, when you put it that way, I suppose it's alright for a girl to cry a bit." She leaned her head on his shoulder and her tears began to flow again.

"Yes, I'd say so. You cry just as much as you want to. I got nothing better to do than sit here and hold you for as long as you need me to."

Lois returned carrying a tray with a carafe of water, a glass, and a wet washcloth and towel. She set the tray on the bench and filled the glass half full and handed it to Poppy.

Poppy took a sip and handed the glass back to Lois. She wiped her face with the damp cloth and dried it with the towel.

"I feel better now," she looked at Lois. "Thank you," she said with a slight smile.

Lois smiled back but didn't reply.

They sat on the bench in silence for a half hour. The door down the hallway opened and Dr. Newly approached them. This time he sat down on the stool next to Poppy and said, "Mr. Johnson's doing fine. The damage to his lung has been repaired, and he's on his way to the recovery room now. You can see him there, but I wouldn't expect him to be conscious till morning."

Poppy began to cry again and buried her head even further into Steele's chest.

Steele looked at the doctor and extended his hand. "Thanks, Doc."

The doctor shook his hand, then turned away and left.

Poppy looked at Steele with red puffy eyes. "I thought I would stay here with Alton but if he'll be unconscious till the morning—perhaps we should go and come back later."

Steele sat down beside her, "I don't see much point in our going to the office now. Why don't I just take you and Lois home."

"That may be best," Poppy said. "If Mother finds out about this she'll be quite upset. I should stay with her tonight—and also ask Barnaby to keep the news from her if he can."

Lois got to her feet and began buttoning her coat, "Mr. Steele, you go and take care of Miss Sinclair. I can take a taxi."

"Are you sure, Lois?"

"Yes, I'll be fine. Miss Sinclair's been through a great deal today. You go and take her home."

Lois tied her belt around her waist as she walked down the hall, the same way Hank and the police officer had gone.

Poppy dabbed at her swollen eyes with the damp cloth, "If you want you can stay at the house tonight. I can have Zoë prepare one of the guest rooms. Would that be okay with you?"

"Sure, no problem." He smiled at her, and they got up from the bench and walked off down the hallway.

CHAPTER 20

A light snow was falling outside. There wasn't a cab in sight when they reached the street. Their overcoats had been left in the Lincoln. It was too cold to stand at the curb and wait on the chance that a cab would drive by so they went back inside. The receptionist called a cab, which rolled up at the curb five minutes later.

The cab pulled up in front of the Conrad's at a quarter past seven. The overcast sky made the night seem even colder and darker than it was. The snow, which had fallen lightly at the hospital, was now falling heavily as they made their way up the walkway. Large wet flakes covered their heads and shoulders by the time they reached the door.

As Steele opened the door, he said, "Looks like a few more feet of snow may get dumped on Boston tonight."

Poppy nodded in agreement, but didn't reply.

A moment later Barnaby opened the door. His eyes revealed the fact the he had seen the bandage on Poppy's head. However, displaying his usual stoic facial expression, he said nothing of it. He bowed with an almost imperceptible bow and stepped back, opening the door wide.

Poppy said to him, "Barnaby, would you fetch Susan and Zoë and bring them to the library? Mr. Steele and I need to talk to everyone."

"Is anything wrong, Miss?"

"Mr. Steele and I will tell you all about as soon as we get everyone together in the library."

"Yes, Miss." He bowed again, turned and went off towards the back of the house. Poppy and Steele went to the library.

A few minutes later Barnaby came into the library, followed by Susan and Zoë. Steele recognized the ladies from the dinner party. Susan was Barnaby's wife, and also the housekeeper and cook. She was in her late forties, stood a full head shorter than Barnaby, and was slightly overweight. Zoë was about thirty, tall with a slim build, with her brown hair pulled back into a bun. The two women wore the same style black dress with elbow length sleeves and starched white bib aprons.

"My goodness, Miss. Your head—what's happened?" Susan said as soon as she saw Poppy's face.

"I will tell you all about it in a moment. In the meantime, will you all please be seated on the sofa."

Poppy took Barnaby by the elbow and pulled him away from the others and whispered, "I have a little bad news for you and the ladies. But first I want you to pour Mr. Steele and myself a whiskey and Susan and Zoë a sherry, and whatever you want for yourself and bring the drinks to the couch."

Barnaby displayed the first real emotions that Steele had seen in him. He frowned and a look of astonishment moved across his face.

"But, Miss—" he began to protest.

"Please, Barnaby. Do as I ask."

"Yes, Miss," he said without further debate. He bowed his head in his usual manner and walked to the bar.

Poppy directed the ladies to the sofa. A few moments later Barnaby arrived with a tray containing the drinks and handed them out. He set the tray on the coffee table and stood at the end of the sofa, with a whiskey and soda in his hand.

Please be seated, Barnaby," Poppy said.

Barnaby protested, "I couldn't do that, Miss—it wouldn't be proper."

Poppy looked at him sternly. "Barnaby, I insist," she commanded. "Please, sit there next to Susan."

"Very good, Miss," he said in a very low voice and took a seat next to his wife on the couch.

Poppy took a small sip of her drink and indicated to the others to do the same.

Steele was standing at the end of the couch and Poppy sat in the chair near him. "Mark, if you could explain."

Steele took a sip from his glass. "You are all aware of Mr. Conrad's being kidnapped last Friday night. We still have no word as to his whereabouts. Tonight after Alton picked Miss Sinclair and myself up at the train station he took us to the police station, where we talked briefly with Lieutenant Williamson. After we left the station there was an accident."

Mrs. Wallace looked intently at Poppy and said in a concerned voice, "Your head—are you sure that you are all right, Miss?"

"Yes, I'm fine, thank you, Susan. Just this little bump on my head, and a few scratches and bruises." She put her hand to her forehead and felt the bandage. "But I'm afraid Alton's injuries are quite serious."

Barnaby and Zoë said almost simultaneously, "How badly was he hurt?"

Steele said, looking at them both, "Alton was shot by a man in another car. That car had chased us through the streets shooting at us and caused our car to crash."

Susan and Zoë began to cry.

Barnaby look at Steele, "How bad, Mr. Steele? He's not dead?"

"No, no, he's not dead. But he's in the hospital. The bullet hit him in the chest and punctured his lung. They operated on him about two hours ago and he's now in recovery and according to the doctor, he's in good condition. The doctor said he could have visitors tomorrow afternoon."

"Miss," Susan spoke up, "Would it be all right if Mr. Wallace and I took a few hours off tomorrow and went to visit Mr. Johnson in the hospital?"

"That's a wonderful idea. Why don't you all go, take the day off, and stay as long as you like."

"Thank you, Miss," Barnaby said in an emotional voice, uncharacteristic of him.

"Barnaby, the car's been wrecked in the crash, so take money out of petty cash and call a Taxi for the three of you. Stop and get flowers too, if you wish."

"Thank you, Miss, that would be just grand," Susan said.

Poppy got to her feet. "Stay here and finish your drinks and then you can all take the rest of the day off."

"But what about your dinner, Miss? Have you eaten yet?" Susan said with concern in her voice.

"No, but I'm okay. Mr. Steele and I can fix ourselves a sandwich in the kitchen later. Has Mother eaten?"

"Yes, Miss, I sent Zoë up to her room with a tray at half past five," Susan said. "She had a bowel of clam chowder I'd made earlier." She paused and smiled at Poppy, "Miss, there's plenty left if you'd like, I can prepare a tray for you."

"No, that won't be necessary. You and Barnaby go and have a nice night off together." Poppy looked straight at Barnaby, "Barnaby, why don't you take the two ladies out to dinner tonight to a really nice restaurant. Perhaps go see a movie, afterwards. My treat."

"Thank you, miss," Barnaby said. He had regained his stoic demeanor. "That's very kind of you, Miss."

"And Barnaby, if you have any trouble getting reservations, don't hesitate to use my name, or Father's. Okay?"

"That's very nice of you, Miss." He revealed a minute smile.

"Go, have a good time."

The three of them got up and left the room leaving Poppy and Steele alone.

Poppy went to the bar and poured them both another drink. "Mark, would you rather have a beer?"

waiting on a customer at the far end of the bar. He called out, "Mr. Barkeep, how 'bout a cold Rheingold for Mr. Crawford here?"

Culp was talking with another customer, but waved his acknowledgment to Steele.

Steele turned his attention back to Hank, seated to his right. "Want to talk about...."

Hank ignored Steele; his attention focused on an attractive woman who had just entered the tavern and taken a seat at an empty table near the far end of the bar.

She was an exotic looking woman of about thirty with jet black hair, a Romanesque figure, deeply tanned olive skin, and wearing a brightly colored floral skirt with a ruffled hem. She also wore a white peasant blouse with embroidered designs around the neck and down the billowing sleeves. The low-cut blouse barely covered her ample breasts. She also wore a floral headscarf, matching the material of her skirt. The scarf was pulled tightly around her head and knotted behind her left ear, which emphasized her large gold hoop earrings. Around her neck hung several gold necklaces. Many gold and silver bangles embellished both wrists.

Steele looked at Culp. "Who's the new lady?" he said, throwing his thumb in an arc in her direction.

Culp glanced at her. "Her name's Lavinia Ghora. She's been comin' in for a couple of weeks now." He rubbed at a smudge on the bar with his rag. "She claims she's a Gypsy. And I've seen her dealin' them there Tarot cards as she talks to people in one of the booths." He seemed to have mastered the smudge—it was gone. He stepped back and threw the bar towel over his shoulder, smiling triumphantly at Steele. "According to what she's told me, and what other customers have told me, she and her family escaped to Cuba after the Nazi occupation of Hungary in '44."

Hank turned back and looked at Culp. "She married?"

"Don't believe so; no wedding ring," he held up his left hand, wiggling his third finger. "And, I've never seen her with anyone except other customers—mostly women," he said hurriedly as he set off to the far end of the bar. A customer was holding up an empty mug.

"Hank," Steele said, "want to talk about the case or would you rather talk to the lady?" He tipped his glass towards the woman's table. The woman, noticing Steele's gesture, smiled at him.

"Wha—?" Hank said as he turned his head to Steele. "What did you say, Steele?"

"Never mind. I can see that your dick has your mind occupied at the present."

"Ah, shit, Steele, don't be a smart ass. I don't... I don't... nothing of the kind."

"Okay, if that's so, then what did I just say to you?"

"Augh, ummm." Hank sputtered.

Culp came back and laid his bar rag on the bar and looked at Steele, "Heard you had a little trouble today, Mister Detective."

"Just a few shots and a small car wreck, that's all. You know, just your typical Saturday afternoon in Boston," he said in his best smart-ass voice, as he looked over at Hank.

Culp smiled. "That's what I heard. That's the second time you've been shot at in the last couple of months, ain't it? Have you been steppin' on the wrong person's toes lately, Steele?"

"Nah, not that I know of anyway. But this guy's aim wasn't any better than the Boomer's. I knew who shot at me then, and I'll figure out who did this, too."

Hank jumped into the conversation. "You seem pretty confident there, ain't you, Mr. Steele?" he with in a sarcastic tone.

"Yeah... shouldn't I be?"

"Maybe," Hank said as he downed the last of the beer, and set the empty glass down with a thump. "How about another, Mr. Proprietor?" He smiled at Culp, who took the glass and headed for the tap.

"Maybe," Steele said.

"We found a partial fingerprint on one of the shell casings in that stolen Chevrolet. So far we haven't been able to match it up with anyone."

"I'm not certain this has anything to do with Conrad's kidnapping. It's more likely that it's connected to one of my old cases; that's the only way it makes any sense."

Culp put a full glass with a large head of suds down in front of Hank.

Hank took a long swig from the glass and said, "I've had the same thoughts." The glass came away, leaving beer suds mustache covering his upper lip—which he licked clean. "Got any good prospects? Anyone that bent on getting you?"

"No. Nobody jumps to mind," Steele said.

"You know, Steele," Culp said as he held up a shot glass to the light, scratching at a spot with his fingernail, "seems to me that you may have pissed off the wrong party pretty badly."

"Yeah... that thought had crossed my mind," Steele said as he pushed his the fedora back on his head. "I've known a lot of bad guys over the years; helped to put a few away myself, but none are so fucked up that they'd do a crazy stunt like this." He sipped his beer. "I mean, yes, I've been jumped in a dark alley and had the shit kicked out of me, but never shot at with a Tommy gun in broad daylight. This was the work of a complete moron."

Hank looked at Culp, and they both looked at Steele and in unison they said, "Boomer!"

A look of shock crossed Steele's face, but it quickly turned to a grin. "Nah. I'll admit that Boomer does qualify as a moron, but I don't believe that he's that stupid."

"He already shot at you once, Steele," Hank said.

"Yeah, don't remind me," he said rubbing his left arm. "Still hurts, and the cold weather doesn't help it a bit."

Culp put his elbow on the bar and leaned in closer to Steele. "Looks to me like Boomer's getting more determined."

"Maybe I should put a tail on you for a few days, my friend," Hank said as he slapped Steele on the shoulder.

"Nah, what happened today is more than likely just a warning."

"What do you mean, a warning?"

"Looking at the car I noticed that most of the bullet holes went high or low. If they'd meant to get me, that line of holes would have been right down the middle of the car. The fact that they did hit Alton, the driver, was only an accident. I'll be willing to bet that if you look at the bullet they took out of Alton, you'll find that it's distorted and bent. I'll wager it's a ricochet."

"Yeah, you hit it, Steele," Hank laughed, "The bullet hit a hard surface first—more than the sheet-metal in the door—flattening it. When I looked at the car earlier, I remembered thinking 'the guy must have been an amateur with a Tommy gun'. But, till you just mentioned it, I didn't see the 'send a message' theme. And you've got a good point, if I'd been the one sending a warning, that's the way I'd have done it—don't hit you, just scare you a bit."

"I'll have Lois check my old files. See if we've received a threat recently that I don't remember right off."

"Might be a con who's just out of the slammer," Culp said.

Steele looked at Hank, who had shifted his attention away from the woman and back to the glass of beer in front of him. "Any noteworthy thugs been released from lockup lately?" Steele asked.

"Fingers Gibson's the only one who comes to mind."

"But Fred's a safe cracker, ain't he, Hank?" Culp asked. "Tommy guns ain't exactly his style, are they?"

"Doesn't really matter," Steele said. "I've heard stories about Fingers, but we've never crossed paths."

"He was before your time, Steele. You wouldn't have had anything to do with his case," Hank said. "Besides, if Fred's after anyone it would be me."

Dexter hadn't involved himself in the discussion, but he had begun to notice that about half of Hank's attention was still focused on the Gypsy woman seated across the bar. Hank kept glancing over his shoulder at her, and she kept looking in his direction with a big smile.

"Not a bad looker. What do you think, Hank?" Dex said, gesturing to the far end of the bar. "Ya don't move on her, I will."

Hank grunted and got off his stool. "I'm goin' to the head," he announced and went off towards the table where the woman sat. However, he walked past her table and went into the men's room.

"You serious about the lady, Dexter? A woman that young, and lively, might kill you my friend," Steele laughed.

"I'd be a willin' to takes me chances on that one, my boy," Dexter laughed and began to get off his stool as Hank emerged from the men's room door and began to walk back to his seat. However halfway there he turned around abruptly and went back to the woman's table and sat down across from her.

"Too late, Dexter," Steele pointed his thumb toward the Gypsy.

"Yeah... ya can't always win when it comes to a woman," Dex laughed.

"What do you mean? You must do okay. Every time I come to your shop there's a gaggle of woman hanging around; young ones, old ones, and a lot in-between. And I'm pretty sure you didn't bake all those baskets of cookies and cakes I've seen in your office. And I don't believe for a moment that all of those ladies are having their oil changed, their brakes fixed, or their tanks filled." He thought about the double meaning of that last one that he'd mentioned and began to chuckle. "Or are they, you sly dog?"

"Ah yes, but peoples been calling me worse..." He took a sip of beer. "But, a gent daren't tittle about such things," he said. He looked at Steele and winked. "I'll just say that I does all right for a fella me age."

Steele pointed his beer bottle toward Hank and said, "He looks like he'll be tied up for a while. Let me make a call and I'll take you back to your place."

"Take your time, me boy, I'm joyin' me beer. And, having a look at the lady, ain't as good as enjoyin' her company, but I'm savorin' it like a fine bottle of wine."

Dexter put his finger together and kissed them in a gesture Steele had often seen Italian men do when he'd visited Rome. Along with the gesture he whispered, "Bella donna."

Steele looked squarely at Dexter, "I didn't know you spoke Italian."

"Don't—but when you've been around as long as I has—youz naturally tendz to picks up a thing er two."

Steele just shook his head at that and got off the stool. He had to walk right past Hank and the woman's table to use the public telephone, located between the doors to the men's and women's restrooms at the far end of the bar. Hank didn't look away from the woman as Steele strolled by. They'd gotten pretty cozy in the few minutes since Hank sat down with her.

It was late but Steele phoned Poppy at the Conrad house anyway. Barnaby answered the phone and it took him five minutes to get Poppy on the line.

"Hi, Mark," she cooed into the phone, "You are going to come by again tonight?"

"I thought I might. How's Alton doing?"

"According to the doctors, he's much better. They say he'll be unconscious and groggy till tomorrow afternoon."

"You sound as tired as I feel. Sure you want me to come over?"

"Yes. I'm sure," she whispered.

"Okay, but it will be late. I'm here at Rivers with Dexter and Hank. Dex just delivered my car and we're having a beer together. You didn't make reservations... did you? It'll be too late to go out—the only thing open will be night dinners; all the club's will be closed."

"My bedroom's the only place I want to go with you tonight," she said in a sexy whisper.

"Penelope Sinclair, we talked about this in New York. I thought we had come to an understanding. I have to take Dex back to his shop, and then stop by the office and do a couple of things. Perhaps it would be better if I just go to my place tonight."

"No—I want you here tonight," she said, raising her voice slightly.

"Hey, I just remembered. What about your mother? I thought you said she would be upset if I stayed there."

"Yeah, but I'm a big girl now and it's time they treated me that way—don't you think?"

"Yes, you may have a point. One would be hard pressed to argue with that school of thought. However, setting that aside for the moment, my attitude on this subject has not changed since our talk in New York. Do you remember that?"

"Okay, yes, I remember. But..."

"But, what?"

"Are you coming over or not?"

"Only if you promise to behave yourself."

"Must I?"

Steele shook his head and then said, "I'll give you a little time to consider things. I'll call you again before I leave my office." He wanted her to think about what he'd said, so before she could reply, he hung up.

On his way back from the telephones he stopped at the table where Hank and the Gypsy woman sat. Hank introduced them, "Lavinia, Mark Steele. He's the private detective I told you about. Mark, Lavinia Ghora."

"Glad to meet you, Lavinia Ghora." He shook her outstretched hand. "Lavinia, that's a lovely name—brings back memories of my boyhood and school. My sixth grade teachers name was Lavinia—Lavinia Atwood... I had a terrible crush on Mrs. Atwood." He sat down in the chair next to her. "I don't believe I've seen you here before."

"No, Mr. Steele, I've only been in Boston a few weeks. I'm here to visit my brother, Alfonso. He works on one of the river boats."

"You have a charming accent. Mr. Culpepper, the owner here, tells me you are from Hungary."

"Yes, Szombathely, Hungary."

"Ah... I'm not familiar with Szombathely. That's not near Budapest by any chance?"

"No, Budapest in eastern sector, Szombathely near the border to Austria in west."

"I went to Budapest, after the war. The people I met there—all very friendly."

"Yes we Hungarians, most friendly people." She took a cigarette from a pack that lay on the table and held it up to her lips. Both Hank and Steele offered her a light. Holding his hand to steady it, she accepted the light from Hank's offering but all the while kept her eyes on Steele. "Was your Mrs. Atwood a Hungarian, Mr. Steele?"

"No, she and her parents came from Nebraska. But, grandparents were originally from Poland."

"There are many Gypsy families in Poland. Your teacher's family could have come from Gypsy blood, or more correctly, Mr. Steele, the Roma people."

"I wouldn't know about that. But, I suppose if you look back far enough we're all related to each other in the distant past."

"Yes, Mr. Steele. That's probably true."

Hank glared at Steele. "Weren't you about to leave, Mr Steele?"

"Yes, I am... I certainly am," Steele said as he got to his feet. He leaned down between the two of them, but addressed Lavinia. "You should get Hank here to show you the sights while you are here in Boston."

She looked at Hank and winked. "I may just do that, Mr. Steele."

Steele patted Hank on the shoulder. "I'm going to take Dex to his shop. If you need me I'll be at my office for a while and then Poppy wants me to come back over to the Conrad place. But, I'm pretty beat; I may just go home."

Hank looked at Lavinia and smiled. "I don't see any reason I'd need you tonight, Steele. We'll talk tomorrow. Come by my office. We'll put our heads together and catch up on all the paperwork on the case."

Steele patted Hank on his shoulder. "Okay, I'll see you tomorrow afternoon." He smiled at Lavinia. "Nice to meet you, Lavinia. You two have a good time tonight."

"Very nice to meet you too, Mr. Steele." Lavinia smiled broadly as she patted Hank's hand. "I'm certain Hank will take good care of me tonight."

Hank looked at Steele as if he could kill him with his bare hands, and with his teeth clenched together said, "I'm almost certain we will."

Lavinia smiled again at Steele, but said nothing.

#

Dexter and Steele left the bar and walked around the corner to where Dex had parked the Cord under a street lamp. When Steele first saw the car he looked at Dexter. "The headlight looks great, Dexter.' Then he frowned, "But now instead of looking like it's winking at you, it looks like it's got a black eye."

"Yeah," Dex replied, "it's just primer."

"Why black and not green to match the rest of the car?" Steele asked, as he ran his hand over the fender and the new parts Dex had installed.

"You'all see, it's like this. I don't have none of that there green paint in the shop. I don't think you would be happy drivin' a car with a pink headlight, so I sprayed primer on it. It'll only be temporary, till we paints that whole car."

"Okay, you're right about that, black's much better than pink. I wouldn't relish driving a car with a pink headlight," Steele said as he stepped back from the fender and looked at it again from a distance. "It will be fine that way, till we can paint the whole car."

"I thought you'd like it better." Dex smiled. "We can order new paint whenever ya'all like."

"Perhaps when I finish this case I'm on now." Steele said as he and Dex got into the car. Steele started the car and cranked the headlight lever to the open position. "Look at that I got lights," he laughed. "You did a fine job, my friend, and it works as smoothly as cranking a window; just like brand new—maybe better." He pulled away from the curb and looked over to Dexter. "I tell you what, Dex. The client in this case has been very generous; why don't you go ahead and order that paint?"

"What color ya thinking 'bout, Mr. Steele?"

Steele pulled to a stop at the sign at the corner. "I don't know, I like the dark green. But, maybe it would look better in another color. Why don't you get a few samples I can have a look at? I'll stop by the shop in a day or two and see what you've come up with."

#

The trip to Dexter's shop in Somerville took ten minutes. Their conversation on the drive over centered, for the most part, on the car and what Steele was going to do next in its restoration. After the car's been painted, attacking the interior seemed the logical next step. The front seat had tears in a few places and was badly in need of re-upholstering. The headliner had started to sag just a little over the back window. The interior could be done a little at a time. The headliner would be first, followed by new floor mats, leaving the seats till last. That way Steele could spread the expenses over a longer time period.

As Dex opened the door to get out, Steele asked, "You serious about that woman in the bar?"

Dex got out of the car, but before he closed the door, he stuck his head back in and said, "Sure thing, me boy. If Hank hadn't made his move, I would've moved in."

"At your age?" Steele quipped. "I know you have many lady friends, but I thought..." he trailed off.

"What you mean, at my age! I ain't dead yet, me young fella. The old pistol still shoots just as good as it ever did... it just take a mite longer to reload than it once did." He laughed as he closed the door before Steele could reply and headed for the garage waving good-bye to Steele as he walked away.

Steele looked at the clock face on the dashboard and addressed his remarks to it. "Now there goes a man after my own heart."

CHAPTER 22

It took Steele less than fifteen minutes to drive from Dexter's garage to his office building. Having two headlights made the trip feel much shorter. He was a bit surprised to find the lobby lights and the elevator still working in the building. It was unusual, but not at all alarming. Fred, the maintenance man, may have had a hot date and forgotten to turn things off before leaving.

Pushing the light question from his mind. Steele had mixed thoughts as he rode the elevator to the third floor. He couldn't make up his mind as to which was more important: Poppy's plea's to rush over there; or making out this report.

Could the report wait? Yes, it could. I could have Hank make a carbon copy of his official report to put in my file.

When the elevator stopped at the third floor, he hesitated a moment, his finger poised above the "L" button. He didn't push it; instead, contrary to his last thought about not doing the report now, he got off the elevator. He had only taken a few steps towards the office when he stopped in front of a red fire extinguisher hanging in a little alcove above a drinking fountain. He began to address the fire extinguisher like a person, "What the hell am I doing here? Right now I could be in a nice warm bed with a voluptuous young woman!"

The fire extinguisher took on a face in his imagination and it said to him, "You know she's still your client. You made a bargain with her in New York."

He blinked his eyes several times and called out, "What did you say?"

Of course, the fire extinguisher, didn't answer his questions. It just hung there in silence.

He turned to leave when he heard a noise coming from down the hallway—from his office—he approached the door cautiously.

After the fire extinguisher conversation, he wasn't totally sure he had heard anything. Was it his imagination? Did his tiredness making his mind play tricks on him? The sound of a woman giggling pulled him back to reality. "That was not my imagination," he whispered softly."

The sound was coming from inside his office. He paused to listen again. This time he heard nothing. Behind him, down the hallway, the elevator door closed automatically, startling him for a moment.

He grasped the doorknob.

Someone may have broken into the office. The door was locked—as it should he—that's a good sign. Although they could have picked the lock, and then relocked it after they entered.

Steele silently took his keys from his pocket, located the correct one, and inserted it into the lock, being as careful as he could not to make any sound. Before opening the door, he withdrew his gun from its holster, quietly switched the safety off, and carefully drew the hammer back with his thumb. He turned the knob. The door swung open silently. The office was dark but the light from the hall threw a triangle-shaped sliver of light on the reception area floor. Even so, it was still quite dark inside. He edged carefully through the outer office door. Once inside he could see that the door to his private office was ajar. This was unusual. He or Lois always closed and locked that door when they left for the night.

Steele held his breath, straining to hear another sound. All was silent, except for the ticking of a small clock on Lois' desk. Steele decided that the sound he heard earlier was more his imagination than anything else.

Steele, for Christ sake, get a grip on yourself.

He reached for the light switch on the wall. His finger had just touched the switch when a soft moaning sound came from the inner office. He decided it might be best to investigate more, in the dark.

The Conrad Kidnapping

He crept across the floor being very quiet. The closer he got to his office door, the louder and more frequent the moaning became.

A rhythmic bump-a-thump, bump-a-thump, bump-a-thump sound; like bearing of drum in a Tarzan movie. He rounded Lois' desk and stood at the partly open door to his office. The moaning got louder and the beat of the bump, thump, bump thump sound began to get faster. The door was open a crack and he gently pushed it further open, just wide enough to get his head inside.

Whoever was there had pulled the window shades closed and the office was in total darkness. He leaned against the wall, gun at the ready and reached for the light switch by his shoulder.

He switched the light on and threw the door fully open, pointing his gun toward the interior of the room. He couldn't believe what his eyes took in. He shook his head thinking that might help... but no, the image remained fixed there in front of him. There, laying on the sofa bed was, Lois, completely naked. Jeffrey Hudson, the mailman, also completely naked, his hips frantically bouncing against her crotch.

Just after the light came on Jeffrey pulled away from Lois and up on to his knees, his erection pointing directly at Steele.

Lois dove for the far edge of the bed, screaming as her derrière disappeared over the edge, followed by a loud 'thud' as she hit the floor. Her scream was loud enough for anyone passing on the sidewalk, three stories below, to have heard it.

She grabbed a discarded sheet lying on the floor, clutched it to her breast and drew herself up on to her knees. The material had pulled in such a way across her thigh that the plush patch of black pubic hair was plainly visible. She saw where he was looking and looked down herself. She yanked the edge of the sheet over her leg. Her eyes grew as big as saucers and her face, neck, shoulders, and chest turned apple red.

In a delayed reaction, her voice finally catching up to the situation, she cried out, "Oh, my god! It's you... Mr. Steele!"

Steele just stood there and started to laugh very hard and very loudly.

"Lois... I thought I'd walked in on a burglar." He continued to laugh, "I could have shot you." He let the hammer on the gun down gently, engaged the safety and put the gun back into its holster.

"I'm sorry, Mr. Steele, I, ugh... we, ah—," She had trouble forming words. Nothing but gibberish was coming forth. She rose to her feet, still clutching the sheet to her chest and ran to a heap of clothing on the floor near Steele's desk. While she managed to cover her front side effectively with the sheet, the way she held it left her whole back side exposed as she ran to the clothing and bent over to pick them up. As she hurriedly scooped up the tangled bundle of clothing, she almost dropped the sheet altogether, but managed to keep a hold on it and her clothing as she ran to Steele's bathroom in the corner. Her bare back and butt disappeared inside and she slammed the door shut.

Jeffrey was still on his knees where he had been just after the lights came on. He looked like the stereotypical deer caught in the headlights; stunned, and now as limp as a wet wash-rag. He seemed frozen to the spot, and said nothing.

A few moments passed and Lois came out of the bathroom. She had dressed, but her hair remained disheveled and her make-up was still smeared. Her face and neck had flushed cherry red.

"I'm sorry, Mr. Steele, I... ugh... we," was all she could get out.

"It's okay, Lois, it's okay," Steele said still laughing slightly, "I've done the same thing myself."

"You have, Mr. Steele?" she looked shocked. She adjusted her skirt which she had put on hurriedly and was nearly sideways on her hips. The look of horror which had covered her face earlier had now turned to a look of moderate relief. She managed a small smile.

"Yes, I have, Lois. More than once," he answered, "when the office was a more convenient place than anywhere else."

"That's it... the most convenient place. You see, Jeffrey lives at home with his mother and doesn't have much privacy and my landlady would throw me out on my ear if I brought a man into my room... and a hotel seemed so illicit—so it all seemed less sordid if we came here."

"It's okay, Lois, It really *is* okay... you can use the place any time you like. I just wish I'd known and I wouldn't have barged in on you, gun drawn and ready to shoot a burglar."

Jeffrey had recovered and was now sitting on the edge of the bed. He was still completely naked. He heard all of what they had said. He got up and went to where his boxer shorts lay on the floor and picked them up. With his back turned to them both, he stepped into them, pulling them up over his hips. The navy blue shorts contrasted with the rest of his body which was now beet red, "I'm terribly sorry, Mr. Steele. This was a terrible, terrible mistake." He picked up all his cloths in a bundle and started for the office door. "I should just go."

The sight of them there struck Steele as being hilarious. Jeffrey still nearly naked and Lois as disheveled as an old dust-mop. He began to laugh even harder.

"No, no, that's nonsense!" he looked back and forth between the two of them. "It was not a terrible mistake. It's perfectly okay. It was just what the doctor ordered, for both of you. I only wish I had known beforehand, and I wouldn't have come by the office tonight." He addressed Jeffrey directly, "It's okay, Jeffrey." He looked back at Lois. "Lois, it's okay. I'm not angry with you—not at all." Steele was having trouble getting the words to come out of his mouth, he was laughing so hard, "So, you two lovebirds just stay right where you are. Stay as long as you like. I just came by the office to make a few notes on the case—but that can wait till tomorrow."

Lois came over to where Steele stood. She looked at him earnestly and said, "I'll pick up my things before I leave, Mr. Steele. And, if it won't be too uncomfortable for you, I will help you find a new secretary tomorrow."

"Don't be an idiot, Lois. You'll do nothing of the kind. I don't need a new secretary. I already have the perfect one." he winked at her. He smiled at them both, doing his best to hold back another bout of laughter. "After all, you did take my advice and accept a date with Jeffrey."

Steele turned to leave but paused at the door, "There's a bottle of Dewar's Scotch in the bottom drawer of the file cabinet. Help yourselves, if you like. And don't forget to make the bed and switch off the lights when you're done."

He went through the door, not closing it, but leaving it slightly open, as it had been when he had come in. He was two feet from the door before he turned and peeked back inside. They stood together in the middle of the room kissing, silhouetted against the drawn shades. Jeffrey had already pulled her skirt up around her waist and was caressing her buttocks with both of his hands. She was giggling.

Steele opened the door and stuck his head inside, "By the way, Lois."

They both turned to face him, their faces beet red. Jeffrey jerked his hand from beneath Lois's skirt, which fell back down around her knees.

"Lois, only have one condition; you must tell me how you two finally got together after saying no to Jeffrey over a thousand times."

She took hold of Jeffrey's hand and with a giggle she said, "Okay." Then ignoring Steele's continued presence, turned back to Jeffrey and they resumed their kiss.

The last thing Steele saw as he turned away was the hem of Lois's skirt as it began to rise again. He closed the door, tightly this time, and left the office making sure that the outer door was securely locked.

Pretty spry for a couple their age.

He waited for the elevator to come from the lobby and remembered what Johnny had said to him earlier in the evening.

Looked as though ol' Jeffrey's pistol worked just fine too.

A broad smile came across Steele's face as the elevator door opened and he entered.

Hope mine'll be working that good when I'm that age.

CHAPTER 23

Steele was very pleased with the new headlamp assembly. The trip over the bridge to the Conrad house seemed shorter with the added light. Being able to see both sides of the roadway, at least made it feel shorter.

It was half past twelve when he parked the Cord at the curb on the side street by the Conrad house. He rang the doorbell and a few moments later he could hear Poppy's voice call-out through the door, "Who's there?"

"Steele."

The small door opened at eye level in the middle of the big door. Through the grill that covered the opening he could see Poppy's eye peering at him. The little door closed, and a second later the big door opened. Poppy peered around its edge. She smiled at him and then opened the door far enough for him to enter. Inside, he turned to greet her and discovered she was stark naked.

She smiled at him and said, "I thought you'd never get back."

"What the hell are you doing, answering the door like that?" he yelled at her as loud as he dared. He didn't want to wake anyone who might be asleep in the house. "What would your mother say?"

Poppy summoned up her most cocky attitude and shot back, "My mother's asleep, has been for hours. And besides, I've already told you, more than once... I often come downstairs for a snack late at night without my robe. But in case it wasn't you at the door, I did bring a robe with me this time—see." She pointed to the fabric draped over the banister. "If it hadn't been you at the door, I would have gotten dressed."

Steele went to the banister and picked up the bundle of fabric. He held it up. It indeed was a robe. A short dressing gown; made of sheer, nearly transparent, pink nylon. The robe was barely long enough to cover a woman's pubic hair, and would conceal absolutely nothing. "You mean this? This thing wouldn't cover a gnat."

"So," she batted her eyelids at him seductively, "you think I should dress like a cloistered nun, just to answer the front door?"

"You're impossible, lady," he managed to mutter as he shook his head.

"I know," she smiled broadly, "isn't it fun?"

"If you think so," he took off his overcoat and folding it in half, laid it on the vestibule table with his hat on top of it. "Yes, I suppose it could be." he smiled at her.

"I was on the way to the kitchen to get a glass of milk. Would you like a glass before we go to bed?" she asked in a sexy voice as she started walking toward the kitchen.

Steele didn't answer. He shook his head in disbelief, and set off following her perfectly shaped naked ass down the hallway.

"Don't you want this?" He extended his hand with the robe to her as he caught up.

"No thanks—I'm just fine." She tilted her head looking sideways at him. The corner of her lip rose.

He held the robe in front of himself, adjusting his trousers, as he walked, to accommodate the growing bulge there.

Once in the kitchen she turned on the light and went to the refrigerator. Bending over to display her feminine assets to their fullest extent, she pulled a half full quart of milk from the shelf.

Steele laid the robe on the back of one of the chairs in the corner of the kitchen where the staff took their meals. He stood, leaning against the counter, his eyes following her every movement.

"Sure you don't want a glass too?" She set the bottle of milk on the counter and went to an overhead cabinet and reached for a glass on the upper shelf.

Poppy made sure that Steele got the full effect of her stretch and how it accented the line of her breast.

She paused, over the glass, before she poured the milk. "You know, on second thought—I'm going to have a hot chocolate with marshmallows instead."

She went to another cabinet near the stove, opened the door, and with her feet planted far apart bent over at the waist to retrieve a small saucepan, making sure he had a full view of her backside. Standing, she unfolded herself to show off her body. After setting the pan on the stove and filling it with milk, she began to stir it with a large spoon. She grinned. "This will be good—sure you don't want me to make you a cup?"

Steele enjoyed watching the little game she was playing, showing off her assets. He sat down on a stool near the counter to conceal the ever-growing bulge in his trousers as he watched her go about her task.

"Sure, why not... I haven't had hot chocolate since my mother made it for me in grade school." He began to chuckle.

"What's amusing you now?"

"Thinking of my mother," he smiled at her. "She had a novel way of making hot chocolate."

"What was so novel about it?" she asked, "Did she use a special ingredient? I've heard of people making it with cinnamon."

He began to snicker. "No, no cinnamon. She didn't use special ingredients. She just left her clothes on."

Her reaction was to scoop a spoonful of milk from the pan and throw it at Steele. None of it hit him, but it did splash on the counter at his side.

"You're just terrible!" She stamped her foot on the floor. "You know most men would just love it if their wife or best girl met them at the door naked or made hot chocolate for them in the nude. Do you know that, mister?"

"You know you're probably right. It's just that I'm not used to seeing all this much skin on one of my clients." He put his finger into a puddle of milk on the counter and then into his mouth. "Although, once I did have a boxer who was my client; but he always kept his trunks on." He smiled at her, "I've never met anyone quite like you, Miss Penelope Sinclair. I guess I'm still having trouble adjusting to your special ways."

"Do you think you will ever adjust?"

"It's a new experience for me. But..." He paused, putting another finger of milk into his mouth and licking his finger in a provocative way. "I'm making a little progress on the project." he winked at her.

"Okay... I can accept that." She smiled, and went to another cabinet and again stretched her legs, arms, and torso to their full extent as she retrieved a can of cocoa from the top shelf. "I'm not a pervert, you know." She placed the can on the counter by the stove. "I wear very fine clothes when I'm out. But when I'm home I prefer the clothes I was born with." She walked to the other end of the counter and brought back a canister marked Sugar and set it near the can of cocoa.

"How do your parents feel about it? You running around the house stark naked, I mean."

"They gave up objecting years ago. Although mother still dislikes it when I come to dinner wearing just lipstick and a smile." She giggled like a little girl as she said it.

"Okay, then I guess the best way for me to react would be enjoy the view. I could bring my camera next time and take a picture for my desk. Lois may not approve, but I have lots of clients who would love it."

Although, after what I saw of Lois tonight, she may not always be as straight-laced as I'd previously thought.

His idea seemed to please her. She grinned broadly, walked over to where he sat and crawled up on his lap straddling his legs. She wrapped her arms around his neck and kissed him. She whispered in his ear, "Bring your camera any time you like, mister. Take as many photos as you like. I'll buy you a silver frame and have a talk with Lois myself."

"Okay, I will."

"Better yet, I have a camera—a really nice Rolleiflex my brother gave me for Christmas last year. I can get it right now—it has film and a flash, and everything."

"No, that can wait till later," he said as he pulled back from her slightly, "but you better watch it if you don't want it to get too hot."

She gave him a perplexed stare, "Too hot?"

He pointed to the pot on the stove. "The milk... it's about to boil over."

She jumped off his lap and ran to the stove, turning it off just as the foaming, frothy liquid crested the rim of the pan. She proceeded to add the cocoa and sugar and after stirring the mixture a minute, poured it into two mugs. She added a marshmallow to each cup. She brought the cups to where Steele sat and placed them on the counter. She crawled up on his lap, straddling his legs again. He frowned, but didn't say anything.

She reached around him and handed him a cup while whispering ever so softly into his ear, "This would be much more fun if you'd take your pants off."

"Maybe so, but for now let's just have the cocoa," he said, taking the cup from her hand and bringing it up to his lips.

"Are you sure? It feels to me like you're ready for more than just cocoa," she laughed as she rotated her hip on his lap.

"Stop doing that or you're going to have a mess on your hands," he chuckled.

She looked down between them. "Really, already?" She rocked her hips back and forth vigorously.

"No, not that. I'm about to spill this hot cocoa down your back."

Her response was to grind herself into his lap even harder as she smiled at him while taking a sip from her own cup. They sat that way a few more minutes, saying nothing, sipping their cocoa.

Steele finished his first. He put his cup on the counter and eased her off his lap. He stood up and went to the sink where he rinsed out his cup and set it on the drain-board.

"Susan will take care of that tomorrow," she said.

"I know, but she's got other things to worry about what with Alton and all," he said. "It won't hurt me to help her a little."

Poppy came over to him and handed him her cup, then went to the stove and brought the pan to the sink. Steele rinsed them all out, leaving them to dry on the drain-board.

She stood behind him, her arms wrapped around his waist, her head lying against his shoulder. "Are you always this domestic?"

"No, but my parents taught me that nearly everyone can use a little help from time to time, and it doesn't hurt to give what you can."

She didn't say anything further. She released her grip on him as he dried his hands on a towel hanging by the sink. Entwining her arm in his she guided him to the service door.

"Where are you taking me now, out to the woodshed?"

"I should." She grabbed hold of his arm. "But after that speech I wouldn't dare." She squeezed his arm tightly. "No, we are going to take the service stairs to the second floor. This stairway isn't as glamorous as the front hallway, but it's closer."

Poppy was true to her word. She led Steele to the guest room. It had a connecting door to her room, which she opened.

She started to leave by the connecting door, then turned back to say, "Would you feel better if I locked this or left it open?"

"Suit yourself, Poppy," he said as he walked to where she stood. He put his hand behind her head and bent her head down and kissed her on the forehead. "Thank you."

"What for? I gave you my word in New York, didn't I?"

"Yes, you did, and that's exactly why I thanked you, for keeping that word. I would also add that I really enjoyed the hot cocoa and the show tonight."

"You did?"

"Yes, I did, very much. You'll have to do it again for me later on—when it's more appropriate."

"Does that mean you may have changed your mind, and you've reconsidered?"

"No, I haven't; it still means you're off limits as long as you're my client. When you're no longer my client, we can discuss the subject again then."

"Okay, I'll keep my word," she took a step away from him, and then turned back. "It's not that I want to, though, you understand?" Her lips pouted.

He smiled at her and winked. "I know, life can be a bitch—when you have to be an adult."

She brought her hand to her mouth, biting her knuckle, before she could start to cry. "If there's anything I've learned about you so far, Mark Steele, it's that you admire people who keep their word."

"Yes, I do."

She winked at him and shut the door. The lock clicked.

CHAPTER 24

Steele woke to find Penelope Sinclair jumping up and down on his bed. She hadn't dressed; she was still as naked as the previous night.

"Wake up, wake up, wake up!" she kept yelling.

"What are you doing? What time is it anyway?"

"It's after seven—time to get up, sleepy head."

"Ah, shit," he said as he pulled the pillow over his head. "Call me again when it's after nine—better yet, make it ten," he groaned.

Poppy plopped down beside him on the bed and threw back the covers. He was wearing white boxer shorts. She frowned, but didn't say anything. She threw her leg over him and straddled him, pulling the pillow from his head. She bent down and kissed him.

He looked up at her. She smiled back. She wiggled her bottom, grinding her crotch into his, and then abruptly stopped. "Don't worry, she said as she rolling off of him and laid down by his side, "I haven't forgotten my promise."

He pulled himself up on an elbow and leaned over and kissed her forehead, "You're an angel. I can't think of anyone else I'd like better to wake me in the morning naked than you. But now we both need to get dressed. We have plenty to do today." He rolled over and sat on the edge of the bed. "I'm going to take a shower, why don't you get dressed?"

"Can I come with you?" she said, running to his side.

"No, you can't." He patted her ass firmly, three times, with his open palm. "Go. Get yourself dressed!"

"Yes, sir," she giggled.

#

They got down to the dining room at eight to have breakfast.

Poppy announced, "I'd like to have French toast and sausage. What do you want, lover boy?" She batted her eyelashes at Steele.

"That will do just fine," he grimaced, "as long as there's plenty of coffee."

"Okay, I'll tell Susan," she said as she darted through the connecting door to the kitchen.

Barnaby came in through the hall doorway.

"Mr. Steele. You have a telephone call. It's Detective Lieutenant Williamson. You can take it in Mr. Conrad's office."

"Thank you, Barnaby," Steele said as he got to his feet, and went to Conrad's office, where he picked up the telephone, "Hey, Hank, you got news for me?"

"How's the girl?"

"Poppy's doing okay... she's up to her old tricks again."

"What sort of 'old' tricks might she be up to?"

"Hank, that's between her and me, and I'm not gonna discuss it with you," Steele laughed.

"Ah, that's a shame," Hank laughed.

Steele ignored Hank's unmistakable sarcasm. "You got any new information on the case or did you just call to chit-chat?"

"Yeah... I do. The fingerprint boys get a couple good prints off those empty casings in the Chevrolet."

"Anyone we know?"

"Yeah, I know him... I don't know if you do. The prints belong to a guy named Sheridan... let's see," his voice faded and Steele heard the ruffling of papers. "Yeah... Jack Sheridan, a small time crook... I put him inside a few years back for robbery and possession of an illegal weapon."

"What sort of illegal weapon?"

"He had a Thompson in the trunk of his car when we arrested him."

"Sure sounds promising—maybe he's the shooter. That name doesn't ring a bell with me, though."

"He works for Big Jake Jacoby."

"Now, him I do know... we've had a couple run-ins in the past. All minor scrapes—I don't think he likes me very much, but I can't imagine anything significant enough between us to make him take a shot at me." Steele paused a moment. "Although, Big Jake has a short fuse and the memory of an elephant... you never know what minor infraction in the past, at least in his eyes, might set him off."

"You're probably right, Steele... I'm beginning to think that this shooting may have nothing to do with the Conrad case."

"Maybe, maybe not... Big Jake has been known to take in outside work, he may have been hired... and the fact it involved me would have made it a priority for him."

"That's an angle alright. But, I'll have a talk with him just the same. Just to see if the name 'Conrad' gets his pulse racing or produces a sweaty brow."

"You ain't gonna pick him up, are you?"

"Nah... I'll just drift by his place and poke around a bit. Sort of unofficially, you know. If he's involved, I don't want to spook him too much. Just drop a few hints, see his reaction."

"Let me know what you find out... You got any word from our kidnappers yet? The Conrad's company ready to pay the ransom? Any other news?"

"Haven't heard another word from the kidnappers since the note. As for Conrad's company, that Veronica Gelding, the treasurer, keeps putting me off. She may be trying to hide an involvement."

"Maybe she isn't. Maybe she's just preoccupied. It can't be easy raising that amount of money—not even for a company like Conrad."

"You may be right... that could be it."

"Have you talked with all the others yet?"

"Sure have. All except Clarence James. It seems Mr. James decided to go deer hunting in Michigan."

"Suspicious?"

"Maybe, maybe not... according to his wife and his secretary, who made the arrangements, he's had this trip planned for several months. His wife said he goes on this same trip every year about this time. Secretary said he's not scheduled back in Boston till the middle of next week."

"He could still be involved. He was in town when they snatched Conrad. And, an after-the-fact alibi doesn't help him much. Unless they're holding Conrad in Michigan."

"I know. I'll check him out from top to bottom and every which way from Tuesday, but I'm not going out to Michigan and bringing him back in irons, if that's what you mean. However, when he does get back, I may just throw him in a cell overnight for leaving town when I expressly told him he shouldn't."

"That's my old pal Hank," Steele said mockingly.

"You're damn tootin'—got to keep the peasants in line or no tellin' what might happen," he laughed.

"Still no word about Lawrence?"

"Yeah... I almost forgot to tell you. The San Juan police picked him up. Lawrence was driving erratically, apparently drunk. He asked them to take him to the U.S. Embassy. They turned him over to the Marine guard at the gate."

"Didn't the FBI say that the embassy had held them there?"

"That's right, they did say that. But the ambassador, in his infinite wisdom, felt that since he had their passports that it would be okay to allow them go back to their hotel until he received a formal arrest warrant. However, as a precaution against them leaving the island, the plane has been temporarily confiscated and put under embassy guard. They allowed the pilot to leave, but he chose to stay with the airplane at the airport."

"If Lawrence's our guy, he has enough money and connections to get a new passport from any country and in any name he likes. Maybe even get his hands on a boat or another airplane."

"Yeah, the FBI knows that. They're keeping a tight tail on him. They know exactly who he sees and where he goes twenty-four hours a day."

"By the way, when I talked to you from New York, you said you had information about Beverly and you would tell me about it later. Okay, it's now later... what's the story?"

"Ah that. I decided that it wasn't important. My source's reliable enough, but it's not official information—just rumor. And, I'm treating it as just a rumor for now."

"Since when did you get so protective?"

"So, it's like this: unless they're both guilty, I don't see a good reason to hang their dirty laundry on the line for everyone to see."

"You ain't getting soft in your old age, are you Hank?"

"Yeah, let's chalk it up to that, and leave it for now."

"Okay, if that's the way you want it I'll just file it in my head for now. But you know, I will bring it up again."

"You do that."

"Meanwhile, anything else I can do to help with the investigation?"

"Yeah, watch the girl and try to keep from getting yourself shot at and killed."

"Okay," Steele said and hung up the phone.

#

"Where have you been?" Poppy asked as Steele came into the dining room, "Your French toast is cold as ice by now."

"Didn't Barnaby tell you that I was on the phone with Hank?"

"No, he didn't."

"Okay—I was on the phone with Hank."

"You said that already."

"Okay." He ignored her sarcasm. "Hot or cold, the toast will be okay. I like it either way." he said as he sat down beside her and poured himself a cup of coffee from the silver urn on the table.

"What did Hank have to say?"

"He said that the FBI had caught up to your brother in San Juan and they are trying to extradite him as a material witness—they suspect that he's involved in the kidnapping too."

"I can't believe Lawrence would be involved in this."

"People can often surprise you." He began cutting the toast on his plate. "And, you must admit, running off on a shopping spree when your father's been kidnapped looks very suspicious."

"Yes, that's strange..." She took a sip from her coffee cup. "Did Hank have any good news?"

"Not really. He also said that Clarence James has gone hunting for deer in Michigan and can't be found for questioning."

"James. He's the research guy at Daddy's company, isn't he?"

"Yes, he is. Why?"

"If anyone knew about a project called *Endeavor* he would be the logical one to know about it... don't you think?"

"Yeah that makes sense," Steele said taking a bite of his French toast.

"Maybe," she said as she dabbed at a drop of maple syrup on the edge of his mouth with her napkin. "We should go and poke around his office and see what we can turn up."

"You're becoming quite good at this sleuthing business, aren't you, Miss Sinclair?"

"I have an excellent teacher," she patted Steele's hand, "and besides that, my father has been gone now for three days. No telling what has happened to him." The tears started to come to her eyes, but she held them back.

The Conrad Kidnapping

"Okay. You're right. We do need to do more digging. And, it wouldn't hurt to do a little snooping around the company's offices—all of them. But, it's Sunday. How can we get inside?" Steele asked as he finished the last bite of French toast.

Poppy looked at him with a blank look for a few seconds, then she jumped to her feet and said, "I know just the thing. Come with me."

She grabbed his hand and pulled him away from the table, then out the door and down the hallway. She almost physically dragged him up the hall and then down the stairs to a door at the end of the hallway. She opened the door quietly.

"Whose room's this?" Steele said.

"Father's," she said holding her finger to her lips.

"Why so quiet?" he whispered into her ear.

"I don't know. It just seemed like the best thing to do. Aren't detectives always quiet?"

"You've been watching too many movies. You need to get yourself a boyfriend," he admonished her.

She looked at him as if he had just hit her with a baseball bat. "Don't be smart with me, Mister Detective. I love movies, and I've been trying to get a boyfriend, but he's being obstinate towards me."

"Obstinate. That's an awfully harsh word. Given the circumstances, wouldn't 'rational' fit the situation better?" He smiled at her, squeezing her hand.

She stopped and looked into his eyes. "Look, Mark, I know you're right, and I respect that you're reluctant to get involved with a client." She put her arms up around his neck and lowered her voice to a serious tone. "I'm very much attracted to you. Much more than any man I've ever met, and there's a part of me that won't let me stop trying to change your mind." She pulled his mouth to hers and kissed him.

She broke the kiss and pulled away.

He gave her a knowing look. "Why are we here?"

She smiled back, recognizing that he knew how she felt. "Father's keys," she answered in her normal voice. "He was completely naked when they took him out of the house, so I'm pretty sure he didn't take them with him."

Steele tried to wash the image of Conrad being naked from his brain and could only say, "Oh."

"Is that all... Oh?" she asked.

"Oh... very smart, Miss Nancy Drew," he answered, squeezing her hand even harder this time. "For a girl detective," he added with a laugh.

She didn't answer him, but extracted her hand from his and punched him in the arm with her fist as hard as she could.

"Hey! That hurt," he yelled.

She rubbed his arm, "I'm sorry, but... you... you, ah." She didn't finish.

He looked at her and smiled, "I don't mind the punch. I probably deserved it," he chuckled, "but next time could you please hit me in the other arm. The one that didn't get shot?"

She threw her arms around his neck and kissed him, "Jeez, Mark. I'm so sorry." She kissed him again. "I didn't think."

He smiled at her. "It's okay. I don't think it'll need a sling."

"Now you're pulling my leg."

"Yeah, and it's a very nice leg indeed."

She giggled and pulled her skirt up almost to her waist, revealing her evenly tanned legs and a pair of pink panties, "I'm surprised you even noticed, me being your client and all."

"Are you kidding? Believe me, I noticed. I've noticed everything about you since we met."

"No, you're not serious. Are you? Tell me what you've noticed."

He ran his fingers through his hair and paused a moment, and looking her squarely in the eye, he said, "You have a mole on your left buttock, and a smaller one near the nipple on your right breast." He grinned at her.

"I guess you've been paying attention. Although I'll have to take your word for the one on my butt."

"You can look in the mirror the next time you take a bath," he grinned.

"I'll do that. Would you like to help me?" she pulled the hem of her skirt up again.

"No, no, no!" he took hold of her wrists, "Okay, enough fun," he pushed her skirt down, "Do you know where your father kept his keys?"

"I don't know for sure, but I'd guess they'd either be in his jacket pocket, on his dresser, or in his briefcase."

Steele said, "I vote for the briefcase. Do you know where he might keep that?"

"Yes." She pointed to a table near the bed. "Over there on the writing-table."

Luckily the briefcase wasn't locked. Steele found the keys inside, along with a dozen papers and a loaded snub nosed thirty-eight revolver. The papers didn't reveal anything that might lead them to whoever was after the *Endeavor project*. Steele held up the gun. "Got any idea why he would have this in his briefcase?"

Poppy shook her head, "No, I didn't know he even owned a gun. He never said anything to me about it."

"Did he carry anything valuable other than secret papers?"

"He never told me if he did, or if he didn't."

"Maybe one of the employees will know about it."

She held up the ring and jingled them. "We have the keys. Why don't we go to the office and see what we can find."

CHAPTER 25

The cab dropped them off at the curb in front of the Conrad Building a half hour later. Only one guard was on duty, an elderly, gray-haired man. He recognized Poppy immediately.

"How are you today, Miss Penelope?"

"I'm just fine, George. That son of yours Bryan get his letter from MIT yet?"

"Yes, he did—but he's decided to go to Stanford instead."

"All the way out to California. That's a long way from home."

"That's for sure. And, his mother's not at all happy about it, either. But Brian thinks Stanford has a better physics department."

"He's probably right," Steele said and George gave him a quizzical look. Steele extended his hand. "I'm Mark Steele, a family friend."

"Nice to meet any friend of the family, Mr. Steele. But, why do you say that about Stanford?"

"I just read an article about it in Newsweek. They said that MIT was still a great engineering school, but Stanford had made remarkable advances in physics."

"I'll have to get that article and see what they have to say. That the new issue?"

"Last week, I believe."

"We didn't come here to debate colleges," Poppy interjected. "We have thing we need to do in father's office, George."

"Anything I can do to help, Miss Penelope?"

"No, George. We'll be fine."

As they entered the elevator Poppy looked to Steele. "No elevator man today. Can you handle it?"

"I don't know. I've seen it done a thousand times. It can't be that hard to master."

He pushed the lever marked "Door" to the closed position and the doors closed.

"Which floor, miss?"

"Ten, if you don't mind."

"Then ten it shall be," he said as he carefully eased the large lever back. He turned to Poppy and grinned as the car began to rise slowly. Turning his attention to the floor indicator dial. He said nothing while they rode. When the indicator dial showed them nearing the tenth floor he began to ease the lever forward slowly. He stopped the car and opened the door. He had missed the mark. The car had stopped two inches above the floor.

"Nice work," Poppy said, "if Father ever needs a new elevator operator for this building, I'll be sure and tell him about you."

"You needn't bother, I'm very happy doing my current job," he laughed.

He left the elevator door open as they exited the elevator, "You think there's anything in your father's office?" he asked as they set off down the hallway toward Roger Conrad's office.

"I don't know. Where else would we start?" Poppy said.

"Arnold Becker interests me the most at this point."

"What makes you suspect him?"

"Besides your brother, he's the only one who's left town without a satisfactory explanation. He went to Canada—why?"

"I don't know, but his secretary may have kept a note," she said, as she turned and began to walk back toward the elevator. "His office's on the eighth floor."

"I know," he took hold of her arm, stopping her, "But, we should take the stairs."

She gave him a questioning look. "What in the world for?"

"It might be better if nobody knows exactly where we are in the building. Let them think we're in your father's office."

"Nobody's here today, Mark—it's Sunday."

"There's at least one person who knows we're here—George, the security guard. He can call almost anyone. Besides others could be here that neither George nor we know about."

"You don't suspect George, do you?"

"Yes, I do—but he's near the bottom of my list." He glanced at her. "Right now, I still suspect everyone except you, Hank, and me." he chuckled. He opened the stairwell door, "This way we can move around the building without being seen."

The stairwell was dark, illuminated only by a skylight in the top of the shaft.

"We should have thought to bring a flashlight," Poppy quipped as she started off down the stairs.

"Do you think you're dealing with an amateur here? Always be prepared: The *Boy Scout* motto is: *Be prepared.* Which is also the detectives' motto."

He pulled a penlight from his inside jacket pocket and switched it on. Its glow was dim, but it shed enough light to see the stair steps clearly.

"Not exactly a flood light," She joked.

"So, a little is better than nothing, I always say."

"That's original," she laughed.

"Stole it from Poor Richard's Almanac."

"The light?"

"No, the *witty affirmation*," he chuckled, "I've had the light for years." He switched it off and back on. "But I admit, it could use a new battery."

Steele opened the stairwell door on the eighth floor cautiously. The hallway was dark except for light coming from a window at the far end.

"If I remember correctly, Becker's office's the last door on the right," Steele said.

Poppy nodded in agreement.

Steele tried five keys from Conrad's key ring before he found the one that worked on Becker's office door. Once inside he turned on the light. He skipped the secretary's office and went straight through to Becker's. The connecting door was not locked. He began to search for anything that looked suspicious or out-of-place. Becker's desk drawer was locked, but with the use of a couple of paper clips lying in a tray on the desk, Steele was able to open it with little difficulty. After going through every paper in the desk drawer he found nothing that helped them.

"I don't think there's anything here," he said to Poppy who was looking through a file cabinet on the far wall.

"Did you find anything in the files?"

"No. Not a thing." She sounded disappointed.

"I say we try Gelding's office next. She's acted suspiciously from the beginning and that's bothered Hank, and I'm afraid it's beginning to bother me too."

"Yeah... it's probably those breasts and legs she likes to show off," Poppy quipped.

"Nah, not that. I'm sure he's noticed both, but it's more serious than that," Steele said, and looked at her more closely. "Do I hear a little jealousy there, Miss Sinclair?"

"No, not at all. I'm just observant." She grinned, but her face also began to flush.

"Just as I suspected," he laughed and headed out the door. Once in the outer office he put his arm around Poppy's waist and said, "You needn't be jealous of anyone. Your figure's better than any woman's I've ever seen."

"Really, I didn't think you even noticed."

"I've noticed," he said as he shut off the lights.

As he was about to close the outer door he stopped, "Poppy, I forgot the wastebaskets! You check the secretary's, I'll check Becker's."

He turned the light back on and headed off to the inner office, leaving Poppy at the door.

"Sorry, the cleaning crew must have come through. It was empty and clean," he said as he came out of Becker's office.

"But hers wasn't," she said smiling, as she held up the secretary's wastebasket. "This was stuck to the bottom by a piece of chewing gum."

She handed a crumpled piece of pink paper to Steele. It was a phone message slip.

The paper was torn in half, crumpled into a small tight ball and discarded. It had stuck to the bottom of the basket by a chunk of chewing gum. The cleaning crew had missed it. Steele opened the two pieces and held them up so they could read it.

The message was from a "Mr. Jones" at "KL 28773" and said "call by 6:30".

"What do you think it means?" Poppy asked.

"I have no idea. Maybe nothing," he said as he took an envelope from the secretary's desk and put the pieces inside. He put the envelope in his pocket.

After finding only the crumpled note in Becker's office they went to Veronica Gelding's office, one floor up and at the other end of the hallway. Her door opened with the second key Steele tried. However, there was no key on Conrad's key-ring that would open her private office door.

Steele set about opening the door using two more paper clips he found on the secretary's desk. While he worked on the lock, Poppy went about searching the outer office. The lock finally ceded to his delicate touch and the door swung open.

A complete search of Gelding's office, including the wastebaskets—netted them nothing.

The next stop was Lawrence's office, also on the 9th floor. The search of his office and files only confirmed that Lawrence did almost nothing at the company. The file cabinets and desk were empty. They found nothing that would help in the investigation.

They ended up in Roger Conrad's office and again they didn't find a single clue to who had taken Roger or where they might be holding him.

Steele made them both a drink from the bar as Poppy, in low spirits, slumped into a chair. "What should we do now? Searching all the other offices, one by one, seems a daunting task, at best," she said. The great frustration of their lack of luck clearly showing in her voice.

"You're right, I don't think we'll find anything more in the other offices." Steele pulled the envelope from his pocket and looked at the small piece of pink paper. He read it again to himself, then said, "I'm going to call Hank."

"We didn't find anything—what can he do?"

"I don't know, maybe nothing... or maybe he can put an address to this phone number," he waved the pink paper at Poppy. "This may get us nothing, but a good detective checks out the small stuff too. You never know in this business."

"Okay, that makes a lot of sense. I remember my father, my real father, telling me a story about an ancient Kingdom being lost for the lack of a nail."

"Yea, that's the idea. I've heard that story... though it may have been an old proverb I heard as a kid."

"Proverb, story, what's the difference."

He smiled at her, "One's shorter that the other; proverb has seven letters while story only has five."

She ignored his snide comment, "We can call from here."

Steele dialed Hank's office. The officer on duty told him that Hank had taken the afternoon off but could be reached at his home. Steele dialed Hank's home number. It rang three times before Hank picked it up. "Hello, Williamson here."

"Hey, Hank, it's Steele."

"Yeah what do you want, Steele... can't a guy even take an afternoon off?" he barked.

"Sorry, old friend, but Poppy and I are at the Conrad Company building. We've been doing a little unofficial snooping of Becker and Gelding's private offices."

"You resorting to breaking and entering, Steele?"

"No, Poppy had the keys."

"I guess it's okay then. Did you find anything interesting?" He asked.

"No, not much. We did find a torn and crumpled phone message slip in Becker's secretary's wastebasket with a phone number on it. It was from a Mr. Jones and said call by 6:30, the telephone number's KL 28773."

"Think it means anything?"

"I don't know, but I thought it might be worth checking it out. Can you get an address from the number?"

"Sure, what was the number again?"

"Klondike 28773."

"Okay, I'll call the office and call you back in a few minutes."

"Right, Conrad's private number—Capital 99642."

Steele hung up. He and Poppy sat in silence sipping their drinks for ten minutes before the telephone rang.

"Hello," Steele said cautiously, concerned that it might be anyone other than Hank calling.

"Steele, that you?" Hank's familiar voice growled.

"Yeah, it's me."

"The telephone company couldn't find anything with that number listed in Boston."

"Okay. I kind of figured you wouldn't; I don't peg these guys as being idiots. Did the telephone company check the number in New Hampshire? The cars involved in this case all had New Hampshire plates. Just maybe, if we're lucky, they did make one big dumb mistake."

"Your right about New Hampshire, I'll call the office and have them check it out."

"Call me back," Steele said and hung up.

Poppy went to the bar and mixed them both another drink. It was twenty minutes before Hank finally called back.

"Any luck in New Hampshire?" Steele asked him.

"Yeah... the number matches one in Salem, New Hampshire."

"Good. Maybe a trip to New Hampshire to check it out would be a good idea. What do you think?"

"I'd love to take a drive in the country with you, Steele, but, I don't have any jurisdiction in New Hampshire. As far as the law's concerned, I would just be a normal citizen there."

"I know that, my license isn't any good there either—but still, as normal citizens it might be easier for us to take a look around. If we find anything useful—we call the local police."

"But I still couldn't go with you. I have a meeting this afternoon, at one, with Assistant District Attorney Jack Murphy to go over my testimony in another case I'm testifying in next week."

"Can you reschedule it?"

"Afraid not. He's even busier that I am, and this was the only time he had free."

"Okay, maybe later. How long will this meeting take?"

"I wouldn't be able to leave till three or three-thirty."

"That's fine. Salem's only forty miles away. We'll be able to get there—check out the address—and get back before dinner time."

"Steele, you do know that it's Sunday. Everything's closed today. I ain't gonna be able to get a search warrant for an out-of-state location today... might take a day or two."

"Yeah, I know that, but it shouldn't be a problem. We're just gonna' have a quick look around. If we find anything suspicious, we'll let the local cops handle it— even the New Hampshire police work on Sunday."

"I guess that would be okay. But I don't want any lock picking, breaking and entering, or trespassing. We just look—no confrontations—understood?"

"Yes, I understand. I'll keep my hands in my pockets all the time. Can you pick me up at my office at three-thirty?"

"Okay, but one more thing, Steele."

"What's that?"

"You'll have to drive," he began chuckling into the phone. "And I get to take a nap in the back seat."

"Sure, I can do that, although... Tell you what, you pick me up in your car and I'll drive the rest of the way there and back... How's that?"

"Okay... I'll be at your place at three-thirty."

Steele turned to Poppy, who'd overheard the conversation.

"You are planning on taking me with you—aren't you?"

"I hadn't thought about it, but I guess it would be okay. We're just going to check out that address in Salem."

"I've never been to Salem. Isn't that where they burnt all those witches years ago?"

"No, that's Salem, Massachusetts. We're talking about Salem, New Hampshire. And, no one was ever burnt at the stake here in America—that only happened in Europe."

"I see... I always thought... umm." she blushed, but quickly recovered. "Do you think we'll find Father there?"

"I have no idea; this whole trip could be a wild-goose chase. Do you still want to come along?"

"Ah, yes—I do."

"I'm going back to the office to catch up on my paperwork while I'm waiting for Hank. Do you want to come with me, or would you rather I drop you off at your home?"

"I should go home and check on Mother. I can take a cab; meet you later at your office."

CHAPTER 26

Steele entered the office to find Jeffrey chatting with Lois as they went about decorating a small Christmas tree Lois had set up on the end of her desk.

"Merry Christmas, Mr. Steele," Lois said as a crimson blush flashed across her face and neck. "Yes, a very Merry Christmas to you Mr. Steele," Jeffrey said as he hooked a red ornament on a limb near the bottom of the tree.

"I'm not really in the Christmas spirit now, Lois, what with Conrad still missing." He looked at Jeffery, "It's Sunday—did you bring another special delivery?" Steele said.

"No—no mail today—just here to help Lois with the Christmas tree." he said, a broad smile across his face.

Lois began to blush and quickly changed the subject. "So, Mr. Steele. Do you have any news about poor Mr. Conrad?"

"No, not much. We have a lead on an address in Salem, New Hampshire. Hank and I are going to run up there this afternoon and check it out."

He went to the door of his office, and then turned, "Lois, after you finish with the tree can you come to my office. We need to update the Conrad file."

Jeffrey looked at Lois and winked, "Merry Christmas, Lois. I enjoyed decorating the tree with you." He turned to Steele, "Merry Christmas, Mr. Steele." Jeffrey went to the coat tree and retrieved his coat and hat. He put the Canada Goose Classique Beaver Fur on his head and began slipping his arm into the sleeve of the Macintosh. "I guess I should go—you two have business to discuss." he grinned broadly at Lois and backed away toward the door.

Steele acknowledged Jeffrey with a wave and went into his office.

As Jeffery grasped the doorknob he turned back to Lois, "Will I see you later, Lois?"

Lois's already red face deepened in color. She nodded, but did not speak as she got to her feet with steno pad in hand.

Steele threw his overcoat across the back of one of the guest chairs and settled in his chair when Lois came and sat in the other guest chair.

She crossed her legs, with her steno pad on her knee and pencil poised. She looked over the desk at Steele.

"Mr. Steele, before we begin, I just want to say that I'm deeply sorry about what happened the other night. It won't happen again."

"It was nothing Lois. You have nothing to apologize for. And, you are welcome to use the office anytime you want to." He leaned back in his chair and began to fill his pipe, "You and Jeffery seem okay."

"Yes. Jeffery's a very sweet man." She smiled, the blush on her face nearly returning to a normal color.

"Okay, enough chit-chat. Let's get this file updated. I'm expecting Hank to come by and pick me up this afternoon and I would like to get this done before he gets here.

#

True to his word, Hank pulled up in front of Steele's building at exactly three-thirty. He was not in his own car, or a police car. He was driving a brand new two-toned Packard sedan—sky blue with a white top.

Poppy had arrived in a taxi a few minutes earlier and she and Steele waited for Hank in the lobby.

"Nice car. Looks brand new," Steele said as Hank got out.

Hank grunted, but didn't respond.

"Police work must pay better now than when I was a cop," Steele said, "you been taking a few bribes, lieutenant?"

"The car's not mine, Steele. It belongs to the department, and it isn't new. If you'd bothered to look, you would see that it's last year's model," he said with a snarl.

"Okay, okay, don't get all huffy about it," Steele said as he held up his palms to Hank in a calming gesture. "Just joshing with you, my friend... no offense."

Hank threw the keys at Steele. "You drive, smart ass," he grumbled.

Hank looked at Poppy. "Miss Sinclair, would you mind sitting up front with Mr. Smart Ass?" He glared at Steele. "I'm going to climb in the back, stretch out, and take a nap."

Before she could answer, he had opened the back door, gotten inside and closed the door again.

Like Hank had said, the car wasn't new; it'd been polished, well-maintained, and was spotlessly clean. A car like this was out of Steele's price range, but after driving it a few blocks, he understood why crooks and gangsters liked these big cars. The Packards, the Chryslers, and the Cadillacs. The car had been solidly built and possessed tremendous power and pick-up.

After leaving Cambridge, Steele drove north. However, it wasn't long before they made a couple of stops—first for gas and a map of New Hampshire. Poppy also bought a thermos bottle from a display at the gas station. She then insisted they make a second stop at a donut shop to fill the thermos with coffee and buy a dozen donuts for the trip. After the second stop, they finally got underway to Salem.

"You do know this trip's a business trip, and not a pleasure cruise?" Steele said as he pulled back out on the highway.

"I know, but it's cold and coffee will help."

"And the donuts?"

"I have a sweet tooth," she laughed. "Don't you like donuts?"

"Sure, EVERYONE likes donuts," He grinned at her. "Even private cops."

"Okay, then I might let you have one later," she chuckled as she fingered the string the sales clerk had wrapped around the box.

According to the map, Salem, New Hampshire's on US-Hwy 28, just over the Massachusetts border from Lawrence. Steele measured the distance on the map and estimated the distance at forty to forty-five miles. Steele judged that the traffic on Sunday would be light and if the weather held up, the trip shouldn't take more than an hour.

Traffic in Boston itself was heavy. However, once they reached the outskirts and were alone on the highway the road conditions worsened. With less traffic the ice and snow accumulated rapidly and wind-blown drifts became more prevalent. Several times Steele found the car headed for a ditch, but was able to get the big Packard back on the roadway safely. The trip would undoubtedly take longer than the hour Steele had originally estimated.

Hank, true to his word, had started to snooze as soon as they got out of city traffic and was no longer being thrown about the back seat as Steele negotiated around the city streets. Poppy laid her head against the seat back, but didn't go to sleep.

Twenty minutes into the countryside north of Boston, Poppy said, without lifting her head from the seat, "Do you think this is a wild goose chase?"

"I'm not sure. It's a long shot. It may actually have nothing to do with the kidnapping and ransom, but for now it's the best lead we have." He smiled at her. Putting his right hand out, he gently touched her arm. "I hope we find your father, there... but I wouldn't be surprised if we found absolutely nothing at all."

Poppy patted his hand and smiled. A few minutes went by and neither of them said anything. Poppy picked up the thermos lying on the seat between them and opened it. She poured coffee into the little lid-cup and took a couple sips. Looking at Steele over the rim of the cup she took it away from her lips and asked, in her sweetest tone, "Coffee?"

"Sure," he said, glancing back at the road and then turning his head back in her direction smiling at her.

"We only have the one cup, so we'll have to share. Okay?"

"Okay with me," he said as he took the little cup from her hand and took a small sip. Handing it back to her, he said, "What kind of donuts did you get?"

"A half-dozen glazed and a half-dozen chocolate covered cake," she said with a lot of pride as if she'd done the grocery shopping for a whole week. "Would you like one?"

"I wouldn't mind one of those chocolate-covered ones," he said, trying to keep his attention focused on the slick road.

To this point in the trip, the box of donuts had sat on the seat between them. Poppy lifted it and scooted over next to Steele. She put the box down on the seat by the door. She opened the lid of the box and took out a chocolate covered donut and broke off a small piece and held it up to his mouth saying, "Open wide." As he did so she put it into his mouth.

"I could do that and drive at the same time," he said.

"I know, but it's more romantic this way. Don't you think?"

"Sure... very romantic," he said in a slightly patronizing tone.

She kept breaking off small pieces and feeding them to him, giggling after each piece, until the donut was gone. Then she handed him the cup of coffee again.

#

The town of Salem was very small. The commercial district consisted of a gas station, a bar, a drug store, a hardware store, and a few other unidentifiable buildings. Steele pulled up to the gas station and sent Poppy inside to get directions to the address that Hank had gotten from the telephone company. She came out a few minutes later carrying a bottle of Coca-Cola.

"The man said 304 North Broadway's in a group of buildings about a half-mile outside of town, where the railroad tracks come alongside the highway."

She smiled and handed him the bottle of Coke.

"What's with the Coke?" he asked.

"The price of information," she smiled at him.

"Yes, I can see that. A nickel for the Coke and ninety-five cents for the directions."

"No, not exactly..." she said as she put the bottle to her lips. "A dollar for the information and the Coke was free." She laughed loudly as she handed the bottle to him.

Steele also began to laugh as he took a sip from the open bottle and handed it back to her.

A half-mile down the road, Steele came upon a group of ten buildings on the other side of the highway that matched the description Poppy had gotten from the man at the gas station.

All the buildings looked old and run down. Only a few still had whole windows intact. Steele spotted at least two doors ajar and hanging precariously from their hinges. Dozens of steel drums and wooden barrels littered the grounds around the buildings. Many were carefully stacked in piles while others lay randomly on the ground. Broken pallets, wooden boxes, and lengths of wood and pipe lay scattered haphazardly around the property. It was hard to imagine that anyone had set foot on the property in ten years or more. Except for the fresh tire tracks and footprints in the snow, the property looked completely abandoned.

Near the end of one building lay the remains of two rusty cars resembling model "T" Fords. One, a sedan, had no hood or radiator and all its windows missing; the other, a roadster, had no doors or fenders. Neither car had wheels. The sedan sat right down on the ground, while the roadster had been set up on railroad ties.

Two sets of railroad tracks ran alongside and parallel to the highway. One, a siding, contained a flat-car and three wooden boxcars, which had begun to rot. The flat-car contained a load of machinery that had rusted badly in the open. Steele recognized a donkey engine, the type used at the lumber mill in his hometown in Nebraska. The chimney of the boiler had rusted through and collapsed, slumping down over the side of the car, nearly touching the ground. Between the nearest buildings and the boxcars lay a stack of railroad ties and a pile of rusty track sections in various lengths—both stacked as high as a man's head.

Amid the mess, one building stood out. Part of it was blocked from view by other buildings, but Steele could see that it still had most of its windows intact and was the only one with a lighted bulb hanging over its doorway. It was also the only building that had a path of footprints in the snow that went from where Steele had parked across the railroad tracks and directly to its door. The path was not fresh; having been covered by a recent snowfall, but it was still quite visible.

Over the door in faded blue paint, almost invisible from where he was, Steele could just make out the numbers three and zero, the last number obscured by a patch of snow that had blown against the building. He could not see numbers on the other building from his location.

Steele turned the Packard's engine off, which woke Hank up. He sat up and looked outside. "Geez... this place looks worse than the Boston dump!"

"Yeah, the Ritz it's not," Steele quipped as he looked around the property. "We need to check out that building over there, that one with the light above the door. I have a hunch it's the one we're looking for."

"Right," Hank replied as he got out of the car and pulled his gun from under his heavy overcoat. "You got your gun, Steele?"

"Yeah. All loaded and ready," Steele said as he got out of the car and pulled it from his shoulder holster.

"You're right. I don't see any activity in any of the other buildings. And it's the only one with a recently traveled path through the snow." He waved the muzzle of his gun at the footprints in the snow. "If they're inside they'll see us if we take the path; I say we go around that other building over there and come up on it from the other direction."

"Sounds like a good plan," Steele agreed. Looking at Poppy, he said to her, "It'll be best if you stay here, in the car, 'till Hank and I check this out."

Steele was expecting a lengthy argument from her but she just said, "OK," kissed him on the cheek. "For good luck," winked at him and got back inside.

Steele grabbed the door before it closed. "Keep your head down. There might be trouble."

Steele and Hank circled around the other building as Hank had suggested. The snow had crusted over a couple of times and was a foot or more deep in most places. Several times Steele sank in to above his knees as he trudged through it. At one point Hank tripped in the snow and fell flat on his face. Steele had expected him to yell or swear but his cop training kicked in and he kept quiet. He'd hurt himself—that was evident—he began to limp, favoring his left leg. Steele could see by the look on Hank's face that his friend was in pain, but not allowing his injury to get in the way of doing the job at hand.

They stood, with their backs to the wall, near the far end of the building away from the door.

"Your leg—it okay?" Steele said pointing to a large red stain on Hank's pants leg.

"Just a little bump... it'll be okay." He then gestured to the back side of the building. "Why don't you go that way? Make sure you check all the windows. See if we can find out how many we're dealing with. I'll do the same on this side. We'll meet at the other end by the door."

Steele nodded and began edging his way along the wall and carefully around the corner. Three windows populated the back side of the building. Steele moved slowly, his back to the wall as he crept up to the first window. He peered cautiously through a corner of the dirty pane. He could see no one inside. The mostly empty room contained twenty to thirty chairs stacked neatly along the wall and a half-dozen piles of wooden crates stacked six-feet high along another wall. A thick layer of dust and dirt covered everything he could see.

Steele could see a large hole in the roof, which had allowed snow to cover part of the room and its contents with deep drifts.

There was only one door in the room, in the center of the front wall. The door was closed.

The second window revealed a room almost exactly the same as the first, except there was no hole in the ceiling and no snow inside. This room also had more furniture. Dozens of desks had been piled three high along with great stacks of chairs, reaching nearly to the ceiling.

The third window was smaller and revealed a bathroom. Compared to the other rooms it looked clean and recently used. The floor was cleaner but still dusty showing a path of footprints from the door to the toilet and to the small sink and then back to the door. Steele could see that the water in the toilet bowl wasn't frozen and the faucet dripped into the sink. Obviously a heat source inside this room had keeping it from freezing.

Steele reached the end of the building and peeked around the corner. He could see Hank's head on the far side of the building, also peering around the corner. Steele waved his gun at him; Hank waved back. They both came around their respective corners as if synchronized. They met at the door, which was in the middle of the building.

Hank whispered, "Did you see anyone?"

"No," Steele said, then added, "mostly dirty furniture, boxes and packing crates... but I did see a bathroom through one of the windows and it's empty now, but it's being used. The water in the toilet's not frozen, so there's heat in the building."

"Be careful," he nodded to Steele, "the building could still be occupied." Hank gently put his gloved hand on the doorknob and tried to turn it. To their surprise it turned easily and the door came open a crack. The glow of a low-wattage bulb came through the open doorway from inside. Hank eased the door further open while Steele hung back to cover him. Neither could see anyone inside. Hank pushed his way into the room through the open doorway.

The room looked unoccupied and sparsely furnished. A table and three chairs stood against one wall. Food containers covered the table—empty beer bottles and a half eaten pizza in an open box. A small pot-belly stove occupied the center of the room, its metal shell still warm to the touch, the fire extinguished for less than an hour.

Against the far wall was a bed covered with a rumpled pile of blankets. The bed appeared empty.

Steele said, "Wonder who's trying to fool who?" as he pointed his gun to the bed. "This set-up looks faked, they're trying to throw us off. Conrad must be at a different location."

Hank shrugged his shoulders, saying, "Got me. But if that's the case, they've gone to a lot of trouble."

Next to the bed was a small table which held a lamp. It was the only light in the room. The table also held an ashtray full of cigarette butts and a half empty bottle of beer. Next to the table stood a chair and a small electric heater. The heater's rheostat had been cranked to the highest setting which kept the room quite warm.

Hank took one of the two doors on the back wall Steele took the other. Steele opened his slowly and went inside. When he came out Hank was already waiting for him.

"This one leads to the bathroom I told you about earlier. No one in there," Steele said.

Hank pointed his gun at the other door and said, "That one goes to a big storeroom. Lots of old furniture and boxes. No one in there either, and by the look of the dust and dirt covering everything, nobody's been in there for years. Didn't see one foot print in the dust covering the floor."

Hank sat down in one of the chairs, slipping his gun back into its holster. He took out a handkerchief and began to wipe his forehead.

"Steele, if this place is a fake, don't you find it suspicious that they keep the place this warm?"

"Yeah, suspicious as hell—wonder why?" he said as he holstered his gun and sat down on a foot-locker at the foot of the bed.

As soon as his weight hit the lid a groan came from the trunk—it had an occupant. Steele jumped up immediately, his right hand instinctively pulling the .32 from its holster and releasing the safety catch in one fluid motion. He looked at Hank, who also had his gun out. Holding his gun at the ready in his right hand he eased the hasp up and opened the lid with his left. Inside, a blanket covered a mass, which moved.

Under the blanket, lying on his side with his legs pulled up to his chest lay a naked man. His hands and feet bound with lengths of rope. A bag, made of black cloth, covered his head.

Hank set about removing the bag from the man's head. The bag had a drawstring tied loosely with a bow. While the cord around the man's neck was loose, Hank had difficulty untying the bow—finally, resorting to his pocketknife, to cut the cord. As soon as the bag came off the man's head, Steele recognized him. It was their kidnap victim, Mr. Roger Conrad. A wadded up cloth, secured with two-inch wide white adhesive tape, gagged the man's mouth. Hank removed the gag while Steele took Hank's pocketknife and set about cutting away the rope bindings.

The door sprang open, hitting the adjacent wall with a loud crack. Steele turned expecting to see Poppy. It wasn't her. It wasn't anyone he had seen before. He was a rough-looking character who had a cigar clenched in his mouth and a Thompson machine gun in his hands. He pointed the gun at them.

"Fingers!" Hank shouted.

CHAPTER 27

Poppy watched Steele and Hank from the front seat of the car as they crept around the building, and watched as he went in. She began to get nervous after they had been inside for more than ten minutes. She opened the car door and was about to get out and go inside herself, when another car drove past the Packard. She closed the door gently and ducked down.

The car, a black pre-war Dodge with two spare tires mounted in its front fenders, came to a stop and parked ten yards in front of the Packard. The windows of the Packard had frosted over, but before ducking her head down, she thought she had seen only one person in the car, but couldn't be certain.

Raising her head a bit, she could see through a small crevice of clear glass, along the top of the dashboard. She watched as one man and then a second got out of the car. The two men wore heavy overcoats. The driver, the more heavy-set of the two, wore a newsboy snap cap with earmuffs. The man on the passenger side wore a fedora, with the collar of his coat pulled up around his ears. Poppy watched as the man on the passenger side opened the trunk and pulled out a short-handled spade. He held the spade at the ready, like a baseball bat, and looked around slowly, surveying the area. He looked directly at the Packard. Poppy ducked down quickly. She waited a moment and cautiously peered through the sliver of clear glass above the dashboard again. She breathed a sigh of relief when she realized the man had not seen her and watched their backs as they trudged through the deep snow toward the building Hank and Steele had entered earlier.

#

Fred Gibson took two steps into the room and yelled, "What the hell you schmucks think you're doin' in here?"

Hank got to his feet, holding his hands high. His voice was calm as he spoke. "Fingers—you aren't gonna' use that thing, are you?"

Steele followed Hank's lead, also standing and raising his hands over his head. Conrad was struggling to get up and Steele turned to him and in a very calm voice said, "Just stay put for a minute, Mr. Conrad."

"You give up crackin' safes for snatchin' people now Fingers?" Hank said as he took a step toward him.

Fingers shifted the gun, pointing it right at Hank. "Just stay put, Lieutenant." He took a cigar stub from his mouth as he spoke again. "Just doin' a favor for a friend."

"You know, you're liable to kill somebody with that thing," Steele said.

Fingers chomped down on the cigar and waved the muzzle of the Thompson at Steele, "Who's your new playmate here, Lieutenant?"

"He's a private dick I'm workin' with. Name's Mark Steele, and like the man said, you should be careful with that thing. There could be an accident."

"Nah, Lieutenant... no one's getting hurt here lessin' I want 'em to."

Steele's eyes narrowed—his chin set and determined—his teeth clenched. He growled, "Y'know, Fingers, they'll fry you for this. Kidnapping ain't a slap on the wrist and five-to-seven inside like cracking safes. It means life in the joint, maybe even the chair."

"Man's got to do what he can to make a livin', don't he? Ain't that so, Lieutenant?" he laughed.

Hank was about to answer him when he caught sight of a figure, silhouetted against outside light, looming behind Fingers in the doorway. Hank glanced at Steele. Steele shrugged. Neither man knew who the new visitor might be. He took two steps into the room and stood behind Fingers.

Steele saw a third, smaller person, again silhouetted in the doorway. The third person swung an object through the air; followed by a muffled *"THUD"* as it hit the second man on the head. The man sank to his knees in slow motion, and then fell forward flat on his face on the floor. Fingers turned and raised the Thompson toward the intruder. Steele sprang at Fingers, hitting his forearm hard with an adept judo chop. Fingers dropped the Thompson, before he could fire it and it, went skidding across the floor.

Steele looked at the doorway. Poppy stood there clutching a two foot long piece of steel pipe in both hands like it was a baseball bat; she looked terrified.

"Oh, my God!" Poppy shouted.

Steele ran to the machine gun and picked it up. Hank moved to Fingers and pulled both his arms behind his back and handcuffed him.

Poppy's voice was calmer, "Is, is... is he, umm, ah, dead?" she pointed her finger at the man lying on the floor.

Steele bent down and felt the man's wrist for a pulse. He looked up at Hank, and then over to Poppy, a somber look on his face. "No, unfortunately he's not dead." He began to laugh as he got to his feet. "But he's sure gonna have one hellishly bad headache when he comes around."

Poppy stood there in a confused and dazed state for a moment. She shook her head, finally realized where she was and what she had just done, and dropped the pipe. It made a hollow thump as it hit the wooden floor. She turned to Steele and grinned.

"Don't look so pleased with yourself. I thought I told you to stay in the car. You could have gotten yourself killed with that stunt."

Hank looked at Poppy, whose face had turned blank. Hank pointed his finger at Steele, "Don't let him get away with that, young lady." He glanced at Steele and then back to Poppy. Steele began to speak but Hank cut him short. "You did a slap-up job, Miss Sinclair, and don't you let this bastard tell you otherwise." He put his hand on Steele's shoulder, looking back at Poppy.

Steele's face also turned glum. "I suppose Hank's right." he went to her and put his arm around her, "You did a good job." He jostled her a bit. "But just the same..." He didn't finish as he glanced over to Roger Conrad, who now sat on the foot of the bed.

Poppy finally noticed her father sitting on the bed and cried out, "Oh, Daddy!" She ran over to where he was and hugged him, "Thank God, you're okay! I was so afraid they had killed you!"

Poppy sat down next to her father on the bed and put her arms around him.

Meanwhile, Steele removed the magazine from the Thompson, pulled the bolt back and ejected the chambered round. He put the magazine and shell into his pocket. He switched the safety on and laid the gun across the foot of the bed. He picked up two pieces of rope he had cut from Conrad earlier and handed one piece to Hank.

"You might want to tie his feet, Hank. Just in case?" Steele said as he went to the man still sprawled out on the floor and began tying his hands behind his back. Once finished, he patted the man down. He found a forty-five automatic in a shoulder holster and the man's wallet in his hip pocket.

"Says here this guy's name's Howard Gibson," Steele said as he handed the wallet to Hank.

"He any relation to you, Fingers?" Hank said as he withdrew the driver's license from the wallet.

"I ain't sayin' nothin'." Fingers grunted.

"Says that he lives here in New Hampshire."

"I wouldn't know nothin' bout that," Fingers smirked.

"Don't you worry, Fingers, eventually we'll get all the answers we need," Hank said as he stuffed the wallet into his coat pocket.

Steele had pulled two chairs near the bed so he and Hank could sit down and talk with Conrad.

Hank began to ask Roger questions. "Did you get a good look at any of them? Do you know either of these guys?"

Roger looked away from Poppy and glanced quickly to Fingers and the man on the floor, then back to Hank. "I didn't see anyone, but I did hear them talking. One of the voices seemed familiar but I'm not sure who he was. I don't know either of these gentlemen."

"If you heard this man again do you think you could recognize him?" Steele said.

Roger looked at Steele. "I might be able to. But I'm not sure." The look in his eye told Steele that Roger was very disappointed that he couldn't be positive.

"This one sound at all familiar?" he pointed to the body lying on the floor.

"I don't know. He could have been here before. But I can't be positive."

"How about him?" he pointed at Fingers who was now setting in a chair across the room.

"Yes, I do recognize his voice, he's been here many times before."

"How long have they been gone?" Hank asked.

"I'm not at all sure about that... if I had to guess—I'd say at least an hour... but it could have been two, or even three," the old man said as he rubbed his wrists.

"Hank, judging from the temperature of the stove I'd say the fire's been out at least an hour. So it's been at least an hour, possibly two," Steele said.

"Did they say anything about where they were going—or, when they'd be back?" Hank asked.

"No. They didn't talk much, nor loud enough for me to hear when they did. They whispered a lot from across the room. I could never make out anything they said, sounded like gibberish to me." He scratched his head and looked straight at Hank, "Although, once I did hear one of them mention *Project Endeavor*. But I can't for the life of me figure out why they would be interested in that project."

By the look on his face and the expression in his eyes, Roger seemed truly perplexed by what had just happened.

"What exactly is *Project Endeavor*?" Steele asked before Hank could get the words out of his own mouth.

"*Project Endeavor* is not a secret government project—it's not even a secret project—it's an internal company project to speed up production in our Roxbury, Ohio plant. It would be of absolutely no value to anyone outside the company," Roger said, shaking his head.

"We received a ransom note demanding all the files on the *Project Endeavor* and a sum of one million dollars for your release," Hank said.

"It doesn't make any sense to me," Roger said still shaking his head. "The money I can understand, but why ask for the files on *Endeavor*?"

Steele said, "We can figure that out later... let's get you back to Boston now and we'll work on the whys and wherefores later."

Roger stood up, a little shaky at first. Steele took off his overcoat and helped Roger put it on.

"Mr. Conrad," Steele said to him, "snow's pretty deep out there," he pointed to the floor, "and since you don't have shoes why don't we carry you to the car?"

Roger nodded his head in agreement.

Hank spoke up and pointed to the man still lying on the floor, unconscious. "Steele, I'm going to need a hand with that sack of shit."

Steele looked at Fingers. "He looks big enough to carry his sidekick." He looked back to Hank. "What'd yeah think?"

"Sounds like an excellent idea to me." Hank untied the rope around Fingers' legs and yanked on his collar. "Get to your feet."

"I ain't gonna carry him. I got a bad back," Fingers began to protest as Hank undid the handcuffs.

Steele picked up the Thompson and inserted the clip and pointed it directly at Fingers. "Hank, on second thought," he said, "maybe we should just shoot him... we could say it happened during the struggle for the gun."

"That's a brilliant idea," he grinned at Steele, "there was a fight, both of 'em them got shot—let the coroner carry them both out on a stretcher."

Fingers jaw dropped and beads of sweat began to pop up on his brow. He held up his hands in a defensive position, "Okay, okay. No need for that. I'll carry him."

"Okay then, get to it," Hank yelled at him, "we ain't got all day."

Steele once again removed the clip from the Thompson and handed them both to Poppy. He pulled out his .32 and held it pointed at Fingers while Hank helped him pull his still unconscious partner upright and lift him up over his shoulder like a sack of potatoes. Once Fingers had his friend in place and balanced, Hank handcuffed the two men together.

When Roger saw how Fingers was carrying the other man he looked questionably to Steele.

"Don't worry, Mr. Conrad I can just carry you in my arms, like a bride over the threshold. If you can put your arms around my neck and help a bit," Steele said.

Conrad smiled. "I believe I can manage that."

Steele looked at Poppy. "Can you bring those extra blankets and that gun?"

Poppy nodded in agreement and pulled the blankets from the bed. She folded them and laid the Thompson across the pile and picked it up.

When they got to the car Steele put Roger in the back seat of the Packard and Poppy wrapped him up snugly in the blankets. She gave him what little coffee was left in the thermos. Meanwhile, Steele put the Thompson and the other guns in the trunk.

Steele said, "With these two mugs along for the ride, we'll need to take both cars. What do you think, Hank?"

"You're right, Steele," he looked to Poppy, "think you can handle this Packard, Miss Sinclair?"

"Yes, I can do that."

"Okay, then," Hank said. "Steele and I will take these two in the other car and you just take care of your father."

"Where are we going? To Boston or to the Salem Police station?" Steele said.

"We'll need extradition papers to bring them back over the state line, or risk a kidnapping charge ourselves. Meanwhile, we can have the locals lock them up on possession of that Thompson. That will hold till the paper work gets done."

"Hank," Poppy cried out, "you've got blood all over your pants leg. What happened?"

"Damn pipe in the snow. I tripped over it."

"Pull your pants' leg up and I'll take a look."

He put his foot on the bumper of the car and pulled up his pants leg to reveal a sizable gash in his shin. The cold had slowed, but hadn't stopped, the bleeding.

"That Packard come equipped with a first-aid kit, Hank?" Steele said.

"Don't know for sure, you'll have to check the trunk."

"Okay, I'll take a look."

Poppy reached into the car and pulled the handkerchief from Fingers' breast pocket and began to clean the wound on Hank's leg.

"Hey, that's genuine Egyptian cotton. It cost me ten bucks."

Hank scowled at Fingers while Poppy worked on his leg, "Fingers, shut up. I seriously doubt you'll have any use for 'genuine Egyptian cotton handkerchiefs' where you're headed."

Steele handed Poppy an olive-green metal box with a red cross stenciled on it.

Poppy looked at the box and gave Steele a bewildered look.

"War surplus," Steele said, "lots of stuff like this on the market, really cheap, since the war."

Poppy opened the box and found a can labeled Antiseptic powder and sprinkled the wound liberally with its pale-yellow contents. She wrapped Hanks shin in several layers of gauze.

"That should do for now, but that gash's pretty big. When we get Father to the hospital you should have it looked at—it may need a few stitches."

"Right ho, nurse Poppy." Hank smiled, as he pushed his pants' leg down over the new white bandage.

Hank retrieved a second pair of handcuffs from the glove compartment of the Packard and he and Steele got Fingers and Howard snugly handcuffed in the back seat of the old Dodge. Steele drove while Hank kept his eye, and his gun, trained on the two prisoners.

Poppy followed Steele in the Packard, but when they passed a diner Steele saw her peel off and stop. He made a U-turn in the highway and went back to see what had happened.

"Poppy, what's wrong?" Steele called out as he entered the diner.

"There's nothing wrong," Poppy said, "I just wanted to stop and re-fill the thermos with hot soup for Father. He hasn't had any real solid food to eat since they carried him off."

"I wish you'd mentioned it before we started. Hank and I both thought you father may have taken a turn for the worse."

"I'm sorry," she looked up at him and began to chew on her lower lip, "I really didn't know until Father said he was awfully hungry."

The waitress brought the thermos and a paper cup of coffee back and set them on the counter in front of Poppy.

"Let's see." The woman consulted her order pad. "The chicken soup's 60¢, and the coffee's 15¢ and with sales tax that comes to 78¢, please," the woman said with a smile.

Poppy handed her a dollar bill. "You can keep the change."

# # #

The Salem Police station was a half-mile further down the highway from the diner. It resembled a residential house; single story, red brick but with heavy bars on all the windows. A sign on the front of the building declared "Salem Police Department" in large block letters. Below that in slightly smaller lettering the sign read "Chief of Police William Edward James".

Hank went into the station while Steele guarded the prisoners. Five minutes later Hank returned to the car.

"The officer in charge said he wasn't authorized to take custody of any prisoners without the Chief of Police's okay."

"I suppose the Chief's not here either?" Steele said with as little sarcasm as he could muster.

"No, 'Chief James don't work no night shifts', the sergeant informed me in no uncertain terms."

"So, the Chief comin' down to the station, or not?"

"Yeah, the sergeant called him at home."

"Good."

"But he's madder than hell that he's been called to the station in the middle of the night."

"Middle of the night," Steele looked at his watch, "it's just a little past seven; not what I would call the middle of the night."

"Yeah, I know." Hank chuckled, "He'll be here in half an hour. He had business at his farm outside of town. It seems we've interrupted him."

"Can we at least take these mugs inside?" Steele waved his gun at the two men in the back seat. "Howard here finally came around a few minutes ago. He's been shooting his mouth off ever since—the guy won't shut-up."

"I don't see why not. He didn't say we couldn't," Hank grinned.

Thirty-three minutes had gone by when the sound of a police-car siren began getting louder and louder until it stopped outside the police station.

A moment later a small, skeleton-thin man wearing a police uniform burst through the front door.

"Where in the hell's this stupid Boston cop?" he yelled in a squeaky high-pitched, ear-splitting voice.

Hank stood up and pulled his badge out of his jacket pocket. "That would be me, I'm the stupid Boston cop," Hank said. "Lieutenant Hank Williamson." He held the badge up with his left hand and extended his right hand."

Police Chief James ignored Hank's extended hand and stomped into his office.

"What's this here all about, exactly, Lieutenant?"

"I have two thugs here that are prime suspects in a kidnapping in Boston."

"Why did you bring them here, Lieutenant? What have the good citizens of Salem, New Hampshire got to do with your little kidnapping?"

"Certain clues led us to a building in your town where we apprehended these two."

"I know that you are aware that you don't have any authority to arrest anyone here, Lieutenant."

"Yes, I know that Chief James. I just need you to hold them here until I can get an extradition order from Boston. A day, maybe two, at the most."

The front door opened and Poppy came in. "How long are we going to stop here, Hank? I would like to get Father to a hospital."

Steele walked to her side, "We'll only be a few more minutes, Poppy. Hank's arranging for the prisoners."

Chief James was now standing toe to toe with Hank and shouting, "This ain't Boston, Lieutenant. This little town can't afford to hold these two, on just your say so."

"Okay, then you can hold them on possession of illegal firearms."

"What illegal firearms? I don't see any firearms."

"They threatened me and my colleagues, Mr. Steele and Miss Penelope Sinclair here, with a Thompson machine gun."

"Where's the gun?"

"It's in the trunk of the car. It has their fingerprints all over it," Hank said. "I can make a citizen's arrest if that will make you feel better," Hank grinned.

"That would certainly help. But it's more a matter of money. I can't afford—the town can't afford-- to feed these Jasper's for two or more days on our budget."

Poppy stepped forward, "If it's just a matter of money, perhaps I can help with that." She opened her purse and took out her wallet. "How much would you need to feed the prisoners for two or three days?"

Chief James suddenly realized that Poppy had called his bluff, "Ah, I don't exactly know. Two, maybe three dollars a day for each of 'em," Chef James said sheepishly.

Poppy pulled a twenty-dollar bill from her purse, paused a second and then returned them both. She pulled out a fifty instead, and handed the bill to Chief James. "Here's enough to treat you and your men to a meal too."

"I don't know if I can do that, miss," he said as he held the bill up to the light, stretching it between his fingers.

"My father, Roger Conrad, who's a very wealthy man, was the kidnap victim. These men held him here, in your town. I want them held until Lieutenant Williamson can make whatever arrangements he needs to make to bring them back to Boston to stand trial."

"However, when you put it that way, Miss, how can I refuse such a passionate request?" Chief James said as he folded the bill neatly and put it into his shirt pocket.

"I believe I should get back to Father, it's rather cold outside in the car," Poppy said as she moved toward the door.

"I'll go with you," Steele said as he followed her out the door.

"There's another small problem, Chief," Hank said as he removed his handcuffs from Fingers and handed him over to a deputy.

"And what would that be, Lieutenant?"

"I'll notify the FBI of the location where we nabbed these two when I get back to Boston. I'm sure that they will want to go over the place for evidence in this kidnapping case. In the meantime I would like for you to secure the place till they get here. Post a man there for the next twenty-four hours. Another member from the gang may show up and we wouldn't want to tip them off that we've rescued Mr. Conrad and arrested his two guards."

"I don't really have the manpower to do anything like that, Lieutenant."

"Would you rather that I call the FBI from here and tell them that the Salem Police don't wish to cooperate on this case?"

"No, that won't be necessary. I guess I can figure out a way of keeping an eye on the place."

"Good, I thought you might," Hank said as he put his handcuffs in his jacket pocket and headed toward the door. He was about to walk through the door when he turned back to Chief James.

"Chief, there's one more thing," Hank said, "There's a car outside, a black Dodge sedan. I believe it's a '46 model. The car belongs to these two bums."

He fished the keys from his jacket pocket and handed them to Chief James. "I'm sure that the FBI will want to look at that too, so I'm going to leave it here."

"Okay, but what happens when they're done with it? I can't keep it here indefinitely," Chief James sputtered, "I don't have enough parking spaces."

"I really don't think the FBI will need it for long, Chief," Hank smiled, "It's a pretty nice car—no dents or dings—and the odometer says less that 30,000 miles. When the FBI's done going over it, it will become the property of the courts until the case's settled. I don't think they would mind if you used it." Hank threw a two finger salute. "I mean strictly for town business, of course."

"Town business you say," he grinned. "Hum... okay, Lieutenant, leave it and I'll take care of it personally."

"Make sure that you put in a claim. Assuming it's not stolen, I'm sure the court will look favorably on awarding it to the town when the trials over. In the meantime, who will know if there are a few more miles on the odometer?"

Chief James face was beaming in a broad grin as he twirled the key ring around his index finger.

As Steele opened the Packard's rear door for Poppy, he said, "You know that the town will never see a penny of that fifty dollar bill?"

"I'm quite sure you're right about that," she smiled at him from the back seat, "but it did help to convince him to do the right thing—didn't it?"

"Yes, I'm sure it did."

"Then I consider it money well-spent."

Steele talked with Poppy while Hank was still inside making the final arrangements with Chief James. Whispering so Roger couldn't hear, he said, "I don't think it's a good idea to tell your father about Alton until after a doctor has looked him over at the hospital."

She nodded in agreement and kissed him on the cheek. "So thoughtful."

Conrad saw Poppy kiss Steele and said, "You two got a romance going? Anything I should know about, Penelope?"

Poppy blushed. "No, Daddy, we're just friends. I'm sure you must remember Mark... um, Mr. Steele's the private investigator—you met him—he came to the house for dinner. I hired him to help find you. He was just reminding me that we should take you to a hospital for an examination, and I was thanking him for his concern."

"I see." The old man looked at Steele while winking at Poppy. "Looked like more than a thank you to me."

"Mr. Conrad, I can assure you it wasn't romantic at all," Steele smiled at him. "But, on the other hand, I've noticed that your daughter has a tendency towards being very affectionate."

"Yes, she does," Roger smiled, and then frowned as realization of what Poppy had said hit him. "What's all this about a hospital? I don't need a hospital!"

"Nonsense, Father. You've been kidnapped—gone for three days. No telling what might be wrong with you. The doctor needs to look at you." She looked at Steele. "We should take him to the hospital here in Salem."

"No, I'm okay, just take me home." Conrad began to get red in the face. "Dr. Gilbert can check me in my own bed."

"I don't think that's a good idea," Poppy said, "but we could wait and take you to the hospital in Boston."

"Okay, but only the Blaxton Medical Center. They'll treat me better—I'm on the board there."

"You mean you can bulldoze them into doing things your way. Isn't that what you really mean, Daddy?"

"Yes, I do. I give a lot of my money to that hospital, and I expect a decent return on that investment," he laughed.

CHAPTER 28

Road conditions hadn't improved during their short visit to Salem. Strong westerly winds constantly blew drifts of snow across the roadway, buffeting the car, at times making the roadway nearly impossible to drive on. Twice Steele had to drive into a frozen pasture to get around a large snowdrift. The trip home took nearly an hour and a quarter.

Once in Boston city limits, Steele drove directly to the Blaxton Medical Center. It was five minutes to eleven when Hank and Steele carried Conrad into the emergency entrance.

Hank didn't stay at the hospital with Poppy and Steele; instead he took the Packard back to police headquarters. He said he needed to make out his report, talk with the FBI and the district attorney about extraditing Fingers and his partner back to Boston, and see if any of the leads his squad had been following had produced any results.

Dr. Arthur Fisher, an old friend of Roger's, was in the emergency room attending another patient when Steele and Hank carried Conrad into the hospital. Dr. Fisher and Conrad often played poker together, along with other influential members of Boston society. He immediately took charge of Roger and sent him off, along with a nurse and another young doctor, to a private room.

"Miss Penelope," Dr. Fisher said, "I'll call Dr. Gilbert, but in the meanwhile, I'll see that Roger has the best of care. Why don't you and your friend get a cup of coffee? I'll send my nurse to get you after I've examined Roger and gotten him settled into his room."

Thirty minutes later a Candy Striper came into the cafeteria and announced that she was looking for a Miss Penelope Sinclair.

"Young lady," Poppy waved to the girl, "I'm Penelope Sinclair."

"Miss Sinclair, Dr. Fisher sent me down to get you. He has finished his examination of your father.

"Is Father okay?"

"Dr. Fisher didn't say. He just instructed me to come down here and retrieve you. I do know that your father has asked about you. He's in room 311."

# # #

Dr. Fisher and a nurse had just left room 311 when Poppy and Steele caught up to them in the hallway.

"Doctor Fisher," Poppy called out to him.

"Ah, Penelope," he said as he turned and came back in her direction.

Poppy asked, "Will he be Okay?"

"He's just fine." He smiled at her. "He's hungry and as cantankerous as I've ever seen him." His forehead wrinkled and his expression turned serious.

"However, he's a little dehydrated."

"It's not life threatening—is it, doctor?"

"No, certainly not, now that we have him under observation, he'll be just fine. However, I don't believe he should have any solid food till tomorrow. I've given orders to limit his diet to soup, pudding, and Jell-O; but he can have as much as he wants. He also has a few scrapes with minor infections, but nothing clean dressings and a few days won't remedy."

"Can I see him?"

"Certainly." He lowered his voice and stepped a foot closer to her. "In fact, you'll be a big help." He almost whispered, "I want him to stay here over night, just in case.

And, true to form, he's adamant about going home. Maybe he'll listen to you."

"I'll be as persuasive as I can be, Doctor." She smiled. "If I can't convince him, I'll just have Mr. Steele handcuff him to the bed." She laughed.

Steele grimaced as he looked at Dr. Fisher, "She's just kidding, of course," Steele smiled. "But between the two of us I'm sure we can convince Mr. Conrad to stay, without resorting to restraining him."

"Good—it would be better if he stays here tonight." He took a few steps away, then turned back to them, "Although, those handcuffs might be a good idea," he began to chuckle as he turned again and walked down the hallway whistling a tune.

Room 311 wasn't your normal hospital room. It was one of the hospital's executive suites. It consisted of three rooms and a full bathroom with a shower and whirlpool tub. These suites are reserved for the wealthy, celebrities, and high-ranking government officials.

The first room, a sitting room, was decorated with expensive furniture: a full-sized leather sofa, two over-stuffed leather wing-back chairs, a radio-television console, and a leather chaise lounge.

The other two rooms, one of which Roger Conrad occupied, looked like standard hospital rooms—equipped with all the paraphernalia one would associate with a modern hospital room.

Poppy sat down on the edge of her father's bed. "Daddy, are you okay?"

"I'm just fine, Poppy. I don't know what all the fussing's about. There's nothing wrong with me that a little iodine, gauze, adhesive tape, and a good night's sleep in my own bed wouldn't fix."

"Dr. Fisher thinks there's a possibility the cuts could be infected."

"Balderdash," he huffed, "I've cut myself worse than this on a fishing trip skinning trout for breakfast."

"Will you at least stay overnight for me? It would make me feel better."

His eyes twinkled and he smiled, as he patted her hand, "So, kiddo... if you're gonna get all girlie on me."

"If it will make you feel better, I'll stay here with you tonight," Poppy said. "This suite has two rooms and I'm sure it won't be a problem."

He patted her hand. "I guess I don't have much choice, do I?"

"Most certainly not—and, I'm glad it's settled."

"How's your mother taking all of this?"

"I haven't told her yet." She grasped his hand and squeezed it. "I thought it would be better if she didn't know anything until we found you. She thinks you are on a business trip to Chicago."

"You're probably right. Your mother's never taken bad news very well. News like this would have had her here in the hospital instead of me," he chuckled.

"Yes. When they told her that my Father, Lord Sinclair, died at Dunkirk defending the soldiers under his command, she took to her bed for six months. Even after being divorced from him for nearly six years, she took his death very badly. She didn't go outside the house for a full year. I was away at school when it happened; but after commencement I came back to live with her."

"I didn't realize. I knew she was quite sensitive, but I had no idea," he said as he squeezed Poppy's hand. "She has never spoken to me about that time of her life—and I've never taken it upon myself to pry into their relationship." He smiled at Poppy, "So, with that in mind, we'll just keep this little outing of mine our little secret. Won't we?" He glanced over to where Steele stood.

"My lips will remain sealed Mr. Conrad. You and your step-daughter are my clients and client information, whatever it might be, is always confidential, and will remain that way as long as you want it to be."

Roger looked back to Poppy. "I like him, I believe you should keep him around."

"I've been trying to convince him of that very same thing," she laughed.

Her facial expression suddenly changed from a smile to a frown. Roger immediately noticed the change in her demeanor.

"What in the world's wrong, Poppy?"

"I have disturbing news and I really don't know how to tell you without troubling you."

"I'm just fine. I can take it whatever it may be." He patted her hand and then gripped it firmly. "The house or the company building didn't burn down, did they?"

"No, nothing like that. It's about Alton."

"What about Alton. I'll bet that rat Councilman Howard Jacobson has tried to hire him away from me. Alton didn't quit, did he?"

"No, he didn't quit. He loves his job, he's told me so. But... um... like you, he's in the hospital."

"What's wrong with him?" Roger called out.

"He... um. He was... um." She began to cry.

Roger looked to Steele, "What's going on Mr. Steele? Do you know what happened?"

"Yes, I do," he answered quickly, but then hesitated.

"Then tell me, man. What's this all about?"

"Alton had picked us up at the police station and was driving us to my office when Alton noticed that a car had begun following us. He did a very skilful job of driving to lose the car on icy, snow-covered streets. We had nearly gotten away from them when they began to shoot at our car. Alton was hit by a bullet and the car went up over the curb and smashed into a telephone pole."

"Is he okay?"

"Yes. He has two wounds. A bullet wound to the head, just a graze. The more serious wound was to his chest. The second bullet missed his heart, but did cause lung damage."

"Will he be okay?"

"Yes, they operated on him to repair the damaged lung."

"Can he talk? I'd like to call him."

"He's doing just fine. He's not up and about yet," Poppy said. "Barnaby, Susan and Zoë have been to visit him; I'm sure he can talk on the telephone."

"Is he here in this hospital?"

"No," Poppy said.

"Then where?"

"The ambulance took him directly to DeBois Hospital."

"Was that the closest hospital?"

"No, this one's closer," Steele, jumped in.

"Why didn't they bring him here then?"

"I wondered that myself, since it was three times as far to DeBois," Steele said. "Later, I found out that they don't treat Negroes here."

"You're not serious," Roger said as he sat up in the bed.

"I'm afraid so, Mr. Conrad," Steele said as he sat down in the guest chair.

Roger leaned over and picked up the telephone from the bedside table. "Yes, Roger Conrad speaking. I want to speak to Alton Johnson; he's a patient at DeBois hospital." He put his hand over the receiver. "This *is* outrageous. Alton should be here, in this hospital."

Steele nodded his agreement.

"Hello, that you, Alton?"

"No, sir, this I'm his nurse, my name's Janet... please hold the line a moment."

Roger could hear two or three muffled voices, but couldn't make out what was being said. After a few moments Nurse Janet came back on the line.

"Who's calling?"

"Roger Conrad. Alton's my chauffeur, and I would like to speak to him."

A weak voice said, "Is that you Mr. Conrad? I thought you'd been kidnapped. Are you okay?"

"Yes, I'm just fine—Poppy, Mr. Steele, and the police rescued me. They also told me that you've been shot."

Alton's voice brightened a bit, "That's true, Mr. Conrad."

"Ah, Alton. What's this I hear about you conducting car chases and gun fights through the streets of Boston?" Roger said with a chuckle.

"Yes, sir, Mr. Conrad. But that gangster had a bigger gun than Mr. Steele had and he got the best of us," he snickered. "Oh, umm, ow."

"You okay, Alton?"

"Yeah, umm, Mr. Conrad... it's just that it hurts to laugh."

"According to Mr. Steele here you gave them hell with what you had. I'm truly glad you're okay. They tell me you'll be as good as new in no time at all."

"Doctor says I'll be here three weeks—maybe more."

"A few days, a few weeks, that doesn't matter at all; you just concentrate on getting well. I'll be in touch."

Poppy drew Steele over near the door. "Mark, I should stay with Daddy, tonight."

"Yeah, sure—by all means you should stay with him."

"But, I also need to tell Susan, Barnaby, and Zoë about Father." She took hold of his hand, "I would prefer to do it in person, not over the telephone. Would you mind coming with me?"

"No, of course not."

Steele left the room and Poppy went back and sat down on the edge of Roger's bed. "Father, I'm going back to the house to tell Mother, Susan, and Zoë that you're safe, and pick up a few things—I'll be staying the night here at the hospital."

"That not at all necessary, I'm just fine."

"I know, but I'd still like to stay here with you."

"If that's what you want. I'm certainly not going to argue with you about it. A little company would be nice," he smiled at her.

Steele came back into the room. "I called a taxi. It will be downstairs in a few minutes."

Poppy was still sitting on the edge of the bed. "I'll be back in an hour or so." Poppy leaned down and kissed Roger on the forehead and she squeezed his hand.

You needn't rush, child. It doesn't seem likely that I'll be going anywhere for a while." Roger chuckled as Poppy got to her feet.

When she got to the door she turned and blew him a kiss before leaving the room.

CHAPTER 29

The taxi was waiting at the curb when Steele and Poppy left the hospital. A light snow had fallen making downtown traffic rather slow; the three-mile ride to the Conrad house took nearly ten minutes.

Steele got out and went around and opened Poppy's door; they walked arm-in-arm to the door. Steele rapped the big brass doorknocker three times. A second later Barnaby opened the front door.

"Miss Sinclair," he said with concern in his voice, "has Mr. Conrad been located?"

"Yes, Barnaby—Mr. Steele, Lieutenant Williamson, and I found him in New Hampshire. Father's just fine, he's at the hospital. They're keeping him for observation."

"New Hampshire? My goodness. Why would they take him to New Hampshire?"

"We do not know, Barnaby. But Mr. Steele and Lieutenant Williamson are still investigating. I'm positive that they will find all the answers."

"Yes, miss." He looked at Steele. "I'm confident that they will." he said as he took their coats and hats. After hanging the coats in the closet, Barnaby continued, "Miss Sinclair, would it be proper for Mrs. Wallace, myself, and Miss Zimmerman to visit Mr. Conrad in the hospital?"

"That's a wonderful idea, Barnaby. I'm sure Father would be delighted to see all of you. You should go and see Alton too." Poppy said as she started up the stairs. "As we did before, when you visited Alton, take money from the household accounts and call a taxi."

"Thank you, miss," he bowed his customary almost unnoticeable bow, "What about this evening, miss? Do you want Mrs. Wallace to prepare a late supper for you and Mr. Steele?"

"No, Barnaby, we'll be fine. I'm not hungry," she looked at Steele, "What about you? Are you hungry?"

"Just a little." Steele turned and addressed Barnaby, "A sandwich and coffee would be just fine."

"Very good, Mr. Steele. I'll have Mrs. Wallace prepare a sandwich for you. Do you have a preference?"

"No, whatever Mrs. Wallace has in the kitchen will be fine."

Barnaby nodded to Steele and turned back to Poppy, "What of Mrs. Conrad? She may need assistance tomorrow."

"I will talk with Mother and explain everything to her. You and the others go and have a good time. In fact, I just had a thought—after your visit to the hospital, why don't you take the ladies out for a nice lunch?"

"I wouldn't know where to go, miss."

"Anywhere you like, Barnaby. I know that Zoë goes out on dates all the time, surely she'll know the best places."

"Yes, Miss." he said as he bowed.

"And Barnaby."

"Yes, Miss."

"Don't worry about the cost, go anywhere you like. It'll be my treat."

"Thank you, Miss," he bowed again. This time he bent at the waist and lowered his head at least six inches.

"Mark, I'm going up to have a talk with Mother, change my clothes, and pack a small bag for the hospital."

# # #

Steele went to the library, poured himself a drink and sat down on one of the bar stools. He picked up the telephone, on the end of the bar, and dialed Hank's number.

"Hank, what do you think we should do now that our kidnap victim has been found?"

"So... even though we found him and he's okay, we still need to find out who's behind all this. Fingers isn't the boss—he didn't set this up—he's not smart enough.""Any suggestions where we should start looking?"

"At this point..." He paused. Steele heard a match strike and the sound of Hank exhaling. He had lit a cigarette. "At this point, I'm leaning heavily toward the son, Lawrence. I have a feeling that he's the brains behind this mess."

"Yeah... his actions have certainly been suspicious. No reason why he shouldn't be at the top of our list. But then again, we did find the crucial clue in Arnold Becker's trash can—we certainly need to lean on him pretty hard, too."

"Don't worry, I will. If he doesn't show up by tomorrow afternoon when he's scheduled back, I'll get a warrant, and have him picked up and arrested as a material witness."

"If he's the one, he could already have a big head start on us."

"I know... but there's not much I can do about that."

"And speaking of Lawrence..."

"Steele, I thought we'd finished talking about Lawrence."

"Ah, nonsense—and it doesn't make any difference, we're talking about him now—aren't we?"

"Yeah, I guess you're right—I can't argue with you over that one."

Barnaby came through the library door carrying a tray with a sandwich and coffee. He set the tray on the bar near Steele. Steele nodded to Barnaby and Barnaby bowed. Neither saying anything, and Barnaby left the room.

Steele brought his attention back to Hank on the telephone, "Anyway, when I was in New York, you told me that your people had found information on Lawrence and Beverly; but you wouldn't tell me what it was. Later, I asked about it again and you ducked my question. Don't you think it's about time you filled me in?"

"It's not important," Hank said. Steele heard Hank exhale again. *Probably blowing smoke rings*, he thought.

"Hank, you know it must have a little meaning or you wouldn't have mentioned it in the first place. You and I both know that you don't let seemingly unimportant things slip by... you investigate even the unimportant stuff. Now, what was it?"

"If I had real proof that the rumor was true, I'd tell you in a minute, but for now—I don't." he said putting his most official sounding voice to the statement.

"So, Hank, have you ever known me to blabber details about a case?"

"No, but—"

"Look, you said you felt it wasn't important, I can understand that. But, what you think is unimportant could be just the piece of information I need to finish the puzzle. As the cliché goes: Two heads are better than one."

"Okay, when you put it that way, I guess it might not hurt to tell you."

In the background, Steele could hear Hank shuffling papers as he talked.

"So, tell me?"

"I have an old high school friend. His name's Jim Howard and he works with the FBI. We have a beer together now and then and he tells me stuff." He paused, took a long drag on his cigarette, and blew out a long succession of smoke rings. "He's not an agent—he's a custodian at the Federal building—and he over-hears things."

"But regardless, you trust him... right?"

"Yea, he's as honest and truthful as they come."

"So, you believe his information's reliable—I get it."

"Yeah, I'm sure it's reliable, it's just not official."

"When did that ever bother us," Steele chuckled, "most of the information we deal with, isn't official, just rumors, innuendo, and supposition until we prove it's true."

"You're right... I wasn't looking at it in that way," he took another deep drag on the cigarette and then snuffed it out in the ashtray. "Okay. My friend overheard a couple of agents talking about Lawrence and Beverly's case in the cafeteria while he was emptying trash cans. It seems that Beverly's not Beverly at all. She's a he, and his name's not Beverly, it's really Bernard."

Steele took a sip from his drink. "Okay, I knew that myself—at least I suspected it—but I didn't really want to believe it."

"What do you mean by that, Steele?"

"I met Beverly, or Bernard, the night before the kidnapping, right here in this room. Roger was trying to teach her, or him, how to play pool." Even though Hank couldn't see him over the telephone, Steele pointed to the pool table.

"How does that tie in... or what does that mean?"

"The night I met her at the Conrad house, she wore a very short dress. It wasn't really a dress, at all; it was one of those new style tennis outfits that barely covered her shorts. Those outfits are normally worn with heavy shorts underneath the short skirt," Steele sipped from his glass.

"So? A lot of women wear that type of outfit."

"Yeah, I know... but usually not in public. Most women, after their matches, would change into their street cloths while still at the tennis club. Other than the fact that she hadn't changed at the club—the thing that was different about Beverly was this. She didn't wear heavy shorts, under her dress; she wore regular panties that night. Shear, nearly transparent, pink panties. And as she bent over the table she exposed those panties, full view, to anyone behind her. At the time I thought the panties concealed nothing more sinister than a sanitary napkin. But being a gentleman, I immediately put the idea out of my head," Steele refreshed his drink and then added, "Perhaps I should have looked closer."

"Maybe, maybe not. I don't know that it would have made any difference," Hank said. "What do you think, now that you know about her? I mean, knowing that she's really a he—does it really have any bearing at all on this case?"

"It's hard to say." Steele took a sip from his glass, draining it. "But I learned a long time ago... almost everything that comes up in a case ends up being of importance in one way or another. Not every small piece will solve the case, but put a lot of them together and they might help. Will this piece of information get us any closer to solving this... at this point, I can't answer 'yes' or 'no' to that, but that doesn't mean in won't fit in later."

"Okay, this discussion of a transvestite isn't getting us anywhere at this point. She/he may be an accomplice like several other people in this case may be—but so what?

Does calling her Mr. instead of Miss make any difference? And, does the knowledge that he's looking to be the next Christine Jorgensen truly get us any closer to who's behind this? I'm not that sure, that it does."

"You're probably right—but where's that leave us?"

"I can make a few phone calls and see if I can get more information on the whereabouts of Becker. I also need to check in with the FBI, see if they've been able to scare up anything of interest in Fingers' car or the warehouse in New Hampshire. What are you going to do, Steele?"

"I don't know... stay here, have a sandwich with Poppy, maybe even go back over to the hospital and see if I can get any more from Conrad. I need to make a few calls, too. I may go back to my office later."

Steele began to pour another drink just as Barnaby appeared at the door. "Miss Sinclair would like to see you, Mr. Steele," he said.

"Is she still upstairs?"

"No, sir, she's in the kitchen talking with Mrs Wallace. I believe they are discussing Mr. Conrad's dietary needs when he returns from the hospital."

He held up his right hand, index finger extended, to Barnaby and picked up the telephone receiver with his left hand. "Hank, I'll call you back later, we can compare notes again then."

"Sounds good to me," Hank said.

Steele hung up the telephone and picked up his glass. "Barnaby, tell Miss Sinclair I'll just finish my drink and be along directly."

"Very good, sir." Barnaby said and left the room.

Steele downed the contents of the glass in one gulp. He sat there on the bar stool for a few moments trying to figure out what he should do next.

I have a vague idea that I already knew what I needed to know to solve this case, but it's stuck in this thick head of mine and I can't get to it yet.

He sat there longer than he had intended, because the next thing he knew a very loud voice was calling his name.

"Mark... Mark—are you okay?"

"Yeah... I was just lost in thought. Guess I blocked everything else out."

"Barnaby said you'd come right away... so when you didn't, I came looking for you."

"I'm okay. Barnaby told me that you and Susan were discussing dinner menus. You expecting guests?"

"No... nothing like that... I just told Susan what the Doctor had told me about Father's meals... she's going to make up a large pot of chicken vegetable soup for when he gets home. Susan made you a sandwich and a fresh pot of coffee; shall I have Barnaby bring it?"

"No, I'm not hungry now. Thank Susan for me and have her save it for me—for tomorrow.

"This case is bothering me. There's a bunch of small details I can't quite figure out by myself. I'm going to head over to Hank's office and see if he can help wrap this whole thing up tonight. You want to come along?"

"I'd love to, Mark, but I told Father I would come back and stay with him tonight. I've already had Barnaby call for a taxi."

"You're right. You should go and be with your father."

She smiled, and wrapped her arms around him, laying her head against his shoulder. She gave him a kiss on his neck and put her lips right next to his ear and whispered, "Thank you for finding my father." She moved her lips to his and they kissed passionately.

"Okay," he said as he turned away to leave. "I'll see you tomorrow then." He headed for the door, and then turned back, "Should I pick you up in the morning at the hospital?"

"No, there are a few errands I need to run. I'll call you after I'm done."

"Okay, but you may have to track me down. I'll either be at Hank's office, my office, or possibly at the Rivers."

"Mark," she pulled him to her and kissed him lightly on the lips. "Thank you."

He stood at attention and gave her his best Marine salute. "My pleasure, Miss."

She laughed and opened the door for him. "My... my taxi's here and I'm not ready. Why don't you take this one and I'll have Barnaby call another."

He saluted her again and said, "As you wish, Miss," and headed off down the steps to the cab waiting by the curb

CHAPTER 30

Poppy awoke to voices, loud voices, coming from the other hospital room. She recognized her father's voice and that of Dr. Gilbert, his regular doctor.

"I don't give a damn, Steven, I want him moved here."

"I'm telling you we can't do that. It would be against hospital policy."

"And what policy might that be, doctor?"

"Roger, you know as well as I do. Your chauffeur's a Negro. We don't treat Negros at this hospital. They're all referred to DeBois Hospital."

"The hell with the policy."

"I can't just ignore it because you say so, Roger."

"So if that's the case, I suggest that you get John Grant down here to talk with me."

"I don't know if I can, the director's a very busy man."

"I don't care how busy he might be. You tell him that Roger Conrad wants to talk with him and he'd better get un-busy really quick and get his scrawny ass over here and talk with me."

Dr. Gilbert eyebrows shot up and his jaw dropped at the words *scrawny ass* but he only said, "I won't promise anything, but I'll see what I can do," as he hung Roger's chart on the foot of the bed.

Poppy had listened through the partly open door between the rooms as her father had argued with the doctor. After the doctor left, she put on her bathrobe and went to talk to her father.

"What in the world was all that yelling about?" Poppy said.

"No, nothing. Dr. Gilbert's being obstinate."

"Sounded to me like he has a good reason. You can't just go around twisting the rules to fit your needs, Daddy."

"It's a stupid rule, that's all. Just a stupid rule."

"What rule's a stupid rule?" a booming voice came from the doorway.

"Hi John... so glad you could come down to see me."

"Roger, what was so urgent that you found it necessary to be rude to one of my doctors?"

"It seems that your fine hospital will not allow me to share a room with my chauffeur, Alton Johnson. He's at DeBois Hospital being treated for gunshot wounds and I would like to have him moved here, to this room. But, I'm told that it's against hospital policy."

"That's absolutely correct," John said as he picked up Roger's chart and began thumbing through the pages.

"Then fix it."

"What do you expect me to do about it?"

"Simple enough, you change the policy," Roger said through clenched teeth.

"That would take a vote of the board of directors. I can put it on the agenda for the next meeting if you like."

"Look, John, you know that by the time the board meets and takes a vote, Alton will be healed and back at work."

"What do you expect me to do then?"

Roger got quiet for a moment, laying his head down on the pillow. "Let me put it in a way that the board of directors will understand immediately." He raised up and took a sip of water from the glass on the bed tray, "My company donates a considerable amount of money to this hospital. As I recall, last year, it was in the neighborhood of $50,000.00. Perhaps one of the other hospitals in Boston could find a good place to spend that money... perhaps I should put in a call to Baptist, St. Mary's, or Boston City Hospital and see what their policies say about this matter."

"You feel that strongly about this, Roger?"

"Yes, I do. You and I both know it's a stupid rule. A holdover from the dark ages."

"Okay, Roger, I'll see what I can do," John said as he left the room.

"You bullied him pretty good, Father. They may just kick you out of here."

"No, they won't, they like my money too much. And if they do, I'm sure DeBois Hospital can use the money."

"Do you really think they'll move Alton in here?"

"Yes, I do. I expect he'll be here before lunch time."

"Okay, Daddy, now that that's been settled would you mind if I leave? There's a friend I need to see."

"Mr. Steele?"

"No, Daddy, not Mr. Steele, I have other friends."

#

The cab driver glanced in the rear-view mirror, "This the place, Miss?"

"Yes, the Rivers Tavern—this is it."

A neon sign promoting Rheingold beer glowed in the tavern's window.

The cab pulled to the curb and the driver looked back over the seat. "Should I wait for you, Miss?"

"Just drop me off. I'm meeting a friend. They'll take me back to town." She looked at the meter. It read $1.03. She handed the driver two dollars.

"You can keep the change," she said as she opened the door.

Poppy entered the bar. Her eyes hadn't fully adjusted to the dim light, but even so, she could tell she wasn't there. "Damnez le!" she muttered in French. *She's not here.* She glanced about the room again. *I should have gone to the office,* she chided herself, but *I was sure she would be here for lunch. I should wait. Perhaps she's in the lady's room,* she rationalized. She removed her coat and moved toward the bar. *I'll ask the barkeep, perhaps he'll know where Lois has lunch.*

She had taken only a few steps when she heard a familiar voice sing out from behind her.

"Miss Sinclair... that you?"

Poppy turned to see Lois seated in one of the booths lining the front wall. "Yes, it's me."

"Please, come sit with me," Lois beckoned with her hand.

Poppy hung her coat on the brass hook at the end of the booth and slid into the seat opposite Lois. She removed her hat and gloves and placed them on top of her purse on the cushion beside her.

"So, Miss Sinclair," Lois began.

"Please, Lois. Call me Poppy."

"Okay, Poppy. What did you say a moment ago? I know it was foreign, and I understand a little Spanish, but I can't tell Italian from French."

"Oh my... you heard that." she raised an eyebrow, then smiled at Lois. "I always curse in French. Less embarrassing that way."

"Interesting. And what was it you said in French?"

"*Damnez le!* It translates as *damn it* in English."

"Very good, I'll have to remember that... Damnez le... is that it?"

"Perfect pronunciation... spoken like a true French woman." She smiled. "Have you been to France?"

"No, I'm afraid not. Born and raised in Kansas City and damn lucky I can speak English without a southern drawl," she laughed. "As I said, I understand a little Spanish, actually very little, and wish I understood more and could speak it as well."

"I learned at Sister Mary's school for young women in Geneva," Poppy smiled. "But I would have preferred to just speak English and have stayed at home with my parents and my brother."

"I'll trade you my brother for boarding school any day of the week," Lois laughed.

"You don't get along with your brother?"

"Yes, I have two brothers; one older, and one younger. I suppose I get along with them better than most sisters get along with her brothers. How about you?"

"I hardly know my brother at all. We attended different types of schools, he to a boys' school and I went to a girls school; and afterwards we moved in different social circles. We do live in the same house now, but it's a large house, and we rarely cross paths."

"I'm sorry to hear that."

"C'est la vie... as wise old Frenchwomen are often heard to say, 'that's life'."

They both smiled.

"I'm a little surprised to see you here, of all places. I imaged you in higher class establishments," Lois said, raising an eyebrow. "I suspect, you're looking for Mr. Steele?"

"Yes. I wanted to talk with him. I went to the office, but nobody was there. The custodian told me that Mark... umm, Mr. Steele, might be here."

"You just missed him. Five minutes before you came in, he got a call on the pay phone and rushed out."

"About my father?"

"I don't know," Lois said as she put her glass to her lips, "he didn't say."

Poppy sank back into the seat cushion and leaned her head back against the wooden booth. "Ah, shit," she huffed.

"That doesn't sound very French to me," Lois laughed.

Poppy sat up and rested her arms on the table. "At times one's choice of words needs to be more explicit, more to the point and damn the embarrassment," she grinned, "the French word for *shit* is *merde*. It just doesn't convey the proper emotion. Don't you agree?"

"Yes, I see what you mean," Lois said with a smile, and they both began to laugh.

Poppy's expression changed quickly, from joyful to somber as she slumped back into the cushion. "I'd hoped to talk to him." She sat up straight again, looking squarely at Lois. "You're sure he didn't say what the call was about?"

"No, he didn't say anything, he just left." Lois pointed to the half-full glass on the table. "Didn't even finish his beer." Lois quickly changed the subject. "You haven't been here before, have you?"

"No, I haven't." Poppy glanced around the room noting two men and a woman seated at the left end of the bar engaged in an animated conversation. The bartender, behind the bar at the other end, was busily filling several small bowls with peanuts from a large can. "My first time... but it seems like a nice place."

"It's a neighborhood spot. Mostly nice people, but it can get a bit raucous and loud on Friday night," she snickered. "Pay-day for the river people. They tend to get a bit rowdy after a few too many beers." She took a sip from her glass. "But the owners a former policeman, and he keeps things pretty much under control."

"I see," Poppy looked around the room again. "Seems well-kept, neat—but looks as if it's been here for a while."

"Revolutionary war," Lois said.

"You don't say?"

"So I've been told," Lois said with a smile.

Poppy looked down at the rough, uneven floorboards and up to the hand-hewn beams overhead. "It's marvelous. And to think it's been here all that time."

"We like it."

"They serve anything here besides Rheingold beer?" She gestured toward the sign in the window. "What are you having?"

Lois held up her glass. "Gin 'n tonic."

"That sounds perfect," Poppy said, sinking back against the red leather banquet cushion. "I don't see a waiter. Do I go to the bar?"

Lois arched her eyebrow, unsure whether Poppy's comment was patronizing or a sincere question. "He'll come to the table," she finally acknowledged, giving Poppy the benefit of the doubt.

The man behind the bar was still busy with his peanut bowls, but he looked up in time to see Lois' hand. She held up her glass and two fingers. He nodded.

"The man behind the bar—is he the proprietor?"

"Yes. That's Jasper Culpepper. Like I said, he was a policeman until get got injured and retired. Most everyone here calls him Culp."

Poppy nodded.

Culp arrived at the table carrying a tray with two glasses.

"Mr. Culpepper, this is Miss Penelope Sinclair, Mr. Steele's new client."

Culp sat one of the glasses on a napkin in front of Poppy and offered his hand to her, "Miss Sinclair, a pleasure to meet you."

Poppy looked up, grasping his hand and flashing him a dazzling smile, "Please, everyone calls me Poppy."

He gave her hand a gentle shake. "Okay, Poppy it'll be. You can call me Culp, everybody does." he said with a broad grin, "And welcome to the Rivers Tavern. Any friend of Steele's will always be welcome here."

"Thank you. Lois tells me this place dates from before the Revolutionary war."

"Sure does," he grinned. "No way to prove it but legend has it that Paul Revere, Ben Franklin, and Thomas Jefferson all stopped here many times on their trips to and from New York and Philadelphia."

"Is that so?"

"That's what I've been told," he smiled.

She glanced around the room. "The place has a friendly atmosphere."

"Yeah, we try to keep it clean and the riffraff out." Culp laughed as he picked up the tray. "You ladies need anything else, just give me a shout."

"He seems quite nice," Poppy said as she took a sip from the glass. "Was he on the police force with Mr. Steele?"

"No, he was with the Boston department. Mr. Steele was with the New York police."

"I see," she said, taking a sip from the drink. She drummed her fingers impatiently on the table. "When do you think Mar... umm, Mr. Steele, will return?"

"I have no idea. Probably downtown to see one of his bums."

"Bums?" Poppy smiled in trying to disguise her annoyance that Lois seemed to know more than she was letting on.

"Yes. Umm... Mr. Steele knows several rather unsavory characters who keep their ears open for him."

"Did he say whether or not it concerned my father?"

"Like I said before," Lois gave Poppy a stern look, "I have no idea."

"What was it you wished to talk to him about?"

"It's umm, ah... it can wait," Poppy fiddled with her glass.

"Shall I tell him you're looking for him then?"

Ignoring Lois' attempts to deflect her questions, Poppy said, "He didn't say who called, or what it's about?"

A frosty look flashed in Lois' eyes. She was getting a little chafed at Poppy's persistence on this subject. She sipped her drink, calming her irritation, and continued, "No, he just left," Lois' voice took on a sharper edge. "He doesn't always tell me where he's going or what he's doing, and, I'm not his mother, so I generally don't ask."

"But you know him better than anyone else, don't you?"

"Yes, I suppose I do," Lois said. "Except for Lieutenant Williamson, I guess I know him better that anyone else in Boston."

"He doesn't seem interested in anything but this case."

"Yes, he's like that. Like a hound dog on a scent when he's working a case."

"Does he...?" Poppy's voice trailed off.

"Does he... what?

"It's nothing." She took a long swallow from her glass. "Really, Lois, it's nothing." She emptied the glass. "In all likelihood, I shouldn't be talking to you about it anyway."

"What's on your mind, Poppy?" Before Poppy could answer, Lois set her glass down sharply and continued, "Look, Miss Sinclair—umm, Poppy. During the war years I was a foreman at Boeing, building heavy-bombers. I had to deal with all sorts of problems from both men and women. If you need to talk it over with me, there ain't nothing these eyes haven't seen, or these ears haven't heard." She leaned into the table and lowered her voice a bit. "Do you know, during a lunch break one day. I found a couple making love in the tail section of a brand new B-24? They might not have gotten caught," she snickered a bit, "but the tail of that airplane was bouncing around so much, you could see it clear across the flight-line. As it turned out, it was one of the co-pilots and Alice a girl on my riveting crew."

"And what happened to them?"

Alice was a very good worker, but I didn't really have any choice—I had to let her go. I heard later that she got a job in a shipyard. As for the co-pilot, I believe the Army put him in the brig for a month and then shipped him out to the Pacific. New Guinea, I believe."

"Too bad," Poppy sighed.

Poppy slid the empty glass to the end of the table. "I need another drink." She waved to Culp, pointed to her empty glass. He nodded. Poppy sat up stiffly and looked straight at Lois, "I was just wondering... about Mark, Mr. Steele... does he have any kind of lady friend?"

"You mean romantically?" Lois' eyes widened in surprise and she shook her head. "I really have no idea. He does date now and then, but nothing serious." She emptied her glass. "He doesn't usually keep that sort of thing a very big secret, but he hasn't spoken of anyone lately. No, I don't believe he's serious about anyone right now."

Culp came to the table carrying a tray with two drinks.

Poppy didn't say anything as she took the glass from Culp and emptied a third of it in one gulp. She looked up at Culp and smiled. "Thanks."

He nodded but said nothing. Her eyes followed him a second as he headed back to the bar. She looked back to Lois. "He and you aren't? Umm, are you?"

Lois laughed. "Culpepper?"

"No, no. I mean umm..."

"Mr. Steele and me? Heavens no!" Lois blushed, "He's just my boss, nothing else." She sat up ramrod straight, "And besides, he's young enough to be my son."

"Sorry... I just thought," Poppy smiled, "It's just... You seem to take such very good care of him."

"More like a mother looking after a rambunctious child," Lois laughed, "he can be completely disordered, unpredictable, and befuddling at times."

"But, you do seem quite close."

"Yes, I suppose we are. But romance?" her rosy-cheek quickly deepened to near crimson. "No, nothing like that." The tint of her cheeks lightened and she smiled. "Although he's very handsome and he does remind me of my late husband, Henry."

"Late husband? Sorry, I didn't know."

Lois gazed at her with a blank look for a moment, and then reached for a pack of Chesterfield's on the table. She shook one from the opening and held the pack out to Poppy, "Would you like one?

"No, thank you. I tried smoking once when I was twelve, in the girl's bathroom at Sister Mary's." Poppy snickered. "I couldn't stop coughing for two hours. I decided then that I didn't like cigarettes."

Lois pulled one from the pack. "You have to want to smoke, usually because a parent or friend does. In the beginning, it takes a little perseverance to keep at it." She put the cigarette in her mouth and then withdrew it. "Do you mind if I..."

"Not at all," Poppy smiled at her.

"It started during the war while building those bombers at Boeing." She lit a match and put it to the end of the cigarette. A billowing cloud erupted around her face. She waved her hand to disperse the smoke. "I really should quit." She took several short rapid puffs and tears began to form in her eyes. She stubbed out the cigarette and quickly opened her purse pulling out a white lace trimmed handkerchief.

"Damn it!" She looked at Poppy. "Or as you say damnez le..." With tears in her eyes she still managed a slight smile. "I thought I'd stopped blubbering about this long ago."

"I'm sorry, I shouldn't have assumed..."

"No, no. It's nothing to do with you or Mr. Steele. It's just that when I think of Henry, I, umm..."

Poppy said nothing. She reached out and laid her hand on top of Lois'.

Lois blotted her cheek with the handkerchief. "It's okay, dear. It was a long time ago. Henry was a fighter pilot. He died in the war."

"I've embarrassed you. I'm terribly sorry, but Steele's gotten me, as you say, befuddled, too."

"Are you confused about the case? I'm afraid I don't know much more than you. Possibly less since you've been with him most of the time."

"No, not about the case. About him."

"What about him?"

"Lois. Look, at me... I'm attractive, wealthy, and I've dated men all over Europe, but I've never been ignored by a man like the way he ignores me. He's courteous, polite, and civil to me and always behaves like a gentleman." She closed her eyes. Her brow knitted into a frown. She opened her eyes again and looked squarely at Lois. "Lois, I don't expect him to grovel at my feet, but he treats me like I'm his baby sister, not a woman he could be interested in romantically. I can't, for the life of me figure out why I'm not getting anywhere with him."

"I'm sure I don't know either," Lois sipped her drink, "I do know that he has certain rules about clients."

"Yes, he told me about that, and I like that about him, the fact, that he has this code that he follows," she grinned, "But still he acts like I don't exist. Not as a woman, anyway."

"That's just his way of coping with the situation he finds himself in. I would be very much surprised if he weren't attracted to you."

Poppy's eyes opened wide and her chin dropped. "I find that hard to believe. Everything he's done has been to push me away."

"I suspect he uses that as a way to manage his feelings. Mr. Steele's one of the most honorable men I've ever known. He doesn't break the rules. Not even a rule he, himself, has made."

"So, can I assume from what you've said that I should look elsewhere for romance?"

"Look, my dear," she grasped Poppy's forearm, "I understand completely how you feel. You're young and beautiful, and men don't ever say 'No' to you. But I can assure you Mark Steele plays by a different rulebook than the men you're used to being around. Once this case's resolved, you may find that things are much different." Lois began putting her gloves on. "I really should get back to the office," she added as she slid out of the booth.

Poppy picked up her hat. "I don't know. In the past I'm the one who had to say no, often more than once." She put the hat on her head. "I can tell you, I've never been in a situation like this before." she began pulling on her gloves. "I had thought that I knew all about men, but he's got me bewildered." She laughed.

"I'm sure you needn't worry. Mr. Steele is a very single-minded man." Lois slipped her arms into her coat and then cinched the belt around her waist, "Right now he's totally focused on one thing—solving this case. Anything else would, in his mind, be a distraction."

Poppy also got to her feet and put her coat on, "Do you really think so?"

"Remember the couple at Boeing I told you about?"

Poppy nodded.

"The story goes to illustrate what can happen when people begin messing around, mixing business with pleasure."

"I see. Not a happy ending?"

"I don't know," Lois smiled, "It also illustrates that, in time, things can work themselves out. Alice still keeps in touch with me. After the war she and Herbert—he was the co-pilot—married. They now live in Denver Colorado and have four kids. He's a flying instructor at Peterson field."

They stepped out into the afternoon, which had turned very cold. The wind swirled snow about the sidewalk. The two women pulled their collars up around their ears and began walking side by side up the street toward Steele's office building.

CHAPTER 31

Culp held a glass up to the light and scratched at a speck on the rim with his thumbnail. "Steele, you're in a bit early today." He turned and sat the glass on the shelf behind the bar and turned back to Steele. "If you're looking for Lois, she and a good-looking broad left about an hour ago."

"Just give me a beer, Culp. Lois didn't say she had company. One of her old friends from Boeing must have come to town for a visit."

Steele retrieved a paper from his pocket, unfolded it and spread it out on the bar. He began studying it.

"What'ya got there?" Culp said as he put the glass of beer down on the bar.

"Nothing special, just a list of people who've been involved in this kidnapping case I'm working on."

Steele took a sip from the glass and smoothed the paper out with his hand again. "The right column's a list of my major suspects, the left column lists other names that have come up during the investigation, but haven't, as yet, aroused any great suspicions."

"Anyone special at the top of the list?" Culp asked as he studied the lists while still polishing a glass.

Steele pointed to the fifth name on the list. "Yeah, so far everything points to this guy, Arnold Becker." Steele sipped his beer as he studied the list. He tapped his finger several times over the name on the paper. "Everything except a motive, that is."

"How's he connected to the case?"

"He's the production manager at the company."

"Not much of a motive there," Culp said as he picked up another glass.

"None that makes any sense to me. He's paid better than most at the company. He treats his secretary like shit, but that only makes him an asshole, it doesn't make him guilty of kidnapping."

Culp held up his hand to stop Steele. "Back in a minute, Steele," he said as he began walking to the other end of the bar. He drew two glasses of beer for two men seated there then returned to where Steele sat and picked up his bar rag and began polishing another glass.

"Wait... did you say Lois was in earlier?

"Yeah, right after the lunch crowd cleared out. She sat in the booth by the door."

Steele's forehead wrinkled. "You also said there was another woman with her?"

"Yeah, she came in about fifteen minutes after Lois."

"What did this woman look like?"

"A real knockout." Culp gave a wolf whistle as his hands drew an hourglass shape in the air. "Five-nine, 135, with red hair. Ooh la la, my friend." He winked at Steele. "A real upper-class dresser too. She wore a mink coat. Lois introduced her as *Poppy*—don't recall the last name."

Steele turned to glance at the door. "Wonder why she would be meeting Lois here?"

Culp stepped back and flipped the jukebox switch on the wall. Hank William's voice filled the room.

♫♪ *Ol' lonesome me...* ♪♫

"So, you know her?" Culp said as he filled a glass with beer.

"Poppy? Umm, yeah sure. She's my client, Penelope Sinclair."

Steele glanced first at Culp, then at the jukebox and finally to the front door. Hank walked through the door.

Hank set down next to Steele and frowned at Culp. "Do you mind, Culpepper? It's been a long day."

Culp set the full glass of beer he had just poured in front of Hank and turned to switch off the jukebox. Hank nodded his thanks, put the glass to his lips, and downed nearly a third of its contents.

"That's better," Hank snorted as he set the glass on the bar.

"Has that extradition order come through yet?" Steele asked.

"It's being taken care of as we speak. Sent two of my men up to Salem to retrieve our guests. They'll be back late tonight."

"You think either one of them knows who's behind this?"

"I'm sure Fingers will talk when we lean on him a bit," Hank said as he drank from his glass.

Steele spread the paper with the names out on the bar again. "I've been going over this list of names," Steele said as he pushed it in Hank's direction. "Almost anyone on the list could have done it. We know, according to Conrad, that it probably wasn't about the *Endeavor* project files. I have a feeling that it wasn't about the money either—that seems secondary to me. There's another piece that I'm missing but I don't know what it is, or even where to start looking for it."

"I don't know," Hank chuckled, "a million dollar's an awful big motivator in my book."

"That's true," Steele said as he picked up the paper again, "but if it's only about the money there would certainly have been more demands for it. We only received that one note. No follow-up, no telephone call, nothing else has happened. We have to surmise from that, that there's a lot more to this than just money. In fact, I'm almost positive that it's not about the money. There's another reason—more personal."

"You may be right, Steele, but we need more than your gut for an arrest. Where are the clues? The proof?" Hank finished his beer and pushed the empty glass toward Culp.

Culp picked the glass up and was about to walk to the tap when he stopped. "Can I see that a minute?" he motioned to the paper Steele was holding as he sat the empty glass back on the bar. "I noticed it when I looked at the list a moment ago."

"What?" Steele said as he handed the paper to Culp.

Culp studied the paper a moment, then said, "It may not be anything but it caught my eye earlier. Two names on this list are anagrams for each other."

"Anagram. What the hell is an anagram?" Hank huffed.

"An anagram, my uninformed friend, involves the rearranging of the letters of one word to form a different word. I've been able to catch things like this since I was a kid." He laid the paper down in front of Steele and Hank. "See this name here *Arnold Becker*, the guy you said was your prime suspect." Culp took a pencil from his shirt pocket and printed the name at the bottom of the paper. "If you re-arranged the letters they also spell out *Clarke Broaden*." He printed the other name below the first, "See watch this." He began to draw lines connecting the individual letters together.

Hank and Steele looked at each other, their jaws dropping.

Steele snatched the paper from Culp and waved it at Hank. "God damn!" he yelled. "That's the motive I been looking for. Broaden's trying to get revenge on Conrad for cheating his father. That's God damn perfect!"

"Steele, we got to have a talk with Becker or Broaden or whatever his name *is* as soon as we can," Hank said.

"We need to find Poppy, too," Steele said. "Culp told me she was here with Lois just after lunch today. Lois may know where she went. Let's go to my office; I'll find out about Poppy and you can call in the APB on Becker from there."

#

"Lois," Steele called out as soon as he opened the office door and saw that she wasn't at her desk.

"Yes, Mr. Steele. I'm here," she said as she came through the supply room door carrying a ream of typing paper.

"You met with Poppy today at the Rivers. Do you know where she was going?"

"I called her a cab. I believe she was going home. What's wrong? What happened?"

"No, nothing's wrong. I just need to find her. We may have discovered who was behind the kidnapping of her father." He looked back to Hank. "You can use the telephone in my office," he said as he turned his attention back to Lois, "Lois, please call the Conrad house and see if she's there."

Lois dialed the telephone. "Yes, Lois Lane calling from Mr. Steele's office. Mr. Steele would like to speak to Miss Sinclair, please." She paused. A frown came over her face. "She's not? Do you know where Mr. Steele can reach her?" She listened for a moment, and said, "I see. Okay, I'll inform Mr. Steele."

"What did they say, Lois? She's not there?"

"No, Mr. Steele. The butler, said that she left the house early this morning and has not returned. She didn't say where she was going."

"Which cab company did you call?'

"Boston Unified."

"Call them and see if they know where the cab took her." He started toward his office door. "I'll be in my office with Hank."

"The APB went out on Becker a few minutes ago," Hank said as he replaced the receiver on the telephone and leaned back in Steele's chair. "The man I had tailing Becker lost him in traffic early this morning after he left his house. He didn't go to his office; he'd been headed in this direction, towards Cambridge," Hank said as he lit a cigarette, sending a long succession of smoke rings jetting toward the ceiling.

"Any news on the whereabouts of Lawrence and Beverly?"

"We may get to talk to them in the morning."

"Good." Steele said as he began to stuff tobacco into the bowl of his pipe. "But, I'm worried about Poppy."

"What's got you worried, Steele? She's not falling for your manly charms and you're upset about it?" Hank puffed on his cigarette, blowing smoke rings into the air.

"No, nothing like that—she's my client. You know I don't chase after my clients." He struck a match with his thumbnail and put the ensuing flame to the bowl of the pipe. "It's not like her to just disappear without letting anybody know where she'd be." He got to his feet and began to pace back and forth in front of the desk. "Lois put her in a cab just after one and nobody has seen her since."

"Maybe she went shopping. She's probably trying on a new pair of shoes, or a dress, as we speak."

"I don't think so. I've been with her too much lately to believe she would go shopping. Not now."

"Do you think it's serious enough to call the cab company?"

Steele sat down in the guest chair leaned over and cupped his forehead in his hand for a moment and then sat up. "Yes, it is serious. I know we suspect Becker but we really don't know who's behind this whole mess. They could be after her now to use as leverage against Conrad."

"Okay, which cab company?"

"Lois said it was Boston Unified. She's calling them."

Steele had no more than gotten the words out of his mouth when Lois came into the office.

"Mr. Steele, I called Boston Unified but they won't give out any information," she said.

Hank sat up straight, snuffed the butt of his cigarette in the ashtray, and grabbed the telephone. "We'll just see about that." He looked at Lois. "What's their number?"

"JEfferson 43000."

Hank dialed the telephone and waited for the connection, looking back and forth between Steele and Lois. "These guys don't know who they're dealin' with." His expression changed as a voice on the line spoke. "Yeah, Lieutenant Williamson, Boston Police Department here, let me speak to Gilbert." Hank turned to Steele. "Tom's a pal of mine—he's an ex-cop too. He started the cab company after he retired. He'll get us what we need.

"Hey Gil, this is Williamson from the station house."

"What you been doing, Hank? Ain't heard from you in ages. You about ready to retire? I could use another good driver."

"No, not ready to retire any time soon. You know how crazy this job gets—you get a hot case, you get focused on that and you lose touch."

"Suppose that's why you called. You workin' on somethin' hot, ain't ya?"

"Yeah. I'm working on a hot lead and I could use your help."

"What ya need?"

"One of your cabs picked up a good lookin' lady at 545 Memorial Drive, Cambridge just after lunch today, maybe one o'clock. I need to know where the lady went."

"That area of Cambridge, it was probably Nolan,"

"This Nolan guy got a first name?"

"Yeah, Jack Nolan."

"Can you get in touch with him on the radio?"

"Sure, just take a minute."

Hank looked at Lois. "Lois, you got any coffee?"

"Sure, Lieutenant. I'll get you a cup right away." She turned to Steele. "How about you?"

"No, not now, maybe later."

"I got Nolan on the two-way radio, Hank. He says he did pick up a good-looking woman at that address."

"Where did he take her?"

"He didn't take her anywhere."

"How's that possible," Hank snorted.

"Hank, maybe you should talk to him yourself."

"He's on his way back to the garage, he just went off duty."

"Good, keep him there. Don't let him leave. I'll be there in fifteen minutes."

Hank hung up the telephone and looked at Steele, "The cab didn't take her anywhere."

Steele shot to his feet and leaned over the desk. "But he did pick her up?"

"Yeah, he did, but..." Hank didn't finish as he got to his feet. "Somethin' feels fishy here, Steele. We need to go to the taxi garage and talk with the cabbie."

Lois came into the office. "Here's your coffee, Lieutenant," she announced as she held the cup out to him.

"Thanks, sweetie, but no time for that now," Hank grumbled as he moved past her.

"What has happened, Mr. Steele?"

"Got to go now, Lois—Poppy may be in trouble!" He put on his hat and followed closely behind Hank as he left the office. "I'll call you when I find out what has happened," Steele called back over his shoulder as he went through the door.

## CHAPTER 32

Boston Unified Taxi Service is located about half a mile from the police station and six and a half miles from Steele's office in Cambridge. Hank switched on the lights and siren and nine and a half minutes later they pulled into the entrance of the taxi garage on North Street.

Hank and Steel rushed to the door marked 'Office'. The room was small and occupied by three people.

Hank burst through the door and called out, "Hey, Gil, that guy Nolan show up yet?"

A man sitting at a desk near the far wall stood up and shouted back at Hank, "Jesus, Hank, not even a polite hello?"

"Sorry Gil, I don't have time for nice."

The lone woman in the office spoke up. "Nolan's a few blocks away."

"Who are you?" Hank shot her a glare.

"Josephine... Josephine Harvey. I'm the dispatcher and I just talked to Jack a minute ago, he's just a few blocks away."

"What the hell's going on, Hank?" Gilbert said.

"We may have a kidnap situation."

"The woman—Nolan's fare?"

"Yeah."

"You don't think he did it, do you?"

"No, but you told me over the telephone that he picked her up but didn't take her anywhere. To get the whole story I need to talk with him."

"That's him there, Lieutenant," Josephine said as she pointed through the office window to a cab that had just come through the garage door.

Hank looked at Gilbert. "I'll give you a call later and fill you in Gil but right now I can't take the time."

"Sure, Hank, I under—" Hank didn't hear the rest as he was already out the door on a dead run, a dozen feet behind Steele. Steele had already yanked the cab door open when Hank caught up with him.

"You Nolan?" Steele barked at the driver as he got out of the cab.

"Yeah, I'm Nolan. What's all the excitement about?"

"You picked up a fare on Memorial Drive a little past noon. She was a very attractive woman; you should remember her," Steele shouted.

He looked at Steele and then over to Hank, who was now holding up his badge. "Yeah, I remember her. A real looker."

"Where did you take her?' Steele said in a calmer voice.

"I didn't take her anywhere." Nolan took off his cap and ran his fingers through his hair. "She got in the cab and told me to take her to 66 Beacon Street. As soon as I started to pull away from the curb a man opened the cab door and took her out."

"And you didn't think that anything was wrong? You didn't think that you should have called the police?" Hank snarled at him.

"No, not really. The woman seemed to know the guy."

"Did you hear his name?" Steele said.

"Yeah," he said as he put his hat back on, "I believe she called him Mr. Becker."

"What exactly did she say," Steele said.

"Let me see," he leaned back against the cab and scratched his chin. "She said, 'What are you doing here, Mr. Becker?'"

"Is that all?" Steele said.

"Did he say anything?" Hank said.

"No, she just gave me a dollar bill and waved me off."

"Did she look like she was in any danger?" Steele said.

"I don't think so. She got into a car with him and they drove off."

"Did she get into the car by herself, or was she forced to get in?"

"By herself. I didn't see anybody force her to do nuthin'."

"What kind of car?" Hank said.

"A Olds... a new Oldsmobile; two tone—tan color with a green top."

"I don't suppose you know where they went, in what direction they drove off?"

"Yeah, sure I do. Like I said I didn't think she was in any danger, until the car passed me and she looked at me through the window. She didn't look at all happy—she looked scared."

He removed his rumpled and well-worn pork-pie hat. The hat had a half-dozen badges and colorful pins fastened to it; including a Purple Heart and an *I Like Ike* pin from the last presidential campaign.

He ran his fingers through his hair and replaced the hat. "I had a strange feeling about her—so I followed the car."

"Do you often follow lost fares? You aren't a pervert are you?" Hank said.

"No, never... it's just the way she looked at me. Like I said, she looked scared."

"Okay, where'd they go?" Steele said.

"I followed them to a small warehouse on Union Wharf."

"Did she go inside willingly?"

"I guess so... didn't seem like the man was forcing her to do nuthin'. They talked calmly to each other, he didn't even touch her. She didn't yell or fight or show any kind of resistance to the guy." Nolan took out a handkerchief and mopped his brow and the back of his neck. "You know, I do remember; the guy had his hand in his coat pocket, and he held it kinda' funny—he coulda' had a gun." He looked at Hank, a sober look on his face.

"Although, the lady didn't seem at all frightened as they went into the warehouse."

"Do you know the exact address of the warehouse?" Hank said.

"Not exactly. It was way out near the end of the Wharf." He stuffed the handkerchief back into his pocket. "But I could take you there easy enough."

"Good, come with us," Hank said as he took hold of Nolan's arm and pointed him at the squad car.

Hank squealed the tires and turned on the lights and siren as he exited the garage parking lot. Traffic was light and he made good time, only occasionally having to weave in and out of traffic. He turned the siren off as he crossed Commercial Street and the lights went off as he entered Union Wharf. The Wharf was busy, with trucks of all sizes and descriptions parked on both sides of the street.

The building that Nolan pointed out was unique; it was free-standing with an alleyway running down both sides.

Hank drove the squad car slowly past the building without drawing attention. Steele examined the building intently as Hank parked the car between two delivery trucks a hundred yards beyond the building.

Hank turned in his seat and looked at Nolan. "You stay in the car and keep your head down."

"You don't need to worry about me, Lieutenant. I ain't the hero type—I ain't even a little bit curious."

"That's good. Just stay put and don't *get* curious," Hank repeated as he removed the radio microphone from its hook on the dashboard.

"402 to dispatch."

"402 respond."

"402 requesting assistance, 10-59 code 2 Bravo at Union Wharf."

"Dispatch—Calling all cars, vicinity Union Wharf, 10-59 code 2 Bravo."

"402 to dispatch—Plainclothes officer on scene. Be advised, suspect may be armed and holding a hostage."

"Dispatch—Car 101 and 305 in route, your location. Will advise—suspect armed with hostage."

"402 to Dispatch 10-4.

Hank put the microphone back on its hook and turned to Steele. "You armed?"

Steele pulled his gun from its holster, thumbed the safety off, and drew back the slide to check the chambered shell. "Yeah."

"I shouldn't do this, Steele; but it might be a good idea if we both go in. Miss Sinclair may not have enough time for us to wait for those two squad cars to get here."

"I couldn't agree more—I'm glad you see it that way. And, just so you know—if anyone asks, you told me to stay in the car with Nolan and I followed you in on my own." He looked back over the seat at Nolan. "Ain't that right, Mr. Nolan, isn't that what the lieutenant said to me?"

"Sure, I heard him say that. Clear as bell I heard it," he grinned and ducked down in the seat. "Whatever you guys say—but I'm staying here."

"Good," Hank said. "Keep your head down."

"Hank, I could see an open door in the back through the big loading door in front as we drove by. You take the front and I'll work my way down the alley and around to the back door. Come up from behind."

"Sounds like a good idea. How long you think it will take you to get to the back door?"

"Give me three minutes, then come through the front door. Keep out of sight, but make a lots of noise, announce yourself, get his attention on the front of the building and I can get the drop on him from behind."

Hank gave him a questioning look.

"A tactic they taught us in the Marines."

Hank gave Steele a thumb's up. "I'm sure it's a good plan then," he said as he pulled his own gun from its holster and checked the cylinder.

Steele got out of the car and leaned back in. "Check your watch. Remember, three minutes from now," he tapped his finger on the face of his watch as he moved away from the car. Halfway across the street, he began to run toward the alleyway between the buildings.

The side of the building abutting the alleyway had no doors or windows. Parked cars and trucks lined the walls along both sides of the ally. Steele ran down the alley as quietly as he could; glancing at his wristwatch when he neared the far end.

Through the open back door he could see the warehouse was full of all kinds of wooden boxes. They made for good cover as Steele dashed through the doorway.

There was no one in sight. Steele checked his watch; it had been two minutes since he left the car. Steele moved further into the building, sidestepping from one box to the next. He heard a muffled sound off to his right. He caught sight of two large rats; one chasing the other, as they scurried away from him toward the far side of the building.

He checked his watch—forty-five seconds remained. From overhead he heard another sound. A flock of birds that had taken up residence in the rafters became agitated by a movement in front of him. They began flying about, flapping their wings noisily. He was nearly half way through the building. He checked his watch again—twenty seconds. Then he heard muffled voices not far, perhaps twelve or fifteen feet, in front of him. He recognized the voices as those of Poppy and Becker, but he could not make out what they said. He crept closer.

He knew that Hank would come through the front door any second now. He needed to take advantage of the commotion to get into a good spot, closer to Becker.

Steele heard a door slam loudly and the sound of a metal can skittering across the concrete floor as Hank began to yell loudly "Boston Police! Boston Police! The place's surrounded. Come out with your hands up!"

Steele could see a man's hat moving, visible over the top of a pile of crates. Whoever it was, he was working his way slowly in Steele's direction. Steele eased himself between two stacks of crates and peered around the corner to get a better look at the man. The man was not Becker, however he did have a gun in his hand.

Steele looked back through the space between stacks of crates; he could see Becker standing behind Poppy. She sat in a chair near a table. Becker held her down, his right hand firmly on her shoulder. Becker held a large hunting knife in his left hand near her neck. He was not threatening Poppy with the knife; his attention was focused on the front of the building. Hank was making an incredible amount of noise, enough for anyone to believe four or five men had come through the door—not just one.

Steele could see movement where Hank should have been. The man with the gun had seen the movements too; he began firing randomly in Hank's direction. Steele saw one of the slugs hit the edge of a wooden box sending splinters flying in all directions.

Hank had moved off to the right, firing two shots at the man as he moved. Neither shot hit anything, they went high, not meant to kill the man, but to make him duck so Hank could move closer in. Hank crouched down behind another crate. He was now six feet closer to Becker's position. He shot one more time, again missing the gunman. He did hit an unopened bottle of beer setting atop the box the man was hiding behind. The beer bottle exploded with a bang, filling the air over the box with a mist of beer and shards of glass. One of the shards of glass must have hit the man; he called out, "Ah shit!"

The man shifted his position, peaking around the end of the box he hid behind. Steele looked over the pile of crates he was using for cover. Hank had a clear shot at the man now and fired. The man fell down to his knees clutching his right arm. He still had the gun in his hand.

He raised the gun and pointed it at Hank, firing one shot. The man glanced back, looking for an escape route. He saw Steele and shot at him too. He missed, but the slug hit the crate inches from Steele's head. Steele ducked down. Hank fired one more time. Steele heard a moan, and the clatter of a gun hitting the concrete floor. He peered around the edge of the crate to see the man slump over, face down on the concrete floor. He had dropped the gun, it lay two feet from his lifeless hand.

Hank moved out from behind his box and scrambled to where the man lay. Hank felt the man's pulse and then picked up the man's gun and put it into his pocket.

"Okay, Becker," Hank called out, "your man's dead, and this place's surrounded. Let the woman go now and come out with your hands up or you'll be next."

There was a pile of crates between Becker and Hank, so they couldn't see each other but from Steele's position he could see both men clearly. Steele waved to Hank and let him know Becker exact location. He also signaled that he was going to get closer to Becker. Hank signaled that he understood and began to move in Becker's direction.

Steele circled to his left around another stack of crates till he could see clearly where Becker stood. There was a clear spot among the boxes and crates; a break area for whoever worked in the warehouse. There was a candy machine, a cigarette machine, and a Coke machine, along with two tables and four wooden chairs. The table where Poppy sat held take-out food containers and drink bottles. She had not been tied up.

Steele was now behind Becker. He caught a flash of Hank's blue jacket as he moved between two stacks of crates. Becker was pacing back and forth near Poppy. He looked nervous, like a man who hadn't really planned out what he intended to do next. Steele moved to another stack of crates about four feet high, and about twelve feet from where Becker was pacing.

Hank, seeing that Becker only had a knife and not a gun, stepped out from behind the stack of crates. He was still nearly twenty feet from Becker.

"Okay, Becker, put the knife down and put your hands in the air," Hank called out.

Becker grabbed Poppy and pulled her to her feet putting her between himself and Hank. His left arm, still holding the knife, wrapped around her neck. His right hand went into his jacket pocket and he pulled out an automatic pistol. He pointed the pistol at Hank.

Becker screamed, "You ain't taken me in copper." The veins on Becker's neck and temples quivered. Beads of sweat began running down his face into his eyes. He blinked. "I'll kill this bitch if you come any closer!" he cried out.

Hank could now see Steele, behind Becker and Poppy and knew that Steele had Becker covered. He put his gun in his pocket and held his hand up at shoulder height. He began walking slowly toward Becker, "Look Becker I put my gun away. Let's talk this thing through. No one else needs to get hurt here today."

"Bull shit lieutenant—as soon as I let this bitch go one of your buddies will shoot me where I stand."

"Nobody's going to shoot you Becker. We need to talk—get your side of the story," Hank said as he took a few steps closer to where he and Poppy stood.

"Nobody's interested in my story, just like nobody ever listened to my father twenty years ago."

"That's not true, Becker. The court listened to your father. The court gave him a lot of money years ago."

"A lot of money! You call fifty thousand dollars a lot of money? It's chicken feed—Conrad got millions from what my father invented. That money should have been my father's, not Conrad's."

"I'm sure that Mr. Conrad would be willing to discuss it with you if you only gave him a chance. I've talked with him and he seems like a very generous man. I'm sure if he understood your feelings he would do his best to fix it."

"He didn't say anything like that when I saw him in New Hampshire. He denied even knowing me."

He waved the gun wildly in the air. Hank saw him pull back the hammer, cocking the gun. "I should have killed the bastard when I got the chance. But I wanted him to suffer, just like he made my father suffer for years. I should have killed the bastard. I should have killed the bastard," he repeated himself, while waving his gun around wildly.

Becker tightened his grip on Poppy. He held his knife near her throat. "I should have killed that bastard," he screamed at the top of his voice. "Now I'm going to kill his bitch daughter instead—that will make the bastard suffer." He inched the knife nearer Poppy's throat and jabbed the gun barrel into her ribs.

Poppy had been relatively clam throughout the exchange between Hank and Becker. She could see Steele standing behind a stack of crates only ten feet away. She smiled at Steele and as she did so she yanked Becker's arm down and threw her head back, hitting Becker in the nose and mouth. Blood began to gush from his nose.

Steele stood up and rested his arm on the crate for support to steady his gun hand. The gun pointed directly at Becker's head. When Poppy made her move he called out as loudly as he could, "Becker!"

Startled by Steele's outcry, and reeling from Poppy's head blow Becker swung around losing his grip even more on Poppy. Poppy tugged his arm further away from her throat with her two hands. Becker was dazed and fired his gun twice wildly in Hank's direction. The shot missed Hank.

The shots caused Hank to back-step a step. He pulled his gun and, crouching, leveled it at Becker.

Becker looked at Steele and then quickly back to Hank.

"Give it up, Becker, before you get yourself killed," Hank called out in a booming voice.

Becker swung his head back again to look at Steele and then back to Hank. He waved the gun nervously and suddenly fired another shot at Hank. The shot also went wild, this time Hank stepped forward instead of backing up.

The next time Becker turned his head back in Steele's direction, Poppy pulled hard against him forcing him to loosen his grip even further. She bent her body over as far as she could—Steele fired one shot.

Becker released his grip on Poppy, his body went limp and he slumped to the floor, both the gun and knife falling free from his hands. Poppy cried out and fell to the floor herself. Steel rushed to her and picked her up, fearing Becker might have cut her with the knife as he fell. The side of her face and shoulder now covered with splattered blood—Becker's blood—but she hadn't been wounded. She threw her arms around Steele's neck. She didn't show signs of hysteria, but she quivered in fear and her legs became rubbery. Steele sat her down on the concrete floor before she fell, and went about wiping the blood splatter from her face with his handkerchief.

Hank rushed over to where Becker lay on his face. He leaned down on one knee and rolled the body over on its back to check for a pulse.

"Nice shot, my friend," Hank chuckled, "More of that Marine Corps training I suppose."

"Yeah, I was first in my platoon on the pistol range at Camp Pendleton."

"Right between the eyes. I wonder what you could do with a rifle," Hank laughed.

"I was pretty good as a kid with my old squirrel gun but not that good with those big Marine rifles. They kick like a mule—ya know?" Steele chuckled.

"Still a mighty good shot my friend."

Steele looked at Poppy and then back to Hank, who was getting to his feet, "What else could I do? He was shooting at my best friend and had a knife at my girlfriend's throat."

"Girlfriend! Did you say girlfriend?" Poppy hollered.

"Yes," he dabbed a spot of blood from the side of her nose.

"Did you mean it?"

"I said it. Of course I meant it," he laughed.

The officers Hank had called earlier came bursting into the warehouse with their guns drawn. "Police! Put your hands up," one of them hollered, which saved Steele from further questioning by Poppy.

Hank, holding his badge up for identification as he called back, "Boston Police, here! Boston Police, here! Everything's under control, boys," as he stepped between the officers and Steele and Poppy.

One of the men, a uniformed sergeant, stepped forward, "Sorry, Lieutenant, dispatch said an officer needed assistance at this address."

"That was me, I called it in Sergeant, but we handled the situation ourselves."

Hank and Steele, along with Poppy—who was still quite shaken by the ordeal—stood silently watching, as the officers went about collecting weapons and checking the bodies for identification.

"These two are dead, Lieutenant?"

"Yeah, I know. You can go call dispatch. Have them send over the paddy wagon and an ambulance. The lady," he pointed to Poppy, "was a hostage, they should check her over."

Hank gathered up two of the uniformed officers—sending them to check the rest of the warehouse for other suspects. "I don't think there are any more," he warned them, "but be careful. There could be more in hiding, and armed—I don't know about."

The two officers moved off cautiously, their guns at the ready.

Within a few minutes they heard the sound of sirens approaching the scene.

It was over.

CHAPTER 33

Two men in white uniforms came running up pushing a collapsible wheeled gurney. "Is someone injured here?" the first man said.

"Nah, but we got two dead," Hank said, 'they'll be needin' the coroner, not you boys."

"That young lady over there," Steele said as he pointed to Poppy who was setting at the table. "Can you check her out? She was held hostage, had a knife held to her throat. Make sure that she's okay."

The two men went to where she was sitting. One took her pulse while the other one wrapped a blood pleasure cuff around her as he talked with her.

Poppy waved at Steele. "Mark," she called out.

Steele went and sat down beside her. "Are you okay?"

"I feel a little woozy. Dr. Brenner here—she pointed to the man Steele had talked to—he thinks I'm suffering from shock and would like to take me back to the hospital for a complete check-up."

"That sounds like a wise idea to me. Hank and I need to finish up here, and there will be a ton of paperwork for us to fill out. I may not get to the hospital for two or three hours."

"Okay, I understand. That will be fine. But why don't you just come to the house instead? I'll visit with Father for a while." She smiled at him. "He may be ready to come home, too—we can share a taxi."

"Sounds like a fine idea."

Hank waved to Steele and called out, "Steele.""Hank needs me to talk with the Captain, I'll call you later." he said as he squeezed her and hissed her on the cheek.

Captain Beadle had arrived shortly after the ambulance pulled up.

"Captain has a few questions for you Steele." Hank said as he sat down on a chair, wiping his forehead with his handkerchief.

"You okay, Lieutenant?"

"I'm fine, Captain. Just a delayed reaction to what happened here. "

"I understand our Mr. Steele here shot one of the suspects. That correct, Lieutenant?" Beadle mopped his brow with his handkerchief.

"Yes, he did, Captain. Lucky thing for me and the woman hostage that he was a Pistol Expert in the Marines Corps.—got him with one shot."

Captain Beadle's eye bulged and he spoke through clenched teeth, "Yes, that's all well and good, Lieutenant." The blood vessels on his neck pulsated, "but, what the hell was a civilian doing here in the first place?"

"Calm down Captain, no need to get excited about this. Mr. Steele came with me. We'd followed a lead, given to us by a taxi driver by the name of Nolan, Jack Nolan—he should still be in my car. As a matter of fact, I left both of them in the car, and told them to stay put while I investigated the situation."

He turned to Steele, the vessels in his neck still throbbing, he approached Steele and with his nose and inch from Steele's he barked, "So, why hell aren't you still in the car, Mr. Steele?" as he poked Steele in the chest with his forefinger.

Steele stepped back half a step, "When we drove by, I noticed through the open front door that there was also an open back door to the building. And since the lieutenant was alone, at this point. I went around to the back to stop anyone from leaving from the back door."

Captain Beadle's face still distorted with rage turned back to Hank, "So, Lieutenant, why did you enter a suspicious place alone? Why didn't you wait for the other cars to arrive?"

"The taxi driver told me that he saw the woman being forced to enter the warehouse by our suspect. I didn't think I had time to wait, since she might be in danger; so I went in by myself to find her."

"And you?" He looked at Steele, the edge of his anger beginning to dull a bit. He lowered his voice, "Why did you enter the warehouse? You said you just wanted to keep the suspect from fleeing out the back?"

"I heard Hank calling out and thought he might be in trouble inside. So, using all these boxes as cover I came inside to see if I could help him if he needed it."

"I see," Beadle said, as he rubbed his chin, and wiped his brow again with the handkerchief. The veins in his neck no longer bulged and throbbed, his face looked nearly normal. "Is that really the way it happened, Hank?" he glanced at Steele momentarily as he spoke, "Tomorrow, when I read your report—that's what it's gonna say?"

"Yes, sir. Exactly—every word—the way Steele and I just told you it happened."

"Okay, if you say so. In any event, I want to see this fanciful work of fiction, with all the details, on my desk the first thing in the morning. That understood, Lieutenant?"

He turned to Steele. "And as for you..." he didn't finish, he just shook his head and then looked back to Hank. "Make sure that you get a full statement from the taxi driver, Lieutenant." He called out over his shoulder as he walked away. "And, Lieutenant," he turned and pointed to Steele, "make sure you get one from your accomplice there too."

## CHAPTER 34

H ank called out as he and Steele approached the car, "Nolan, you still in there?"

The crown of a rumpled pork-pie hat appeared in the rear door window followed by the brim and then Nolan's face.

"Yeah, Lineament. I told ya I wasn't going anywhere—I heard shooting. Did someone get shot?"

"Just a couple of bad guys," Hank said as he opened the driver's side door. "Nolan. I'm gonna have to take you down to the station house and get an official statement from you."

"Ah, Lieutenant, I got a living to make. I'm loos'n all kinds of money just coming over here with you."

"The dispatcher said you were off duty for the day," Steele said as he got into the passenger side seat.

"Yeah, I am off duty with B U; but I got more than one job. I also drive a limousine for the Hilton—driven' folks to and from the airport."

"Sorry, but this has to be done now. If it'll help, I can call the Hilton and tell them that you're a material witness in this case and we need to ask you a lot more questions." Hank said as he started the engine. "And, if you're quick with your answers, this shouldn't take more than an hour."

Nolan grunted but didn't answer as he slumped back into the seat.

Hank sat Nolan down at Sargent McDoodle's desk. He took a brand-new stenographers note pad from the bottom drawer of McDoodle's desk and handed it to Nolan. "I want you to write down everything that happened since you first got the call to pick the woman up on Memorial Drive." He plucked a sharp pencil from a cup full of pencils on the desk and pointed it at Nolan, "And, don't leave out any details."

Nolan took the pencil, "Everything?" he asked.

"Yes, everything—if you had an itch on your balls I want to know about it."

Hank turned to Steele and they went into his office.

"Little tough on the guy, don't ya think?" Steele said as he removed his overcoat and put it, along with his hat, on the coat-rack in the corner.

"Na," Hank said as he threw his own coat and hat across a chair and sat down at his desk. "Most of the time if you scare a witness just a little—they're more truthful."

"That hasn't been my experience—being nice to withes usually gets me better results. I agree, leaning on a suspect can produce result, but not a witnesses."

"Okay, it's not worth arguing about. You do it your way and I'll do it my way—agreed?"

"Sure Hank, just don't lean on me."

"I wouldn't think of putting pressure on you, Steele. You always tell me the truth—don't you?"

"Sure, when the situation demands it."

Hank looked at Steele, a frown on his face. And then he burst into laughter. "You're pullin' my leg ain't you Steele?"

"Sure, Hank. You got me pegged."

"Okay, then let's put the joking aside and get this report filled out." he opened a drawer on his desk and rummaged through a pile of papers till he found what he'd searched for. He handed a sheet of paper, with two carbons attached, to Steele. "Shooting report... you need to fill it out."

"This is for a Police officer involved in a shooting."

"I know that, Steele." He sat down in his chair and lit a cigarette. "But, it's all I have; we'll just have to make do. Scratch out anything that bothers you, and fill out the rest the best way you can."

Steele sat in the chair across from Hank and began to read the sheet of paper; satisfied with it, he grabbed a magazine, a *Police Gazette*, from Hanks desk, and using it as a knee desk began to write in the spaces on the paper. Hank had pulled an identical form from the drawer and began filling one out himself.

Five minutes passed before a knock on Hank's door. Hank looked up to see Nolan coming in. "This okay, Lieutenant?" he said as he handed the steno pad to Hank.

Hank took the steno pad and began to read. "Looks good, Nolan," he said as he reached for the telephone. He dialed a number and said, "McDoodle, come in here, I got a little typing job for you."

"Can I go now, Lieutenant?" Nolan said as he put his hat on his head.

"What ya got, Lieutenant." McDoodle said as he came through the open door.

"Lieutenant, I um..." Nolan said.

Ignoring Nolan, Hank addressed McDoodle, "Take Mr. Nolan, and this statement to your desk. Type this up, adding the usual stuff: Address, telephone number etc.. When you've finished, have Mr. Nolan sign it. When that's done you can have an officer take him back to the Boston Unified garage."

"Sure thing, Lieutenant," McDoodler said. He turned to Nolan, "Mr. Nolan if you'll come with me this will only take a few minutes and we can get you out of here and back to work."

McDoodle took Nolan and they left the room. Hank called after them, "McDoodle, close the door." McDoodle stuck his head in, didn't say anything, but smiled as he shut the door.

"You got that sheet filled in yet, Steele?"

"Sure, as best as I could, considering."

"You'll also need to write out a civilian statement, just like Nolan did. And I'm going to need your gun."

"What for?"

"They'll want to run a ballistic test on it."

"You already have the guns ballistics on file for my investigators license."

"I know all that, Steele. But I got word to have the gun tested again. I'm sure it's just a formality, you'll get the gun back—probably tomorrow. "

The telephone on Hank's desk rang.

"Williamson here, whose calling?" He adjusted the head-set, holding it with his shoulder as he lit a cigarette, "Mr. Conrad, you okay? You still at the hospital?"

"No, they released me this afternoon. I'm at my office."

The receiver went quiet, Conrad had covered it with his hand, but Hank could hear a muffled unrecognizable voiced just the same.

"Lieutenant, can you come to my office? I've called a few people together here for a meeting and I would like you to be here."

"Of course I can. But, what's the meeting about?" He put the cigarette in the ashtray.

"I'd rather not talk about it over the telephone. I'd also like Mr. Steele to be here, do you know where I can get in touch with him?"

"Sure, he's right here in my office, I'll ask him." He held his hand over the receiver and turned to Steele. "Got Roger Conrad on the line. He wants you and I to come to a meeting he's called at his office."

"What kind of meeting? What's it about?"

"He wouldn't say, he just wants us to come over... it shouldn't take long."

"Okay, I don't see why not. Better than filling out paperwork here."

"The paperwork got to be done in any event, Steele." He removed his hand and spoke into the receiver. "Sure, we can both be there. What time?" he glanced at Steele, "An hour... that should be okay. Steele and I have paperwork to finish up, but we can be there in an hour."

CHAPTER 35

George, the same guard that Poppy had introduced him to, greeted Hank and Steele at the reception desk in the Conrad building lobby. Steele's watch read three-fifteen when he filled in the time on the sign-in sheet.

"Good afternoon, Mr. Steele. Mr. Conrad's expecting you."

Steele glanced at the man's ID badge, "I'm surprised you remember me, George. With all the people you must have coming and going here."

"I was able to get a copy of the Newsweek article you mentioned about Stanford. Very impressive, Mr. Steele. I passed it along to Brian."

"Glad I could help." Steele said and he handed the sign-in sheet to Hank. "Mr. Conrad has asked the Lieutenant and me to attend a meeting in his office."

"Yes, he gave me a list. Your name as well as the Lieutenants is on it." George pointed to a sheet of paper on the counter, containing half a dozen names.

George picked up the paper, "All but one—a Mr. Hollis has not yet arrived. The others have gone up to Mr. Conrad's office."

"Who's Mr. Hollis?"

"I have no idea who any of them are, Mr. Steele. Mr. Conrad handed the list to me personally when he came in this afternoon. His instructions were to allow the people on the list to come up to his office."

At that point the outside door opened and a man came in.

"This may be Mr. Hollis now," George said.

"I know the way, George. Hank and I will go ahead." Steele said, not waiting to see who was at the front door. He went directly to the elevator and entered it.

"Aha, Steele," Conrad's booming voice came from across the room, "right on time."

Steele walked to Conrad and shook his hand across the desk. "What's this all about, Roger?"

"All will be revealed in good time, my boy, all in good time." he gestured to the bar with his hand. "Come make yourself a drink. We have one more guest to arrive and then we'll get started."

Steele looked around the room. Two men he did not recognize were seated in the wing-backed chairs near the sofa. The man nearest to Steele got to his feet. He was a tall slim man—over six feet—with dark brown hair that had begun to turn gray around his temples. He wore a black suit and a solid red tie. He extended his hand to Steele. "I'm Gerry Bollinger, Assistant District Attorney here in Boston."

Steele took hold of his hand. "I'm Mark Steele, private detective. My office's in Cambridge."

"Ah, you're the young man who was instrumental in Roger's rescue—I have read all the police reports. Nice job, Mr. Steele."

"Nothing special, just your basic detective work. I'm sure Hank, here," he gestured to Hank at his side, "could have done it just as easily without my help."

Conrad leaned forward, "Nonsense. My daughter has told me that Mr. Steele was a great deal of help. Isn't that correct, Lieutenant?"

Hank grunted, but didn't say anything, as his face began turning red. He went to the bar and began to pour himself a drink.

Conrad came around his desk and put a hand on Steele's shoulder. "I've recommended that the mayor give Mr. Steele a medal and special recognition for his excellent work on the case."

Steele now turn red himself, "I don't think that's really necessary, Mr. Conrad." He reached into his jacket pocket and retrieved a piece of paper, which he handed to Conrad.

"Lois, my secretary, said she received this obscenely large check from you in the mail. This wasn't necessary—Poppy has already paid me more than enough for my services."

"Balderdash, my boy." Conrad said with a laugh as he stuffed the check into Steele's breast pocket. "You keep that. It's the least I can do—besides, you're worth every penny."

The second man who had remained seated till now, stood up. He was tall, but not as tall as Bollinger. He wore a dark blue suit with a fine gray pin stripe and a more conservative blue tie. He extended his hand. "Mr. Steele I'm Herbert Taylor—Mr. Sinclair and Mr. Manners lawyer."

At that moment the office door opened and another man came in. He was an elderly man, quite short—just over five feet tall. He was also at least a hundred pounds overweight and completely bald. He wore a dark brown suit with a yellow and brown plaid vest which shone like a beacon from under his jacket.

"Prentice," Conrad called out and approached the newcomer with his hand extended. "I'm so glad you could make time to attend my little gathering."

"You're a very persuasive person, Roger. The Attorney General was quite insistent that I should come over and see what you had to say."

Roger turned around and with his arm lying across the man's shoulders announced. "Everyone let me introduce Prentice Hollis. Prentice's from the Attorney General's office in Washington. Luckily, he's in town for another matter and I convinced him to squeeze our little meeting into his schedule."

Conrad introduced the others in the room and got Prentice a drink from the bar. When everyone had taken a seat around the conference table, Conrad seated himself at one end.

"I'm going to get right to the point. The reason I've called all of you together today..." he paused and looked at each person around the table. "I want to talk about my step-son Lawrence and his friend Bernard Manners. I've spent a good deal of time with both in that last few days. Lawrence has been very honest with me about what exactly he has done with regard to the kidnapping. He freely admits that he was the one who sent the ransom note, however he's adamant that he had nothing to do with the kidnapping itself."

He took a cigar out of the polished walnut humidor on his desk. He lit the cigar. "I'm not here to make any excuses for either of them." He placed the cigar in a large crystal ashtray and leaned forward in his chair, placing his palms flat on the desk top. "Especially Lawrence!" He remained forward in his seat and picked up the cigar, puffing it for a moment. "I am, however, here to see if we can work out an amicable punishment for him that will not kill his mother."

Hollis spoke up first. "Roger, the government looks on kidnapping as a rather serious offense. I don't see why the government should show any leniency to these two on this matter."

Steele spoke up. "I'm not so sure that Lawrence had anything to do with the kidnapping."

"That's right," Hank said, "we've found no evidence, none whatsoever, that he's involved in the kidnapping. He has confessed to sending the ransom note, but he did that after Mr. Conrad had already been kidnapped."

"Like I said earlier... that's precisely what Lawrence has told me," Roger said as he puffed the cigar, "he told me that once he learned about the kidnapping he did send the ransom note, hoping to get a large sum of money, but he maintains that he had nothing to do with the kidnapping itself."

"Didn't he realize that by doing that he became an accessory after the fact?" Bollinger said.

"He's not a lawyer... and I don't believe he thought it through." Roger said. "He needed money, and I believe that was all he thought about."

"Why didn't he just ask you for the money?" Steele said, Poppy tells me that you've never turned either of them away when they needed money."

"He was mortified—he didn't want to tell me why he needed the money."

"And why would he be embarrassed to tell you?" Hollis said.

"The money was for Beverly—Bernard."

Hank jumped in, "I knew about Beverly from very early in the investigation. We didn't know his name, until later, but we knew Beverly was a man."

"I had my suspicions of her, but nothing concrete," Steele said.

"This homosexual relationship didn't bother you, Roger?" Bollinger said.

"I believe we've drifted off course here," Conrad said skirting Bollinger's question.

"What exactly did you have in mind, Roger?" Hollis said.

"I have discussed this with Lawrence. He realizes that what he did was wrong and is willing to plead guilty to a lesser charge."

"What kind of lesser charge?" Bollinger said.

Lawrence, Herbert, and I have discussed this at great length. We feel that a moderate sentence for extortion, and perhaps interfering with a police investigation would be appropriate."

"I'm not sure we can ignore the kidnapping," Hollis said.

"I can tell you—at this point in our investigation—we have no real evidence that Mr. Sinclair or his gir.... Umm, boyfriend, participated in the kidnapping," Hank said.

"I have reviewed the evidence myself," Bollinger said. "Admittedly, the evidence's a bit thin—and it won't be the easiest case I've ever prosecuted—but I'm convinced that we have enough to convince a jury."

"That may be so, Gerry. But, why not go with a sure thing—he'll plead guilty to extortion and save the government the cost of a trial," Conrad said.

Bollinger scratched his head, got to his feet, and paced around the room. After two trips back and forth he said, "If he pleads guilty to extortion, I wouldn't be happy with anything less than ten years."

"Herbert and I felt that a sentence in the range of four years would be adequate."

"No, no... that's impossible, not a day less than six years," Bollinger shot back.

"I'm sure the Attorney General would accept six years," Hollis threw in. "Seems like a good compromise, and we avoid the price of a trial."

"How about this," Roger said as he too got to his feet and came around the desk to stand near Bollinger, "Lawrence serves two years, and then eight years probation—and you'll have your ten years, Gerry."

Bollinger downed the rest of his drink and went to the bar and poured another. "What do you suggest for Mr. Manners?"

"Lawrence maintains that Bernard had nothing to do with anything he did. He knew nothing about it at all."

"I see, so you believe their story," he said sipping from his now half full glass.

"I have no reason to not believe it, and there's no evidence to the contrary," Conrad said.

"Mr. Bollinger," Steele said as he pointed to Hank, "Lieutenant Williamson and I tried our best to find any evidence that Lawrence had anything to do with this kidnapping. His actions at the time of the kidnapping cast strong suspicion on him, and he was our only suspect for a good part of the investigation. And I believe, for a time, even his sister, Miss Sinclair, was convinced, that he was guilty. However, we didn't find any connection at all to the kidnapping—only to the ransom note. Especially after he ran off to New York and then left the country."

"He told me he was very sorry he reacted that way. After he sent the note to Mr. Steele, he felt quite guilty and just wanted to run away and hide like a little boy."

"About that ransom note," Hollis said. "Those files he wanted—what about them?"

"I talked with him at length about that," Roger said. "He tells me that he really didn't know anything about the project—the name on the file *Endeavor Project*, looked important to him, and that's how he chose to use it in the note."

"Is that even plausible? He must have known about it," Hollis said.

"Yes, it probably is," Roger said, "and it's my fault. I didn't give Lawrence any responsibility in the company. He wasn't really in charge on anything. I gave him the job, but didn't really give him much to do."

"And, what about Beverly... Bernard?" Bollinger said. "Why did she go along with him?"

"He too was confused by what happened. He had no idea why Lawrence was upset." Roger poured himself another drink. "He just wanted to stand by Lawrence and help him deal with whatever it was that was bothering him. 'Like any wife would do for her husband.' was how Bernard... um Beverly, explained it to me."

"So, Roger. What do you recommend that I do with him?" Bollinger said.

"Nothing," Roger said, puffing on his cigar. "Thanks to Mr. Steele, the ring-leader's dead."

"And, what about Frank and Howard Gibson?" Bollinger barked.

"They're career criminals. I believe we should throw the book at them," Hollis said. "We have irrefutable evidence that they were responsible for kidnapping Mr. Conrad and then transporting him across state lines, to Salem New Hampshire, and holding him captive there."

"Are we agreed then, gentlemen?" Conrad said as he looked first at Bollinger and to Hollis.

Neither Bollinger nor Hollis said anything, but both nodded their heads at Roger.

# # #

Steele approached Roger after all the others except Hank had gone. "If Lawrence will be going to jail for two years, what are you going to tell his mother?"

"I'm going to lie to her, that's what I'm going to do. I will tell her that I have put Lawrence in charge of one of the company's subsidiaries in Europe."

"Okay, but won't she expect him to come home for the holidays."

"I will just have to manufacture a crisis within the company that will keep him away during the holidays for those two years."

"But, she will want to write to him or at least speak with him on the telephone."

"It will be simple enough to have his letters sent to Europe and re-mailed to her from there. As for the telephone, I'm sure I can work that out with Prentice; he can be quite reasonable when he wants' to be," Conrad chuckled.

"And Beverly, what will happen to her? I'm convinced that Lawrence's very much in love with her."

"I'm sure that you are correct. And, as soon as they release him I will have a long talk with him. If he still wants to go through with this operation, I'll see that he has it."

"What about Poppy, why wasn't she invited to this meeting?"

"She was still at the hospital when I was released. They will keep her there until this evening."

"Steele how bout I buy you a beer at the Rivers?" Hank said, "it's been a long day. Would you like to join us Mr. Conrad?"

"No, I believe I'll just go home now."

Hank walked with Steele to the door. As they entered the elevator Hank said, "Why don't you go ahead, I need to stop by the office to do a couple things and I'll meet you at the Rivers in an hour or so."

CHAPTER 36

The Rivers was quiet. Steele had finished half the beer in his glass, when the jukebox began to play. He turned around on his stool and a minute later Hank came through the door.

♫ ♪ Why can't I free your doubtful mind and melt your cold, cold heart? ♪ ♫

Culp put a glass of beer on the counter in front of the empty stool next to where Steele sat. Hank walked to the bar, picked up the glass of beer, and downed nearly half of it before he sat down.

"Can you cut that off, Culp? Steele and I need to talk."

"Something important happen at the station? Another homicide or kidnapping?" Steele asked.

"No nothing like that. Just as I was leaving the office the DA's office called and informed me that the Police Review Board and the DA's office have ruled that the shootings are justifiable homicide and no further action will be taken against either you or me by the state of Massachusetts, Suffolk County, or the City of Boston."

"That sounds like good news."

"Just what I expected." Hank said as he pulled Steele's gun from his pocked and laid it on the bar top. "They're all done with this. It's all yours."

"Thanks," Steele said as he popped the magazine out of the handle—the magazine was empty—as was the breech when he pulled back the slide.

"They took the bullets."

"Yeah, that had to fire it... didn't they?"

"That's three bucks in bullets."

"Shut up Steele," Hank sipped at his beer, "they could have kept the whole thing as evidence, you know?"

CHAPTER 37

It was nearly nine in the evening when Steele knocked on the front door of the Conrad house. Poppy opened the door. Not surprisingly, she was once again stark naked.

"Haven't you learned your lesson about opening the door without getting dressed?"

"I've been waiting here by the door for fifteen minutes." She pointed to a wine glass, still half full, and a plate with a half-eaten sandwich on the vestibule table. "I heard you drive up and park, and then watched you through the peep-hole as you came up the pathway to the door." She giggled as she began to peel his jacket back over his shoulders.

"Whoa, wait just a minute." He grabbed hold of her wrists. You just got out of the hospital."

"Oh, that was nothing. I'm just fine. There were fussing over me for no reason." She began to peel his jacket off again.

"Slow down, woman."

"What's wrong, Mark?" She smiled at him. "I'm not your client now."

"Yes, I guess that's technically true enough."

"So what's the problem? Don't you want me?"

"There's no problem, Poppy, I just think we should proceed at a more modest pace."

"Okay, what did you have in mind? We can't go much slower that we've been going."

"For one thing, I'm still wearing the same clothes I put on the morning we went to New Hampshire. I need a shave and I would like to take a shower and get cleaned up, change my clothes. Does that seem unreasonable?"

She grinned at him. "Yes, very." Her grin broadened and she threw her arms around his neck and kissed him. Pulling back, she said, "Unless we can shower together!"

He bent down and picked her up in his arms and began walking up the stairway with her. "Whatever you say, you wicked woman."

When they reached the landing he set her down. She grabbed hold of his hand and pulled him down the hallway to the second doorway on the left. She opened the door and ushered him inside. The room was obviously her bedroom.

"What happened to us in separate rooms?" he said.

"You want separate rooms?" she asked.

"No, not really. But we've had this discussion before Poppy... I thought... what about your mother?"

"Just a minute, I'll be right back," she said and left him standing there. In two minutes she was back, "I'll just tell Mother you used the guest room. She'll never know the difference. I messed up the bed sheets so that if Mother questions Zoë about it, she can tell her the bed was used."

"You're a devious, devious woman, Miss Penelope Sinclair and I love it," he said as he pulled her to his chest, kissing her passionately.

Her lips parted from his; she moved back an inch. "I try my very, very best," she purred.

His hands closed about the two white orbs of her buttocks and pulled her hips into his with great urgency.

Their kiss lingered, but soon she forced their bodies apart as her dexterous fingers got to work un-buckling his pants which soon lay in a heap, along with his boxer shorts, around his ankles. She began to nibble on his ear as her deft fingers began to explore places they'd been denied to go, until now.

ILLUSTRATIONS

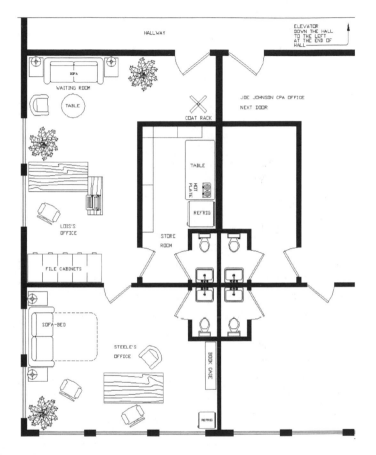

Illustration: 1: Mark Steele's office
545 Memorial Drive, Suite 9, Cambridge, Massachusetts

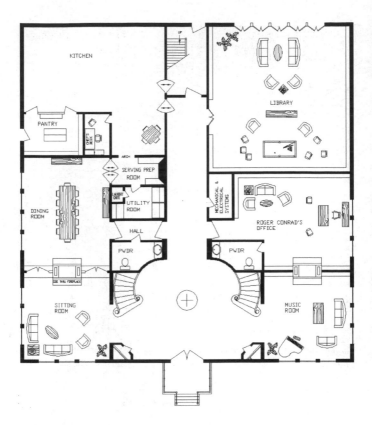

KITCHEN

LIBRARY

PANTRY

SERVING PREP
ROOM

UTILITY
ROOM

DINING
ROOM

MECHANICAL &
ELECTRICAL
SYSTEMS

HALL

ROGER CONRAD'S
OFFICE

PWDR

PWDR

SITTING
ROOM

MUSIC
ROOM

Illustration: 2 Conrad Mansions - First Floor Plan
66 Beacon Street, Boston, Massachusetts

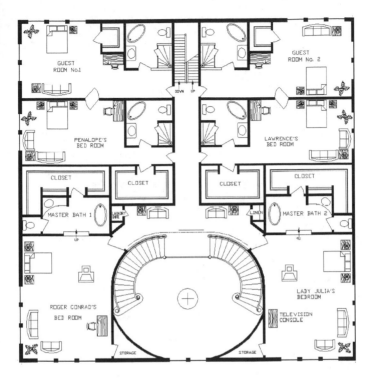

Illustration: 3 Conrad Mansion - Second Floor Plan

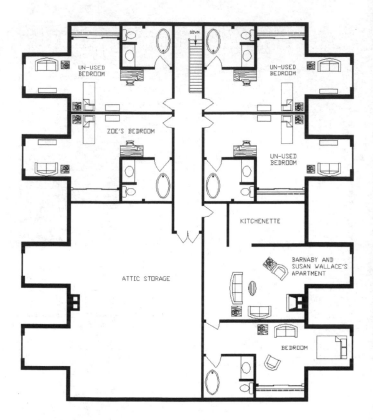

Illustration: 4 Conrad Mansion –
Third Floor Attic Plan and Servants Quarters

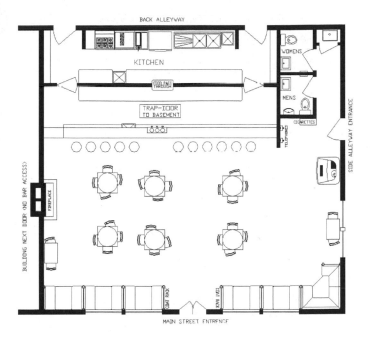

Illustration: 5 The Rivers Tavern
581 Memorial Drive, Cambridge, Massachusetts

Look for the next Mark Steele Mystery entitled:

" Pepper Creek Murder"

Mark Steele was delighted when his daughter, Janet showed up at his Boston office for a surprise visit. However, Janet has come to Boston, not just to visit her detective father, but also to enlist him in a little inquiry. "No big investigation," she declares, "come up to Vermont, bring your fiancée, relax by the pool and snoop around a little—that's all."

Janet and her husband Thomas own and manage The Pepper Creek Resort in Vermont, and it seems someone has been purloining small items: watches, rings, necklaces, and other little items left unattended by the guests, on poolside tables.

Steele has no way of knowing that his daughter's innocent invitation for a restful weekend will be anything but a vacation. Relaxing by the pool will come to an abrupt end when a horse, ridden by one of the guest's, returns to the stable without its rider. The search for the missing woman will escalate quickly into a murder investigation and thrust Steele into the dogged pursuit of a ruthless killer.

Concurrently, Steele also consults with his friend, Boston Police Lt. Hank Williamson, over the phone lines. Steele will aid his friend in tracking down the killer of an underage stripper who was murdered savagely in her Boston apartment.

Altogether, Pepper Creek Resort, and its unusual guests, will hold more surprises for the semi-hard-broiled ex-Marine MP and NYC cop now turned Boston private detective than he ever dreamed of.

ABOUT THE AUTHOR

Tom Saine is a retired mechanical engineer with a long history in the American space program. During the early part of his career, while working at HRM in Burbank, CA, he was privileged to be on the team of engineers who designed the gimbal actuators for the F-1 engine of the Saturn V moon rocket. Later at Parker-Hannifin in El Segundo, CA, he was also privileged to be on the team that designed the "Oxygen Control Assembly" of the Lunar Excursion Module (LEM) for the Apollo moon landing missions. Tom has also worked for such well-known companies as Lockheed Aircraft, Bell Aircraft, Hewlett-Packard, Polaroid, and IBM. Tom was born in Indiana and went to school in Southern California. He has also lived and worked in Atlanta, GA; Boston, MA; Raleigh, NC; Cedar Rapids, IO; and Buffalo, NY. After he retired, he moved back to his native Indiana where he now lives with his fiancée Faith Duncan and his cats Rusty and Smoky.

As a writer Tom didn't get started until he acquired his first computer in 1990. Even then he didn't really begin writing seriously until he retired in 2001. While a late bloomer, Tom has written a dozen novels since then and has several new titles in the outline and planning stages.

The Conrad Kidnapping is the first in a series of Mark Steele Mysteries stories to be published; the second, **Pepper Creek Murder** (See a brief synopsis on a previous page) will be released in the near future.

Other Mark Steele Mysteries: *Murder at Sea, Cloak and Dagger, and The Museum Caper*, are all well along in the revision pipeline and should be ready for release sometime in the not too distant future.

Be sure and look for these and other titles by Tom Saine at your local bookseller or online at www.amazon.com and www.createspace.com. Tom's books are also available for Kindle at www.kindle.com